THE VESPUS BLADE

SPACE ASSASSINS 2

SCOTT BARON

"The path of the warrior is lifelong, and mastery is often simply staying on the path."

– Richard Strozzi Heckler

CHAPTER ONE

Normally, the light of the nearly full moon would have reflected brightly from the Ootaki woman's golden hair. The natural magic storing property of her kind's resplendent locks made them something to behold under the right circumstances.

These, however, were not the right circumstances. Mud and debris werematted into her hair and were likewise smeared over most of her body. Her hasty escape had been the cause of that. It was also the reason she was still free.

For the time being at least.

The woman ran on even faster than before, pushing herself far beyond her own perceived limitations. Ootaki might have been capable of storing massive quantities of magic in their hair, but as a people, they were unable to tap into it themselves. A cruel joke of fate, for the mostly enslaved race.

But not all Ootaki were slaves. Some small pockets of free folk still existed at the periphery of the systems. Places where the peaceful, pale-yellow-skinned people with their golden hair could live unmolested by ruffians and scoundrels.

Usually, at least.

Hers had been a tranquil existence. A quiet life with her

friends and family, all living in a small commune in a quiet corner of a quiet world.

Then the horror fell upon them, shattering all semblance of peace they had ever known. And it wasn't just a random group of pirates or thieves. Those they could hide from as they'd done in the past. But not this time. This time, they'd been discovered by Tslavars.

They were a disgusting race of mercenaries. Slave traders. Strong arms for hire, working for the highest bidder. The deep-green-skinned men and women were more than that, however.

They took great pleasure in their profession, making them even worse than mere thugs for hire. They *enjoyed* the dirty work. And that made them a particularly popular tool of the Council of Twenty as that group of power users strove to expand their control over the known systems.

And that was what they were doing here, undoubtedly. Rounding up the magical beings for their masters. All of them to be collared and enslaved, their hair to be charged with even more magic until such time as it was ready to be harvested, even though some of that power would be lost in the shearing process.

The first cut was always the most potent, and for that reason, the younger Ootaki were a great prize. One that could be groomed their whole life until a rainy day. Or a day their owner *wanted* it to rain. Fire and brimstone, that is, for their harvested magic could be a fearsome thing.

But to preserve the power without loss upon cutting, an Ootaki could give their hair freely. It was rarely done, though, and their locks always knew their owner's intent, even if they did say the words, "Freely given."

If their heart wasn't truly in it, the hair would know and only be a tiny fraction stronger than that taken by force.

There were tales that Ootaki hair given not only freely, but out of love, held immense power, exponentially greater than what it appeared to initially contain, binding it forever to the recipient. But that was no more than a myth. A legend. For Ootaki could not use their own kind's power, and giving it in love to another of their race, even out of love, would have no effect.

A ship roared through the air nearby, powered by a team of Drooks, the enslaved men and women focusing their particular flavor of magic to make the craft fly. Free Drooks were even more rare than free Ootaki, for without them, interstellar travel would be impossible.

Such was the way of this magical galaxy.

The golden-haired woman raced through the sparse woods that bordered the fields at the far end of her people's enclave. Her clothing was torn, her pale-yellow skin bleeding from the myriad scrapes and abrasions acquired in her hasty flight. And, of course, her hair was a mess of dirt and grime.

A faint whiff of fresh moisture greeted her nose and exhausted lungs. The river. It was close by.

She pushed on, racing as fast as her feet could carry her on the uneven ground, even as the trees grew thicker close to the water's edge. Her father had told her to run. To run far and find water. Only there could she hide her scent from any tracking animals the invaders might possess.

Another ship approached, much lower and much closer this time. The young woman quickly jumped into the muddy water at the river's shore and tucked herself beneath a partially submerged log near the water's edge. It was not a moment too soon, for footsteps could be heard growing near. *Many* of them. And not all of them belonging to the men and women hunting her.

There was something else. A sound besides that of the clomping boots of the mercenaries. When she heard the nearby snuffling of the Tslavars' beasts, she realized her father had been correct in his assumption. Trackers, no doubt.

She shifted ever so slowly, allowing herself the tiniest of glimpses of the animals padding along the shoreline. They weren't terribly large, nor were they particularly fierce in appearance. Nothing like their massive, distant cousins often used as guards for royal families of particular note and wealth.

But these smaller versions, with their wiry hair and long snouts, had a keen sense of smell, and for that they served the Tslavars well. And there was more to them than mere animal tracking.

These animals, in addition to sweat and fear, could also sense magic. And that was something the Ootaki girl had in abundance. Fortunately for her, the flowing waters of this world possessed ambient magic of their own, though minor. Nevertheless, it muddied her scent, preventing them from getting a proper fix on her.

She felt a tug on her head. Her hair was of great length, having never been cut, as was the Ootaki way, and the weight of it in the water was threatening to pull her farther out into the fast-moving current. The same current that was also beginning to rinse away some of the mud caked in her hair.

She felt her grip on the slippery log failing as the pull of the river drew her farther into its depths. Any moment now, she would be swept free, a golden-haired treasure for all to see. She clung as tightly as she could, but as she had feared, the river finally took her into its embrace.

Only not as she'd imagined.

Rather than floating along the surface, making an easy target for the hunters along the shoreline, she was hit by a piece of debris and pulled underwater, swept out to the middle of the torrent.

Drowning was suddenly a very real possibility, and as her lungs burned with the need for air, the thought of slavery was beginning to sound a lot better than that alternative.

Pulling frantically, she felt her head begin to go light as stars coalesced at the periphery of her vision. Her body was starting to go weak, the lack of oxygen taking its toll. She was going to drown, she realized.

Fear shot through her body, the surge of adrenaline giving her the energy for one last burst of strength. With a final, mighty pull, she freed her hair from whatever it was she'd been caught up by and burst through the surface, gulping in huge lungfuls of air.

She expected to hear shouts, then be snatched from the water. Instead, she heard nothing. Drained, she collapsed at the shoreline.

"Where am I?" she wondered as she pulled herself from the waters.

It seemed that the current in the middle of the river was far faster than that at the shoreline, and she had been transported a great distance in a short time. Far enough that her home was now a significant distance away, in fact.

Scared, wet, and alone, she sloshed from the shore into the relative cover of the woods nearby. Her hair was golden once more, she realized. She had to get out of the moonlight before the shine caught someone's eye.

Deeper into the woods she walked, fighting back tears with every step. She was worse than lost. She was alone. *Truly* alone, for her entire family had been captured just after her father told her to flee. She'd never seen such urgency in his eyes before, and she had reacted immediately without question. It was the only reason she'd escaped.

And now she was on her own. On her own and far from home, walking through woods she'd never before set foot in.

She moved farther from the rushing water and stopped to listen. Far away, the faint sound of Tslavar voices could be heard carrying over the water. But sound was funny like that, and those men could be miles away.

It was quiet here. Quieter than back home. There were no

laughs of children, nor the sounds of livestock and those tending them. Just her own faint footsteps on the soft soil.

This would not be easy, but she owed it to her father to survive. To make sure at least someone could recount what had happened here this night. With her will renewed and her back straightened, she began walking, her home to her back. She could never return. That was simply how it would be. But she would make the most of it.

A magical stun spell slammed her to the ground, nearly knocking her unconscious.

Snarling Tslavar mercenaries stepped out of the shadows, shedding their magical camouflage. They wore shimmer cloaks, though not very good ones. Adding to that was their lack of proficiency in the spells to utilize them, which led to mediocre camouflage at best.

But for the distracted Ootaki girl, they had proven more than enough and served their purpose well in the dim light. Certainly, any with a fair degree of training would have spotted them, but a scared Ootaki girl with no off-world experience didn't stand a chance.

"Skree back to Captain Moratz we've got another one," a Tslavar said as he loomed over the fallen girl.

"She's young. And her hair is long. We'll get a nice bonus for this one," his associate said.

"Yeah, and it's about time," his friend replied. "Work's been picking up lately, and I gotta say, I'm getting a bit antsy for some shore leave."

"I couldn't agree more. I'm looking forward to a stiff drink and a warm woman, once we get paid."

"You said it," the other Tslavar said as he threw the young woman over his shoulder. "Come on, let's get this one back. We might get lucky and find a few more if we hurry."

The two carried her back to the hastily constructed pen the other captured Ootaki had been corralled into and unfastened the gate. A golden control collar was slapped around her neck, magically sealing into an unbroken band, keeping her under the control of her owner. She was no longer free. She was now someone's property.

Just like all of the other slaves in the galaxy.

CHAPTER TWO

Death came in many shapes and sizes, and while it was sometimes delayed, eventually, it would visit all. The specifics, however, were a crapshoot for the most part.

Time, place, method. Some people simply met the shadowy specter of their demise sooner than others, and they never knew who, or what, would herald its arrival.

Some deaths came via bearers that were long in tooth and claw, stalking their prey with bloody focus and intent. Other bringers of death walked on two legs, or ambulated on rippling tentacles or cushions of magic, and wielded all manner of weapons, conventional and magical alike.

In their grasp one would find swords and knives, blades both enchanted and not, and each non-magical variety was well capable of ending life in its own manner with brutal efficiency.

And then there were the magical devices. Items that did not look like violent implements at all. And some were not. At least, not in their original design.

The magic-storing konuses, their metal bands resting around the wearer's wrist, holding often vast stores of magic for later use. Whether the smallest of service units used to power the casting of day-to-day housework spells, or the heftiest of battle konus, they were alike in that they were tools used by nearly everyone, as only a tiny portion of the galaxy's inhabitants possessed actual power of their own.

In addition to konuses, there were slaaps, the heftier versions more military in design, and not often used for anything but fighting. However, those devices were extremely dangerous and required far more training to handle, the absence of which could result in a tragic end to an unskilled wielder as well as those around them.

Other, far rarer magic storage and concentration items existed, but for the most part, those were the two most often encountered in daily life. But on this evening, in this dimly lit maze of alleyways and corridors, despite the danger in the air, only limited magic seemed to be in play.

A well-muscled woman, fairly tall, but by no means what one would call lithe or statuesque, moved from shadow to shadow with a smooth grace that belied her stockier build.

She possessed great physical strength, that much was clear, despite the layer of womanly padding that provided her the curves she had often used to her advantage to distract a target. Just before ending their lives.

Her name was Demelza, and she was a Wampeh Ghalian. An assassin of the highest order. And this particular pale woman was on the hunt.

Demelza's long, dark hair was woven into a snug braid that barely moved behind her as she stalked. It served two purposes; not only keeping her locks out of the way in case of battle, which was pretty much a given on this evening, but the braid also possessed multiple weapons hidden in the tight bindings.

There were numerous guards and sentries stationed in the area, nearly all in varying degrees of concealment. Any lesser killer wouldn't have stood a chance, but she wasn't just any killer.

Demelza slid into place behind a young man who believed himself shielded from view without so much as a whisper of a sound. Even her clothing was utterly silent, laced with a handful of muffling spells––one of her strong suits––that kept her movements unnoted by all.

Her arms wrapped around the youth's neck fast. So fast he didn't have the chance to sound an alarm before the blocked blood flow to his brain rendered him unconscious. Demelza carefully bound him, applied a magical gag spell, then hid the body before continuing toward her ultimate target.

Two more guards fell in quick succession. One in much the same manner as the first, but the second possessed a fair amount of skill, managing to evade the initial choke and sound the alarm. Unfortunately for him, his attacker had been prepared for that, and the air around them absorbed his shouts, dissolving them to less than whispers in the wind.

He resorted to martial engagement immediately, drawing his knife from his belt and settling into a fighting stance. Demelza was on a ticking clock, however, and simply didn't have the time for a knife fight. So she did the last thing he expected. She lunged right at him.

The knife brushed her side as she pivoted away, bringing her elbow crashing across her opponent's face, right into the corner of his jaw, striking it just so. The way she'd been practicing for what seemed like her whole life, making it second nature. The guard fell in a heap and was quickly trussed up and hidden with the others.

On she progressed, unseen, unheard, taking down guard after guard. Even the most camouflaged of them were no match for the deadly assassin. Ten had fallen to her skills by the time she reached the outer door to the building the target was hidden within.

She approached cautiously, senses on high. This was too

easy. Sure, there had been guards in some numbers, but it still didn't feel quite right.

She was just deciding whether or not this was a trap when the answer was provided to her in the shape of the foot that crashed into her chest, blindsiding her and sending her flying backward.

Demelza dug her feet into the ground and pulled a bit of the stolen magic flowing in her body, bringing her feet to an abrupt stop. She then leapt into action, not allowing her attacker another moment to formulate a next step.

The two fought fast. So fast it was almost impossible for the naked eye to register the strikes and counterstrikes being exchanged. Demelza was amazing, skilled, and driven. Unfortunately, the man she was fighting was, almost impossibly, simply better. And *much* better, at that.

A trio of combinations stunned her, knocking her back on her heels as the man shifted his angle of attack to her weak side just as she launched another counter. It caught her off guard for only a moment, but that was enough.

He swept her feet, a move that would normally take an opponent to the ground in short order. But this assassin was fast and nimble and twisted aside, somehow staying upright. But that was what he had been expecting, and the stronger man was already in place, locking her arms up while gently resting his blade against her throat.

"Damn. Well done. I yield," she grumbled.

Hozark smiled and released his grip, the knife in his hand vanishing back to its hidden sheath.

The lighting around them brightened, and all of her now freed victims moved in closer, as did the other students who had been watching from the wings. This wasn't a true assassination attempt, but a very, very realistic training exercise, put on for the benefit of the young would-be assassins in the Wampeh Ghalian training house.

Hozark, the man who had triumphed against her, was one of the handful of masters of the order, the other four spread out across the systems visiting the other Ghalian training facilities between contracts, as was their way. He was more than just another assassin. He was one of the Five. The best of the best.

"A most impressive showing," the master assassin said. "Ten students incapacitated, and all without raising the slightest alarm."

"Thank you, Master Hozark," she replied. "But, ultimately, it was not enough."

"Perhaps not, but failure is a valuable lesson as well. Even for the best of us," he said, turning and surveying the attentive students' faces. "In fact, topped up on power as she is, had magic been allowed in this contest, she very well might have bested me in a purely magical contest."

A murmur would have quietly flowed through any other body of students had a teacher admitted as much. But these were older trainees, and the silent, attentive ways of the Ghalian were as ingrained and natural as breathing by now.

Demelza, however, and quite in spite of her training, felt the beginnings of a blush rising to her cheeks. Redirecting her attentions, she forced it down, her face remaining as pale and emotionless as a statue. But *inside,* the blush had spread into a broad smile.

For Master Hozark to simply say such a thing was enough. He was not one for overt shows of flattery, nor did he lie to his wards. But for him to admit this in front of the students? Demelza's ranking had just taken a serious bump upward in the eyes of all within the training house.

And Demelza *was* topped up with magic. A *lot* of it, in fact. She had been born without any significant power of her own, as was normal for the vast majority of those in the galaxy. But she had also been one of the fraction of a fraction of a percent of

Wampeh born with a *different* gift. The rarest of abilities that only the tiniest amount of her race possessed.

A grain of sand on a beach. That was how rare it was. And yet, it was an ability all aspirants to the Wampeh Ghalian order possessed. One that made them feared even more than the deadly skills they spent their lives perfecting.

It was their ability to take another's power.

And they did so by drinking their blood.

CHAPTER THREE

Only a few weeks prior to their demonstration at the assassin training house, Demelza had been working in the service of a violet-skinned, elderly man residing on the deadly, gaseous planet of Xymotz. It wasn't a permanent gig, but in between contracts, she was assisting him in any way he asked.

Master Orkut was his name, and he was one of the last surviving swordsmiths possessing both the magic and the arcane knowledge needed to craft the rarest of Ghalian weapons. The vespus blade.

It was a sword made of a magically enhanced blue metal. A weapon capable of causing great damage regardless of who swung it. But in *Ghalian* hands, it was far more, its magic allowing the sword to absorb and redeploy the power a Ghalian assassin had stolen. Few enchanted blades could match its power, and Hozark had visited the old man seeking such a weapon.

Given whom he was about to be facing at the time, he knew full well he would need it.

It was there, while seeking Orkut's services, that he had met

Demelza and joined forces. Not *met*, technically, since he'd known who she was from her time as an aspiring trainee not too many years before. *Partnered* would be a better choice of words. And an odd one, for Wampeh Ghalian almost always worked alone. But, then, he wasn't the one who had decided on their unusual pairing.

Orkut had.

Demelza was working in the swordsmith's service in order to earn favor enough for the man to craft her a weapon. Nothing so elegant as Hozark's vespus blade, but a fine weapon worthy of a Wampeh Ghalian just the same. One day, perhaps, she would be worthy of a vespus blade. But for now, she would gladly take what he might offer her.

Hozark, however, was one of the Five, and *he* had visited the man in search of the finest sword the master artisan could craft. And, after passing Orkut's many tests, the man had agreed. But at a price.

His requested payment, however, would not be in simple coin. This particular weapon would be used against one of the Council of Twenty's key players, and that same group of power-hungry vislas and their hangers on were threatening more than just some random systems this time. Their activities had put Orkut's homeworld at risk.

"The Council has always been a thorn in the side of free men," the swordsmith had said, and it was true. The Council was one of the main forces behind the magic-user slave trade. "But these times are becoming even more dangerous. Greed and lust for power is threatening all but the most stable of systems. This chaos they are causing is even threatening my own home and those I hold dear."

It seemed Orkut had a family far away, including a son who shared his father's swordmaking gift. The youth *could* craft weapons to nearly his father's level of skill, but all the man wanted was for his children to be able to live a normal, safe life, hopefully never being called upon in service of the Wampeh Ghalian, or any others, for that matter.

But war and conquest were in the air, and the Council of Twenty was engaging in far more than their usual quest for power and control in the known and newly discovered systems. They were threatening the order of things, including Orkut's home planet. It was for that reason he made Hozark a deal.

Fight the Council and kill his target. Stymie them and their plans. And in exchange, he would receive the finest vespus blade ever crafted by his hands. A weapon that would feel as natural in his hand that it would seem as though it had always been a part of his body.

Hozark had accepted and returned to his ship to await delivery of the blade. Three days later, it arrived, delivered by Demelza at Orkut's request. And it was everything he had ever hoped for and more.

It was at that moment that Hozark learned the other component to the swordsmith's price, and it was an unusual one. He was to bring Demelza on this contract and utilize her skills to ensure success.

It wasn't insulting, exactly, but the Wampeh Ghalian always worked alone, especially one of the Five. It was simply their way for as long as any could remember. But on that particular occasion, an unlikely partnership had been formed, the two thrown together at the insistence of Master Orkut.

As it turned out, it was a good thing, for while Hozark was battling their target's bodyguard and right-hand killer, Demelza had snuck up on the man and completed their task, sinking her fangs into his neck, draining the man of his life and his power.

Visla Horvath had been a moderately powerful visla, and that magic now belonged to Demelza until such time as she utilized it. Unfortunately, once it was gone, it was gone. A Wampeh Ghalian could only take the power that was present. The ability to *create* power from within died with their victims.

And while the assassins only drank from power users, the general public didn't know that, and the sight of a Wampeh's deadly fangs sliding into place was enough to loosen the bowels of even the hardiest of men.

But Visla Horvath hadn't had that opportunity, nor the chance to deploy any of his powerful spells. He had been too engrossed watching Hozark battle his bodyguard, their vespus blades clashing with bright, magical sparks, for his right-hand man was a woman. And she was a Wampeh Ghalian.

Samara was her name. A deadly assassin possessing one of the few vespus blades still known to exist. But the Wampeh Ghalian did not work for the Council, nor did they take this sort of employment.

Samara was different, however. She was dead.

Or so they had all believed when she had been lost on a job a decade prior. Finding her alive had been a shock to the order, but to none so much as Hozark, for not only had they grown up together, working their way to full-fledged Ghalian assassins side by side, but there had been more. While bonding was simply not something the Ghalian did, the two had been lovers from time to time, and they were as close as two could be without crossing that invisible line.

But she had perished.

Again.

Killed in the aftermath and chaos following their hit on Visla Horvath. She had fled, and her ship had been destroyed in the process, her remains scattered to the stars. Yes, Samara was dead again. Everyone had seen it.

But Hozark still harbored doubts.

CHAPTER FOUR

"Your form is impressive," Hozark said to the younger woman as they walked from the training site hidden within the facility's grounds. "And I mean what I said. Had you utilized the magic currently residing within you, I might very well have been unable to best you."

"Because the rules of this exercise precluded lethal force," Demelza noted.

"Well, yes, there is that," he admitted. "But regardless, it was a good showing. It was only your counter-counter that I felt could use a bit of refining."

"Oh? I appreciate any knowledge you are willing to impart to help me improve my combat skills. One never ceases learning, even after becoming a full Ghalian."

"I could not have said it better myself," Hozark replied with a little grin. "Come, this practice space is unutilized at this time of day," he said, stepping into a nearby chamber.

Demelza followed, ready for a sneak attack to test her skills, as her teachers had so often done under the guise of a simple, innocent bit of practice. But Hozark had no need for such games with her.

She had more than proven herself in combat. This was merely helping her achieve an even higher level of proficiency. And as Orkut had more or less saddled him with her as a partner, he thought it wise to help make her the deadliest woman possible, given their resources.

"Stand here," the master commanded.

Demelza complied, standing before him where he had indicated.

"Turn. Face as you were when I first engaged you during the exercise."

She did as he asked, waiting for his arms to slide into place. But this time, he did so slowly, so she could better feel the angle of attack, as well as her best means of evasion.

"There. Do you sense it? The weak point you failed to exploit previously?"

"I do," she said.

"Now, move through the sequence and counter."

She did, and his muscle memory began countering her counter without requiring thought.

"There. Do you feel that? The control shifting once more?"

"Yes. And it was there that my form was unequal to your attack previously."

"But now, taking your time, you see the way, do you not?"

Demelza paused a moment, her body feeling the pressure exerted at each contact point between them. At full speed it would be a very different sensation, but the principle was the same. And, she was pleased to note, the correct counter-counter was suddenly as clear as crystal.

She moved slowly, ensuring her motions were perfect.

"Yes, that's it," Hozark said, pleased at the speed with which she realized and corrected her prior error.

They flowed through the sequence, then moved into a freestyle adaptation on the theme, utilizing each of their own particular techniques. That was the thing about Wampeh

Ghalian. While they trained in dozens upon dozens of martial styles, each Ghalian assassin ultimately developed their own unique form, special only to themselves.

It was what made the assassins so difficult to handle. Where other orders and military units would drill in a fixed set of styles, the Ghalian took what worked for each of them and blended it until they had a deadly series of moves that none could foresee. And, better yet, they knew the rote patterns most of their opponents had memorized, making their slaughter all the easier.

Twenty minutes passed in a flash, as time often did when skilled fighters were practicing their art.

"I've greatly enjoyed this session," Hozark said, dabbing the light shine of sweat from his brow. "We will practice further at a later time. For the moment, however, it is time for the meeting of the Five."

"The others are here?" Demelza asked, surprised. "*All* of them?"

"Yes. After what so recently occurred with the Council of Twenty, as well as the reappearance of a formerly deceased Ghalian working for them, it seems we have quite a bit to discuss."

"Understandable," she agreed. "May your meeting be productive."

"And the remainder of your training day be rewarding," he replied, then took his leave.

The Five rarely gathered in one place for several reasons, the least of which was the concern of what should happen if all of the Ghalian masters guiding the order fell in an attack.

Their training houses were robustly reinforced with year upon year of defensive spells and wards layered into and around the structure every single time any entered or exited the locations. As such, it would take an attack of extraordinary magnitude to have even the slightest possibility of breaching their defenses.

On top of that, in addition to the assassins and their trainees residing within the walls, if the Five were present, and with the extensive weapons caches at their disposal, their combined, deadly skills could make a five-on-one-thousand battle seem almost trivial, depending on the enemy.

Master Corann, the head of the Five, was in her seat atop the low platform the masters often used while observing the young trainees as they demonstrated their progression in the Wampeh Ghalian's deadly arts. But today, there were no students present in the chamber. Today, they had things of great weight to discuss.

The others were there as well. Master Varsuvala sat to Corann's right, as she often did. Masters Falsam and Prombatz were chatting off to her left, the young, androgynous assassin and the elder Ghalian engaged in an energetic discussion.

Hozark completed the group, and he had to admit, it was nice having all of them together again, even if for just a short while.

"The youngster is quite talented," Varsuvala said as Hozark took a seat with the others. "Not only is she proving quite adept in her continued training, but she is also a great help teaching the novices."

"It is our way, Varsuvala," he replied.

"Yes, but not all thrive as she does. The woman possesses skills."

"That she does," Hozark agreed. "She is exceptionally talented for one of her years."

"And she took down a full-blooded visla. A rather powerful one at that."

"To be fair, he was distracted by Hozark and Samara's battle," Master Prombatz noted.

"True, but regardless, it was still no easy task, especially for less than a master of the order."

"On this we are in agreement," the older Ghalian replied. "She is a valuable asset, and a credit to her teachers. We are fortunate she was paired with you, Hozark."

"So it would seem," he replied.

Corann sensed his reticence. The Wampeh Ghalian always worked alone, and having a partner thrust upon him had been a bit disconcerting, to say the least. Nevertheless, the young woman he had been saddled with had done an admiral job, and even Hozark had to admit his pleasure with her performance.

"It seems Demelza's attempt to acquire a blade from Master Orkut has proven beneficial in unexpected ways," Corann continued. "While she was successful in finding the man in the first place––no easy task, I would add––it will take time for her to work her way into his good graces enough for him to forge her an enchanted blade. And even then, he'd likely never make a vespus for her."

"Honestly, I'm surprised he made yours, Hozark," Master Falsam chimed in. "Though he only makes them for masters of our order, he hasn't crafted one in many, many years. In fact, I thought he'd sworn off the practice entirely."

"I learned why," Hozark said. "It would seem Orkut has family he wishes to keep safe from possible reprisal if it should be known he is working with the Wampeh Ghalian. Apparently, one of his sons possesses his father's gift, and he has been trained in the crafts."

"Another bladesmith of Orkut's line? No wonder he went silent," Varsuvala mused.

"Indeed," Hozark replied. "He hopes his family will be able to live a normal life, free of the dangers associated with working for our order. But should the old man fall one day, and we truly be in need, the five in this room now know of his son's existence. Of his gifts."

"And it shall be kept in the closest of confidence," Corann said. "Only the Five."

"Agreed," the others said. And so it was that Orkut's son was out of harm's way. For the time being, at least.

"Now, Hozark. About this last contract. We know you had an unexpected run-in with our presumed dead sister. But you also learned something else?" Corann asked.

"Yes. My two recent contracts appear to have been quite well acquainted. But more than that, they were involved in some shady affairs with one another for some time."

"Visla Horvath was working with Emmik Rostall?" Falsam asked.

"Indeed. And he was sending magically charged weaponry to Visla Horvath before I even engaged him."

"Fascinating," Corann said. "It seems there is a quiet power struggle at play within the Council of Twenty. And it seems these two were making serious moves to snatch up more control."

"Yes and no," Hozark interjected. "You see, there is more. A rumor. Word that there is another pulling their strings, and quite possibly without their even knowing about it."

"Do we know whom?" Corann asked.

"A few names have been bandied about, even Maktan."

"Maktan?" she said. "He's one of the most docile of the Council of Twenty. In fact, he's always seemed rather benign. For a Council member, that is."

"Appearances can be deceiving," Hozark noted, citing a Ghalian adage they lived and died by.

"As we know quite well," Corann replied. "But whatever is at play, his Ghalian advantage is no more. Samara is dead once again, courtesy of your friend's ship blasting her from the sky."

"Uzabud's new partner, yes. Quite a shot, that one. But I still have my doubts about her demise."

"Caution is prudent," she replied. "But let us also not forget that the details of the event have been corroborated by our agents in the system. Her ship was destroyed trying to flee after you executed her employer. She was shot from the sky as she attempted to flee her lost cause."

Hozark nodded slowly. "This is true, Corann. Yet, again, I still have my doubts."

"Of course. This is Samara we are talking about, and you do know her better than anyone else," she said, careful not to twist the emotional knife still stuck in Hozark's back.

Samara had faked her death and vanished, and none would take it as personally as he.

"She always was a rather talented swordswoman," Corann said, shifting the topic. "One of our best, in fact. I take it your new vespus blade proved worth the effort to procure?"

"More than you can imagine."

"I can imagine quite a lot, my friend. But we have matters at hand we do not need to imagine. Several high-end jobs have just been accepted by the order. Risky, difficult, and Council-affiliated targets, most requiring a master's touch."

At this news, the others perked up. "Oh, really?" Falsam said, relishing the thought of a new contract.

"Indeed," she replied. "I will get each of you details for your contracts, and we shall begin at once."

CHAPTER FIVE

"Master Hozark, your presence is requested at the entry hall," a young aspirant informed the seated master as he studied one of the ancient scrolls of Ghalian spells.

"Oh?" Hozark said, looking up at the young woman.

"Yes."

"What is it?" he replied.

"Something most unusual," the young Wampeh replied. "There is a man. He entered the foyer and has been pounding on the inner doors for nearly five minutes."

"And no one has disposed of him?" Hozark asked. "You realize, it is somewhat out of the norm to request one of the Five for so simple a matter, do you not?"

"Ah, apologies, Master Hozark. But, well, that's the thing," the youth replied. "You see, this man. He is calling for *you*."

Hozark's face remained neutral, not betraying his surprise. "This man. Does he happen to wear any pirate's garb in his attire, by any chance?"

"Actually, he does. How did you know?"

"Uzabud," the master assassin said, sighing quietly. "What in the worlds are you doing here, old friend?" He turned to the young Wampeh. "Thank you. I shall handle our guest from here."

"As you wish, Master Hozark," the youth replied, leaving him to deal with the unexpected intruder, allowing her to return to her regular duties.

Hozark quickly strode through the halls to the entryway. As was the case in every Wampeh Ghalian training house, it was a false entry, of course, and warded to boot. There was no worry whatsoever of anyone actually breaching the interior of their facility.

Still, most gave up and walked away upon a lengthy lack of reply from the property's overseers. But Uzabud was camped out in the foyer and didn't seem to be going anywhere. He was stubborn, for certain, but not impulsively foolish.

For him to actually fly all the way to this world and come to the training house's door was beyond unusual. And unusual could be fatal, where the Wampeh Ghalian were involved. Especially if one were to be perceived as intruding on their privacy.

Fortunately, the young aspirant had notified Hozark rather than another of the masters, likely avoiding what could have been a rather unpleasant end for his friend. After so many years working together, that would have been a terrible shame.

The unusual thing about this was they had actually only parted ways a short time before. Mere weeks, in fact. Their last job together had gone a bit sideways, even though Master Horvath had fallen as intended when the contract was completed.

But at the end of it all, Samara, back from the dead, much to Hozark's surprise, had thrown them for a loop before meeting her death once again. It was an unusual turn of events, and a particularly difficult job, during which Bud had performed admirably.

Despite his somewhat checkered past, Uzabud had always

been a rock-solid and trustworthy asset, and one Hozark could call upon without any concern for his abilities or discretion. For him to now show up unexpectedly at the secret training house that only a handful of non-Ghalian even knew existed hinted that something of great urgency was afoot.

And Hozark would be finding out what that was far sooner than later.

"You know, dropping in on a Ghalian training house unannounced and pounding on the doors is a good way to get yourself killed, Bud," Hozark said as he approached his friend from behind in the entryway.

Uzabud spun at his friend's voice. "How did you get over there? I didn't see you come in."

"I have my ways, my friend," the assassin replied with a little grin.

Despite the many skills he'd learned in his stint as a pirate and overall man of action and adventure, Uzabud was nevertheless an unpowered man. He had no magic within him whatsoever, and no knack for sniffing out wards and illusions on his own.

And his konus was not attuned to the particular spells used to detect hidden doorways such as the one Hozark had just used. Even if it was, it wouldn't have mattered. Not here, anyway. This was a Ghalian compound, and anyone short of a visla would be very hard-pressed finding the *actual* entryway.

"So, you've come all the way to this place seeking me out. You could have simply skreed me, you know. Or reached out to Demelza. She'd have relayed your message."

"I did call you, but you didn't answer your skree. And I had no idea Demelza was still with you. I thought she'd have gone back to serve Orkut by now. She was pretty anxious to have him make her that blade."

"Yes, but there were valuable things for her to learn before returning. And so long as she is away from his service, she and I are bound to work with one another, as Orkut required of me when he completed my vespus blade, as you know."

"So why didn't you just answer the call, then? It's not like you were on some top-secret assignment," Bud said. "You weren't on another job, were you? I mean, if you were, you know you could have called me if you needed a hand."

"I was not on a contract, Bud," Hozark replied. "And inside of these walls, I do not carry my skree with me at all times. To do so is distasteful. But I would have seen your message soon enough, so why the impatience?"

"I'm sorry, but there was just no time to wait, Hozark. Something's gone wrong."

"Normal, for our lines of work."

"Yeah, sure. But this time, it's something different. Laskar has been taken prisoner."

Hozark shook his head. Uzabud's new copilot and partner grated on his nerves more than a little bit. Yes, Laskar was a skilled pilot, and he had proven his worth on their recent, disastrous job. But his cocky overconfidence grew tiresome quite quickly.

"Taken prisoner, you say? Once again, you illustrate the reason that you and I do not normally *have* partners, Bud. We are men of action, and of a particular type. We work far better alone, you and I."

"Normally, yes. But he's proven himself to be a really good asset. I mean, you saw how he flies. And the guy is fearless."

"True," the assassin replied, "but, again, it is precisely this sort of incident that drives home why we do not have partners."

"You and Demelza have made a good team," Bud noted.

"Yes, she is quite skilled. But this is temporary, and it was not by intention. I was saddled with my partner at the direction of Master Orkut. I'd not have accepted her otherwise. You, on the other hand, selected yours of your own free will."

"And he was captured."

"Indeed, the fool," Hozark said with a bit of disdain.

"Sure, he's a bit of a pain at times, I'll admit. Hell, I know I've wanted to smack that cocky grin off his face more than once. But this is different. He was gathering information on what Visla Horvath and the Council of Twenty were up to when he was caught, Hozark. How Samara came to not only be alive, but working with her former enemies. He was digging up intel for *you*."

"Why would he do that?"

"After what happened on the job at Visla Horvath's compound, he felt he owed you one and wanted to do something to be helpful. So he was snooping for dirt on who else Visla Horvath had been coordinating with, in hopes it would prove useful to you."

Hozark sighed, shaking his head. "And just as I was satisfied disliking the man, he has to go and do something like this," the master assassin said, pondering the situation a long moment. "I see where this is going, Bud. You have an abundance of skills, and a treasure trove of unsavory contacts and shady friends from your pirating and smuggling days. If you've come to me, it must truly be bad."

"It is. Trust me, it is."

"Very well, then," he sighed. "How bad is it? Where exactly is he?"

"Uh, yeah. That's the problem," Bud said. "Laskar's being held in Visla Sunar's estate. On Ahkrahn."

Hozark sighed. It was even worse than he'd imagined. "It's never easy with you, is it, Bud?"

"But that's why you love me."

"A Ghalian loves no one," he replied with a straight face. "But let us see about retrieving your friend. Ideally, before his head is separated from his neck."

CHAPTER SIX

Hozark watched the two young Wampeh locked in battle. Each was in their early twenties, fighting with great focus as they moved through a flowing combat session, sparring at top speed with both blades and konuses. The weapons, unlike those used by the younger trainees, were honed to razor sharpness, though their konuses were operating at a somewhat reduced level.

To feel the brunt of one of their magical attacks would likely not be fatal, but it would certainly cause damage. The blades, however, could prove deadly, though they were moving for mostly less than fatal strikes. It was training, after all, and though the healers could remedy any damage incurred, none wished to have to visit them.

The pair were the most senior of the training house's students. Both young men had grown up in the facility, steeped in the order's deadly arts nearly their whole lives. They had done smaller hits for the order for years, but nothing of high difficulty. Now, however, it was time for them to take the final step. To be assigned their graduation contracts.

They had been ready for some time, but the order waited

until the right job presented itself for the final test. Wampeh Ghalian, even senior students, normally went on contracts alone, but for their final test, they would be accompanied by one of the masters. One who would remain close and keep a watchful eye on them, either disguised or under cover of shimmer cloak.

Hozark had recently been with a particularly talented student named Enok on his final test. A test where things had gone horribly wrong. The target, an emmik by the name of Rostall, had surprised them with a rare and utterly unexpected weapon. One that could kill a Ghalian on contact.

The Balamar waters were a healing fluid, beneficial to all they touched. All but Wampeh Ghalian. For *them*, the rare waters would not heal, but rather immolate them instantly, reducing them to ash. They were incredibly rare. And yet, somehow, Emmik Rostall had a small vial in his possession.

Enok had stood his ground without flinching as Rostall randomly splashed suspected assassins hiding in his guards' ranks. He didn't possess enough to spray all of the men, and it was an incredible fortune he was throwing away in the process. But luck was not on Enok's side that day, and he was one of the randomly selected targets within the emmik's reach.

He died instantly in a plume of flame.

Hozark had been standing beside him, observing the student on his final test. But there was nothing he could do to save the youth from this unforeseen event. It was so utterly unexpected. Those waters were worth a fortune. And yet this lower-level emmik not only possessed them, but chose to use them so freely.

Hozark had ultimately completed the task, killing Emmik Rostall and taking the deadly waters for himself, originally intending to lock them in the order's vaults.

But then his former lover had proven herself very much alive, and in the employ of a Council of Twenty member. At that news, he kept the waters for his own final option. He just hoped he would never need to employ them.

Given what had happened so recently, Hozark would not be the master accompanying either of these particular students. But he wished to observe their final training session just the same. If he could impart any additional knowledge to them before the undertaking, he would gladly do so.

When he quietly joined them in the training chamber, Demelza had just stepped into the mix between the two, refocusing their attacks and subtly nudging them toward more effective style variants against one another.

She was not a master, nor even a teacher. In fact, she had been out of the order's grounds for some time, but in this moment, her skills shone through.

Each of the youths had their own particular style, but she adapted to each, and modified both her own response,s as well as the manner the other student fought, to better combat them. It was masterful, the way she fluidly guided them in improving their own forms.

Demelza had gone from merely observing and directing the combat to being a full-fledged participant, making the whole event into a three-way battle with magic and blades alike.

She blocked and countered, using her konus while saving the internal power she'd recently taken from Visla Horvath. To waste her stored magic in training would not be acceptable. To utilize one of the order's many konuses, however, was not an issue whatsoever. They were far, far easier to come by than a visla's power, and she didn't know when she'd drink from one of those again.

Hozark watched the combat with silent appreciation. The man at his side, however, was not so tactful.

"Holy shit, man. She's kicking ass!"

"Bud, please," Hozark said.

But the disruption had been enough, and the three

combatants ceased their attacks and counters as if by silent agreement and stepped back, bowing slightly to one another.

"Thank you, Teacher Demelza," Aargun, the older of the two, said.

"You are welcome. But please, I am not a teacher in the order. Merely a sister Ghalian."

"We appreciate your tutelage regardless, Sister Demelza," the other youth said. "Your unusual style has proven most enlightening. I think both Aargun and I will benefit from your instruction, whether you are officially a teacher in the order or not."

"Her skills are indeed impressive," Hozark noted. "I have seen her in true action, and rest assured, despite her non-teacher status, her skills are more than adequate for her to bear that title. If she so desired, that is," he added, flashing her a little look.

The two students nodded respectful bows to Master Hozark, mopped the sweat from their brows, then took their leave.

"Hey, Demelza," Bud said. "Sorry to interrupt. But wow, that was really cool."

"Uzabud. This is a surprise. We only parted ways a short while ago, and yet, here you are. You are well, I see."

"Well, yes and no."

"Yes and no?" she repeated.

"He has lost Laskar," Hozark clarified.

"Oh, I am sorry to hear that. He was a brave companion."

"He's not dead," Bud said.

"Ah, a pleasant mistake on my part."

"He's not dead. But he *is* being held on Ahkrahn," he added.

Her mood shifted to a far more serious one. "Oh. That is not good. Not good at all."

"No, it isn't," the former pirate agreed.

"Ahkrahn is ruled by a particularly nasty visla, if I am not mistaken," she said.

"You are correct, Demelza," Hozark said. "Visla Sunar controls that world. That entire system, for that matter. He runs the Ootaki trade, and it spans many, many systems."

"And he's got my copilot," Bud said.

Demelza read the look on both of the men's faces clearer than any book. "I am not going to like what you say next, am I?"

Hozark smiled with deadpan Ghalian mirth. "Likely not," he replied. "It seems Laskar was taken prisoner while attempting to retrieve information beneficial to us. Information about the goings-on between Visla Horvath, Emmik Rostall, and how it all ties in to the Council of Twenty. That, and how exactly Samara came to be embroiled in their affairs."

"Interesting. He did this of his own accord?"

"He did. And from what Uzabud has told me, it seems he may have succeeded."

Demelza nodded, taking it all in. She already knew whatever plans she might have had in the works would be delayed indefinitely. Hozark saw the realization in her eyes.

"Yes, Demelza. We are delaying both of our contracts for the time being. There is a cushion built into them, and we will utilize it to the fullest."

"We are going to get him, aren't we?"

"We are," the master assassin replied.

It was an inconvenience, putting their officially sanctioned contracts on hold. But this was more than a rescue of a friend's partner. This was an intelligence-gathering operation, and Laskar, it seemed, possessed some most valuable information indeed.

"It's gonna be tough," Uzabud said. "I mean, this guy has a shit-ton of Ootaki hair at his disposal."

"So, you're saying it is going to be a particularly challenging endeavor," Demelza mused.

"Yes, it will be *most* difficult," Hozark agreed.

She smiled broadly. "Excellent. I will gather my gear."

CHAPTER SEVEN

"I must admit, while I am quite looking forward to this challenge, I do find it somewhat hard to believe we are undertaking this task for the likes of Laskar," Demelza said as she stowed her gear aboard Bud's larger ship.

She'd already attached her much smaller craft to the ship's hull, as Hozark had done with his shimmer ship, fastening it securely with several spells locking it in place for transit.

She had minor shimmer ability to her craft, but nothing like that of the master Ghalian. His ship could become entirely invisible, even in space, though the cost in magic was great. Fortunately, the Wampeh Ghalian were by no means a poor order.

"You are not alone with your surprise on this," Hozark replied. "But, despite his somewhat abrasive personality, he *has* proven himself in combat at our side."

"Many have. And many have fallen," she noted.

"True. But this one may possess vital information toward understanding exactly what the Council of Twenty is up to. And for that, we must retrieve him."

"Guys, do me a favor," Bud interjected. "If we do manage to

spring him from Visla Sunar's cells, try to keep the, 'We don't need him,' and, 'We only did it for his intel,' stuff quiet, okay? He's a cocky bastard, sure, but that would kinda suck, and I'm the one who's gonna be flying with him when this is all through."

"Of course, Bud," Hozark replied with a grin. "Tact is one thing we are not lacking."

"Nor is candor, when called for," Demelza added with a grin.

They had geared up quickly for the rescue attempt. Being within the walls of a secret Ghalian training house, all they could possibly need was at their fingertips in the many storerooms contained deep within. It had been one hell of an eye-opener for Uzabud.

He'd always known the wealth and assets of the Wampeh Ghalian simply *had to be* immense by now, given what they charged for their services and how long they'd been around. But to see the neatly organized shelves and tables covered in everything they could possibly need, all of it neatly arranged and left out for any of the order to utilize should they have need, well, it was enough to make the sticky-fingered former pirate in him itch just a bit.

But he knew far better than to steal from the Ghalian. Not only was Hozark his friend, but his people were the deadliest assassins in the galaxy. And besides, Uzabud knew he would most likely get to keep much of what they used in their endeavor as a little thank you payment, as was Hozark's habit. Maybe he'd even let him keep one of the Drookonuses they'd brought for this mission.

The devices held a vast amount of Drook power, more than enough to drive their ship for months if need be. And Hozark had brought an extra. For the assassin to take that level of precaution spoke volumes of just how difficult this might be.

"We should be underway," Hozark said. "Time is of the essence with Laskar in Visla Sunar's grasp."

"Lifting off in two minutes," the pilot replied.

He appreciated Hozark and Demelza delaying their order-sanctioned hits to come with him on this dangerous rescue mission. It was not something Ghalian did. *Ever*. But Laskar, all of his faults aside, had performed well under pressure, and he had been captured attempting to help Hozark learn more about his former lover's ties to their enemies.

Samara may have been killed during their last mission, and just after she had been discovered alive, no less, but at least they would know how she'd been wrapped up in that mischief. Hozark owed the man for that. For closure, where his unlikely enemy––his former lover––was concerned.

Loyalty was something the Ghalian took *very* seriously, and though he didn't particularly like the man, and still harbored some doubts about him, Laskar had fallen into captivity while attempting to acquire intel on his behalf. A bit of closure for the man who, though he hadn't shown how Samara's loss affected him, had been shaken by it all the same.

And that had taken him to the world of Ahkrahn, of all places. Of course, Hozark knew it. Everyone did. A planet ruled by a powerful visla. Powerful not by his own internal magic, but rather, by the slave trade he controlled. For in addition to all manner of other races, from Drooks to basic laborers, to gladiators, Visla Sunar also ran the Ootaki trade for many, many systems, and that made him a very powerful man indeed.

His home of Ahkrahn was a lush world in a large system, its twenty-seven worlds and moons orbiting a blue giant sun, the rays of which gradually fed a small trickle of additional power into the Ootaki slaves' hair, making it an ideal system for Sunar to set up his base of operations.

People came from the distant ends of the galaxy to seek out Ootaki from his stables. And while many coveted his wealth of the magic-bearing men, women, and children, none were foolish enough to attack him at home. He was simply surrounded by too much power. Power he'd carefully deployed in traps and wards all around his estate's grounds. To attack his compound was to court death.

And Visla Sunar *never* ventured far from home.

His inner estate's safety behind the Ootaki hair-fueled defenses made it a place of relaxation, and his most trusted allies and favored clients were occasionally granted visits within his walls, where the elite lived it up the way only the truly wealthy could.

Lesser visitors stayed outside the grounds in one of the neighboring cities. Ahkrahn may have been known for Sunar's slave trade, but it was also a tranquil world in a pleasant system, one sought out for the restorative rays of its sun.

"We can't just barge in there," Uzabud said as they exited the fifth jump en route to Ahkrahn. "He has way too many wards in place. And with all of that Ootaki magic at his fingertips..."

"You are correct," Hozark agreed. "We will need to find other means into the estate. And from what our spy network has heard, Laskar is not being held in the cells near the outer guard station, as is the norm. Apparently, he is being held within the main compound itself."

"Your spies know that? How did they even get inside?"

"The Ghalian have paid off a great many people for a great many years. So much so that the flow of what is seemingly innocuous information to them has become something of a mindless habit. We do not ask more than that of them, and their handlers sort the intelligence and refine it as needed. In this case, a simple observation of the arrival of a man fitting Laskar's description was all it took to weave the threads together."

"I knew you guys were dialed in on a lot of worlds, but this is more than I expected."

"Ahkrahn is a place of particular interest due to the nature of its slave trade. Power moves are made there. Resources for expansions of power are acquired. For that reason, we pay particular attention to worlds of this type."

"Makes sense," Bud admitted. "Get an idea who's about to stir up trouble just by seeing if they're stocking up on Ootaki or Drooks. Pretty clever, actually."

"We've not survived as an order for this long by being sloppy, my friend," Hozark said. "Now, as for Laskar. If he is indeed being held in the innermost reaches of the estate, this will make his extraction particularly difficult."

"What in the worlds did he do to warrant that?" Demelza wondered. "I mean, being captured for snooping is one thing, but to be held within Sunar's sanctum? It is highly unusual."

"I don't know, but he must've really pissed the guy off," Bud said.

"Knowing Laskar, I do not find that hard to fathom," she replied.

Though he wouldn't say it aloud to Hozark, Bud was glad Demelza was coming with them. He had no concerns or doubts about his friend's legendary abilities, but the woman joining them had not only proven herself quite a badass on their last outing, she had also been the one to take down Visla Horvath.

He had been a powerful man, and when she fed on him, that power became hers. She was topped up on magic, and as this would quite possibly be a magic-heavy mission, having someone on their team with that kind of internal supply, as well as her robust konuses and slaaps, was a great force multiplier for them.

"What are you staring at, Uzabud?" she asked, noting his gaze.

"What? Oh, nothing," he said, blushing slightly. "I'm just glad you're part of the team is all."

Hozark's face remained impassive, but inside, he cringed slightly. *Team.* He was not fond of that word. Wampeh Ghalian worked alone. It was their way. But they adapted when need be. They improvised. They did whatever was necessary to overcome the obstacles placed before them and complete their objective. Even if it meant working with others.

"How many more jumps, Uzabud?" Hozark asked.

"Only two more. It's a good thing you brought extra Drookonuses. I doubt we'll need 'em, but man, it's a long way to Ahkrahn."

"We have Drook power to spare, Bud," he replied.

"Yeah, I guess so. And no need for a crew of Drooks to feed and house," the former pirate replied.

He'd flown on plenty of ships with crews of Drook slaves powering them. In fact, that was the norm. The race had been bound into slavery, their very specific manner of magic powering craft of all types since longer than any could remember. It had simply always been that way.

They were a slave race at this point, and while some might be mistreated by the basest of rabble, Drooks were treated far better than even lower ranking ship's crews, for the most part. It was an enslaved life, but at least it was a comfortable one. And since they ran the ships, that was how it needed to be.

But their stored power channeled into a Drookonus provided a freedom of movement between vessels that was a great advantage, if one had the coin to procure one, that is. But for the millenias-old order of high-price assassins, money was really no object, though they never spent their coin frivolously.

"Okay, we should be there in two jumps," Bud said. "Hang on to your bootstraps; we're almost there."

Moments later, the ship jumped away in a flash of magic.

CHAPTER EIGHT

Uzabud's jumps were expertly plotted, and their arrival within Ahkrahn's system went about as smoothly as could be hoped for. They'd exited the jump just within orbit of the twelfth planet from the blue sun, a common destination and safe enough distance from their target world so as to avoid any scrutiny.

So far as any could tell, they were just another ship on another run-of-the-mill trip to one of the system's many planets for trade or recreation. But *this* ship carried not one, but two Wampeh Ghalian. And they had dangerous work ahead of them.

That, however, was not something they could launch into headfirst. There was simply no way they could hope to come at Sunar's compound head-on and survive. They had to come up with another plan. And, thanks to the Ghalian spy network, an unexpected alternative presented itself.

"You want to do what, now?" Bud blurted when Hozark floated his idea. "I mean, we've done some crazy shit, don't get me wrong. But this?"

"I understand your concern, Bud, but this is literally killing two Borzinghi with one stone," Hozark replied. "The opportunity to complete not only my tasked contract, but to also utilize my target's resources to further this rescue attempt is too good to pass up."

"But you're talking about Captain Dortzal. *The* Captain Dortzal."

"And?"

"*And?* And he's one of the most dangerous slave traders in the systems. The guy's brutal, and vicious, and––"

"And the perfect cover for us to land within Visla Sunar's defenses once we eliminate him and commandeer his ship. The good captain has been raiding smaller systems of late, apparently taking a great number of slaves for the Council. His ship will be the perfect entry vessel."

"I agree with Hozark," Demelza said. "It seems to be a perfect ruse. We eliminate the captain, completing Hozark's contract. He then takes his place, and we land within Sunar's defenses as if it were a normal visit. Thus, we bypass any nasty business working our way inside, and no one shall be the wiser."

"But what if they catch on? And what if they make us land outside the compound? Then we'd still have to find our way in through all of those defenses. Have you thought about that?"

Hozark chuckled. "Bud, your very reaction to hearing Dortzal's name should answer that question for you. A man of his reputation would not be treated as an ordinary visitor."

For all of his uncertainties, Bud knew the assassin was right. Though Visla Sunar was a powerful man, capable of demanding fealty of most who passed through his doors, one such as Captain Dortzal would be treated with a certain degree of deference.

And as a slave trader, and one who had likely provided many Ootaki to the visla over the years, no less, Dortzal had undoubtedly earned that respect.

"So, I guess that's it, then," Bud grumbled. "I can't believe we're doing this."

"Yet you were all gung-ho and ready to charge into Visla Sunar's compound," Demelza noted.

"To rescue Laskar, yes. He's my crew. I have a duty of care."

"And yet, taking out a far easier target is what has you concerned," Hozark chuckled. "Oh, my dear Uzabud, you continue to surprise me."

"Glad to provide some amusement," Bud groused. "So, what's the plan, then?"

"We will utilize one of the more disposable of the spare craft you keep mounted to the hull. I think the Fahkran skimmer should do just fine."

"That piece of junk? It's pretty fast, but its defensive spells are incredibly glitchy."

"Precisely."

"So we do what with it, exactly? Leave it floating out in space for them to salvage? I mean, it's not good for much. It doesn't seem like they'd waste their time on an empty junker like that."

"Empty? Oh, it won't be empty," Hozark said with a wicked grin.

"I do *not* like the sound of that."

"I'm sorry, Bud, but for this plan to succeed, I'm afraid you will need to be 'captured' by Captain Dortzal. It's the only way we can be certain the crew will all be on board with the story we are creating."

"But he might just as soon kill me, Hozark. Have you considered that?"

"Of course, my dear Uzabud. But never fear. It will not be the real Captain Dortzal you encounter."

"No?"

"No. I will have entered the ship and taken his place long before you ever set foot aboard."

"But how do you plan to do that?"

"We have our ways," he said with a wry grin. "Demelza, I shall require you to accompany Bud on his capture."

"I had assumed as much," she replied.

"But if she's captured too, what good does——"

"She will not be captured, Bud. She will be under cover of a shimmer cloak aboard your craft when it is taken."

"Exactly," she said. "I will then follow you aboard Captain Dortzal's ship, where I will shed my camouflage and disguise myself as a new transfer to the ship, upon which I will blend in with the actual crew well."

"You see, Bud, if all goes according to plan, the only actual person we will need to eliminate will be the captain himself. It is far easier to complete the illusion we require if the entirety of the crew is actually comprised of true Tslavar mercenaries."

Bud didn't like it. Not one bit. But he had to admit there was a certain elegance to the plan. Using the real slave-trading mercenaries to complete the disguise, and all without their knowledge? It was a stroke of genius. But then, that was why Hozark was one of the most sought-after and highest-paid assassins in the galaxy.

While others might waste the blood and magic of thousands storming the gates of such a facility, his Wampeh friend would stroll right through the front doors. Better yet, he would be readily invited in.

"All right," Bud grumbled. "What do I need to do?"

CHAPTER NINE

Captain Dortzal's ship was a fearsome thing to behold. Decades spent clawing his way to the top of the slaver/mercenary heap had seen him amass a small fortune, and along with it, the salvaged spoils of his many conflicts. He had also secured the good graces of a number of powerful vislas and emmiks, more than a few of them affiliated with or actual members of the Council of Twenty.

The magical stores aboard his craft were abundant, and his crew was one of the most well-armed and well fed in the galaxy. His stable of Drooks were likewise treated to a lifestyle far superior to even the typically comfortable existence they were usually afforded.

Of course, he did not actually *need* the Drooks. More than one grateful visla had provided him with a Drookonus in payment for his services. At this late stage in his career, he had nearly a dozen of the devices tucked away in his ship's innermost vault.

It was a cache he would never need to use, though. For his Drooks to run so low on magic as to require him to break into that secret stash would mean he had driven them to exhaustion, and that would mean he had encountered a foe that could either best him or flee from him.

Neither event was likely.

He was one of the biggest sharks in a vast sea, and short of falling on the Council's bad side, he was more or less free to do as he pleased with no fear of reprisal.

That was about to change.

Captain Dortzal had been spotted in orbit above the planet of Augus, a trading world a mere three systems away. It was a fortuitous location. The jump would barely drain Hozark's Drookonus at all.

"Shall we?" he asked as he and Demelza settled into his shimmer ship.

"Indeed, lets," she replied. "I shall be back shortly, Uzabud. I will skree you for pickup when I've completed my task."

"I'll be here," the pilot said from the comfort of his ship. "Safe travels."

With that, Hozark released his docking spells and his little craft drifted away from Bud's mothership. A moment later, he engaged his Drookonus and jumped.

"There," he said, pointing out the sizable craft orbiting the green-blue orb.

"Bigger than I expected," Demelza noted.

"A sizable craft, yes."

"Good. The extra unoccupied spaces within should make it easier to go unseen during your incursion."

"I was just thinking the same thing," Hozark said as he slid his shimmer-cloaked craft up to the larger vessel's hull and fastened to it with a delicately placed docking spell.

Anything more substantial might trigger any one of a number of possible safeguards a ship of this sort might have in place. But this wasn't Hozark's first stealth insertion. Not by a long shot.

He muttered the words of the umbilical spell, providing himself a small corridor of air from his craft to the ship's hull.

"I shall see you soon," he said, then unsealed the door and stepped out into space, maneuvering himself quickly to the larger ship's skin.

He cast a sensing spell, ensuring no one was directly on the other side of the craft's hull, before casting his breaching spell. Without wasting another second, he uttered the words that parted the ship's body like an expert surgeon would a patient, slipping silently inside and sealing the breach in an instant.

He slipped under his shimmer cloak as he worked, rendering himself invisible as he carefully restored the violated section of hull to its former state. A few moments later, none would ever be able to tell there had been a breach at all.

Demelza carefully dissolved the docking spell and drifted away from the Tslavar ship, waiting until she was well clear of it before jumping back to the dangerous planet, where Bud was already waiting for her on the surface.

"I am back," she sent over skree. "Meet me at the rendezvous point in ten minutes."

"Will do," he replied, warming up the little hopper ship for departure.

She then dropped down into Ahkrahn's atmosphere, carefully guiding the cloaked craft to the wooded area not too far from Visla Sunar's estate. A recreational location that they had determined to be rarely frequented.

Demelza sealed the craft behind her as she exited, then cloaked herself and took off at a run for the nearby clearing where Bud had been waiting.

"I am aboard," she said from inside the gangway while Uzabud stretched lazily outside, putting on a show for any prying eyes that might be watching.

He was just another man out for a relaxing long lunch, or so it seemed. He turned and casually stepped back into his ship, sealed the door, and took off, all as slowly and relaxed as could be.

"How'd it go?" he asked.

"Perfectly."

"It's Hozark. I'd be surprised if it hadn't, to be honest." He steered the ship into space, heading to a nearby moon, where he'd left his mothership safely tucked away, awaiting their return. "So, I guess this is it, then."

"Yes, this is it."

"Damn. I still can't believe I'm doing this."

"It will be fine, Uzabud. Hozark's plan will work. You will be taken prisoner in no time."

"I know," he said with a groan. "That's what worries me."

The pair loaded into the Fahkran skimmer docked on the hull. Uzabud then released the binding spell and pulled away into space while Demelza donned her shimmer cloak and settled into a comfortable spot near the doorway the enemy would breach through. While they were busy with Bud, she would slide into their craft unnoted.

"Jumping," he announced, then cast the spell that would take them to the same system as Captain Dortzal's ship. Bud just hoped Hozark had been successful in his end of the task.

Hozark had not wasted a single moment upon his entry into the Tslavar ship. No sooner had he sealed the breach than he was on the move, taking a little bit of time to observe Dortzal as he ordered his men about, then stealthily making his way to locate the precise location of the captain's private quarters. That would be where he made the kill.

Of course, he was a master assassin and could eliminate Captain Dortzal pretty much anywhere on the ship, but the quiet seclusion of his personal rooms would be best. Once in his quarters, no one would dare interrupt their captain for anything short of an emergency, and that would give Hozark enough time to not only steal the man's physical identity, but also take a moment to practice his speech patterns and body tics and movements.

Fortunately, none of the captain's crew were remotely strong enough in natural magic to detect the Wampeh disguise. In fact, until they landed on Ahkrahn, he would be quite safe from prying eyes.

Once on the surface, however, it would be another matter entirely, for a sufficiently powerful visla might have a chance of piercing his disguise, and Visla Sunar was just that sort of man, if he chose to channel some of his Ootaki hair magic to those ends.

Hozark would worry about that when the time arose. Odds were Sunar would not waste valuable magic boosting his own innate gifts while safely within his innermost walls. It was a bit of a gamble, but given the security of his compound, it seemed a fair bet. Innate magic users knew its true value, and they tended to hoard rather than squander it.

For now, he had a captain to dispose of and a crew to deceive.

The captain walked the corridors, passing the shimmer-cloaked assassin without sensing a thing, then entered his chambers and shut the door. This was the time to act, but quite interestingly, Hozark was fortunate to have observed a rather unusual interaction.

It seemed the captain had taken a shine to a very young and very green new crewmember. The lad couldn't have been in the mercenary game more than a few months, and for whatever reasons, be they savory or not, Sunar seemed to favor the young man.

It was perfect, and precisely the sort of thing Hozark could exploit.

CHAPTER TEN

"What the bloody hell do you want? This better be important!" Captain Dortzal growled, shirtless and with damp hair, as he pulled open the door to his quarters.

"I...I'm sorry, sir. It's just, I was unsure about how you wanted..." The young Tslavar hesitated as his gaze flicked to the many scars on the captain's muscular torso. His cheeks went a bit deeper green. "Uh, never mind. I'm sorry I bothered you, sir."

A little smile teased the corners of Dortzal's lips.

"No, you did the right thing, Tür. Come in, and let's discuss this. In depth. I know it can be hard for you at times."

Tür swallowed hard and nodded, then quietly entered the captain's quarters. The captain gave the youth an appreciative look as he passed, then sealed the door behind him, redoubling his muffling spells to ensure privacy.

His intention was to keep prying ears from hearing what he did in his spare time. The unintended side effect was those very same spells muffling the lone, brief, desperate cry of a dying man.

Hozark dropped the Tslavar disguise as soon as the little blade in his hand had snuffed the spark from Captain

Dortzal's eyes. Such a tiny thing, the blade. Not even enchanted. And yet, it had taken so much from him. Everything, in fact.

It was something even the roughest of mercenaries often had a difficult time with. Ending someone with a knife. There was a visceral connection to it, watching the life fade from their face mere inches away. It was for that reason most opted for swords or magic in combat.

But Hozark was a Wampeh Ghalian, and he had taken lives more up close and personal than this on countless occasions. It was only because the captain possessed no power of his own that he didn't drain him, feeling him shift from a living person with hopes and dreams to an inanimate bag of meat and bones growing cold beneath his lips.

Any observing the scene from arm's length would have witnessed what appeared to be Captain Dortzal killing Captain Dortzal. Hozark had uttered the specialized spells and begun shifting his disguise to that of the dying man before his body hit the floor.

Shirtless, his torso riddled with old scars, just as the captain had been, the assassin quickly stashed the body in one of the captain's private lockers and cast a sealing spell upon it. No foul odor or inadvertent opening would give away its true contents. Not until long after the task had been completed.

A knock at the door.

Hozark double-checked his appearance in a looking glass, ensuring everything was just right, then answered the call.

"Uh, Captain Dortzal?" the young Tslavar said, hesitantly.

It was Tür. The *real* Tür, Hozark noted with a degree of amusement at the lad's timing. He noted his eyes dart to the scars on his broad chest, each of them matching those of the real captain. Assuming the confident posturing of the dead man, he leaned into the role, an air of disquieting intimacy to his authoritarian tone.

"What the hell is it?" he growled as he looked the youth up and down.

"Uh, we just received word of a possible salvage, sir."

"You know I don't care much for mere salvage."

"Yes, but this is different. There seems to be someone aboard. Someone from a distant system."

"No one knows they're here?" the disguised assassin asked.

"It seems not, sir."

A wicked smile spread across the ersatz captain's lips. "Excellent. You've done well."

"Thank you, Captain."

"Relay my command to the bridge. We make for the distressed ship at once. Have Starnnik skree down and inform the men gathering supplies on the surface we will return for them straightaway. For now, they are to continue their tasks."

"Aye, aye, sir," the young man said, then turned and hurried off to his duties as his captain watched with an unsavory leer.

Hozark closed the door and adjusted his disguise spells, locking them in place firmly. *Was that a bit overboard?* he wondered.

Then he reflected on the way the real captain had looked at him only a few minutes before and realized that no, it was not overboard at all. In fact, it had been perfectly in character.

So far, the plan was going smoothly, but he knew all too well how easily things could take a turn for the worse. But until that happened, it was full speed ahead.

"Status?" Hozark barked as he strode into the command center.

The men and women were mercenaries, but nevertheless, they snapped to attention as their captain entered.

"We have the ship in range and have deployed a series of blocking spells to inhibit it from jumping away, Captain," a woman with a long scar across her cheek said from her station.

"It looks like they've only got minimal power to their ship. It seems to be run by a drained Drookonus."

"So, no Drooks to sweeten the score?" Hozark said. "A pity. Is this piece of refuse even worth our time?"

"Well, there is one person aboard," she replied. "Though he's been rather pathetic in his skree communications."

"Pathetic?"

"The usual, sir. Whining. Telling his sad tale. Begging for mercy. That sort of thing,"

Hozark laughed, the captain's gruff voice coming from his mouth, courtesy of his Ghalian magic.

"No mercy. Not when there is coin to be had," he said. He spotted the young crewmember across the command center. "Isn't that right, Tür?"

"Uh, yes. Never leave coin on the table, Captain," he said, both thrilled and terrified to be singled out in front of the others.

"Well said," Hozark replied with a grin. "All right, then. Stun spells, but go light with them. No sense wasting resources over just one man."

"Aye, aye, Captain," the weapons specialist said as he prepared to cast.

The words flowed from his lips as the konuses mounted to his station delivered the magic needed to overwhelm the hapless man within the little derelict craft. The small spell was easily enough to render anyone unconscious. Anyone who didn't know what was coming, that is. And Hozark had made sure that Bud and Demelza both had ample shielding power to protect them.

They moved in quickly to secure the drifting ship and its crew, assuming its pilot to be incapacitated. But that was far from reality, for once the spell had hit the craft and dissipated, Demelza would collect the defensive konuses from her colleague and hide them on herself beneath her shimmer cloak.

To the average observer boarding the little ship, it appeared as though Bud had been knocked unconscious. But he was alert.

Playing a part. And Demelza? The assassin stealthily followed him into the invading party's craft.

"We have taken both the ship and its pilot," Hozark was informed.

"Good. Place him in holding and secure his craft. I know just the place to go to see if any coin is to be had for it."

No one was the wiser, it seemed, and the plan was getting underway just as they had hoped. Now they just needed to take their time, resupplying and acting completely normally to avoid drawing any suspicion from the crew. Then, and only then, they would head to Ahkrahn.

"Ahkrahn?" the scarred woman asked when told their eventual destination.

"Yes. It is time to offload some of our cargo, and Visla Sunar will give us a good price for our wares."

"Of course, Captain," she replied, still a bit unsure.

This could be a problem. Apparently, visiting Sunar's estate was a bit more of an unusual occurrence than he'd originally expected. Hozark had to improvise, and fast.

"We will be flying hard after this. I want my cells full and coffers overflowing in a month's time," he growled.

"Yes, Captain."

"*But*, given the tasks that await us, it is my desire that the crew have a little shore leave before we embark on such a strenuous task. *That* is why I have selected Visla Sunar's estate as our destination. The cities around him are ideal for the men to recreate while I deal with the visla."

Heads turned ever so slightly at his words. The crew knew better than to tempt fate and express their disbelief and excitement at the prospect of shore leave on Ahkrahn. Compared to most worlds they stopped on, this would be a downright luxurious respite, though one man couldn't help but say something.

"Your generosity is appreciated, Captain. And *two* shore leaves in so short a period? Thank you, sir. Thank you!"

The others glared at the man, silently willing him to just shut the hell up before he made the captain change his mind.

Shit. They just had shore leave? Hozark silently lamented. *Incredible. Just my luck. Well, there's nothing to do about it now.*

"Yes. A second respite break is warranted," he said to the assembled crew. "But it is not out of the kindness of my heart, I can assure you." His steely glare made it clear he was speaking true. "I noted an increase in productivity after the last shore leave. This pleases me, and I wish to see this trend continue. But do not mistakenly think this is about your happiness. It is about your work improving. Disappoint me, and it will be a long, long time before it happens again."

Silent nods met his gaze as the crew set back to work.

Good. This is working out after all, he mused.

All that remained now was the tedium of returning to orbit and completing their resupply. After that, the interesting part would begin.

CHAPTER ELEVEN

With one of his and Demelza's previously delayed contracts completed, and the dead man's ship now under his command, Hozark settled into the captain's quarters to study the cargo manifest and familiarize himself with his new assets.

Distasteful as it was, he was a slave trader, for all intents and purposes, and he had to act the part. And that included potentially selling or trading some of his cargo upon arrival on Ahkrahn. Fortunately, despite his often brutal ways, Visla Sunar was a businessman first and foremost.

The slaves in his stables were always well cared for. Not for their benefit, of course, but because a healthy slave fetched a higher price. And it looked like he would be adding a few more to those numbers soon. The one question that lingered, however, was why Laskar had been moved to the innermost part of the visla's compound.

Regardless of their landing within the inner walls, this would nevertheless be a far from simple rescue. Something, Hozark again reminded himself, Wampeh Ghalian simply did not do.

But this was different, and it was not for hire. This was saving a part of his––he hated to say it––*team*. Those to whom he owed a debt of gratitude. There was simply nothing else for it.

A knock at his door rang out right on schedule.

"Come," he called out, releasing the door's locking wards.

A pair of guards entered the room, a somewhat disheveled prisoner shoved in front of them.

"This is the newest addition?"

"Yes, Captain. As you requested."

Hozark eyed their new prize with interest. "Very well. I'll take it from here."

"Will you be wanting this, Captain?" the man asked, holding out a gleaming golden band.

"Of course. Leave it on the table. I will not require it for now," he said, adjusting the konus on his wrist with a menacing grin.

The guards nodded, then left both the control collar and prisoner in their captain's more than capable hands.

"Well, that sure sucked," Bud said, taking a seat once the door had sealed and the silencing wards were once again put in place.

The captain stared at him silently a moment.

"Uh, that is you, isn't it?"

Hozark cracked a grin. "Indeed, it is, Bud. Good to see you, my friend."

"They stuck me in a cell with the most disgusting creature I've ever seen. Stumpy little legs that only came up to my knees. And rolls of dark-gray skin that it actually hid bits of food in."

"Ah, that sounds like a Faroon. Quite unusual to find one outside of their own system. Did it happen to have external gill apparatus?"

"You mean the weird frilly stuff sticking out of its neck?"

"To aid in gas exchange as it breathes. Yes, a Faroon, most certainly. Not a true amphibian race, mind you, but they can draw breath from many environments not suited to most other species."

"Well, gee, thanks, Hozark. I feel so much better about being stuck in a box with a stinky, frilly-necked, food-hoarding, non-amphibian. Totally makes it all right."

Hozark chuckled. "You knew this would be a difficult mission, Bud. And I remind you, it is *your* copilot we are rescuing."

"I know, I know," Bud groused. "So, I see you had no trouble assuming Dortzal's place."

"The transfer went smoothly, yes. I also learned a bit more about our cargo, now that I have full access to all of the manifests. It seems we are carrying not only the regular retinue of run-of-the-mill slave laborers, but there is apparently a contingent of Ootaki aboard."

"Not terribly unusual, though."

"No. But *these* Ootaki were free-folk."

Bud blanched. "You mean, they found one of the uncharted enclaves?"

"It would appear that way. Mind you, it was a small group, and the larger, neighboring communities appear to have caught wind of the attack before the Tslavars reached their homes. But nevertheless, there are roughly a dozen Ootaki aboard. And all of them unshorn."

Bud realized what that meant. Power. A lot of power. And their ticket into Sunar's innermost sanctum. But there was a problem.

"You know how I feel about slavery, Hozark."

"And you know I am in agreement with you," the assassin replied. "However, this group is already in slave trader hands. And at least on Ahkrahn, they will be well treated. It seems Dortzal's original intent was to bring these directly to a member of the Council of Twenty, bypassing the normal channels."

"That's weird," Bud said.

"Indeed. And more unusual is that there is no mention of the person's name. It seems the captain was being far more cautious than normal in keeping this a secret."

"It's like what happened with Visla Horvath and Emmik Rostall," Bud noted. "They were pulling some sneaky shit too."

"There seems to be a silent power struggle going on within the Council of Twenty. And someone is amassing Ootaki, likely gathering up all the power they can before making their move. By depositing these Ootaki with Visla Sunar, we are disrupting their plans, though not by design."

"Call it an extra bonus, then," Bud said with a grin. "So, what's next?"

Hozark's eyes fell upon the golden control collar resting on the table, and the smile fell from Bud's face.

"Captain Dortzal! Visla Sunar has asked me to wish you a warm welcome to his humble estate."

The estate was anything but humble. Opulent in its splendor was more like it. But Hozark merely nodded offhandedly to the visla's servant.

"Where's the visla? I don't deal with lackeys," Hozark said, playing the role of cocky slaver captain to the hilt.

"Ah, yes. Well, you see, we were not expecting you, Captain," the man continued.

"No, you were not. But when I came across this cargo, I knew the visla would be most interested in them, so I plotted a course straight here to give him first pick."

Seventeen collared slaves were ushered out of the craft as they spoke. The inner walls were too small to accommodate the slave captain's ship, but given the nature of his cargo, he was offered a landing spot inside the main walls and right up against the entry to the central enclave.

"The visla wished me to invite you to dinner later. He should have time after—Oh, my!" the servant said as the flow of slave offerings shifted from laborers and gladiator fodder to a small group of Ootaki, their golden hair long and unshorn. "The visla will be most pleased indeed!" he exclaimed. "Please, follow me. The visla is, of course, most thrilled to have you with us. Allow me to show you to a room we have readied for you."

The man then nodded to the guards. The slaves would be taken to the holding pens, where they would be fed and allowed to rest before being inspected by the visla himself.

"You, there," Hozark called out to one of the slaves.

"Me?"

"Yes, you. Come here."

The recently captured man stepped out from the line and made his way to the Tslavar captain.

"Those bags there. Pick them up and follow me," Hozark commanded, then turned back to the visla's welcoming party. "This one seems strong enough of back and weak enough of mind. I think I will utilize him as a manservant until the trade is complete."

"Of course, Captain. Now, please, if you'll follow me."

They started walking, but Uzabud was staring at the opulence of the visla's home, and as a result was a little slow in picking up the captain's bags.

"*Nari pa!*" the visla's servant said.

Bud fell to his knees as the stun spell surged through his control collar.

"You would do well to remember your place, slave. Now, pick up your master's bags and follow."

Bud bit his tongue and grabbed the bags. To mouth off would only result in more shocks, and though Hozark had modified the control collar as best he could to reduce its potency, there was simply no way he could be brought into the grounds without one.

A false collar, though useful in lesser worlds, was out of the question. Something like that would be noticed almost immediately. So it was that Bud was forced to wear an actual control collar in order to gain access to the visla's grounds. For the moment, Bud really was a slave.

"At least give me the release spell," he had begged Hozark.

"I will tell it to you, but you are an unpowered being, Bud. Without a konus to power the spell, you will be unable to cast it."

"Still, I'd feel better having it."

"Very well. The spell is Captain Dortzal's own modification. '*Ngthiri oolama tzaldor.*'"

"Got it."

"Remember, Bud, it will not work for you without a konus."

"I know."

"And prepare yourself for what is to come. As a slave, you may experience some... *discomfort* while within the visla's walls."

"How bad can it be?"

Hours later, Bud had indeed experienced a little taste of what his friend had warned him about. Fun, it was not. Shifting into his role as slave, he shouldered the bags and followed Hozark and Visla Sunar's servant into the depths of the innermost chambers.

Hozark turned to his crew as they departed. "You men, tell the others once the ship is clean and secured, they're released for shore leave in the city. Recreate and enjoy yourselves, but remember, you represent Captain Dortzal while on this world, and I expect you to not sully my reputation. You know what'll happen to any who do."

The Tslavars indeed knew full well what it meant to incur the wrath of their captain and merely nodded respectfully, then set about their tasks, looking forward to the many pleasures to be had in the nearby town.

Bud trotted behind Hozark and their guide, his bags hanging from both shoulders and across his back. For so short a stay, the captain certainly did seem to have a fair amount of luggage. But for one such as Captain Dortzal, allowances for eccentricity were made.

Still, a perfunctory magical examination of the bags was made as soon as they'd been placed within the compound walls. Clothing, a few bottles of spirits, but nothing more. No hidden weapons or magical devices of any sort. He was obeying the rules of the house, as was expected of one such as he.

What Visla Sunar's staff did not know was that the 'slave' he had then called over to carry his bags was actually armed to the teeth, with all manner of magical and conventional devices fastened to his body beneath his loose-fitting slave's garb.

He wore a control collar. He was a slave. He was less than a person in their eyes, and no one would ever think he would be carrying forbidden weapons. And Hozark was taking full advantage of that fact.

CHAPTER TWELVE

"That was *not* cool," Bud grumbled as he ran his fingers across the skin of his neck beneath the smooth metal collar. "That shit *hurt!*"

"It was a stun spell, Bud. It was supposed to hurt," Hozark replied. "Maybe if you'd been paying more attention to the part you were playing rather than sightseeing, you would have avoided the discomfort. Though, to be fair, it did reinforce the illusion quite nicely."

"Illusion? The bastard actually shocked me."

"Yes. And with that, he felt completely at ease with you, henceforth viewing you as nothing more than a mere slave and not worthy of any more of his attention. Sometimes being invisible has nothing at all to do with the use of a shimmer cloak or camouflage, Bud. Sometimes, being of a certain class is enough. And with that, you often find you will have access to places otherwise unreachable."

Bud thought on it a long moment. Of course, Hozark was right. The man had infiltrated countless high-security establishments, killing their inhabitants and escaping intact every time. He was one of the five Ghalian masters. When it came to this sort of thing, only a fool would question his expertise.

"So, we're inside now. But how do we find Laskar? I didn't see any sign of him when we were escorted in."

"Once again, this is where your less-than-a-person status comes in handy. I obviously cannot inquire of the man, but you are a servant. And servants see all. Here, put this on," Hozark said, tossing a clean tunic to the collared man.

"What's this?"

"Proper servant's attire. The more you look like my personal assistant and not a run-of-the-mill slave, the more likely the other staff will speak freely with you."

Hozark's plan was suddenly beginning to become a bit clearer. He would play the part that had allowed them access into the innermost reaches of the visla's private estate, but it was Bud who would likely have the most success finding out the actual location of their endangered friend.

Hozark summoned one of the residence's staff via the convenient house skree located in his chamber. A few minutes later, a pale blue woman with enormous eyes and an opalescent sheen to her skin appeared at his door.

"Yes, Captain? You summoned?"

"I am hungry, and it looks like I won't be dining with Visla Sunar until much later. I need some food."

"Of course, Captain. What can I bring for you?"

"My servant knows my tastes. I am going to take a hot bath and wash away the aches from far too much time out in space."

"It would be my pleasure, Captain," Bud said, leaning into the role.

Hozark merely grunted, then strode off into the bathing chamber, sealing the door behind him. Uzabud and the blue woman were completely alone.

"Sorry for his abruptness. He was a little put out that the visla was making him wait," Bud said.

"Oh, that's all right," the woman said. "We know how stressed powerful men can be."

"That we do. But why would Visla Sunar be stressed? It seems he's got the world in his hand."

"Perhaps, but he's a very busy man. Now, what would your master like to eat?"

"Vinarus fruit are a favorite of his. And some shaved bundabist meat, if you have any."

"Of course we do."

"Great. And what do you mean, busy? I can't see how Visla Sunar could be that much busier than most?"

"He has had a great many visitors of late. And with the slaying of several of the Council's key members and associates, things have been in a bit of a mess."

"I heard about that. We were near a system where a man named Rostall fell. I believe he was loosely affiliated."

"Oh, more than that," the woman said. "He was a regular guest here, in fact."

"A mere emmik?"

"An emmik who swam in deep waters, and with much larger fish."

"I heard he knew a Visla Horvath, but that was just a superficial business dealing."

She smiled. She knew something this newcomer obviously didn't. "Rostall and Horvath traveled *together*. They were far closer than others realized, I think. Regular guests of Visla Sunar, in fact. It was quite a tragedy to learn they had both fallen."

"Yeah, terrible," Bud agreed, the gears in his mind churning.

Hozark would find this tidbit *most* interesting. Visla Sunar was known for not taking sides. He was in it for coin. But this did not sound like neutrality. Not at all, in fact. It sounded like far more was at play than they'd realized.

But that was secondary. First and foremost, Laskar needed to be saved. After that, *then* they could dig deeper into this new wrinkle in the mysterious goings-on within the Council of Twenty.

"You know, I've heard that there have been a lot of spies captured in a whole bunch of systems. Might be what happened to Visla Horvath. I guess they're infiltrating all kinds of powerful people's estates."

"Not here, that's for sure," she replied. "No one would be so foolish."

"So, no high-value prisoners, then?"

"Not in the visla's prisons, no."

A look of surprise flashed across Bud's face. "Really? I thought Visla Sunar was known for his, uh, *proclivities*."

The woman looked around with a conspiratorial look and lowered her voice. "You didn't hear it from me, but there is *one*, I suppose. None of us see him, though. The visla keeps him locked up in a private chamber near his own quarters. Rumor is, he can interrogate him at his leisure that way."

"Well, I suppose even a visla needs a bit of recreation at times," Bud said, a sinking feeling settling into his gut.

"And what could be more relaxing than a little bit of torture, right?" she replied with a grim laugh.

Bud chuckled, an utterly false bit of levity, beneath which the cold, hard determination set in, tinged with a healthy bit of anger. Hozark had been right. Staff knew far more than one would expect. And the news had been anything but good.

His friend and copilot was being held nearby, and he was being tortured. And he and Hozark were going to put a stop to it, whatever it took.

CHAPTER THIRTEEN

Uzabud had relayed the revelation about Laskar's whereabouts and dire circumstances to his assassin friend as soon as they were alone in their chamber once more. Hozark had been less than thrilled at the news.

"You realize, this will make recovering Laskar difficult."

"I know, I know."

"*Very* difficult."

"I said I know, Hozark."

The Wampeh paced the room for a few minutes, mulling over the new information and how they might best utilize this knowledge to their advantage. Unfortunately, as he was expected to be present in the guise of Captain Dortzal, Hozark simply did not have the freedom of movement to make an attempt to free Laskar. And Bud, while granted the social invisibility of the slave class, was sadly lacking in access to areas of the compound where his 'owner' was not.

That left but one option.

"Come along, Uzabud. We are taking a little stroll," Hozark said as he opened the door to their chambers and stepped into the corridor.

"Are we—"

"Follow silently, *slave*," the disguised assassin said sharply, reminding his friend of his role while putting on the expected show for the pair of servants walking down the hallway.

"Apologies, Master," Bud said, his eyes lowered as he fell in behind Hozark.

"You two. The inner courtyard is up ahead to the left, is it not? I desire fresh air before I meet with Visla Sunar for dinner," Hozark said to the approaching servants.

"Yes, sir. It is."

"Excellent," he replied, then strode off down the hallway. "An impressive building, Visla Sunar has," he said to Bud, but not. "The chambers adjacent to his quarters seem like they would be quite an interesting place to visit, were they not occupied by his *other* guest."

Hozark did not look at the empty spot adjacent to the small pedestal on which a bust of the visla rested. He did not even pause as he walked past. But Demelza, hidden and invisible in her shimmer cloak, knew he sensed her. That conversation was not for Bud's benefit, but for hers.

She was good with a shimmer cloak. Very good, in fact, though nowhere near the master Ghalian's level of skill. Hozark could utilize his at a full run, wielding spells and weapons, no less, while she needed to remain nearly still when others were close by to maintain her invisibility.

It was something that came with practice and age, and Master Hozark simply had more of both. But that did not matter at this moment. The mission was squarely in her hands. She would make her way to Visla Sunar's private chambers while Hozark did his best to impersonate the dead Tslavar captain.

No pressure.

Visla Sunar kept Hozark waiting for only ten minutes when he and Uzabud arrived in the smaller dining hall they'd been directed to. As it was an intimate affair, and one the visla had not been planning on, a less resplendent setting would suit them just fine.

The interesting thing about this particular situation was that Hozark had quite unexpectedly placed himself in the perfect position to eliminate Visla Sunar. This deep within his compound, the assassination would be a very feasible thing, and none would be the wiser until he was long gone.

But Sunar was not a contract, and the Ghalian did not kill randomly. Someday, that job might come their way, but until that time, Visla Sunar would live.

It was not lost on Hozark that for this rescue of their annoying comrade, he had stumbled upon an unusually fast and efficient means into the visla's grounds. It was the sort of thing that would often take months of planning, steering the pieces from systems away until they all lined up just right before he could act. A plan more difficult than the killing itself.

But Laskar was leading a charmed life, it seemed—aside from the capture and torture, that is—for they had found a way to reach him in record time. And more than that, it had actually worked. And while eliminating a contracted target, no less.

Demelza had taken the side corridor toward the visla's private chambers as soon as Hozark and Bud had passed her, but the visla had several wards and booby traps laid on the approach. They weren't difficult for the experienced assassin, but they took time, for she had to reset them after she passed each one, hiding her entry should any follow in her wake.

Hozark would be dining with the visla for at least another ten or fifteen minutes, she figured. Of course, that was assuming the man had kept his guests waiting, as was almost always the case with men of power such as he.

Bud, standing quietly against the wall near his master, was carrying weapons secreted on his person should they be required. Once again, none thought to even look at the lowly slave.

The master assassin was fortunate, however, that Visla Sunar was somewhat distracted by other things on his plate, and the thought of casting probing spells that might pierce Hozark's disguise had not even crossed his mind.

For one, he knew Captain Dortzal, and that was indeed his ship parked outside and his crew recreating nearby. And on top of that, there were a dozen new Ootaki in his possession now, and despite the price paid for them, they were not the sort of thing an impostor would part with easily.

And so it was, they had casual chatter over a light meal. It was apparent the visla had other guests awaiting his attention as well, but he did his best to at least give the bearer of such valuable merchandise enough time to make him feel special.

Everyone had to be made to feel special, he had learned. It fostered loyalty and goodwill, and though he really didn't give a damn about anyone but himself, some things had to be done in the interest of expanding his power. This was simply one of them.

Two-thirds of the way through their light repast, a servant— a well-dressed woman *not* wearing a control collar, Hozark noted—entered the dining hall and whispered in the visla's ear. The visla's face remained impassive, but his guest had been at this game a long, long time, and reading microexpressions was as second nature as breathing for him.

"I'm afraid I am needed," Visla Sunar said, rising from his seat. "Please, make yourself at home. Enjoy the grounds, perhaps utilize the spa facilities. I have some wonderful masseuses on hand who can relieve all manner of tension."

"Thanks," Hozark said in Captain Dortzal's gruff voice. "I may just do that."

The visla nodded once, then turned and left the room, his retinue following behind him until all that remained were Hozark and his faux slave.

"A bit early," Hozark noted. "But it should have been enough time. We should head to the dead drop straightaway. If she succeeded, the marker will be there."

He rose and strode from the chamber, Bud close behind. They crossed the nearby inner courtyard, reaching the bust of Visla Sunar. There at the base was a tiny marking, no more than a smudge. But to Hozark's eye, it was a welcome sign.

"Success," he quietly said as he obliterated the mark with the toe of his boot. "Come, slave, we have things to do."

CHAPTER FOURTEEN

The door had barely closed and the sound-dampening spells secured in place when Bud shed all pretense of a demure slave and began pacing the room like a caged animal.

"Okay, we have to get the hell out of here. You saw that, right? That was *not* normal. Did you see how she whispered in his ear? He knows, Hozark. I'm telling you, he knows."

"Relax, my friend. If the visla suspected anything, we'd have likely engaged in battle right then and there. I agree that it is entirely possible that there is *something* afoot on his grounds, but *we* are not the cause for concern. At least, not at the moment. And by the time we are, we shall be long gone."

"How can you be so sure? We don't even know if Demelza's been caught or killed! Oh my gods, what if that's what it was all about? What if they––?

"Bud, please," Hozark calmly interrupted. "Really, you are beginning to whine as badly as Laskar. Using an expression you are so fond of, please chill the fuck out."

Bud froze, his expression trapped between shock and amusement. Finally, the latter won out, and he burst into chuckles. Hozark, the stoic, deadly, quiet master assassin, had just made a funny.

"Okay, okay. Message received," Bud said, regaining his composure. "But we need to contact Demelza and have her speed up whatever she has planned."

"Bud, please," Hozark replied. "She has already completed her task."

"I'm sorry, she what?"

"Demelza has freed Laskar and is awaiting us in an antechamber just down the hallway."

"You didn't tell me anything about us meeting in another room."

"No, I did not. Had you been captured, you would have likely been unable to withstand the visla's torture. And, as you know, you cannot disclose information you do not possess."

Bud blinked. "You thought I might get tortured?"

"It *was* a possibility. You are carrying a variety of weapons, after all."

"That *you* told me to carry. And you didn't think to warn me about this?"

"Again, had I done so, your attitude would have reeked of paranoia and drawn unwanted attention," the assassin replied. "Uzabud, you are a trusted companion, and one of the best pilots, pirates, and smugglers I've ever known. But your acting skills? Let us just say there are still a few areas in which your abilities could use refinement."

"Gee, thanks."

"Honesty is far more useful than empty flattery. Now, let us cease this chatter and make haste. I need to help her apply a disguise to Laskar to aid in his escape."

Hozark and Bud stepped into the hallway once more, the faux Tslavar captain strolling casually as if he and his servant were merely out for a relaxing walk of the grounds. Three minutes later, they arrived at a nondescript door just past a servants' storage area.

The tiny smudge on the floor disappeared beneath Hozark's boot as he quietly knocked twice, then once, then three times. The door opened, and he and Bud quickly slipped inside.

"Laskar! You're okay!" Bud exclaimed as he wrapped up his copilot in an enormous embrace. The man may have been in his mid-thirties, but his demeanor was nevertheless that of a far younger man. Sadly, so was his maturity at times.

"Hey, easy there," his rescued friend replied. "Don't bruise the merchandise."

Bud pulled back with a little chuckle. "Sorry. Are you hurt?"

"What? Oh, no, nothing like that. I'm okay."

"He was in good condition when I found him," Demelza noted. "No obvious signs of torture. The visla is a talented man, and his magical violence does not leave marks."

"We would do much the same," Hozark noted as he studied the man. "So, you are in sound enough condition to walk?"

"Yeah, I think so," Laskar replied.

"Good. We need to apply a few layers of disguise spells on you before you make your exit from the compound. I'm afraid as a non-Wampeh, this may hurt a little."

"How bad can it——Holy shit!" he blurted as the first spell took hold.

"I warned you," Hozark said, uttering the next spell, fixing the altered visage in place. "It will hold up to close scrutiny by all but the most powerful of users, but only for a short while. You and Demelza will have to make haste in your exit."

"Hang on. We're not going too?" Bud asked.

"We have things to do first, Bud. And you are Captain Dortzal's slave assistant. I'm afraid I shall require your presence at my side to complete the disguise."

"Well, shit," Bud grumbled. "I guess we'd better get to it, then."

After a few more minutes of unprofessional grousing, Laskar was thoroughly changed in appearance. Where the man was a tall and fairly handsome fellow under normal circumstances, he now sported the visage of a much older Bantoon.

Making his skin appear blue and loose, as that species' flesh so often was, had been relatively easy. Altering his height, however, had required a bit of finagling. Finally, his body had bent as required to fit the visual output of the spell. It would not be comfortable, but if all went according to plan, he wouldn't have to stay in costume long.

"We will meet you at the ship as soon as we are able," Hozark said as Demelza and Laskar prepared to leave. "The corridor through the servants' quarters will bypass the regular security posts and deposit you in the marketplace."

"Won't they be checking us?" Laskar asked.

"They only check on the way *in*," Hozark replied. "Those who make up the innermost staff have a certain degree of freedom of movement once within the walls. It is only when entering from the outside that they face true scrutiny. The regular cells are on the other side of the compound, and aside from that location, people would normally try to break in, not out."

"Come on," Demelza said, opting for a servant's disguise rather than her shimmer cloak. "Keep your mouth shut and let me do any talking. We could change your appearance, but I worry your voice may still sound like you, and we don't know who would take note of that."

Fortunately for her, they were largely able to avoid any conversations with other staff on their way through the servants' areas, though one curious older woman did inquire who these two newcomers were.

The busybody. Every estate seemed to have one.

Her explanations were good, and any other would have been satisfied and let the newcomers go about their work, but this particular woman continued to poke and prod. Demelza could not tell if she sensed something wrong or not, but time was of the essence.

"*Inoculo termus,*" she hissed, the almost silent spell striking the older woman down with a terrible, body-shaking trembling.

"Someone, help! She's having an episode!" Demelza said.

Staff came running, as expected, giving the assassin the opportunity she needed. "We'll get help!" she said, then took off at a hurried pace with Laskar following close behind.

A few minutes later, the woman and man who had gone to get help were out of the estate and nowhere to be found.

CHAPTER FIFTEEN

Hozark and Uzabud were clear across the facility, heading toward the exit into the outer courtyard where Captain Dortzal's massive ship was resting.

"We are done here," the disguised assassin barked to the men standing guard at the ship's entry. "Notify the crew on leave. They are recalled immediately. We are departing at once."

"Sir?" one said, puzzled.

"Yours is not to question. Only to obey, is that clear?" was the snarled reply.

"Of course, Captain," the man said, his back stiffening to attention.

"Good. The visla should have provided me my new toy by now. Has she been brought to my quarters?"

"Uh, I'm not sure, Captain. We've only been on duty for an hour."

Of course, Hozark knew full well when the shift change had occurred, and he was now using it to his full advantage.

"No matter. She will have been delivered by now," he said with a lustful grin. "When the crew has returned, we are to liftoff and make for Sinthall. I will be in my quarters, and I am not to be disturbed until we arrive. Is that perfectly clear?"

"Yes, sir," the men replied.

Their captain had a new toy aboard, and he was going to be putting her to good use, it seemed. The flight to Sinthall was a long one, and would afford him plenty of time to recreate to his heart's content.

Hozark strode through his ship with purpose and was about to step aside and alter Bud's appearance to aid in his escape from the ship when an unexpected youth rounded the corner. It was bad timing, but there was little that could be done.

"Captain. You're back early," young Tür said.

"I am. My business is done here."

"But didn't you want to––?"

"I said my business is done," he repeated far more forcefully.

"Of course, Captain. Apologies."

"You are to go to the command center and relay my orders, Tür."

"But I am new. Perhaps one of the more senior––"

"*This* is how you move up in this world," Captain Dortzal growled. "You don't wait for opportunity, you seize it. You want to be a captain yourself one day, do you not?"

"Yes, sir."

"Then start acting like it. Now, go tell them to set course for Sinthall. I want five jumps, back to back. And before you say it will wear out the Drooks, I know that. But it's good to give them a little run every so often, just to keep them on their game. I've been too easy on them of late. On all of you, for that matter."

Hozark leveled a firm stare at the young Tslavar. Yes, this had worked. The lad would do as he was told with no further questions.

"Go. I am to be left undisturbed until we arrive."

Tür nodded once and took off at a double-time run to inform the command center crew of the captain's orders. He actually seemed like he might have the stuff to make a captain one day, but Hozark would be nowhere near when that happened. And the youth would quite likely not survive that long.

He pulled Bud into the captain's chambers and spoke the words to remove the collar from his neck.

"It's about time," he said, rubbing where the metal had rested.

"Shh. Hold still," Hozark said. "And do not make a sound."

Bud had done this before, and he knew it was going to suck. But unlike Laskar, he bit his tongue and remained silent while Hozark worked his magic. A few moments later he looked like a Tslavar.

It wasn't Hozark's best work, but given the rush with which everyone was returning to the ship, he wouldn't face much scrutiny at all. And on a craft of this size, new crew was coming aboard with some regularity.

The assassin then slid into his shimmer cloak and opened the door. The coast was clear.

"Go. I will be right behind you."

"I'll have to take your word for it," Bud replied to the thin air.

The shimmer offered an additional degree of safety as they made their escape. Should Bud be stopped for any reason, Hozark could strike out of nowhere, eliminating whoever stood in their way and clearing their path without breaking stride. But they made it off of the ship without incident.

"Just making a last rounder to be sure there are no stragglers," Bud said to the visla's guards as he stepped outside the gates leading toward the city.

The men merely nodded. A steady stream of Tslavar mercenaries had been returning to their ship, so this was not unusual in the slightest.

Bud ducked down an alleyway once they'd made it into town, where Hozark removed the disguise from his friend and restored him to his normal appearance.

"Oh, that's much better," Bud said with a sigh. "That is really uncomfortable, you know."

"I do. And you are far more professional than your friend."

"He's just new to it, is all."

Hozark was too professional to roll his eyes, but Bud knew he was doing it on the inside.

The pair walked the marketplace and casually made their way out of the center and toward the shimmer-cloaked ship parked not too far away, just as Demelza had left it prior to beginning their mission. Behind them, Captain Dortzal's ship lifted into the sky and pulled up through the exosphere, where it then jumped away in a magical flash.

The unexpected departure would be a source of much discussion when the visla's prisoner was discovered to have gone missing. Soon, all eyes would be looking for that ship, and the multiple linked jumps would make it both hard to find, as well as reinforcing the impression that the good captain was running from Ahkrahn.

The ship would be found eventually, of course, and Visla Sunar's men would undoubtedly slaughter the Tslavar crew without mercy. None could anger the visla in his own system with impunity, and an example would have to be made.

Perhaps a few would be allowed to live. The youngest and least seasoned, most likely. But that would simply be to bear witness to what was done and give warning to any who would think to do likewise.

It was something the Wampeh Ghalian had done on occasion for much the same reasons, though that was typically while in the employ of a particular party who wished to make that point.

"Here," Demelza hissed as they approached the shimmer-cloaked ship.

Hozark and Uzabud made a slight course correction and strode toward the emptiness, stepping up and vanishing into the invisible craft a moment later. The door sealed behind them, and the ship gently lifted off and headed into space. They then parked in orbit to see what the visla's reaction might be.

They'd been watching for nearly an hour before a dozen of the visla's ships hastily rocketed into space and jumped away in all directions.

"And the search begins," Hozark said with a smile. His plan had worked to perfection.

Laskar watched the whole thing in silence, which, for that chatterbox was quite uncharacteristic.

"You've been really quiet," Bud said. "You okay?"

Laskar turned to him, then looked at the two Wampeh who had come with his friend to rescue him.

"I... I didn't think anyone would come for me," he said quietly.

"Of course we would come for you," Bud replied. "Isn't that right, guys?"

"It is," Hozark said, taking the hint. "You are a part of the team."

Laskar's eyes flashed with a flicker of amusement. "We're a team now? I thought you worked alone. I thought you hated teams."

"Dude, shut up. You know what he meant," Bud said, smacking him on the arm.

"Just saying," the copilot shot back.

"Aaand, the old Laskar is back," Bud said with a chuckle. "Okay. If you're done watching the visla's response teams, I think it's about time we get back to my ship."

"Agreed," Hozark said. "Demelza, would you please?"

She nodded and muttered the spells engaging their Drookonus. A moment later they jumped, leaving Ahkrahn and Visla Sunar in their wake.

CHAPTER SIXTEEN

Laskar was pensive and unusually quiet for a long while after they'd departed Ahkrahn. Whatever had gone on there, he did not wish to talk about it, and given what his friends knew about torture methods often employed by the more powerful men and women in the galaxy, they couldn't really blame him.

After sitting around silently for a bit, he finally retired to his quarters to be with his thoughts a while, and the others left him to it.

"So, signs of his torture?" Hozark asked.

"None. Whoever had worked on him was very, very clean. Expert, I would say."

"And the accommodations were up to the standards one would expect of a chamber within the visla's innermost rooms?"

"It appeared so," she replied. "Though we did make a hasty departure once I'd located him. But the space did seem quite comfortable."

"All the better to put an interrogated prisoner at ease before laying into them once more."

"I was thinking the same," Demelza noted. "He even had a small exercise yard that afforded him fresh air in an outdoor setting, though it was walled off from the rest of the compound. That was where I found him, actually."

"It was still a prison," Bud groused.

"He does not realize just how fortunate he was," Hozark said. "It could have been far, far worse, as I am sure you know. I will be interested to learn what exactly Sunar thought he might provide him to have warranted such treatment."

They would have their chance a few hours later when the copilot rejoined them after a hot meal, a hotter shower, and a bit of quiet time alone.

"Hey, I wanted to say thanks again for saving me back there."

"You'd do the same for us, man," Bud said, slapping him on the shoulder.

"I know, you just couldn't live with the thought of having to fly without me. But I'm back now, so you can relax."

"Aaand, there's that asshole we all know and love," Bud grumbled.

"Love is quite a strong word," Demelza said. "Though I can think of a few other strong ones that might apply."

"Laskar, I wish to better understand how you managed to land in such comfortable accommodations within the compound," Hozark said, heading off any potential name-calling. "It is highly unusual for a prisoner to be treated to such luxury."

"Luxury?" he replied. "Sure, it may have *seemed* luxurious, but a prison is a prison, even if it has gilded bars."

Hozark cocked his head slightly. "Surprisingly sage words, Laskar."

"Good looks and piloting prowess aren't the only things I excel at, you know," he replied.

"But you have not answered my question."

"Oh, that. Well, when I was captured sniffing around, they were going to throw me in that pit of a prison, but I lucked out. The visla's personal valet happened to be present when I was brought in, which was a total fluke, I might add. But anyway, he overheard my telling the guards I was just a clueless guy hired for a secret mission. For whatever reason, the word secret got his attention, and he brought me to see the visla personally."

"There is much subterfuge within the upper ranks of the Council at the moment. You may have stumbled upon the one thing that made you of interest and worth to the man," Hozark mused. "But why did he keep you there so long?"

"He couldn't break me," Laskar replied with a bit of braggadocio. "He was trying to get information from me, but I honestly couldn't tell him who I was working for."

"Because you were there of your own accord."

"Exactly. But he didn't phrase the question the right way, so when the truth spells and torture wouldn't yield a suitable answer, he decided to keep me nearby so he could repeat the process as often as it took to get what he wanted."

"But all he needed was to properly question you," Hozark mused. "Fascinating. I'd heard of some interrogation spells being too specific to allow the questioned party to answer if the phrasing was not exactly precise, but I'd never personally known any who had actually undergone such an ordeal."

"Well, it wasn't fun, let me tell you. I mean, I could have just said it was my own doing, but by then he had convinced himself I was somehow withstanding his spells. After that, there was no way he would believe me if I said I truthfully didn't come on anyone's orders."

Bud couldn't help but chuckle. "Holy crap, man. That's the most ridiculously good luck I've ever heard of."

"I was tortured, Bud."

"Well, yeah. But you lived it up in a posh estate instead of some filthy cell."

"As a prisoner."

"But still."

"Gentlemen, please," Hozark interrupted. "Now, Laskar. Bud

has filled me in on the particulars of your capture. How you were rooting out information about how Visla Horvath and Emmik Rostall were working together in secret long before I was engaged for that contract."

"Oh yeah. There's some nefarious shit going on," Laskar said. "Real cloak-and-dagger stuff."

"Two tools of which I am most fond," Hozark noted. "But what of their dealings within the Council of Twenty's affairs? And did you learn how Samara came to be in Visla Horvath's employ?"

Laskar looked at the three so intently staring at him and paused. It was nice being the center of attention, even if for so unpleasant a reason as his capture. Finally, he answered.

"It runs much deeper than we thought," he said. "Those two were in cahoots, and from what I could tell, your ex was––"

"She was not my ex," Hozark corrected.

"Uh-huh. Sure. Anyway, the Ghalian working for Horvath seemed to have been attached to his service at the request of another. Really, all of this points to all of them just being lesser players with someone else pulling their strings."

"A visla and a Wampeh Ghalian being manipulated?" Bud said. "Highly unlikely, if you ask me."

"I'd have said the same thing, but that's what I heard. And I'll remind you, I got tortured over it."

Hozark nodded thoughtfully. "Do you have any idea who this person might be? What their name is?"

"I had a lead I was going to follow up on when I got captured, so no, not yet. That lead still needs to be run down."

"Then we shall do so while completing Demelza's contract," Hozark said.

Uzabud leaned in to his friend. "You've done enough, Laskar. We can't ask you to do any more. Just tell us what we need to know and we'll drop you off for some downtime and take it from here."

His shoulders stiffened. "No, I want to help. I need to finish this."

"We must first engage Demelza's target," Hozark noted. "It is going to be a somewhat difficult endeavor. And time-consuming. Are you certain you are up for this?"

"I am. I want to contribute. I'm part of this team, so where you go, I go."

Hozark studied the man a long moment. The resolve in his eye was firm, and unlike many who had fallen under the gaze of the assassin, Laskar did not waver.

"Uzabud, may I have a word, please?" Hozark said, rising and walking to the adjacent chamber.

"What do you think?" Bud asked quietly.

"I was going to ask you the same thing," the assassin replied. "He did do the legwork, and he seems to have regained his former demeanor, though I cannot help but wonder if it is partly an act. Perhaps he would be best left behind for this outing."

"Yeah, I know. But I worry about what he might do if he's left alone. You know he'd probably get into some mischief."

"True."

"It would be good for him to have something to do. And if he's with us, we can at least keep him occupied but also out of harm's way."

"When are we ever out of harm's way, Bud?" Hozark joked.

"Valid point. But still, you see what I'm saying."

"That I do," the Wampeh replied. "Very well, it is decided," he said, then walked back into the adjacent chamber. "You are a valued member of this group, Laskar, and we have decided that you will accompany us on this contract."

"Excellent!"

"*But*, this is Demelza's contract, and we must all do as she wishes. Is that clear?"

"But you're a master Ghalian," the copilot said.

"That matters not. I assist on this contract at the pleasure of my Ghalian sister. It is her task, and she is more than capable of planning and executing this mission without any of our input."

"Funny you should say *executing*," Laskar said with a laugh.

"Actually, this is largely an intelligence-gathering contract," Demelza said. "There will be killing, no doubt, but that shall not occur until after I have obtained the required information."

"Someone hired the Wampeh Ghalian to gather information? Wow, I thought you guys were all killing and stuff, not skulduggery."

"It is uncommon, but not unheard of. And our target seems to know the rumored location of a world of some value, though for whom and for what reason, we simply do not know. But the contract is from a legitimate and well-paying source, and the order accepted it," Demelza said.

"Well, that settles it, then," Laskar said, perking back up with the promise of adventure. "So, who exactly are we looking for?"

CHAPTER SEVENTEEN

Billian was the man's name, and he was quite a sight to behold. Nearly a full head taller than most, his deep ochre skin and old brick-colored hair made him stand out as much as his height.

Then there were the bone ridges protecting his spine, kept out of sight by his loose-fitting clothing.

He didn't appear that tough, but a blow to the rigid protrusions would quickly rectify that miscalculation as his incredibly strong muscles and tendons would aid him in crushing the life out of his attacker.

For all of that deadliness, though, there was one silver lining to this job. Billian possessed no magic of his own.

"*That* is what we're going after?" Laskar said when an image disc Demelza had activated from her contract package presented their target. "What the hell is that thing, anyway?"

"He is a Mahgwhamp," Hozark replied. "They are a brutish race, and not often seen in polite company."

"Let me guess. This guy doesn't hang with *polite* company," Bud said.

"Very astute of you, Bud. Now, you should know, despite his great strength, Mahgwhamps possess limited lateral movement capabilities. Just an evolutionary flaw in their hips that presents their one notable weakness."

"I'll keep that in mind if I wind up face-to-face with him," Bud joked.

"You would do well to. A quick lateral dodge could save your life," Hozark noted.

"So what are we supposed to do? Just go up and talk to the guy and ask him what he knows?"

"No, Laskar, though that would be nice if it would work," Demelza said. "I will handle that part of the contract. And once the intel is acquired, his lips will be sealed forever."

"You almost make it sound poetic," the copilot said.

"In a way, it is," she replied. "Now, before any of the interesting bits can occur, we must first achieve objective number one."

"Which is?" Bud asked.

"Which is finding his whereabouts."

"And how exactly do we do that?" Laskar asked. "You know all about this guy, so what do we have to do?"

Demelza grinned at the thought of the mission ahead of them. It was challenging. It was dangerous. It was difficult. It was everything she could hope for in a contract.

"Billian runs a junker fleet," she finally replied. "It's made up of hundreds of small ships that cluster together and form a sort of hive during downtime. Then, when a target is acquired, they scatter and swarm, converging on their prey from all directions."

"Sounds like a dangerous enemy," Bud mused. "How do we even get close?"

"They are a deadly foe, yes, but they are one that avoids conflict at most times. They just go about their business, interlocked in a giant mass of vessels."

Laskar studied her expressions, a small grin creasing his lips. "You don't know which one of those hundreds of ships he's on, do you?"

"No, I do not," she replied. "Nor do I know which system they are in. They are constantly on the move, in fact, making tracking them near impossible."

"And, yet, we are going to track them," Hozark said with confidence.

"Yes. That we are."

"But how? I mean, you're not exactly making this sound like an easy job here," Bud noted.

"Oh, it is not easy by any means," she replied. "But there is one weak link in their system. You see, they can't resupply all of their ships at once. To do so would negate their tactical advantage. So, instead of a hundred ships descending on a trading world, only a few of their number break away to gather goods for all and resupply the rest of the fleet."

"Kind of like hive insects bringing nourishment back to their kin," Laskar mused.

"Precisely. Only, this hive is comprised of a few hundred craft, any one of which could contain Billian," Demelza said.

Bud pondered the facts he'd learned so far. "So, let's say we do somehow manage to locate this fleet. A mess of ships like that? That's hundreds of defensive wards, all operated by different crews. How do we even get close?"

"Hozark?" she said, looking to the master assassin.

He turned to Bud. "That's where you come in, Bud. You and Laskar."

"Oh?"

"Yes. Because we are going to steal one of their ships."

Laskar raised his hand. "Uh, excuse me, but I have a crazy question. How is it going to do us any good to steal one of their ships if we don't know where the rest of their fleet is, and if we have no idea how to get past their defenses?"

Hozark looked to Demelza.

"We will extract that information from the crew before returning to the fleet, the same as if we were actually a part of the collective," she said. "The whole group is comprised of all manner of people from systems far and wide. A true multi-species conglomerate. As such, none will question our disparate appearances."

"If we have the right spells to disable the defenses, that is," Bud added.

"Obviously," she replied. "But those should be easy to wrest from the craft's crew. And with them, the passive wards and active countermeasure guards will recognize us as a friendly vessel and let us dock back into the fleet without raising a single alarm."

"You make it sound easier than I think it's gonna be," Laskar said.

"Perhaps. But it is quite straightforward. We just have to find the supply ships when they make a run."

"But how do we even do that?" Laskar grumbled.

She fixed her gaze on the man. "Legwork, dear Laskar. A lot of legwork."

"You know, I've still got plenty of ties to my old pirating buddies," Uzabud said. "I know you have your Ghalian spy network, but, if you like, I can reach out to them and see if they might be able to dig up a little information for us. You know they've always got an eye out for a potential score."

"So long as it can be done with the greatest of anonymity and subtlety," Demelza said. "Two things pirates are not exactly famous for."

"Oh, don't worry about them. If there's the opportunity for some plunder, they'll keep their mouths quite sealed. And if we're going to scatter a few hundred ships, I bet they'll be more than happy to scavenge a few of them in the process."

"That's all it would take?" Laskar asked.

"Booty is booty, my friend. And they aren't all that particular what they take, so long as they can sell it on the market."

"I know you talked about your old pirating days, Bud, but I

thought it was just bragging," Laskar said. "You really think you can convince *pirates* to help us? And for free?"

"Well, it's free in that we don't pay them. But there's plenty for them to profit from if all goes well."

"And the Ghalian possess a spy network vast enough to pin down a few supply ships across hundreds of inhabited systems?"

"In time, yes," Hozark replied.

Laskar looked at his companions with a newfound appreciation for the immense resources these seemingly ordinary people had at their fingertips. It was inspiring.

"Well, then. This should be fun!" he said. "Let's get this party started."

CHAPTER EIGHTEEN

Five days of utter boredom later, the foursome finally received word from a Ghalian envoy of a single ship spotted in a not-too-distant system. One that might actually be one of Billian's supply craft. Hopefully, *this time,* it wasn't another wild goose chase.

The hunt had begun with excitement and high spirits, and even after the first three leads turned out to be dead ends, the group's energy was good. But after nearly a week of incessant waiting, punctuated with periodic disappointment as Bud's pirate friends identified wrong ship after wrong ship, the tension was growing.

Of course, the Ghalian assassins were as tranquil as always. In fact, Hozark had been rumored to have sat almost perfectly still for nearly two weeks once while lying in wait for a target. But the order trained their aspiring members in stillness of body as well as mind from their earliest years.

Bud, however, was getting antsy. And Laskar? He was absolutely climbing the walls. A tough thing to do when inside the confines of a spacecraft, even one as spacious as Uzabud's mothership. And with his increasing agitation, Laskar's annoying personality tics were turned up to eleven.

"Oh, thank the gods," Bud said with palpable relief when they finally got word of the likely target. "It's about time."

"Yes, it sometimes takes our spy network a bit of time to properly track a target," Hozark said, calm as ever. "Fortunately, this time was relatively fast, all things considered."

"Okay, I'll admit it, they were harder to find than I anticipated. A lot harder," Bud said.

"Your friends' efforts are appreciated nonetheless," Demelza said. "They identified a fair number of craft."

"Yeah, the wrong craft," Laskar groaned. "We were on wild Bundabist chases more often than not. The letdown is almost worse than just waiting."

Hozark understood his sentiment. Just because he didn't show it did not mean he did not feel the boredom as well. He was just used to tamping down unpleasantness and clearing his thoughts of the tedium. "Well, this appears to actually be one of Billian's supply ships," he said. "So sharpen your minds and prepare yourselves for action."

Bud had begun the jumps required to reach the planet the Ghalian had identified as soon as their envoy had departed the ship, wasting no time to get them doing something other than waiting. After arriving in the system, the black sun at the center radiating its power well into the ultraviolet spectrum, he directed them on what appeared to be a casual approach to the dark world of Faloon.

But they were anything but casual. Bud and Laskar were buzzing with energy at finally having something to do.

"There," Laskar said from his copilot's seat. "That's the one, I know it."

"Patience, dear Laskar. We must confirm before we act. Haste is the downfall of many," Hozark said.

"It looks like any other ship," Bud noted. "How are you so sure?"

"I just am, okay?"

Demelza and Hozark glanced at one another. Laskar could be an issue if he didn't rein in his impulsiveness. But they also noted something else as they drew closer. It seemed Laskar was right.

"Ingenious," Hozark admired as they flew a casual pass over the parked ship and lined up their descent to a relatively close available landing site.

"Quite elegant, really," Demelza agreed.

"What is?"

"Look closer, Uzabud," she said.

"I am looking closer. What am I missing? It's just another ship. It looks like any other of the smaller craft dotting the landing area."

"Yes and no," Hozark noted. "It's a very clever means of avoiding scrutiny. And if the main body of their ships were to be forced to scatter, they could hide among any number of craft innocuously. But there is something to them. Laskar was correct in his instinct."

"See? Told ya," he said.

Hozark ignored the comment and continued. "Note the faint markings on the craft's hull. Do you see the glyph that is worked into the skin of the vessel? How it is masked by the lines of the hull itself, appearing almost as if it were residual damage markings from atmospheric entry?"

"But spells protect the hull," Bud noted.

"Yes. A unique flavor of magic. We can use that to our advantage, actually."

"But why the damage?"

"We've all seen craft that have had issues with their shielding spells. It's quite common, especially with lesser-powered craft. And as these are all smaller ships, it's the sort of thing we see every day and don't even think about. Much like many Ghalian methods of camouflage, actually."

"Ooh, really?" Laskar said, perking up. "You'll have to show me those!"

"No, I do not," Hozark replied as politely as he could.

Some things were not shared outside the order. Laskar was part of their trusted team, but even so, the Ghalian had a great many secrets guarded to the death.

"So, the crew's gonna be just as hard to recognize, I assume?" Bud said.

"Oh, I would expect nothing less, seeing their ship. It will take a bit of careful observation to find our mark."

"This is going to be a pain in the ass," Laskar groaned.

"You said you wanted to come with," Hozark reminded him.

"And I do. It's just, this is all a lot more boring than I expected. I thought we'd be getting into some *real* action."

Again, Hozark and Demelza shared a glance. One that Bud caught and understood. Laskar wanted action, but a true man of adventure never *really* wanted action, per se. Sure, they were deep in it at times, often over their heads, but survival often meant in and out without anyone the wiser.

He'd flown with Hozark on a lot of dangerous jobs, and they'd barely made it out of more than a few. Even for one of the deadliest assassins in the galaxy, shit still went sideways sometimes.

"While I appreciate your enthusiasm, Laskar, the Ghalian way is one of efficiency and stealth. We do not telegraph our presence, nor do we leave trace of our work, unless specifically needed to send a message. We complete our contract and are systems away before anyone knows we were ever there."

"But you said you send a message sometimes."

"Yes. But that is exceedingly rare, and usually not reported outside the victim's household. Often, the slaying is enough to prevent others in their circle from pursuing the target's plans, you see."

"Oh. I guess that makes sense," Laskar mused.

"And more often than not, we try to not leave any body at all," Demelza added. "When people go missing, it is hard to attribute it to an assassination. And sometimes, the job entails making it *appear* the target has simply fled for greener pastures."

"Or you make it look like an accident," Bud noted. "Those are always fun."

Laskar laughed at the idea. "Ha! Like how Emmik Zingal got crushed to death when the Malooki he was riding slipped and landed right on top of him? That was such a humiliating way for a man of his power to go. And funny as hell."

Hozark and Demelza looked at him, their expressions impossible to read. Well, *almost* impossible.

"No way. No freakin' way! There's no way you could have made that happen!" Laskar blurted.

Neither assassin replied, but the twinkle in their eyes and faintest of twitches to the corners of their mouths spoke volumes.

Bud had settled the ship into a low hover, the magical cushion keeping his ship a few inches above the ground. It required only a small amount of magic to sustain that particular spell, and should they need to depart in a hurry, it would give them those few seconds of additional speed that could prove the difference between success and failure should pursuit, or flight, be warranted.

"I shall be going into the city to locate, then gather information from, whichever members of the crew I can find. Laskar, you have been exceedingly patient. Why don't you come with me?"

He jumped out of his copilot's seat in a flash. "Hell yes. I've got your back!"

Hozark and Bud shared an amused look at the man's enthusiasm. He was accompanying a full-fledged Wampeh Ghalian. He most certainly did not need to 'get her back.' Demelza was on a simple, non-violent part of the task, and this was simply her way of affording the man an opportunity to get some fresh air and let off some of that pent-up energy.

"I'll hang back and keep this baby ready in case we need to make a quick run for it."

"And I shall enter the target ship and await Demelza's return," Hozark said.

"What about the crew?" Laskar asked.

"What crew?" Hozark said with a smile. One that implied that once he was through with them, there would not *be* a crew aboard when his friends joined him.

CHAPTER NINETEEN

The oppressive feel of a black-sun solar system varied, depending on the strength of the dark orb throwing off its rays that were well past ultraviolct, as well as a particular planet's distance from it. Given that, the little world of Faloon was actually not terribly unpleasant, all things considered.

Of course, all of the cities were illuminated with magical lighting, as there was no visible sunrise or sunset to brighten the day. Not to the naked eye, at least. And with the lack of an obvious day or night, most venues and shops were open round the clock, staffed by an ever-shifting group of employees who had adapted to their particular work schedule.

It was the sort of system that Wampeh thrived in, their pale skin right at home in the dark environs. Other races lived on these worlds as well, and over time their skin lightened as well, all of them fading to lesser shades of blue, or green, or whatever color they might be.

On rare occasion, a black sun's unusual power could enhance the magic of certain users. Typically not much, but occasionally more than expected. It could also make one's spells fail in a most spectacular manner, the invisible solar power flares causing magic cast at an inopportune time to react in all sorts of ways, often detrimental.

For that reason, Demelza and Hozark had decided before they had even landed that they would only use magic if absolutely necessary. Especially as Demelza was carrying a hefty load of stolen magic inside of her.

Visla Horvath's power would be used eventually, but given the power the man had possessed when she took it, Demelza had to be extra careful wielding it, lest she damage herself in the process. This system's sun didn't *seem* to be particularly strong, but safe was far better than injured or worse.

The curvy assassin walked the city in the most minimal of disguises, again keeping her magical output to a minimum. All she did was shift her complexion from pale white of the Wampeh to a light bronze. It was a little thing, but she had found it to be one of the skin tones most likely to draw the sort of attention she wanted. The sort that could earn her information from loose lips.

The topmost buttons of her tunic were unfastened, revealing far more cleavage than she would normally expose. But the deadly woman had more than one way to manipulate her targets, and this was one of the oldest known. And simplest.

Laskar walked at her side, eyes wide as he took in the sights of the unusual world. Magical lighting and buildings that seemed dark from the outside, but revealed a warm glow when patrons would filter in and out of their doors.

"Would you look at that!" he blurted as a swirling green glow wove across the sky then dissipated.

"It is just an aurora. I thought you'd been to all sorts of worlds, the way you talk."

"I have, but never Faloon. This place is legendary, and it's famous for its gladiator arena."

The air was pierced by a shrill cry as if to punctuate his words.

"What was that?"

"You said you know of the arena," Demelza said. "Did you not know of the *other* combatants it houses?"

"You mean... *Zomoki*?"

"Your grasp of the obvious is inspiring, Laskar. *Yes*, they are Zomoki."

The man's eyes went even wider with excitement. The thought of seeing actual Zomoki was turning this into a very, *very* interesting outing indeed.

The feral beasts were enormous, winged things, with a tough, scaled hide and huge, deadly teeth. Dragons, some in a distant galaxy would call them. Fire-breathing creatures of some magic, capable of jumping from world to world with their innate powers.

Centuries earlier, there had been immensely powerful Zomoki, huge, intelligent creatures capable of not only great magic, but also speech. The Old Ones they were called. The Wise Ones. They had been Zomoki of incredible power. And they were all dead, the last of them killed off in the destruction of Visla Balamar's domain.

The visla had possessed a singularly unique gift in his lands. A small flow of magical waters he had learned to focus into a healing elixir capable of enhancing not only magic, but granting great longevity. To bathe in the waters would restore one's power and health.

But there was a catch. Any could bathe, but for all but the most powerful, to drink them, would cause instant death. And for Wampeh Ghalian, merely touching the waters would make them burst into flames. A funny quirk of the normally healing waters that only affected the tiny subset of Wampeh who possessed the Ghalian's innate power.

The Council of Twenty had long coveted Visla Balamar's waters, and they had tried to cajole and pressure him into joining them for many years. But he had wanted nothing to do with their machinations of power and glory. And with the Zomoki who had befriended him and resided on his grounds, there was little the Council could do about it.

That is, until the Council decided to take his waters by force.

It had been the single greatest use of Ootaki hair in history, and that, combined with the full magic of the Council's strongest members, had blended into a doomsday spell even deadlier than those casting it had intended. The result was the obliteration of Visla Balamar, his Zomoki friends, and his entire realm, turning it into a barren wasteland as far as the eye could see.

It had been the end of the Wise Ones, and the loss of the Balamar waters. The few traces still remaining in private hands were immediately rendered priceless.

Zomoki hadn't gone extinct that day, but the best of them had. Now only the most feral and mindless of their species remained, and those were routinely captured and bound, forced to act as guard beasts or gladiator fodder.

The shrieks of the Zomoki rang out again, as did the sound of the clashing of blades. The gladiatorial combat in the arena was underway, it seemed, and Laskar's eyes gleamed with excitement.

"Might we see a bout?" he asked.

"We are not here for recreation," Demelza reminded him. "The job always comes first."

"But after?"

She sighed. "Perhaps after, yes."

He was a grown man, and skilled in many areas. But sometimes he could be as unintentionally annoying as a demanding child.

Demelza cast a seeking spell, carefully pulling a tiny bit of power from her konus, testing the air to ensure there was no interference from the dark sun. It seemed there was no alteration to her spell.

Good.

She cast a little more forcefully, the intent behind the words driving the spell more than what she spoke.

Of course, the spell would not work if not spoken aloud, but the intent was what made it function. It was why lesser casters could not perform greater feats of magic despite knowing the words. It was something that could take years to learn. For some spells, a lifetime.

Her casting reacted far sooner than she had anticipated, a faint tug pulling her toward an ordinary-looking man casually walking toward the arena. He possessed traces of the same magic that was unique to his ship's shielding. Just a trace, but at this proximity, it was enough.

"Well, it looks as though you are in luck, Laskar," she said. "For it seems our target had a similar desire."

"You mean?"

"Yes," she replied. "We are going to the gladiator bouts."

CHAPTER TWENTY

Demelza produced coin and paid their admittance into the arena. It was a thick-walled structure, with multiple levels capable of holding a respectable number of spectators. Not all contests warranted the capacity, though. Many of the bouts were lower-level fighters trying to claw their way up in the rankings.

Today, however, it seemed there were going to be a few particularly interesting fights. Apparently, they had arrived in time for some of the best combat of the month. Possibly why this was the chosen resupply time, and likely why their target was headed into the arena rather than stocking his craft, as was his task.

A few hours' delay wouldn't be noted, though, and how often did he get to see the likes of this? Rarely, was the answer.

"Which one are we——?" Laskar began to say when Demelza elbowed him somewhat hard and flashed a cold look. "Oh, right. Sorry."

The fool was blurting out things without care for those around them, and if he wasn't careful, he could tip off their target without realizing he was doing so. Demelza was beginning to regret bringing him along. But a Ghalian made do with the cards they were dealt, and she would make this work, whatever it took.

She nudged him and gave an almost imperceptible nod toward a thick-necked man with elongated upper arms but far shorter forearms. His hair was such a deep green it almost looked black in the artificial light.

Demelza had dealt with this kind before. Strong laborers, but not the brightest more often than not. Likely why he had been selected to resupply the others. She wondered what the rest of his crew was like. That didn't matter, though. Hozark would have that handled long before they reached the man's ship.

The man strode into the general admission area and took a seat with a fair view of the field of battle below. Demelza and Laskar did likewise, seating themselves several rows behind him so as to avoid the possibility of his unintentionally noticing them. He'd have had to spin entirely around to see them. Not likely. And that was precisely what she wanted.

Laskar leaned in and spoke in a quiet tone. "What do we do now?"

"We watch the bout, of course," she replied. "There is no more we can accomplish here. It is far too public a place, and entirely non-conducive to discourse, let alone intensive questioning."

"So, we really get to just sit here and enjoy the show?"

"Yes, Laskar. So long as he stays, we stay."

A huge grin spread across his face. "Fortune is smiling on us today."

"That remains to be seen."

Down below, the dirt arena had been cleaned of blood from the prior bout, and a new group of gladiators were ushered out. Novices, this lot, and all of them using underpowered konuses in addition to their conventional weapons.

The match began without fanfare while patrons were still milling about. It was unimpressive, to put it nicely.

Watching the novices was light fare that only the diehard fans paid much attention to. But for the combatants, it was an opportunity to hone their skills, and without the certainty of death. That would come later, as they became much more proficient in the combat arts. Then death was more likely, but still rather uncommon.

In fact, most gladiatorial engagements were fought until there was a victor, but given the time and coin required to train up a gladiator from a novice, rarely were the bouts to the death. And with these green combatants, there was simply no excitement to be had in the killing of a lesser opponent.

That said, if they did become too injured in their contest, the cost benefit analysis would be performed, and if it was too expensive to heal their wounds, they were fed to the Zomoki more often than not.

That was something that always amused the audience to no end.

The combat ceased nearly ten minutes later with a few of the gladiator slaves victorious, the others injured but not terribly.

"That was pretty pathetic," Laskar grumbled.

"We all start from somewhere," Demelza noted. "Even the greatest warrior was once a novice."

"Well, yeah. But it's boring to watch, is all I'm saying. And it took *forever*."

Demelza agreed with him on the inside, but she didn't say as much. When Wampeh Ghalian fought, contests were decided in seconds, not minutes. In fact, if she had gone against all of the young fighters they had just observed, she would have achieved victory in the time it took to pick up a dropped blade.

"Give it a few more contests," she said. "I believe the later ones will be much more to your liking."

Indeed, after one more novice contest, a battle between three small teams consisting of three gladiators each began. This time, there was much more efficient use of magic, and the fighters were doing some impressive maneuvering to protect their strongest caster while fending off attacks of both magical and physical nature.

Unlike a simple two-sided contest, having three teams, each striving for victory, meant paying attention to more than just one opponent. If a gladiator got over-enthused in his pursuit of an opposing team member, he would very likely be separated from his group and taken out.

Just as Demelza was about to comment to that effect, a man from the yellow team found his insides suddenly on his outside. The combination blow of blade and spell had opened him like a piñata, only, rather than candy, it was entrails that fell to the soil.

"Yes!" Laskar shouted, clearly enjoying this much-improved level of combat.

"Not too enthusiastic," Demelza reminded him.

"Right. Sorry. But did you see that?"

"It was rather hard to miss."

"So cool," he said with a huge grin.

Apparently, his bloodlust was greater than she'd assessed. That, or being among the throngs of enthused spectators was amping him up. He wouldn't be the first to fall victim to such a crowd mentality.

Demelza nudged her partner. The target was heading inside while the arena was cleaned for the final bout.

"He's on the move. I need you to keep an eye on him."

"Aren't you already doing that?"

"There are places I cannot follow him," she replied.

"What do you... Oh," Laskar said. "Got it."

"Yes. Just ensure he does not depart the arena. I will be nearby at the refreshment stand."

"Got it. See ya in a minute."

The two of them blended in with the flow of spectators

heading to either relieve themselves or acquire more snacks for the upcoming finale. Demelza lingered at the vendor's stall a long while before purchasing a small bag of roasted kernels of a local plant. The aroma was actually rather pleasing, and the flavor not bad.

A few minutes later, Laskar came hurrying back to join her. He eyed the bag she was holding.

"Did you wash your hands?" she asked.

"What?"

"Your hands. Did you wash them."

"Of course I did," he replied.

Only then did she tilt the bag and allow him to grab a handful of the toasty snack.

"Come, we should return to our seats," she said, nodding toward their man heading back into the arena.

They had just settled back into their seats when Laskar noticed a trio of vislas casting a protective spell around the combat zone of the arena. For not one but three vislas to be placing the spell, something good must have been coming up.

"Why so much effort on that spell?" he asked.

Demelza smiled. "You shall see."

She was certain Laskar was going to love the final contest.

A loud horn sounded, and heavy gates at either end of the arena floor slid open. What came forth was enough to draw a huge cheer from all in attendance. Not one, but two Zomoki came out from opposite ends. And with them were a half dozen men per side.

"What are they doing?" Laskar asked.

"A team event."

"But why aren't the Zomoki just eating everyone?"

"Do you see their control collars?" she asked, noting the thick golden bands around the animals' necks. "There are limiters placed on them. Spells to keep them from attacking their own team's colors."

Laskar leaned forward in his seat, studying the crackling power visible from the collars every time one of the beasts thought to try to devour one of the men alongside it.

Now the containment spells made perfect sense. These were pretty big Zomoki, and if they could manage to get outside of the containment spell and overcome their collars, they could possibly manage to harness their magic and jump away somewhere the collar's control could not reach.

Or they might try to eat the audience.

It was really anyone's guess.

The fight began without warning, just a quick smattering of deadly magic cast as the two teams jockeyed for position, attempting to take down their opponents while also avoiding the beast partnered with the other team.

It made for a fluid battleground. The gladiators all knew their offensive and defensive spells and were casting them expertly, but the Zomoki threw an unknown factor into the mix.

Any misstep could lead to incineration and death. And that was if you were lucky. Worse still would be finding oneself eaten yet still alive, slowly digesting in the beast's belly.

The gladiators fought with great skill, but soon enough the first fell, his head separated from his neck by a swirling counterattack that caught him off guard. Laskar's bloodlust seemed to be back, Demelza noted as she saw the look of glee in his eyes, but at least he was keeping himself restrained, so that was something.

One of the Zomoki bellowed in pain as a spear found a weak spot in its armored hide. The flames it spewed missed its intended target, but a spray of its blood landed on the hapless gladiator, some of it directly contacting his skin.

The man crumbled to the ground, writhing in agony before succumbing to the magical blood's deadly properties. To injure a Zomoki, one had to be exceedingly careful for precisely this reason. Contact with Zomoki blood was almost always fatal.

Soon enough it became clear one side was about to lose. Down two of their number, they simply could not stop the onslaught from the other team. They fell in short order, injured but alive. But this was not a novice's event, and the crowd demanded blood.

With a simple spell, the visla in charge of overseeing the beasts released one of their restraints. In a flash, the Zomoki descended on the wounded men, and a few screams later, they were removed from the arena, courtesy of the hungry beasts. The handler then directed them back to their pens, guiding them with shocks from their control collars.

The excitement was done for the day, it seemed, and what a showing it had been.

"Are you sated?" Demelza asked.

"That was fantastic!" Laskar said in reply.

"I thought you would approve." Her attention shifted down several rows. "Time to go," she said as their target rose to leave.

Blending in with the rest of the patrons, the assassin and her over-enthused sidekick followed. They'd have answers soon enough. What remained uncertain was how much work would go into prying them loose.

CHAPTER TWENTY-ONE

The crowd leaving the gladiator arena was a somewhat gregarious bunch, the excitement of the final bout leaving them buzzing with a slightly aggressive energy. But it had been others doing the fighting this day, and the spectators, while feeling the flush of battle, were not inclined to violence of their own.

It was one of the reasons those with a more tenuous grip on the worlds they oversaw tended to favor such exhibitions. A means to quell the masses and distract them from mischief of their own. And for the most part, it worked.

Laskar seemed to have been greatly energized by the display and was walking with a bit of a spring in his step as they trailed their target from afar. The man was no more than fifty meters ahead of the pair, though the crowd flowing around them made it feel like a hundred.

"Shouldn't we get closer? I lost sight of—?"

Demelza held up her hand to silence him and kept walking, her eyes focused on the man far ahead, but all while moving her body like the other mildly inebriated fight patrons.

She was, however, very skilled at what she did, and where Laskar might have had a hard time keeping track of a single person in a crowd of hundreds, Demelza could follow him with little difficulty. If pressed, she could even tell you what the twenty people nearest him were wearing.

Of course, when you might need to get as close as, say, one of twenty people nearest your target, that was a particularly useful skill to have. And *that* was why it had been drilled into every Ghalian aspirant since early in their training.

"Let's get a drink!" Demelza abruptly said with a gregarious laugh totally unfitting her normal demeanor.

But she was on the hunt and had slipped into this character with such ease that it seemed as if she had always been a jovial, bronze-skinned woman of mirth and leisure. Tugging Laskar by the arm, she swam upstream through the river of people toward one of the many pubs dotting the dimly lit street.

"This one looks good," she said with an exaggerated wink.

She then popped open two more buttons on her top, flashing her curves even more than previously. They were moving on to a different part of their game, and *now* was the time for *that* sort of attention.

Laskar couldn't help but notice the appreciative glances she was garnering. Even without a disguise, Demelza's thick and curvaceous build was enough to draw attention from those appreciative of a strong, well-built woman.

She possessed curves in all the right places, and when she chose to flaunt them, she was quite the sight to behold. And with her magically applied bronzing of her skin, her womanly form was even more accentuated.

On a world of no light, where everyone was particularly pale for want of sun in a different spectrum, the warm-toned woman garnered much attention from locals and visitors alike.

She was particularly appealing to the locals for her exotic look, and it was that additional attention that would increase her desirability and make her more intriguing to her target.

People always seemed to want what everyone else wanted, and she would use that weakness to her advantage.

"Stay here," she quietly instructed Laskar, nudging him toward a seat at the far end of the bar nearest the door.

If the target were to unexpectedly leave, he would be in the perfect position to casually follow without Demelza having to abruptly jump up and follow him. Laskar slid onto a seat and ordered a drink. Not a terribly potent one, the assassin was pleased to hear.

With a womanly sway to her hips, Demelza casually walked the length of the bar while looking over the room with a bored glance. Nothing seemed to interest her, so she pulled up a seat. Conveniently, that seat happened to be right next to the man they had been tailing.

"Whew. I'll never get used to these dark systems. Is it always like this, or does it ever get lighter out?" she asked casually as she ordered a drink.

"Pretty much the usual," the man replied, then went back to his own beverage, gazing off across the bar.

This was not going quite as she had planned. Demelza sat quietly a moment, shifting in her seat in a way that better accentuated her cleavage but without being too obvious about it. The man didn't seem to notice.

"Quite an exciting bout," she said offhandedly when her drink arrived.

She'd ordered a strong one, and a double at that. All the better to play up her inebriated role. But she had cast the spell Hozark had taught her, directing the fluids that passed her lips to materialize in an alleyway a few hundred meters away.

She could drink heavily yet remain stone-cold sober. A useful trick for an assassin. But the man still didn't seem to react to her.

For ten minutes she tried making small talk, and for ten

minutes she was shut down. No matter what she said, it seemed he was either incredibly shy, or simply not interested.

Demelza took a big gulp from her glass and swayed a bit in her seat, leaning into the man, pressing her breasts against his arm as she did, making him spill a bit of his drink.

"Oof, I'm so sorry," she slurred. "That's a bit stronger than I'm used to."

"No problem," he replied, not even glancing at her.

"Oh, I spilled your drink! Silly me. Lemme make it up to you. I can get you another."

"That's really not necessary," he replied.

It was perplexing. The man was being handed an opportunity on a silver platter, yet he was not interested. He did, however, seem to keep glancing at the door.

Demelza wondered if he might be waiting for one of his shipmates to join him. If that was the case, he'd have a long time waiting. Hozark would have taken care of them a while ago by now.

She followed his gaze once more when he glanced that direction and realized what was up.

Of course. She chided herself for not noticing sooner. Swaying a bit, she rose to her feet and made her way to the restroom.

After staying there a reasonable amount of time, she returned to the bar, but took up a seat at the far end, by Laskar. She sat with her back to the bar, as if observing the crowd. What she was really doing was hiding her face from their target so he would not see her conversing.

"Don't make it obvious we're talking," she said quietly. "He's not interested."

"Not interested?" he replied in a low voice, appearing to glance the other way. "Are you serious? Look at you. All boobs falling out and flirty drunkenness. What man wouldn't--?"

"He's looking at *you*," she said, cutting him off.

"I'm sorry? What?"

She took a casual glance around the room, looking anywhere but at the man seated next to her. Laskar was a good-looking man, she had to admit, and it seemed his accompanying her on this contract had been a fortuitous thing after all.

"You need to go talk to him," she said. "Get him to invite you back to his place, which conveniently happens to be his ship."

"I'm not interested in men."

"You don't have to be interested. You have to get the job done. You said you wanted to be of help. So, help."

Laskar's face struggled to remain impassive. An internal struggle was underway. Finally, reluctantly, he slid up from his seat.

"You *so* owe me," he hissed as he walked past Demelza.

She almost felt sorry for the guy. Almost.

While fluid sexuality was as common as breathing, some people were not only set in their ways, but also became uncomfortable when directly faced with a situation such as this. It seemed Laskar was one of them, but now he would have to overcome that and get the job done.

She nearly smiled when she turned back toward the bar to order another drink. Laskar had not only taken a seat next to their target, he was actively engaged in conversation. More than that. He was flirting, and he was doing it well.

Another round of drinks was acquired, and the two men chatted away, thick as thieves. Eventually, she noted Laskar even appeared to rest his hand on the man's knee, drawing a little lip bite from the fellow, along with a look of great interest.

She had to hand it to him. For not being his thing, the guy was actually handling himself like a pro. It was only five minutes later that Laskar leaned in and whispered into the man's ear, cupping his cheek with his other hand as he did so.

Demelza could see the man blush from across the bar.

The two quickly settled their tab and headed out into the

dark night. A moment later, the assassin followed, her curves hidden once again, and her skin returned to a far cooler tone. She no longer wished to be seen. She was going to become as plain as she could. And once she found a suitable alleyway, she'd don her shimmer cloak.

It was a short walk back to the waiting swarm ship, which was resting exactly as it had been left. Even the external wards were in place protecting it.

"*Ahznal provicto*," the man said, the passphrase lowering the defenses and allowing him and his guest into the craft. "I'm back!" he called out. There was no reply. He grinned. "The others must be sleeping. Come on. My quarters are this way," he said in a husky voice, eager to reach his accommodations.

"I like your ship," Laskar said in a similarly excited tone. "It's nice and cozy."

"My room is cozier," the man replied, taking him by the hand.

A few short corridors later, they stepped into his room. A Wampeh sitting on his bed was not what the poor man had been expecting.

He turned to run just as Demelza dropped her shimmer cloak, blocking the doorway. He looked at the two Wampeh, then turned to his amorous would-be lover.

"Sorry, dude," Laskar said with an amused grin.

"Shall we begin?" Hozark asked.

"Oh, we shall," Demelza replied, her fangs sliding into place as she smiled.

Laskar knew it was an act to loosen the man's lips, but say what you would about the woman, she most definitely put the *terror* in interrogation.

116

CHAPTER TWENTY-TWO

A few days later, an unassuming ship jumped into the relatively remote system where Billian's swarm fleet was residing. An unassuming ship bearing the subtle markings identifying it as one of their own, and responding with the correct countersigns when contacted over skree.

The hundreds of craft were eager to head to their next destination, but they waited as patiently as spacefaring scavengers could. They'd be moving on soon enough, but they all knew a proper restock was vital before they did so.

Fortunately, the ship that had just arrived was laden with supplies, though it had made it back a day later than the other craft out on resupply runs. But that sort of thing was common among those existing on the fringes of society.

"You're clear to dock," a gruff man called out over skree.

"Be there in a minute," Hozark replied in an equally gritty tone. "We've got a full load ready to go."

"Excellent. Be seein' ya soon," the man replied, then shut off the skree.

When the assassins had commandeered the hapless crew's ship, it had already been largely filled with the items on their procurement manifest. But the Wampeh were well accustomed to the necessity of a little something extra to ease passage, and as such, they picked up a healthy supply of items *not* on the manifest.

Fine foods, sweets, and, of course, all manner of alcohols with which to dull one's mind and brighten one's spirits. All were carefully tucked away, ready to be offered as needed.

The thing about the swarm was it was a conglomerate of craft and crews, all of which contributed to the general welfare of the whole. It had worked quite well for them so far, and there did not seem to be any reason to change it any time soon.

Palms could most certainly be greased, however. A socialized system in no way meant that particular way of doing business had been done away with, and having someone trade for the finer things in life, either for goods and services, or simply to look the other way once in a while, was as common as black market hooch and gambling.

Bribes weren't needed here. But favors? Everyone could use a little help from time to time.

"Get these distributed," Hozark growled to the men boarding his stolen ship as they began sorting the stacks of crates, then cast floating spells to aid them in offloading them from the craft.

Only the captain of the ship would have been of any note, and as such, Hozark had taken on his appearance in case their contact upon arrival happened to know the man. But in a swarm of so many craft, those odds were slim.

But slim had a way of turning into substantial, in his experience, so the additional precaution was worth the minimal expenditure of magic. As for Demelza, Bud, and Laskar, they were just crew, and crew was constantly changing.

It seemed the foreman didn't know the man Hozark was impersonating. That was a nice surprise. Also a nice surprise was the small box the disguised assassin handed the man when the others weren't looking.

"A little thank you for your help offloading only *those* crates," he said to the gruff man.

The foreman looked inside the little box, and his eyes widened with pleasant surprise. Finarkian snuff was hard to come by, and quite pricey. How this particular transport captain had known to bring it to him was something he didn't care about in the slightest. All that mattered was his little box. His precious.

"Those ones, eh?" he said, eyeing the several smaller crates that would be left aboard. "Of course, friend. Happy to oblige."

He then turned and began bellowing to his workers once more, directing them what to move and where to disburse the cargo. As for the containers not on his manifest? He was quite happy to look the other way.

"How did you know he'd go for that?" Laskar asked when the last of the designated crates was offloaded. "That was a really lucky guess."

Hozark laughed. "Luck, my friend, has nothing to do with it."

He opened a nearby crate and showed the contents to the startled man. Multiple small boxes were nestled inside, each of them containing a different item. Something for every vice.

"You saw the tremble in his hand, didn't you?" Uzabud asked.

"Yes."

"And the discoloration just inside his nostrils," Demelza added. "Though that was a bit harder to see, for obvious reasons."

"You guys are something else," Laskar marveled. "Like, that was *actually* impressive."

"The rest of it wasn't?" Bud asked, rhetorically.

What he was referring to was the manner in which they had not only stocked up the little cargo ship, but how they had gained full control of it and its magical countersigns without having to resort to a single bit of torture.

Demelza's target, the *true* captain of the little craft, had been so utterly terrified at the sight of not one, but two Wampeh Ghalian in his quarters, that he had shit himself with fear.

Literally.

It was a smell that required a fair bit of cleansing spells to eliminate.

Of course, his being rather inebriated at the time hadn't hurt. Lowering inhibitions for making sexytime with the local talent he'd brought home from the pub was one thing. But when it came time to spill the details of his task, he had readily volunteered far more information than they even wanted.

Yes, they got the passphrases and countersigns that would allow them to approach and dock with the swarm fleet, but they'd also gotten an earful of intel about the assorted ruffians running much of the conglomerate's business.

Most was trivial information, but a few tidbits actually seemed like they might be useful. And all were given up freely in hopes of them sparing his life.

Little did he know, they had no intention of killing him. Nor his crew, for that matter, though he had assumed the worst when they were nowhere to be found. Those had been easy enough to render unconscious and remove from the craft long before Laskar had lured him back to the ship.

Hozark had simply used a strong stun spell on the men and women aboard the craft. All but one, that is. He did question that sole individual briefly to ensure there were no additional crewmembers who might return at an inopportune moment.

But they were it. The entire crew in one place. It was almost laughably easy for the master assassin to carry out the rest of their plan. Each of the stunned crew was hidden in a crate, which he then loaded onto a conveyance that dropped him at an alleyway in a seedy part of town.

He then dumped the slumbering men and women, but not before he turned out their pockets to make it seem they'd overdone it at a pub and been robbed. To complete the picture, he also dosed them with a liberal amount of a rather potent alcohol native to that world. Copious quantities were also spilled on their clothing to complete the effect.

But that would be slept off in a day, and word of what had happened would get out. So, Hozark added a little something special to the liquor. It was a somewhat dangerous recreational drug refined from a mold that grew on the bristling quills of a little creature indigenous to a few blue sun systems.

It had been banned on several worlds, and for good reason. The drug, when taken in any significant quantity, could cause weeks of hallucinations and paranoid delusions. When the crew woke under its influence, anything they might claim would be shrugged off as mere side effects of the drugs.

On his way back to the now-empty ship, Hozark slipped a youth some coin to make sure they were discovered before any *real* muggers had their way with them. By morning they would wake in the local constable's holding cells, and it would take weeks for them to properly come to their senses.

The captain, having coughed up any and everything they could possibly have needed to dock with the swarm, was dosed as well, though in his case, he received an extra-strong portion, just to be absolutely sure. They then acquired the last of the items on the manifest—with the coin aboard the ship, no less–and left the hapless crew behind.

There was no honor in killing innocents, and though these poor saps were part of the path to their ultimate target, they had done nothing to warrant losing their lives. But a few weeks of memories? That they could afford.

"I'm taking these," Demelza said, slipping a few of the more exotic treats they had held back into a grubby satchel she'd found in one of the crew's quarters.

"Here," Hozark said, handing her a small konus. "It was on one of the crewmembers. Pathetically underpowered."

"Perfect," she said as she slid it onto her wrist. "Keep the ship ready. If all goes as planned, I should be back in no time."

With that, she stepped into the linked network of spacecraft, following the path to Billian's own vessel that the hapless captain had given her. It was a winding route, and she would have to pass through several attached ships to get there. Her bribes would help her with that part of her transit.

"So, now we wait," Bud said, settling down into a seat.

"Are you sure she doesn't need our help?" Laskar asked.

"You may trust me on this," Hozark said with a wry grin. "It is not she who will be requiring help."

CHAPTER TWENTY-THREE

The walk through the interlinked craft to find Billian's command ship would have been worthy of King Minos with all of the twists, turns, dead ends, and double backs. But Demelza walked with confidence. And unlike Theseus, she didn't need a thread to help guide her.

With the swarm's latest configuration of ships firmly locked away in her head, the Wampeh assassin was walking the route as if she had always known it.

"Where do you think you're going?" a particularly muscular guard said as she drew close to the target vessel.

"Just delivering a few last packages from the supply run," she said demurely.

"Go around."

"But it's so much longer if I do. Can't you make an exception, just this once?"

"No exceptions. Go around."

She had expected some pushback, and considering how bad things could have been, this really wasn't all that bad. Demelza reached into her satchel and pulled out something this sort of man would find irresistible.

Not drugs to dull the mind or alcohol to relax it. No, this was a martial man. One who enjoyed his physical prowess. And what better to tempt him than with a beautiful phallic offering. And this one faintly glowed.

"I really am in a bit of a rush, but I'm sure we could come to an understanding," she said, 'accidentally' dropping the enchanted blade on the ground and not seeming to notice.

Her intent was as clear as the fresh pools at Lake Sarkan, and, despite his knowing better, the guard couldn't help but be tempted by the bit of shiny at his feet. An actual enchanted blade? Sure, it wasn't a super powerful one, but a weapon such as this would still be a world of improvement over the dull knife strapped to his hip.

Exactly as she'd thought when she noted the old blade dangling from his belt. Just as Hozark had done, Demelza had quickly found the man's weakness and exploited it.

"Well," he started to say. And with that, he was lost.

She reached out and opened the door, flashing a bright smile as she passed through before he could change his mind. The door closed behind her, leaving the guard to collect his new prize and forget he ever saw the delivery girl.

What he didn't know was the enchantment was temporary, and if he attempted to use it against a Ghalian, the limited magic she'd stored in the blade would backfire on its wielder. A little trick she'd used on more than one occasion.

She ducked into a side corridor that led to a small passage allowing her to access the outermost layer of Billian's craft. She was aboard. All that remained was extracting the information she sought from the man and making her escape.

With a confident stride, she walked the route to the salvage captain's inner set of chambers. The guard she came across this time was much easier to handle. She'd made it this far, after all, and in order for anyone to do so, they would have had to have the proper clearances.

"Passphrase?" the guard asked.

"Delmarian Salingahr," she replied.

He nodded once, then stepped aside. Demelza reached out and opened the door, stepping through into the chamber. It was a rather ornate room, The better bits of salvage had obviously been held back by Billian for his own use. But there was no time to gawk at his gaudy display. There was work to do.

Not the one to her right, but the door straight across the chamber was the one she sought, and it would lead her right into the heart of her target's den. She pushed the door open and stepped inside.

Rough hands grabbed her and spun her around, forcing her against the wall at knifepoint.

"Who the hell are you?" a deep, gravelly voice demanded in her ear.

"I'm just the delivery—"

"Liar!" the man growled, spinning her around until she was face-to-face with him.

Billian was even more striking in person, though not in a pleasant way. His jaw flexed angrily as he sized up his captive. Behind him, five guards strolled into the room, all with the same amused expression. One, she noted, was a familiar face and was carrying her enchanted blade.

"I was just trying to finish my rounds. I have things to deliver," she said, reaching for her satchel.

"Take it," Billian ordered.

One of his men snatched the pouch from her shoulder and dumped the contents onto a nearby table.

"Not much," the captain said as he looked through the little treasures. "But still enough to bribe some of my ship's guards."

The man with the enchanted knife stood still, hoping to remain anonymous a bit longer. Lucky for him, with the curvy woman in front of him, Billian was a bit distracted, and the man's wish was granted.

Billian menacingly ran his hands over his captive, admiring her form before stopping at her hands. "Pathetic," he said as he snatched the little konus from her wrist. "Barely enough magic to make me dinner, woman. But I'm sure I can find other uses for you."

A loud slap punctuated his words, and Demelza's head jerked to the side. Another followed, then another, until tears began streaming from the poor woman's face, punctuated by rough sobs.

This seemed to please him greatly.

"Bind her. Tie her to the chair," he ordered.

The men swung into action, forcing their captive to sit as they quickly tied her hands and feet. In mere moments, she was totally immobilized.

"Oh, yes. You are going to be my little plaything," Billian said, pacing in front of her like a cat studying a mouse, but unsure exactly what he was going to do with it yet. "I will have you. I will break you," he menaced.

"Like you did to Minara?" she spat back at him.

He stepped back. That was a name he hadn't heard in a long time. And more importantly, there was no way this woman could possibly have known about her.

"How do you know that name?"

"I know things," she replied. "I know *you*."

He looked at the fierceness in her gaze and couldn't help but appreciate her spirit. And that would make her all the more fun to break.

"There is more to you than meets the eye, my trussed-up intruder."

"And the same could be said about you," she replied. "A simple swarm fleet, salvaging and avoiding notice? Is that what you've told your men?"

The guards looked at one another, a bit confused.

"That *is* what we are doing. I've not lied to my men."

"Minara was from Vassitar. She and her people were my friends, and believe me, I've heard all about your little raiding missions in their system and a dozen others nearby. You killed her family."

"You're mistaken. Cocky, but mistaken."

"You lie to your men. I know you were there."

His men chuckled, as did he. "Oh, dear. You're trying so hard to get a rise out of me. Why? To buy yourself a little time? That won't help you in the long run. And you may as well cease your little game. I might go easier on you if you do. At first, anyway."

"You were there, and I can prove it."

"Oh, give it a rest, woman. I've not been anywhere near Vassitar, or that system, in ages, and my men know it. I heard of the attacks in the area, but we were systems away."

"Yeah, we were clear across the galaxy at Garvalis. Just ask Visla Horvath," one of the guards said with a laugh.

Billian flashed him an angry look that immediately silenced the man. Tormenting the prisoner was one thing, but loose lips were not allowed.

And speaking of lips, Demelza's had acquired the faintest hint of a smile.

"Garvalis, eh? What in the worlds is at Garvalis? It's almost entirely empty, from what I've heard."

"It's nothing you should concern yourself with," Billian replied, leaning in closer. "But tell me. Did you actually come here seeking revenge for a friend, only to discover it wasn't me you should be after at all? How delightful!" he laughed. "Oh, that's just rich. And now you are mine to do with as I please. And I have a *lot* of things in mind for you."

Strangely, the smile on the captive woman's face only grew as he continued his intimidating rant. It was decidedly *not* the intended effect. In fact, her smile was beginning to feel downright unsettling.

Billian knew she was unarmed. He had stripped her of her

only magical weapon himself before she was bound to the chair. And all of her other possessions were strewn on the table well out of her reach even if she weren't tied up. Yet still she smiled.

Just to be safe, he quickly uttered a binding spell, fastening her arms and legs even more securely to the chair. It may have been unnecessary, but there was something about this one. Something deeply wrong.

What the captain didn't know was that while she had indeed had her magical devices taken from her, Demelza was still brimming with magic. Visla magic, saved for just such a moment.

With no effort, she snapped both the magical and physical restraints as if they were tissue and rose to her feet.

"How did you––?" the nearest guard began to say. His words ceased moments later as she crushed his throat with a devastating punch.

Bedlam and chaos broke out, the men shouting for more guards as the woman they had terribly underestimated made quick work of them, starting with the one she'd identified as the best fighter of the bunch, judging by how he carried himself.

She quickly disarmed him, literally, then moved through the rest of the men with ease while their comrade screamed about his missing limb. But those screams were silenced by the layers of dampening spells she had been quietly casting over the doorways, creating a soundproof killing jar while her 'captor' was busy with his pompous monologuing.

He'd been so busy with his self-aggrandizing bluster that he hadn't even noticed her doing so. And that cockiness was his, and his men's, undoing.

It was a ballet of death, wrought by a woman who was in no way the victim they'd thought her to be. And while she moved with power and grace, the men attempting to stop her found their weapons turned against them as they tried first to attack her, then to escape.

At both of those endeavors, they failed miserably.

CHAPTER TWENTY-FOUR

"That didn't take terribly long," Laskar said when Demelza returned to their stolen ship. "Were you able to find the guy?"

She wasn't carrying the satchel any longer, but her clothing was as pristine as when she left. Then he looked down and noted the tiny spatter of blood on her left boot.

"Uh..."

"*Flarus colinsa*," she said, the cleansing spell erasing the last traces of her battle. It seemed one of the dead men still had a bit of the red stuff pumping in him––or *out* of him, as the case may be––after she had done her final clean up. A tiny splash managed to reach her foot, but no one looks at boots in space.

"So, things got hairy, I take it? I mean, did you have to fight a lot of people?" he asked.

"I wouldn't call it much of a fight," she said. "Though, to be fair, one of them did appear to have at least a little bit of training."

"But you found that Billian guy?"

"Oh, yes. We had some words," she said.

"I've seen what you can do. There were bodies, I take it?"

Bud asked with a knowing look. "Are we good? I mean, we're still tied into the swarm fleet, and if they go on lockdown––"

"Yes, there were bodies, Bud. And no, you do not have to worry about them being discovered. They are about to be disposed of."

"About to be?"

"Yes," she said, glancing up in thought as she tapped into the mental countdown she'd been maintaining since she left the captain's ship and set her spells in action. "The alarm should be sounding right about *now*, in fact."

On cue, a magical warning blast flashed through every one of the linked ships like energy rocketing through a ganglion of neurons. In an instant the entire fleet was on high alert.

"What the hell?" Laskar blurted as the ships all began breaking their bonds, separating with great haste and jumping away as soon as they were able.

The poor pilot hadn't been expecting to be so abruptly thrown into a flight situation, and he all but dove into his seat to activate the Drookonus and keep them from spinning into one of the hundreds of fleeing craft all around them.

"What did you do, Demelza?" Bud asked as he raced to his seat to take the helm from his copilot. "They're running like a herd of spooked Hookatsa."

"As intended," she replied, casually taking a seat of her own.

Hozark, utterly calm through the entire ordeal, simply gave her an appreciative nod. She had performed admirably, and her contract had been completed. And that meant she had obtained the intelligence they were after, no doubt. Information that would be relayed back to Master Corann to then transfer to their client.

A nearby ship's defensive spells surged and connected with their own, once more shaking the craft violently.

"I've got this," Bud said confidently. "Hang on, I'm pulling us clear."

He maneuvered the craft through the scattering swarm of ships until they were in a patch of relative calm. It had all happened so fast, it was hard to tell exactly *what* was happening. Demelza saw the quizzical look on Laskar's face.

"I noted a flaw in their defensive alert systems while I was making my way to Billian's ship," she said.

"I didn't see anything," he replied, a bit defensively. He prided himself in not only his piloting skills, but his understanding of magic as well. He was a weak caster, possessing so little of his own magic that neither of the Wampeh would waste their energy drinking from him.

But despite his lack of power, he did seem to have a fair grasp of the castings others placed. But this one he had somehow missed. And it was clearly bothering him.

"You would not have been able to detect it from where you were docked, Laskar," she said. "That particular spell was tied into their leader's craft alone."

"And by boarding that ship, you were able to sense it. And then you were able to exploit it," Bud said. "Nice one, Mel."

"Thank you, Uzabud."

"But what did you do? I mean, look at them!" Laskar said of the score of scattering ships. "There are hundreds of them, all armed, and yet they're running away."

Demelza flashed an amused grin. "This is where having one centralized node controlling the actions of the entire swarm proved a weakness," she said. "While Billian was a capable leader, and his direction was largely responsible for keeping the fleet coherent, his cockiness and overconfidence also provided for a most enticing opportunity."

The gears turned in Laskar's mind. "Are you saying you used his own spells against him?"

The main body of ships had broken into their individual components at last and were finally getting the distance needed to run. The whole thing had only taken a minute. Their vessel rocked as another fleeing ship jumped away far too close to their craft.

"It is exactly that," she said, amused. "They are a formidable adversary, no doubt, but against some foes, they do not wish to have any part of an engagement."

"What did you do, Demelza?" Bud asked, a hint of amusement sneaking into his voice.

"Why, I merely altered the alarm spell to react as if it had detected a group of magical signatures they did not want any part of. A fleet of Tslavar mercenaries, to be exact. While the swarm could survive an engagement, it would be incredibly costly, and for no good reason. The only logical option would be to jump away and flee, regrouping at their predetermined rendezvous point for just such instances."

At that moment, Billian's command ship, which looked much like the others in the swarm but for its somewhat distinctive markings, burst apart in a huge blast, fallen victim to what appeared to be a massive magical attack.

Frantic, the ships around it began jumping immediately, ignoring the proximity of their fellow craft. A few were terribly damaged in the process, but less than thirty seconds later all of the swarm ships were gone, fled to wherever it was they would regroup. Regroup, and mourn their leader.

"Oh, that was very well done, Demelza," Hozark said. "A master stroke."

"What do you mean, well done? Their ship just got blown to hell in all the panic," Laskar said. "I thought subtlety was the goal."

"You are correct," Hozark said. "But realize the true skill with which she carried out her contract. You see, to all of Billian's comrades, it now appears as if their leader was lost tragically during a surprise attack. It is the perfect cover. And while this was a contracted killing, when whoever it was who had hired Billian gets wind of this incident, they will believe it to have been a tragic incident, the sort of thing that happens to men such as him. All while remaining none the wiser as to the dear captain's true fate and the information he gave up before his demise."

"But how did you make it happen? There isn't really a Tslavar fleet out there, and that was a very real magical attack," Laskar said.

"That would be me," Demelza replied.

"You?"

"Yes. Though it was an unfortunately large expenditure of magic on my part, especially after healing the little wounds I received during his pathetic power play."

"You had *that* much power saved up inside you? I mean, I know you took Visla Horvath's magic when you drained him, but to blow up a ship like that would require nearly all of that power."

"As I said, a particularly significant expenditure of power. But I feel it was worth it to maintain our anonymity and complete the contract in a manner that not only satisfied our employer, but also kept whoever Billian was working for in the dark."

"So, you're saying we know what he knew?"

"Yes. I was able to extract the requested location prior to his demise."

"So, it's a planet? That's what this was about?"

"Among other things."

"But we now know which world this was all about, right?"

"Yes."

Laskar waited as the silence drew out. "Well?"

"Perhaps I was unclear as to that aspect of this task. You see, that was contracted information and will be reported to Master Corann, who will then relay it to the client. As for us, our work is done."

"But aren't you even the slightest bit curious? I mean, we just went through all of that to find and kill the guy. Don't you want to know what this is all about?"

She turned her calm eyes to Laskar and gazed upon him as one might look at a small child about to throw a tantrum. "I know the world he spoke of already. You can rest easy in the knowledge that there is nothing there."

"Nothing?"

"No. Not that we know of, at least," she said, then turned to their pilot. "Bud, would you please set a course for Inskip. I am to meet Master Corann in the capital city."

"Will do," he replied, then began the many jumps needed to reach their destination.

Hozark and Demelza rose and walked to one of the storage compartments farther back in the ship. A little privacy among assassins.

"So, you extracted the information."

"Indeed. The world is Garvalis. But what I said to the others was true. There is nothing there."

"I know."

"But there was more."

"Oh?"

"Yes. Billian was careful, but one of his men had looser lips than he and let a detail slip. A very interesting one at that. It seems they were at Garvalis with someone we've dealt with. Visla Horvath, in fact."

Hozark's slightly cocked eyebrow was all that showed of his surprise, but he was most certainly not expecting that bit of information.

"It seems there is a web of intrigue greater than we were previously aware of. We only completed the Horvath contract recently. It is possible that this crew did not even know of his demise."

"I had thought the same."

"But then this new question remains. How are all of these pieces connected?"

"I do not know," Demelza replied. "But at least we have a lead."

"Yes. But to what, we do not know," the master assassin replied.

Strange things were afoot. Things that seemed to tie back to Horvath, and possibly even Samara. They were going to have to get to the bottom of them, no doubt. But for the moment, they had a duty to perform.

"You shall make your report to Corann. And while you do, I will take my shimmer ship to Garvalis."

"Oh?"

"Yes. I will join you on Inskip shortly. But for the moment, I think a bit of digging is in order."

CHAPTER TWENTY-FIVE

Hozark had boarded his shimmer ship with the pretense that he had merely been called away to attend to a bit of Ghalian business for the Five.

In a sense it was true, he could rationalize, but nevertheless, it was not pleasant having to lie to Uzabud. The man had been through much with him, and he trusted him as much as a Ghalian could trust anyone outside of the order.

But this operation had to be quiet. Stealthy. Secret. And there was one in their party with a propensity for blurting out the wrong thing at the wrong time. In fact, Laskar didn't seem capable of efficiently lying—or keeping his mouth shut, for that matter—to save his life.

Or, in this case, protect Hozark's.

It was a risk he was not willing to take.

So, his excuses made, Hozark said his farewells and released his docking spells, drifting away from Uzabud's larger craft a moment before engaging his jump spell. And just like that, he was gone.

Hozark was still carrying some of the residual power he had stolen from Emmik Rostall not too long ago. Power he had taken just as Demelza had claimed hers from his secret partner, Visla Horvath. What exactly the two had been up to was still a lingering question, and one that would likely be resolved later rather than sooner.

It took a fair number of jumps to reach Garvalis, and even though his Drookonus was more than capable of making the trip many times over, Hozark couldn't help but notice just how distant the planet really was. A true backwater system at the edge of everything.

And for some reason, it had attracted the attention of some very powerful players.

Hozark engaged his shimmer cloak and approached the world. It *seemed* like all was quiet, but one could never be too careful. Especially when the Council of Twenty could be in play. Their thirst for power was bound to spill over into outright war one of these days, and woe unto whoever was in their way when that happened.

His first pass seemed to confirm what Demelza had said. There was essentially nothing there. Nothing to speak of, anyway. Just some small settlements populated by the sort of people who liked a quiet life off the grid, far from the interference of others.

But the idyllic scene shifted as he dropped into a lower orbit. Yes, inhabited regions were still sparsely populated, but there were signs of recent construction and expansion in one area in particular. And as he shifted his flight pattern to get a better look, he noticed something else. Something far more ominous lurking above.

A small armada of Tslavar craft.

Not all were mercenary ships, however. Some were supply and transport vessels supporting the larger militarized ones. And a number of craft were of a luxurious design he was unfamiliar with. Power users of some sort, he wagered, but which variety was guesswork.

Regardless, whatever was going on, something was definitely afoot, and it looked like he was going to have to go deeper into the action than he had originally anticipated. With a contingent like that, he couldn't just walk in and dig for intel.

He would have to resort to Ghalian ways. He would have to infiltrate.

Shimmer ships were rare, and most did not possess the power to properly camouflage the craft, nor the skills to control the shimmer properly. As a result, most were often mostly visible despite their users' best efforts.

The Wampeh Ghalian, however, had perfected them many centuries earlier and could not only maintain the cloaking to near perfection, they could also do so in space, a setting where shimmers notoriously failed their users.

For this incursion, however, Hozark would be setting down as close to the main town's borders as was feasible while maintaining a safe distance to avoid detection. And he would have to do so slowly.

While the ship was invisible to the eye, the shifting of winds around it at speed would still be detectable to an alert lookout if there were any clouds or vapor in the air. After a few minutes of careful study of the terrain, a suitable spot made itself apparent.

It was a small copse of trees, beneath which a thick tangle of brambles had grown. The thorny bushes would not harm his craft, nor would they interfere with his shimmer cloak, but they would prevent unwanted guests from accidentally walking smack into the invisible ship.

He dropped low in the empty clearing that ended just a few meters from the trees, then spun the ship and backed it carefully into place, dropping it down into a low hover so as not to crush the plants below. It was as good a hiding spot as he'd likely find on short notice, and he was actually quite pleased with it.

Hozark then set to work adopting one of his favorite characters for this sort of infiltration. A jovial trader, fond of drink and quick to laugh. Alasnib was his name, and he had a reputation for making friends wherever he went.

Of course, he was also unarmed and harmless, meaning Hozark had to shed all of his weapons and magical accoutrements, even his vespus blade. But that was of little concern.

For one, he was perfectly deadly without his tools and toys. For another, something as rare as a vespus blade would draw much attention. And last and most importantly, an unarmed and inebriated man tended to be underestimated and not seen as a threat.

That, he had taken advantage of on more than one occasion.

Hozark opened the door and cast a small protective spell allowing him to cross the thicket of thorns safely. He then cast several deadly wards and traps on his ship, ensuring an unpleasant demise for any who might try to enter it should it somehow be discovered.

But that was not ideal, and his stealthy incursion would be for naught if his ship happened to be found. So he also cast a few unpleasantness spells. Foul odors and an itching sensation as if being bitten by tiny insects, both of which would intensify should one draw close to his ship's hiding place.

Satisfied at his precautions, Hozark began the walk into town, a healthy, red blush to his cheeks and a small satchel of goods to trade with once he arrived at his destination. As was so often the case, a floating conveyance driven by one of the locals happened to be passing by as he walked.

With a friendly hello and a bit of cheerful banter, he had acquired a lift the remainder of the way. This served twofold. One, he didn't have to walk all the way to the town center. But two, it also let him casually acquire information as to the nature of the town, its layout, and what exactly the strange newcomers seemed to be doing there.

He was a trader, after all, and perhaps there was coin to be had dealing with these Tslavar visitors, regardless of what they were doing on so remote a world.

His new friend deposited him in town and pointed the way to the nearest tavern at which he could continue his drinking if he so desired, or perhaps add a little food to his belly to help absorb some of the copious booze he seemed to have been marinating in.

Of course, the strong alcohol smell was magical in origin, and Hozark was stone sober, as was always the case when he was on the prowl. But those who knew him as a stoic and proper man with a somewhat stiff demeanor and precision with words would not have recognized the man who now stumbled into the tavern, bleary-eyed and grinning like a fool.

"I'm Alasnib," he said with a slight slur as he flopped down at the nearest table. "Just got in, and I'm *starving*. A lovely fella named Jodpur said this was the place ta get something to eat."

"Yes, of course," a barmaid said. "What would you like? We have a hearty stew just made fresh this week. And there's––"

"Yes! Stew sounds wonderful!" he gushed.

"I'll get your order going."

"Wait. One more thing," he said. "Jodpur also said you have fine drink in this lovely establishment."

"Oh, that we do, friend."

"Well, then. A bottle of your finest local brew to wash down my meal, if ya please."

"I'll bring it right out," she said, rolling her eyes at the bartender as she hurried back to the kitchen.

In short order, Hozark was merrily slurping down his stew and engaged in a most hilarious conversation with one of the locals. Hozark was sharing his alcohol, and as a result, the two had become fast friends.

And while he ate and drank, he observed the Tslavars and other offworlders who were likewise having a repast, taking note of each and every one of them, from their clothing to their voices to their mannerisms. He hoped to avoid killing any of them, but if the need arose, by the time he'd finished his meal he was sure he could convincingly impersonate most of them.

But for now, he was a drunken trader, and that was all the better to casually make information slip from unguarded lips.

CHAPTER TWENTY-SIX

Stumbling out of the boarding house he had acquired accommodations in the night before––after waking the proprietor with loud, but good-natured shouts for a bed–– Hozark rubbed his hands through his hair and yawned deeply.

A moment later, he belched loudly and scratched his crotch, then flopped down onto a convenient seat on the porch of the building. Most of the structures were simple and squat, and none of the towering spires were held aloft by magic as you might find on the more wealthy and populous worlds.

Garvalis was, for lack of a better word, *homey*. It had that little town feeling. And it was charming for it. Well, if not for the Tslavars traipsing up and down the streets on their way to and from their labors.

It seemed the recent expansion had been undertaken without the consent of the locals. Those pulling the strings wished to build here, so here they would build, the desires of the preexisting inhabitants be damned.

But it wasn't all bad. The influx of workers also meant more coin flooding the coffers of local establishments so long accustomed to scraping by on the meager business of the local clientele. With the newcomers came opportunity, and the taverns and businesses that embraced them readily soon found their pockets filled.

It wasn't a lot of money by any standards, but for this backwater planet, it was more than some might see in a year, casually spent in but a few weeks by their visitors. Soon there were two menus in most restaurants. One for visitors, and one with lower prices for the locals.

It was done surreptitiously, of course, as no one wanted to bite the hand that fed them. But as the amount of coin flowing was not only ample, but also coming from their employer's vaults, the interlopers didn't seem to care one way or another. It was always nice spending someone else's money.

One of the more noticeable changes to the overall feel of the place since the Tslavars began their work was a greatly increased military vibe about the place. The new structures were erected with great speed and efficiency, but something about them felt transitory. Temporary. Like an invading army making camp that might be uprooted at a moment's notice.

But for now, it was a functioning model, and they were all making do as best they could.

Hozark spent his first day in the area simply wandering aimlessly, striking up conversations and making friends with all he met. Sharing the alcohol he always had on his person went a long way in furthering those interactions, and by nightfall, he had more than a few invitations to join his new acquaintances for meals or drinks.

As a trader, and one with at least some coin to his name, many of them did so in hopes he would treat. And the first few nights, Hozark did just that.

"What's that?" he asked on his third day as he strolled toward the far outskirts of the town in a direction he hadn't yet traveled.

"That? Just another of their new buildings, is all," the man trudging along the road beside him said.

"Nothing special? It seems bigger than the others."

"Nah, there's not much going on there. Not much anywhere, to be honest. They build all of this stuff without really putting any of it to use."

"Are they expecting more of their friends to come?" Hozark asked.

"Who knows? Your guess is as good as mine."

"But I've only just arrived here."

"Exactly," the man said with an exaggerated wink. "Anyway, no sense worrying about it. They've got coin and power, so they'll do whatever it is they want to do, like the wealthy always do."

Hozark and the man parted ways shortly thereafter. Alasnib the trader veered along the path running nearer the large building that had caught his eye. He had actually noted it immediately upon his arrival, but keeping with his character, he made a point to go nowhere near the obvious focal point of Tslavar activity until he was a somewhat familiar new face.

The building had an almost warehouse or factory feel to it. Far more modern-looking than any of the other structures in the town, or on the planet, for that matter. Three sides of it sat exposed, facing the town, while the fourth abutted the small hill that arose behind it.

With his usual inebriated cheer, Alasnib wandered over to a shade tree and flopped down, taking a break from the effort of walking. From his new vantage point, he could easily count the actual guards patrolling the building, versus the regular laborers moving to and fro.

At a glance, the men and women appeared to be just like the others. But to his trained eyes, the differences stood out even from a distance. Their demeanor, for one, made them easy to pick out. The way their eyes kept moving, always scanning for a threat, even though, by the bored looks on their faces, none had presented itself in a very long time.

Then there was their clothing. Similar to the garb of the regular workers, but a bit better fitting. More functional. And with pockets that no doubt contained dangerous implements to be deployed should the need arise.

The visible weapons—knives strapped to their belts—had the appearance of regular work tools, but the assassin knew a killer's blade when he saw one, and these were most definitely not layman's weapons.

All of that aside, the guards could not hide their boredom. They shifted in place, or paced back and forth from the tedium. Whatever the job might be, it was not exciting for people of action, and eventually, boredom could make even professionals sloppy.

Which was perfect for his needs.

Hozark spent a little while longer studying the men and women. Most were Tslavars, but there were a few other races mixed in. Apparently, this was not an *entirely* mercenary force. At least, not a Tslavar one. And that could be potentially useful should things go sideways. Any flaw in their defenses could be exploited if need be.

But for now, he just studied them, noting their routines and patterns from his spot beneath the tree where he seemed to be sleeping, and snoring quite loudly as well. Eventually, the sun began to set, and he snorted himself awake, his carefully applied stream of drool stuck to the side of his face.

He rubbed his eyes and rose unsteadily to his feet.

"Excuse me, I think I may be turned around," he said to a group of workers who just so happened to be coming off shift at that precise moment.

Obviously a coincidence. The type of coincidence that so often followed masters of this deadly craft.

"You trying to get back to town?" a woman asked, elbowing her friend in amusement at the disheveled man's dazed look.

"Uh, yeah. That's it," Hozark said, pulling a fistful of coin from his pocket, dropping a few in the process. "I must've dozed off. But I'm really hungry."

"We know a good place to eat," another worker said. "We'd show you and join you for a meal, but I'm afraid it's a bit out of our budget."

"But you're such lovely people. Come, let this meal be my treat. In the spirit of new friends," he gushed.

"If you insist," the man replied with a grin.

They walked into town together and settled in for a meal at what really was a pretty decent establishment. Hozark found himself impressed by the cook's ability to work with such limited fare and wondered if he'd ever spent time off world.

Drinks flowed, and heady laughter was thick in the air until well into the evening, when the conversation took a somewhat more serious turn.

"I tell ya, I'm sick of tha trader thing," Hozark slurred. "I mean, sure, I get to travel, and yeah, I earn pretty good coin. But tha thing is, it's not stable. Like, take this place, for instance. You all have a great life. Work is steady, you know you'll get paid every week without having to scratch out a living trading baubles, and it's a pretty place to live."

The exhausted workers looked at one another with amusement, but also a degree of consideration for this outsider's fresh eyes on their lives. Maybe he was onto something?

"Thing is, I wish I could just have a stable life like you do," he continued.

"Why don't you, then?" his new friend asked.

"Why don't I what?"

"Join up with us. Stop doing what you obviously don't enjoy. And if you find you don't like this either, you can always go back to trading."

Alasnib the trader squinted hard in concentration at the man's suggestion.

"You know what? Maybe I'll do just that!"

The next day, the newcomer stuck to his assertion and followed his new friends to the foreman to ask about joining the labor force.

"You're sure this is for you?" the stout man asked.

"I'm sure. I need a change of pace, and this is it!"

"Well, okay. But you need to carry your own weight. You can't rely on the others to keep you going, we clear?"

"Clear as can be."

"Great. Then welcome to the team, Alasnib."

And like that, he became one of them. Another face in the group, growing more and more familiar with each passing day. And those days stretched on and became a week. And with that familiarity, those around him let their guard down more and more.

They worked long hours together, joked together, talked shit together. He was one of their team, and as such, he enjoyed a degree of freedom that mere residents did not enjoy.

On his eighth day as a laborer, Hozark "accidentally" stumbled into a sentry spell near the large edifice while delivering a load.

"Oops! What's that?" he asked innocently as guards came running, excited to finally have something to do.

"It's just the new guy," the closest guard said, then uttered the disarm and reset spell.

Hozark made note of it. He might not have possessed a konus to power the spell, but the careless guard didn't know he still had Emmik Rostall's power within him.

Out of the corner of his eye, he noted something else the alarm had brought. Something none but the most observant would see. A trio of shimmer-cloaked sentries. They were actually quite skilled in their use of the shimmers, but he was a Ghalian master, and for him, they were only a little more difficult to pinpoint.

"I tell ya, the guys running this show need to unclench their assholes, right?" he joked as he and his friends walked away.

It was the kind of comment that you could get in trouble making about a visla. The kind of thing you'd only say when you were sure you were alone. And he had said it in front of the invisible guards. To turn him in would reveal their presence, and they knew it. Just as he had intended, but his "blunder" cemented him in their eyes as a fool. Just like every other low-level, whining laborer. He was normal.

In reality, however, he was anything but.

CHAPTER TWENTY-SEVEN

"He's been gone a pretty long time, now," Uzabud said as he sipped on a cup of frothy arambis juice blended with crystalized ice.

Laskar sat beside him, drinking a similar beverage. "Yeah. This can't be normal, right?"

The motherly looking woman sitting with them on the porch smiled as one might to a little child. She was the very picture of sweet, tender compassion. The sort of woman children and adults alike felt an immediate warm affection toward.

She was safe. She was home. She was the embodiment of all the calming and comforting traits a mother could have.

She was also the head of the Five, and arguably the deadliest woman in the galaxy.

Master Corann had not merely excelled in her climb up the ranks of the Wampeh Ghalian. She had thrived. And her body count at this point was higher than that of some military units. The *entire* unit, that is. In her early days, she had outright slaughtered many, often with no more than her bare hands and fangs.

Corann was what the locals colloquially called a "badass," though they'd never in a million years think to apply that term to that sweet woman they all knew as Arlata, the kindly widow who adored the local youth but never had any children of her own.

It was the perfect cover. And when a young Wampeh woman came visiting with her two friends in tow, the locals were thrilled for her having company. For this was surely the niece she'd mentioned on occasion. A girl she cherished as if she were her own.

When Demelza had arrived at Corann's primary city of residence, she had felt a little odd approaching the head of her order outside of one of their training houses. She was vulnerable here. At risk. Why she had communicated the desire to meet here instead of one of their secret facilities was beyond her.

But Corann had spoken, and that was that. And once they saw how beloved she was by the locals, her safety and security seemed far more stable than originally believed. If anyone raised so much as a finger against that kindly woman, the entire neighborhood would descend on them in an angry mob.

Of course, she had also installed countless wards and defensive spells, all ready for her to trigger at a moment's notice, wiping out every living thing for miles as she made her escape, if need be.

It would be a shame, that. She really *did* like the locals. But she was a Ghalian assassin, and that aspect of her nature would always win out.

"Master Hozark will come when he has completed what he set out to do," she said to her guests as she rocked casually in her chair, soaking in the morning sun.

"But what if he doesn't? What if he needs our help?" Bud asked. "He's been a little off ever since we ran into his old girlfriend."

"Well, we did blow her out of the sky," Laskar noted. "After she tried to kill him, that is."

"Yeah. That sort of thing can mess with a man's head," Bud agreed. "But he's a Ghalian. And a *master* at that. He should be immune to that sort of thing, shouldn't he?"

Corann smiled and glanced over at Demelza, who had been silently contemplating the private discussion they'd had when she first arrived, eager to share what she had learned.

There was more at play than anyone knew, and the sooner Hozark returned and could be filled in on the developments, the better.

"Samara was *not* his girlfriend," she told them. "While they may have had a dalliance in the past, they were in no way a bonded pair."

"Sure, whatever you say," Bud said. "But you didn't see the look on his face when she died."

"There was no look on his face," Laskar noted.

"Precisely. And you don't just take that sort of thing without it messing with your head a little. You need to let things out or it'll eat you up inside."

Corann took a sip from her steaming mug of local herbs as she sized the men up. Both seemed to care about Hozark, and while the new one was somewhat of an untested variable, Uzabud had worked with Hozark for a long time, and she knew he trusted him implicitly.

"Master Hozark is something of an *unusual* man. Even for a Ghalian," she said, carefully choosing her words. "But he will be fine, I assure you."

Bud and Laskar looked at Demelza, confused. She said nothing, but just shrugged. Whatever Corann was getting at was news to her as well.

"Unusual?" Bud asked.

"Let's just say that Master Hozark was able to attain his

ranking within the order largely because he overcame his own innate foibles."

"Well, he's the best at what he does that I've ever seen."

"An assessment I would not think to contradict," she replied. "But he was not always this way. In fact, as a youth, there was much doubt as to whether or not he was even Ghalian material."

"Hozark? We are talking about the same fella, right?" Laskar said. "Scary guy with pointy teeth who mows down his enemies like they were made of tissue paper? The one with a freakin' vespus blade and the power to wield it? *That's* who you had doubts about becoming a Ghalian?"

Corann smiled as she thought back to her friend's early years. "Oh, yes," she said. "He has always been different, even among our order. You see, what you say about his connection to Samara rings true, to an extent. In his youth, *Aspirant* Hozark continually proved to be too emotional for our kind. He *felt* too much, and it affected his performance."

"My turn," Bud said. "We are talking about the same guy, right? The one who puts on a happy face, acts like a jolly drunk, making friends with everyone he talks to, then slaughters the entire roomful of people without breaking a sweat? *That* guy's overly sentimental?"

"*Was*," she corrected him. "He overcame that weakness, in time."

"Obviously," Bud cracked.

"And now his stoicism is legendary even among the Ghalian. His ascendance taught us all a little lesson about judging an aspiring candidate too soon."

Bud couldn't believe what he'd heard. Hozark was a softy? It was just so incongruous with all he knew of the man. Sure, he expected his ex's death to get to him, but he had no idea those still waters ran quite so deep. It seemed there was still a lot to learn about his friend.

Demelza finally broke her lengthy silence. "Whatever he is

up to, I am sure he will be successful in his endeavor. One thing I have learned about Master Hozark in the short time we have traveled and worked together, is he is not one to leave things to chance, and he never takes a task lightly."

On that they were all in agreement. And so it seemed they had naught to do but patiently wait for the return of their friend. When exactly that would be, however, was anyone's guess. As was whatever in the worlds he was up to.

CHAPTER TWENTY-EIGHT

It had been an uncommonly long infiltration by many people's standards. Weeks spent essentially doing nothing but laboring and toiling in the company of the motley band of workers building out the expanding development.

But the Wampeh Ghalian were legendary for their results, and this showed why. What people failed to realize is those incredible and seemingly impossible assassinations were often the result of weeks, months, or in rare instances, years, of hard work gathering intel, building "friendships," and gaining proximity.

It was akin to the great Bantoo philosopher Aukratzi's saying: "The ease of mastery comes with the effort of training."

In this, the Ghalian were certainly of the same mind, though they had also adopted a much more martial mantra as well: "The more one sweats and bleeds in training, the less one bleeds and dies in battle."

Thus it was that Hozark did what seemed like the most un-assassin thing possible. He worked as a menial grunt, whining about his day and drinking away the aches and pains every night with his new comrades.

Of course, his lifelong training regimen had given him the muscle tone that made these labors seem trivial by comparison. But he grumbled and groaned all the same, endearing himself to his likewise whinging friends.

He had found a groove, and as a good worker––but not so good as to stand out particularly––he had been shifted to more important tasks. One of which was using the smaller floating conveyances pushed by hand to deliver containers to the mysterious building on the outskirts of town.

It was being worked on inside, so whatever was being done to it was still hidden from view. And for whom it was being made was still a question mark. But Hozark had spent enough time in proximity to the structure now to have marked out all of the actual guards blending in with the workers, as well as the handful of shimmer-cloaked sentries who shifted positions like clockwork.

Sentries on a fixed schedule. It was the sort of thing people like he so enjoyed coming across. It was almost like a gift-wrapped roadmap to incursion. Truly well-versed guard captains knew better. They knew to mix up the routine daily, if not hourly, so as to not allow one such as Hozark to learn their patterns.

But these men were lax in that regard. And the master assassin was certainly not going to look this gift Malooki in the mouth.

After weeks of observation, it seemed clear that the multiple entrances to the large facility were unimportant. Not decoys, per se, but they led to parts of the structure that were seemingly benign in nature.

The back of the building, however, where it abutted the hill, possessed a small, hidden entrance. Very few deliveries were made in the vicinity of that one, and they were never taken inside, but merely deposited nearby, as if being stored temporarily.

Hozark knew better.

Of course, the door was hidden, and as such, no one had seen it used who wasn't supposed to. No one but Hozark, that is. He had adopted the habit of taking surreptitious naps on his breaks beneath a nearby shade tree. It was a position that allowed him just the slightest glimpse of the rear of the building.

It was all he needed. In just a few days he'd observed everything he required for his next steps.

At the end of the third week he found himself delivering a load of crates to the area at the rear of the building. It seemed the man who normally made that delivery had gotten sick after breakfast that morning.

The little droplet of toxic slime mold that grew on this world that Hozark had mixed in with his meal might have had something to do with it.

"Are you sure you don't mind?" the man asked as he caught his breath between bouts of vomiting.

"Of course," Alasnib the trader had replied. "You're a good friend, Tiku. I'm sure you'd do the same for me if positions were reversed."

"Thanks, Alasnib. You know, I'm really glad you decided to stick around and join us."

"It's been exhausting, I'll admit. But also a lot more stable than trading, though I do miss it a bit."

"Well, you can alwa––" he started, then spun away as a fresh stream of bile rose from the depths of his belly.

Hozark patted him on the back. "You just feel better, my friend. Good old Alasnib will make sure your deliveries are handled. You won't be docked any pay on my watch!"

Tiku merely nodded his thanks as his body trembled from the dry heaves that took hold of him.

Hozark headed off to hurry through his own work so he would be free the rest of the day. He knew it might draw a little attention that he was suddenly so efficient, but he reasoned a

SCOTT BARON

single day of faster work would likely not catch anyone's eye. Especially not while they were preoccupied with their own tasks, as people typically were.

He finished up the bulk of his work, then gathered up Tiku's deliveries and headed to the back of the structure to deposit the full crates, which would be brought inside later by the as-of-yet unseen denizens of that secret area.

He was unloading the cargo when he noted a nearby guard scrutinizing him. He must have noticed this was not the usual delivery person. Hozark hummed and went about his work, stacking the crates high and putting the floating conveyance to the side where it would eventually be loaded with empty container for re-use. Then he casually trotted back to get his next load, quickly blending in with the other workers.

On his return trip, the same guard was still on shift, and he once again kept an eye on this particular laborer working in his area. Hozark was mildly inconvenienced by this development, but he had learned many tricks in his day, and it seemed this was the time to utilize one of them.

He unloaded the crates, then leaned against one of them and began picking his nose.

Not just casually picking. He was really digging in there, then examining his finger with great interest before thrusting it into his nose again, digging like a dwarf mining for gemstones.

It was a funny psychological trick, and one that worked more often than not.

When under scrutiny, simply picking one's nose tended to make people look away. It was a completely involuntary action that had been observed and exploited by masters of mental trickery. It was like being caught looking at something you shouldn't. An instinctive reaction that could be used to one's advantage on occasion. And today was one such day.

The guard looked away, making an effort to scan the other workers in the opposite direction. Hozark didn't waste a second, quickly bypassing the magical wards on the door he had been casually studying for days from his siesta vantage point. The magic was hard to sense at that distance, but with the benefit of time and focus, he had worked out the basics of the mechanism even from afar.

The door's safeties released, and the threshold appeared where a wall had been. Without missing a beat, the assassin scanned for further traps within the doorway, then, when he was satisfied there were none, slipped inside and sealed it shut behind him.

Outside, a stack of crates was neatly in place, just as they were supposed to be. When the guard finally turned his head in that direction once more, it would look as if the laborer had simply gone off to continue his work. And working he was, but not in a manner any would have expected.

CHAPTER TWENTY-NINE

The interior of the secret door appeared to be nothing terribly out of the ordinary. At least, not to a layman's eyes. Once inside, Hozark found himself in a dimly lit corridor that stretched nearly five meters before reaching another door.

It was wider than a normal hallway might be, designed to allow for the passage of larger items, such as crates and supplies, he reasoned. The faint glow overhead was cast by an overlapping series of spells rather than a single one. Should one fail, the others would keep the space illuminated.

It was that little detail that made Hozark stop in his tracks. Something about this felt far too familiar. He had dealt with seemingly straightforward things such as this in the past. Most recently when he tracked down the legendary swordmaker Master Orkut to entreat him to craft him a vespus blade.

Ultimately, after overcoming a lengthy series of traps, pitfalls, wards, and snares, Hozark had proven himself to the bladesmith, and the weapon he had desired had been forged. In the process, he had also found himself saddled with an unwanted item. A partner.

Demelza had been part of Master Orkut's deal, but what had

seemed to be an inconvenience and intrusion on his lone wolf style had proven to be a most beneficial arrangement.

She was more than just a talented assassin. There were scores of them within the order. But she was also particularly clever. And it had been her masterful subterfuge that had allowed them to complete their first contract together.

But that was a different time on a different world, and the obstacles he had faced leading up to that were of a far milder variety. Those might have hurt and even maimed, but the spells he was beginning to sense hidden in *this* seemingly benign corridor were deadly.

This was not a test. This was a trap. One giant trap waiting to be sprung on any so unfortunate as to enter without first knowing its secrets.

Hozark reached out with his internal magic and plucked at the strings of power all around him. It was almost like a web waiting to snare its next victim. Hozark stood stock-still and *felt* the space. After several minutes––one does not rush when surrounded by deadly traps if one can avoid it––he opened his eyes. Yes, there was a way through this invisible gauntlet.

It was the lights that gave him the clue he needed. Most would have begun undoing the wards one by one as they went, clearing the way to the door at the far end of the hallway. And most would have perished.

It was quite clever, and he certainly gave whoever devised this little trap full kudos for their ingenious design. This was a functional entrance to an important facility, and whoever came through the outer door would be on their way to whatever task they were engaged in. Likely something that would simply not do with lengthy delays.

This hallway was one *giant* delay. Even with the correct counter-spells, it would take time to deactivate and reset them as you went. Each light above was keyed in to a series of spells, and their visual shifts would act as a confirmation of progress, leading the intruder farther down the hall, closer to their goal.

But the doorway at the far end was a trap in and of itself.

"Oh, you are a clever one," Hozark said with a low chuckle.

Logic dictated that workers would need to be efficient. Speedy, even. This entry was by no means fast.

Hozark closed his eyes and shut down his senses once more, focusing on ignoring the tangle of magic laid out in front of him. Slowly, it all faded until it was just him standing within the entryway and nothing else.

He then let his power trickle out to either side, gently feeling for a tug on his magic.

"Yes, there you are," he said, slowly opening his eyes as he reeled in that thread of connection.

It was almost invisible to the naked eye. A tiny discoloration on the wall to his left. And within that mark was a very subtle magical ward. A lock. He grinned.

Locks were meant to be picked.

In just a few seconds he had disabled the warding spell and released the hidden doorway, the section of wall silently and effortlessly swinging open on a magically linked cushion of power.

Hozark stepped inside, the door sealing behind him as he did. This was the *true* interior of the facility, and it was far different than what any would have guessed from seeing the rest of the structure.

It was dark, for one. Not pitch-black, but merely measured in the use of power to illuminate the space. No additional magic was floating through this area, and when the sharp, acrid smell of hot metal and the clanging of enchanted tools reached his ears, Hozark suddenly had a very good idea why.

This was a weapons factory. And the forming and powering of konuses and slaaps had to be done in a very particular manner. Once they were completed units, they would be robustly safeguarded against all sorts of mishaps. But in the creating process, too much ambient magic could make the initial charge misfire, and that could be catastrophic.

It was for that reason that most konuses and slaaps were only minimally imbued with magical potential at first, then shipped for proper powering up afterward. It greatly reduced the likelihood of mishaps that way.

These, however, were being fully charged on creation. And while they were stable once that task was completed, each unit still in production could prove deadly if the wrong magic mingled with its new charge.

Hozark stealthily moved through the shadows to get a better view, utilizing the side effect of the reduced magic to his benefit. The creatures forging the devices were a deep green with blotches of black smattered across their skin.

He had come across their kind before, and always in the employ of nefarious types. Weapons makers of some talent, but with such a malevolent nature that only the most powerful, or the most twisted, would employ their skills. And it seemed that this lot was making some *very* powerful weapons.

A few small crates lay open, exposing their contents. Konuses, in one crate. Slaaps in another, the more powerful weaponized version of a konus being of particular use in purely martial endeavors. Yes, this confirmed it. Someone was gearing up for a conflict, though most of the devices did not appear to be charged yet.

A flash of golden light caught his eye. There, in the dark, a pale-yellow-skinned woman sat chained to a heavy ring in the floor. No control collar for her. Not in this place where magic had to be carefully contained. But she was an Ootaki, and she possessed a vast quantity of magic of her own. Magic that she herself could not access.

So, that's how they're doing it, Hozark mused.

Without a visla or other high-level power user to actively

feed magic into the new devices, they would be no more than inert pieces of metal. And it was clear that whoever their master was, he or she was nowhere near. Had they been, they would not have needed the Ootaki, though a visla conserving their own power would often use the stored magic in Ootaki hair to preserve and enhance their own.

Looking closer, he could see she had already had a large chunk of her long hair crudely chopped off, undoubtedly used to power some of the devices. Movement in the shadows caught Hozark's attention, and even in the dim light, he could make out the shapes of several other Ootaki, all huddled together, bound by non-magical restraints.

They were being treated like refuse, not the valuable tools their kind were seen as. But one look at their heads revealed why. Shorn, the lot of them, robbed of their magical hair, undoubtedly by the creatures currently enslaving them.

Yes, their hair would grow back, and it seemed as if several were of the age where they'd likely had their locks harvested more than once. But that would take years, and until any sizable amount had grown back, they were just more mouths to feed and look after, their value diminished with their loss of hair.

Hozark watched in silence as another swath of hair was unceremoniously cut from the woman's head. It seemed to be her first growth. The most powerful. But she was not freely giving it. Not in these circumstances. And as a result, much of the power faded as soon as the hair had parted from her head.

But the weaponsmiths didn't seem to care. The apparent leader took the hair and held it over a newly forged konus, then uttered a series of arcane spells. The very particular magic that would grant the device the ability to hold and disperse power as its wearer desired.

It was a difficult task, and one that most lacked weapons-grade proficiency at. But this man seemed to know his way around the tricky magic, and moments later, the golden hair faded to white as its power drained into the metal band. He held still a long moment until the konus ceased glowing. Then, when it was safe to pick up, he transferred it to the nearest crate to join the other completed konuses.

A trace of something made the assassin spin, his senses sharp and hands ready for combat. But no one was there. Still, there had been *something*. A sense of a familiar magic.

Horvath, he realized, identifying the subtle hint of magic from the visla he and Demelza had been contracted to kill. But there was more. *Emmik Rostall, as well*, he noted, feeling the residue of the dead man's power reach out to the same power still residing within him from the assassination. The magic seemed to be mixed together, and it was coming from some of the other crates. Crates containing finished weapons.

The two men had been here. *Here*, of all places. And they were apparently more than just in cahoots to wrest power from the Council of Twenty in a few systems. No, this seemed to be far more than that. They were involved in a plot much more dangerous.

And there was more.

Another magic was present. Far, far stronger than the others. Hozark had simply failed to notice it at first as his senses were so flooded with the fresh Ootaki magic being harvested in front of his eyes. But this other trace? It was incredibly strong, yet also disguised. Expertly hidden. Just a scent of it was present, and not enough to identify. But it was strong, whomever it belonged to.

Someone was preparing for action, and it seemed many of his recent encounters were tied into it somehow. Hozark simply didn't know why.

CHAPTER THIRTY

The acoustics of the smelting facility were not the best. Sound had a funny way of bouncing and echoing off of the hard surfaces and angles, making it incredibly difficult for even one as skilled as Hozark to listen in.

If he'd had his shimmer cloak, that would have been easily remedied, at least normally. But here, with this volatile mix of magic in the making, even if he hadn't left it aboard his ship, using the magical cloak could very well set off a chain reaction.

So, strained ears it would be. Fortunately, the smelting had ceased, at least for the time being, and the green and black men's voices carried with a degree of clarity for the moment. And the subject matter of their discussion was of great interest to the lurking Wampeh.

The men closest to the forge were talking over details of their magical resources as they loaded the last konus into a full crate and sealed it tight, stacking it atop another identical crate nearby. There were not terribly many of them––certainly not enough for a proper military action––but more than enough to cause all manner of mischief in the right, or wrong, hands.

"We need to speed the process. Are there any more Ootaki

inbound?" the stockiest of the group asked. "This is our last one."

"Dunno," the apparent leader of the workers said, pulling on the poor slave woman's golden hair. What was left of it, anyway. "There were supposed to be more coming, but then that idiot Horvath went and got himself killed, and that screwed up the whole thing."

"Too bad about that. I liked him. He brought us drinks when he came to power those konuses," another said.

"Idiot, that was just to keep everyone happy and working harder. And apparently it worked. I swear, you're so gullible."

"Call it what you like, I still thought it was a nice gesture."

"Well, it doesn't matter now anyway. Whatever is completed is set to be shipped out soon. Visla––"

A terrible clanging rang out as a red-hot crucible was pulled free and tipped, the molten metal inside merrily pouring into the konus mold.

What did he say? Hozark wondered, more than a little frustrated at their horrible timing. *It sounded like Visla Akta. Is that right? I've never heard of such a man. Or woman.*

Whatever had been said, the moment was now lost as the workers settled back into their routine.

"...picked up at the depot," he heard one man say.

"The Fakarian will handle the delivery," another said.

Hozark was surprised to hear that tidbit. But he had heard correctly. A Fakarian was involved. Normally you didn't see members of that amphibian race on bone-dry worlds. It wasn't that they couldn't go there, it was just they preferred not to.

For one, their skin was sensitive to drying out in dryer climes. For another, they simply felt more secure with water at their backs to provide an easy escape should it be needed.

More clanging rang out, and the next bit was simply too garbled to understand, but Hozark was able to pick out a few key words. It seemed the Fakarian was going to carry the cargo and then await distribution orders.

Wherever the visla wanted them to go, he would handle the delivery. As for the metalsmiths, all they had to do was wait for more power-holding bodies to arrive for them to drain to charge the weapons.

A whiff of a very familiar smell suddenly cut through the sharp tang of the molten metal. It was a smell Hozark knew as intimately as any lover. It was the smell of death. Somewhere nearby, corpses lay.

Carefully, the assassin moved around the periphery of the room, following his nose until he discovered the smell's source.

A dozen bodies lay piled against the far wall. Most bore the markings of magical draining, and others still had signs of torture. Whatever they'd done here, it had been an attempt to utilize power wielders other than Ootaki. Even a Pair of Drooks lay in the heap, and to sacrifice users of that value, whoever was in charge must have *really* wanted to complete these weapons in a hurry.

Something caught Hozark's eye among the dead. A sight that chilled even him. He moved closer for a better look, a look that confirmed his suspicion. It was a dead Wampeh, his pale body tossed aside. Tortured by the look of it. Experimented on. But why? Wampeh weren't a magical race.

Whatever the reason, Hozark had seen enough. This warranted breaking cover and returning to the other members of the Five to relay what he had learned. What manner of nefarious plotting was afoot. It looked like an attack was imminent, and given what he'd seen so far, it could upend some systems and lead to all-out war in others.

With a stealth that came as naturally as breathing, he slowly melted farther into the shadows in the dim chamber, moving farther from the workers and closer to the exit.

From where he was standing, it seemed the adjacent storage

room would provide him not only cover from being seen by the workers, but also a more direct route back to the hidden door he had arrived by. It was a fortuitous bit of luck, and one he would gladly accept.

Hozark stuck to the walls, lurking in the shadows as the Wampeh Ghalian were wont to do, until he finally reached the doorway to the room. Peeking his head inside, he saw his hunch confirmed. There *was* a door at the other end of the room that appeared to empty out into the far end of the larger chamber, right by the secret entry.

Double checking that no one was looking his way, Hozark reached out and felt for wards or snares on the doorframe. None were to be found. It was just a doorway. Satisfied that for once things were going easier than expected, he stepped through the doorway and found himself abruptly falling straight down, tumbling to what might very well be his end.

CHAPTER THIRTY-ONE

It was only pure instinct that saved Hozark's life, the blocking spells he cast as he fell drawing deep from the internal magic he carried, forming a protective bubble around him. The act was not something that could really be taught, it was more of a visceral reaction, and one that he had done without even thinking about it.

A good thing, too, for when he impacted the bottom of the deep pit into which he'd fallen, a sharp cracking sound heralded his abrupt arrival.

Ahh, spikes, he quietly noted. Even having fallen into a deadly trap, his calm remained, as did his attention to maintaining silence.

Given the depth of the pit, however, he was relatively certain any sound, such as that of the cracking spikes, would have been directed straight upward. And as the room containing the trap was set away from the main labor area on the smelting floor, odds were none would have heard a thing.

Hozark loosened his grip on the magic cushioning him and settled down onto the dirt.

"Illumino azminus," he quietly said, casting the faintest of

illumination spells. One that would be utterly unnoticed by any above unless they gazed directly upon it.

The dim light revealed what he had deduced from his abrupt landing. The floor of the pitfall was indeed covered in sharp spikes pointing upward to welcome whatever surprise visitors might make an appearance. Any lesser man would have found himself dead, and in a most unpleasant way.

He examined the ends of the broken spikes, careful not to touch the points or any part near them. A habit drilled into him since his earliest days, but one that proved unwarranted in this particular instance. No poison had been applied to the wood, as was common in this type of trap.

But given the secrecy of this particular section of the facility, it seemed unlikely the Tslavar mercenaries with experience in that arena of combat would be allowed into this obviously secret and sensitive area. Whoever had set the trap knew the basics––and had done an admirable job of it––but was ignorant of the finer nuances of pitfalls.

Hozark looked up at the smooth walls. They were cut from the soil beneath the building, not bedrock. That was an interesting wrinkle to things. Apparently, the security of the hillside shielding the entrance was worth the slight lack of stability from building atop soil, not rock.

But the dirt had been altered. Hardened. Made into a smooth surface as if it was rock. Hozark had no choice but to admire the craftsmanship. Far superior to anything a mercenary could have achieved with his konus.

This was the work of a powerful caster. And given the location and nature of the masterfully laid trap, it was one who knew a thing or two about Ghalian ways, it seemed.

He chided himself for only a moment as he replayed the incident that had led to his current predicament. All of the usual precautions were taken, and there had been no traps or wards placed on the door, nor directly inside the threshold.

However, the piece of stone lying on the ground keyed him in to the novel trigger mechanism. Whoever it was who had caught him in their snare had been clever. Exceptionally clever.

They had placed a perfectly normal, solid, real piece of stone where one would tread upon entering the room. But it was suspended in place by a magic cushion. Only when a person's other foot had left the ground to take their next step would the connection to solid ground be broken and the spell released.

The resulting tumble would have caught those with even the quickest of reflexes.

Hozark had been holding his power at the ready for a few minutes as he waited for the mind behind this endeavor to make an appearance, but none appeared at the lip of the pit to gloat at his folly.

They are not present, he realized. *If they were, they would undoubtedly have sensed their trap having been sprung. Interesting.*

Hozark slowly released his grip on the spells he had ready on his lips. The deadliest of arcane Ghalian magic. Killing spells known to but a handful, and even then, rarely used due to the power they required.

But whoever had placed this trap was a powerful caster, and in his precarious position, he would have only one shot at them. If he missed, all would be lost. But they never came. Only workers and lackeys were present, and unattuned to magic as they were, and with any ambient spells that might have notified them deactivated due to the risk of magical reaction with the fabrication, Hozark found himself in an unusual position.

He was trapped, but no one knew. Not yet. He was left alone for the time being. And that meant he could be down there a while. He glanced around for a better look and noticed the white of bones littering the pit floor. Rather than feel any fear, he almost laughed.

It was startlingly amateurish. There was simply no way a body would have decomposed to bleached bones in the time in which the facility had existed. Not even close. Someone had scattered them to terrify any who might fall into the trap and survive.

No wonder the spikes were not poisoned. The maker of this trap was a bit of a sadist, apparently, and while the spikes *might* have killed their victim on impact, the odds were more likely that whoever fell in would be terribly injured, then left bleeding and broken, with plenty of time to stare at the bones as they bled out.

But Hozark was no ordinary victim. Not by a long shot. And this silly little ploy by a petty tyrant could quite possibly have provided him his means of escape.

Several of the bones were simply too small for his needs, but some of the leg bones strewn about were sturdy enough. Hozark picked one that held the most promise and then carefully applied a precision strike with the edge of his hand while channeling a little of his power to reinforce the bone everywhere but where he was making contact.

The crack was not terribly loud. Certainly nothing that would be heard outside of the pit. And the sharp points that were the result of his first attempt seemed like they would suffice. If they didn't, he would only have a few more tries before he used up the suitable bones. After that, he could have a very, very long wait in the bottom of a pit.

Hozark tucked the bones into his belt, then walked around the pit, taking his time studying the smooth walls, running his fingers across the surface. It was not stone, but the magic applied to the dirt had made it into a particularly slick and robust surface. Climbing it would be impossible, and chipping hand and footholds simply wasn't an option.

But Hozark had other plans.

Yes, this is the spot, he noted as his fingers found an irregularity in the surface just above head height.

He withdrew one of the sharpened bones and began casting,

slightly at first, the magic reinforcing the bone's natural matrix, making it far harder than it would otherwise be. He then drove it into the wall as hard as he could, pushing it with not only his muscles, but also additional magical force.

The bone pierced the slick surface and wedged into the obscured crack, sinking in a few inches once it had found its way through the hard exterior. Hozark whispered an unusual spell. A slight variant of a ship's docking spell now used in a most novel way. When he felt the bone actually lock in, he applied more magic still, binding it to the softer dirt held behind the firm wall.

With one arm, he heaved himself up, then felt the wall above for another weak spot. After a moment, a sufficiently irregular line presented itself. He drew the other bone spike from his belt and once more drove his makeshift piton into the hardened soil.

The amount of magic he was forcing into the bone and soil was substantial, but he had enough still saved within him from the last magical victim he had drained. But this escape was taking time. Far more than he would have liked.

He continued up the wall, magically shoving the spikes into the surface, then pulling himself up and searching for where to drive the next one. He could feel the magic within him being drained. Used up from this lengthy period of expenditure.

Magic was used in spurts, normally. But this constant casting was pulling the power from him at an alarming rate. So much so that he was beginning to worry it might not last long enough to get him to the surface. And if that happened, he wouldn't have magic left to cushion his fall a second time, and if *that* happened, it was a very real possibility that the next set of bones at the bottom of the pit would be his own.

Up and up he went, quietly repeating his spell over and over. His arms burned and his hands were beginning to cramp from the sustained effort, but on he climbed. Failure was simply not an option. To fail was to die. And that was something he had no intention of doing.

After what seemed like an eternity, his hands finally felt the rough soil at the lip of the pitfall trap. And it was good timing, as he had almost no power left within him. As he rolled to the floor, his hands uncurling from the bone spikes they clutched, a deep lungful of relief found its way into his lungs.

He lay there for two long breaths then rolled to his feet. Any longer would be folly, even for a master assassin. Looking down, he saw that the illusion of the pit's floor was still intact. Even the stone he had stepped on appeared to be in place, though he knew it was at the bottom of the long shaft.

This was good. Unless someone actually touched the stone, it would seem as if the trap had remained unsprung. One small slip-up by the caster, and one that could buy him time. His triggering the pitfall might even go entirely unnoticed. Whoever had cast the spell was powerful, yes, but also overconfident and a tiny bit sloppy. Never a good combination, in his experience.

He tucked the sharpened bones into his clothing to either dispose of elsewhere––there was no sense in revealing the caster their error in their plan––or to be used as makeshift weapons should the need arise.

Careful to ensure there were no other traps or snares in his path, Hozark made his way through the room to the far end, then re-opened the secret door and made his way back outside.

It was getting dark out, and the guards had changed shifts in the time he was delayed in the pit. His friends would be wondering where he was, but that would be a topic easy enough for them to rationalize without his needing to make an explanation. He had gone missing, but it really wasn't that much of a surprise, the seeds of his plan in place and taking root for weeks now.

More likely than not, they would simply believe their friend Alasnib the trader had finally grown tired of the manual labor he had been increasingly less fond of and had returned to the seemingly easier life of world-hopping and trade. It was a bit earlier than he intended, but this new information he had unveiled needed to be shared with the Five. He had done all he could on this world for now. It was time to leave.

Hozark stepped out of the hidden door and ducked down behind a small pile of crates. He studied the area around him. Empties were ready for return to the depot, and an empty transfer conveyance was sitting nearby.

Perfect.

He picked up several crates, stacking them high on the floating device, then headed back along the pathway, keeping the crates between himself and the new guard, blocking his face as he walked at a leisurely pace.

As soon as he was out of sight of the guards, however, he left his load and veered into the brush at the side of the trail. Yes, Alasnib the trader was going missing. And Hozark the master assassin was going home.

CHAPTER THIRTY-TWO

Freed of the guise of his bumbling and often alcohol-hindered trader persona, Hozark made exceptionally good time through the scrub brush and trees as he moved back toward town. The dimming light of the approaching dusk only added to his stealthy approach.

When he arrived, all appeared to be calm, but he had to be sure. Before he could depart, it was imperative he first make sure no alarm had been raised among the others. It was unlikely, given what he knew of the secret facility thus far, but one didn't live to his age in this line of work by taking things for granted.

Fortunately, all appeared quiet in town. The late shift was finishing up their labors, and the earlier work group of which he was a part was milling about in a mildly inebriated state, as was their typical status after a hard day's work and a hard night's drinking.

And it appeared they had begun their nightly merriment without so much as missing their new friend.

It was all as Hozark had hoped. Better, actually, for no one was even questioning where he was. It seemed quite likely his absence would go unnoted until the morning, and perhaps even longer, depending on the severity of the others' hangovers.

That established, he skirted the rest of the town, taking the long and less-traveled route via game tracks through the trees. The more direct path was simply too visible, and he hadn't enough magic left in him to effectively don any disguises.

It was a strange sensation for him. He'd had a konus or stolen power at his disposal for so long these days that the absence of both left him with an oddly thrilling sense of vulnerability. Not since his youth had he been so completely on his own. The challenge, rather than worrying him, raised his spirits.

This was interesting, and he loved interesting.

That attitude changed, however, when interesting of the annoying variety reared its ugly head as he reached the outskirts of town. Signs of new arrivals were visible up ahead. He'd been entrenched within the town and its workers for weeks, and this was relatively far from their environs. That was why he'd parked his ship there in the first place. It was remote enough to be safe from discovery, yet close enough that he could reach it relatively quickly should need arise.

Only *this*, he had not planned on.

Hozark stayed in the tree line as he drew closer to the clearing that abutted his shimmer ship's hiding place. The craft was undisturbed, tucked deep within the bramble patch beneath the copse of trees, but the empty field he had previously traversed after landing was not.

In fact, it was anything but. It seemed that in the time he had spent living in disguise, the Tslavars had set down a number of new arrivals, but rather than housing them in town, where he would have noted them, they had set up a separate camp a ways away.

Unfortunately, they pitched their tents and arranged their supplies in that very same field. Directly in front of his vessel's hiding place. And even if he could make it to his ship undetected, lifting off and flying forward out from under the trees would definitely garner attention.

While the shimmer-cloak would protect the craft from visual observation, the air around it would move, and if that happened, word of an invisible craft lurking in their midst would certainly put everyone on high alert. Exactly the opposite of what he wished to achieve.

The cooking tents were closest to his little bramble patch, Hozark noted. At least *that* was fortunate. Typically, the more important encampments would be set up far from where the noise and smell of food preparation was taking place. The dining areas, however, would be relatively close. And with them, there would be dozens, if not more, Tslavar mercenaries.

There seemed to also be a few recreation tents erected toward the outskirts of the little encampment. "Entertainers" from town had likely been ushered out to service the lonely crew who had been brought down to the surface for shore leave.

That meant the large craft in orbit had been joined by more. They'd not have allowed their crews to be diminished in such a manner otherwise. Whether they were preparing to depart after this break and were simply being relieved by the new ship, or whether the newcomers were adding to the existing force stationed above was unknown. All that mattered at this point was that Hozark's departure had just become even more difficult.

He was going to have to run them off, somehow. It was the only way he could take off safely. But to do so, he would need the devices stored safely aboard his ship. The same ship he could not reach at the moment given his diminished power. Even if he had his shimmer cloak, he doubted he had enough magic remaining to utilize it.

No. He was going to need to come up with something different. Something he could do with no magic, and with the very limited resources at his disposal. After his ordeal in the deadly pit, it seemed yet another trial was before him. If he were a superstitious man, he'd almost have thought some sky deity had it out for him.

But the Ghalian did not believe in such fairy tales. They dealt in cold, hard facts. And death, of course. And all of his instincts told him it would take something exceptional to move so large a body of men from the area without the use of any magic.

Gears were turning in his mind as he ran through possible scenarios, no matter how unlikely they were to succeed, when a whuffling sound reached his ears from not too far away. Several, in fact.

Hozark smiled to himself. *Oh, yes. This might work*, he mused, then set off in the direction of the sound.

A half hour later, the encampment was both quiet and loud. Quiet with all of the men contained therein gathered together, eating their nightly meal, and loud with the clamor a gregarious collection of mercenaries that size could generate. By his estimates, there were over a hundred of them, all counted, but that wouldn't make a bit of difference in a minute.

The men were eating and drinking to their hearts' content when a thundering rumble began to cause their beverages to ripple and shake. A few noticed the disturbance sooner than the others, but soon all were looking around in confusion. They were obviously not under attack, they had lookouts for such a thing, as well as defenses against magical attacks.

Yet the ground shook harder. Soon a faint red glow was seen approaching from the far end of the clearing. And it was getting closer. Fast.

"Stampede!" someone shouted out in alarm from the perimeter of the camp.

The men and women leapt to their feet and scattered in a panic, unsure which way to run. It wasn't an attack they were experiencing. It was dozens of spooked Malooki racing right toward them.

The animals were massive, horse-like creatures with mighty hooves and a long hair that shifted color with their moods. It had made taming and utilizing the creatures easy, enabling their trainers to easily tell when they were calm and at ease simply by looking at them.

And now their manes were flushed deep red with panic and agitation as they thundered straight into the camp. Normally, they were quite harmless. Tranquil beasts that no one feared. But their size could make them a danger when they were spooked and in numbers. Times like this, for instance.

Tents toppled, and tables were overturned and smashed as the Malooki tore through the area with wild abandon. Whatever had set them off had been enough to not only make them break from their enclosure, but also to charge quite uncharacteristically into a populated area.

Of course, Hozark would have no idea who could have done such a thing.

With a satisfied grin, he watched the Tslavars flee, rushing for the safety of anywhere but their own camp. A minute later, the space was devoid of his primary obstacle. Malooki were still there, trotting to and fro with displeasure, but the assassin had no intention of interacting with the enormous animals any more than he already had.

Quietly and with great speed, Hozark darted through the trees and brush, racing to the tiny camouflaged pathway that would take him aboard his ship. There were still some Tslavars in the area, trying to figure out what to do next, but in all of the commotion, no one even noticed the man who seemed to vanish into a section of brambles.

Nor did they take note of the slight shift of wind as the invisible ship lifted off and slowly slipped free from the brush and trees, though the latter did shift from the force of the ship as it moved. But everyone was so preoccupied with the danger on the ground that they were completely oblivious to the one above.

With great restraint, Hozark guided his shimmer ship away from the commotion below, taking a wide path around the town, just in case any new detection spells had been placed since the arrival of the newcomers. Then he lifted up into the welcome safety of the vacuum's embrace and jumped away.

He was finally free and clear, and he needed to get back.

CHAPTER THIRTY-THREE

"Where the hell have you been?" Uzabud blurted as he rushed up to his friend's ship as it settled into a hover beside his larger craft. "It's been weeks. *Weeks*, man. You said it was just going to be a quick detour for some Ghalian business."

"And it was," Hozark replied calmly.

"For over three weeks? You and I obviously have very different definitions of the word quick. We've been waiting for you, wondering if something went wrong."

"I am fine, Bud. Though I do appreciate your concern. It is most flattering."

"Flattering? Shit, Hozark, you've got some strange workings going on in that head of yours."

"Perhaps," the Wampeh replied with a little grin.

"Well, come on, then. Corann wanted to speak with you as soon as you landed. We should go tell her you're here."

"My dear Uzabud, you should know by now, Corann knew of my arrival before I had even touched down."

"Is that some sort of Wampeh Ghalian thing?"

"No. Just the simple courtesy of a call," he replied with a chuckle. "I skreed her from orbit as I was making my approach."

Bud flashed an amused, yet annoyed look at the man. He drove him nuts at times, but they'd made a good team, and it was something he hoped to continue for many, many years.

Provided the damn fool didn't get himself killed, that is.

"All right, then. Let's head to Corann's place. I'm sure Demelza and Laskar will be glad to see you too."

"A sentiment I share."

The duo walked the short distance from the landing pad to the leader of the Five's home. Hozark had not visited Corann on Inskip for quite some time. It was not something the Five often did. Not for respect of each other's home bases, but the practicality of not wishing to approach their "ship number."

Bud had once asked what the hell a ship number was when Hozark had made him take a circuitous route after a particularly hairy contract so as to pass nowhere near Master Prombatz's homeworld, which happened to be in the same system.

"A ship number is the maximum number of individuals in charge of an organization that may be aboard a ship at the same time."

"What, like some sort of weight limit?"

"Hardly. It is far more practical than that. A ship number is the maximum quantity of casualties the organization could sustain while still functioning properly. For the Ghalian, it is three, though the remaining two would have a difficult time of it at first."

"Morbid, dude. Just morbid,"

"You asked, and I explained. It is not my fault you do not appreciate Ghalian practicality," Hozark said with a chuckle.

But here on Inskip, there were only two masters present. And these two would present a particularly difficult target should anyone have learned their true identities and gotten any clever ideas.

Many had met their ends thinking themselves smarter than the Ghalian masters, though none would ever hear of their attempts—or failures—nor would they ever find the bodies. More often than not, not enough of one remained for them to be identified anyway.

Corann was resting comfortably on the porch with the others when Hozark and Uzabud approached. Laskar jumped up and rushed over to offer a warm welcome. Demelza and Corann, however, merely nodded their casual greeting, as if he had merely returned from a trip down the road for some tea.

"An eventful trip?" Corann asked, casually

"Nothing terribly exciting," he replied. "Just handling that bit of Ghalian business we discussed took a little longer than anticipated. I'll tell you about it later, if you wish for details."

He knew she would certainly want to know all about what he had learned. It *was* an uncommonly long delay, and she knew Master Hozark well. Something had most definitely come to light, but that bit of business was not for mixed company.

"Tell him what happened," Laskar blurted.

"Please, Laskar. I will get to that in due time," Corann replied, turning her gaze back to Hozark. He, Demelza, and Corann all shared the briefest of looks. One that confirmed that the Ghalian assassins already in the know felt it okay to discuss the matter further in front of the others.

"'Well, I suppose now is as good a time as any," Corann said. "Something has come to light, Master Hozark. Something nefarious."

"Oh? What has happened?" he asked, sensing the seriousness of her tone.

"A tragedy, I am afraid."

The look on Demelza's face was so faint none but another Ghalian would have noticed it. But for Hozark it was plain as writing on a parchment. She was upset. And for that to occur, something truly bad must have happened.

"What sort of tragedy?" he asked.

"It's all kinds of messed up," Laskar blurted.

"Hey, shut up. Not cool," Bud hissed, elbowing the man.

Corann continued. "I am afraid Laskar is correct in his assessment. It *is* all kinds of messed up, to use his parlance. While you were away completing your contracts, Master Prombatz took one of the aspirant Ghalian on his final trial. The perfect contract to prove his skills and become a full-fledged member of the order."

"Who was the youth?" he asked, directing the question to Demelza rather than Corann.

"Aargun," she replied.

He knew the student, of course. He knew all who were reaching the age of their final trials. But this one in particular held some significance to Demelza. He had been one of the youths she was helping train so recently, just before they left for their mission.

"He was quite skilled," Hozark noted, a sinking feeling settling into his gut. "He showed great promise."

"That he did. But his contract was a failure, ending in catastrophe," Corann said.

"That is most unfortunate," Hozark replied, the memory of his own recent brush with death when Enak––an aspirant under his very own wing––had met his end at the hands of Emmik Rostall.

The youth had performed admirably, but was nevertheless reduced to smoldering ashes by an unexpected splash from the emmik's damned bottle of Balamar waters. It was so rare, and so valuable, no one ever thought he would possess such a thing. And it had cost Enak his life. A life that Emmik Rostall quickly repaid with his own under the fangs of a very displeased Hozark.

"Prombatz must have been upset by the youth's failure," Hozark sympathized. "I assume he completed the contract. With some malice, of course."

"This is where the problem comes to light," she said. "He

was unable to do so, Hozark. In fact, he used so much of his power, and was nevertheless gravely injured, and unable to feed on a magic user in order to heal himself, that he barely made it out alive."

"He is currently recovering under the care of Denna Finnleigh," Demelza noted.

The healer was not a Wampeh, but she possessed great skills and was willing to put them to use on his kind when the need arose. She also happened to enjoy not only the coin of the Ghalian, but also their protection and thanks. A gratitude that had resulted in more than one member of her family being saved from difficult circumstances over the years.

Master Prombatz would heal, but it would take time, judging by Corann and Demelza's demeanor.

Hozark scratched his chin as he pondered the situation. "This is indeed unfortunate news. Aargun is dead, and one of the Five is wounded."

"No, he is not dead," Corann corrected. "Or, he was not the last we heard."

"I am afraid I am not following."

"This was not a job gone wrong, Hozark. This was an ambush. A group of many Council casters were there, and all of them had prepared specifically for a Ghalian attack."

"Members of the Twenty?"

"Not all. Perhaps one, maybe more. But their lackeys were there, and they are skilled casters, who we know can be dangerous enough, in numbers."

"How would they have known?" Hozark mused. "There are safeguards. *Many* safeguards, known only to us."

"I can think of but one explanation," Corann said. "Impossible as it may sound. But, then, our recently deceased sister seems rather fond of the impossible, wouldn't you agree?"

"Samara?"

"Who better to betray the order?"

Laskar couldn't help himself any longer. "Wait a minute, but we saw her die. I cast right at her and her ship blew to pieces. We all saw it."

Corann ignored the pilot and focused on her fellow master. "Hozark, I see you have doubts."

"I do. Perhaps it might be within the realm of possibility that Samara yet lives. But if she does, I do not believe she would commit such an act against the order. Whatever conflicts we may have, we are her family, and have been since her childhood."

"What else could it be?" Demelza asked. "You must admit, given what we know of her, Samara is a likely suspect."

"I understand your reasoning, but I have another theory," he replied. "One that is equally disturbing if it proves true."

All eyes were upon him, wondering what other explanation he might have for them. They would not like it. Not one bit.

"What if this was not a specific target, but a wider attempt on Ghalian masters? What if someone engaged in a contract not in hopes of its completion, but with the intent of snaring one of us? The other masters had high-level contracts given to them roughly when we received ours. Have they been set upon as well?"

Corann looked as calm and pleasant as always, but inside, her mind was ablaze with activity as she connected the dots between all of the contracts and Ghalian fulfilling them.

"No. Not as of yet," she said. "It seems as though this was the only trap."

"Were all of the contracts made by the same party?" Demelza asked.

"On their surface, no," Corann replied. "But given the rapid proximity of them all being made, and despite coming from different sources, I have already anticipated that particular concern and have sent messengers far and wide. All who have not already gone dark engaging their target will be recalled until we can verify the true identities of the parties involved. So far, it *appears* as if it is just one person."

"Then you know what I must do."

"Yes, Hozark, I do. His name is Tikoo. A Fakarian smuggler who was last seen in the markets on Obahn."

"A Fakarian?" Hozark mused. He wouldn't divulge what he'd heard in the smelting factory until he and Corann were alone, but it seemed to be far too much of a coincidence. Fakarian were uncommon, and for two to be involved so close to Ghalian affairs seemed near impossible.

"I've never seen a Fakarian," Laskar said. "They're amphibious, right?"

"Yes," Corann replied. "A blue-green-skinned race. Bipedal, but with webbed feet and a short, powerful tail to aid while swimming. They also use it as a weapon, striking out at their enemies."

"So, they really do live on both land and water?"

"Yes. They've evolved for just such a thing, and they possess two sets of eyes. A pair for their time under the bright lights of the surface, and another to see in the murky deep."

Corann rose and asked Hozark to join her inside so she could give him something that might be of use on his journey. It was no more than a bauble, of course. What she really wished was for his update on what he had found.

"Things are far more unclear than we had believed," she said after hearing his tale and word of a Fakarian involved with amassing arms for the Council. "And it looks like far deadlier times are coming."

"Indeed," he replied, his jaw set with determination. "I will find him, Corann. And I will get answers."

She looked at her friend and knew he would. Or would die trying.

"Of that I have no doubt," she said. "Happy hunting, Brother."

CHAPTER THIRTY-FOUR

The private discussion with Master Corann had been brief. The intelligence Hozark relayed was both detailed, yet concise, and there was no need to talk in circles about who or what might be in play. Balls were in the air, and when they landed, everyone could be affected. That was all they needed to know for the moment.

As for the other part of their chat, it was decided that the trio who had been spending the past several weeks as her guests would be a fine addition to his mission. Despite preferring working alone, both masters agreed that this was simply too big and too crucial to forego any assistance, even that of Bud's chatterbox copilot.

"We're gonna do what?" Laskar blurted when he heard the plan. "You want us to track down a Council agent? That's the kind of thing that'll get a fella from alive to dead in a hurry. Chasing Council of Twenty agents is a whole new level of dangerous."

"Which is why only Demelza or I will engage the target," Hozark said. "You and Uzabud will act as our eyes and ears as we narrow our search and close in on the man. But once we find him, you are to step back and remain safe, is that clear?"

"You don't have to tell me twice," Laskar said with visible relief.

"All talk," Bud grumbled.

"Hey, I just don't have a death-wish is all," he shot back.

"Gentlemen, enough," Hozark said. "We have much to do, and not a great deal of time to do it in. The intelligence we have received from our spy network indicated that the target is indeed currently on Obahn, in its capital city."

"Isn't that a pretty wet world?" Uzabud asked.

"Yes, it is, and that is likely why he has chosen to utilize it as a base of operations. His kind always feel more secure with water close by."

"So, what are we supposed to do? I mean, we can't exactly go around asking if anyone's seen a Council agent," Laskar said.

"No, obviously not. Rather, we will break into teams and casually search, and occasionally inquire, until we develop leads that take us to the man."

"If he is still a man," Demelza added.

"I'm sorry, what?" Laskar asked, a puzzled look on his face.

"Fakarian are not only an amphibious race, but also one that comes from rather remote and isolated pockets across the galaxy," Demelza explained. "Over time, they developed the ability to change their gender depending on the reproductive needs of their society."

"So he could be a she by now?"

"Potentially. Though it is unlikely. Most tend to stick with the gender of their birth unless a breeding predicament presents itself. And with modern jump transit spells, they are no longer isolated as they were thousands of years ago, so that sort of thing really happens far less often than before."

Demelza's words made sense, but Laskar still seemed to have a hard time wrapping his head around how a he could become a she, and without the aid of magic or surgeons. The galaxy, it seemed, was a far more interesting place than he had realized.

"So, do I get to fly this time?" Laskar asked, clearly putting the quandary behind him and diving headfirst into their pending adventure.

Normally Uzabud would do the flying, leaving navigation, peripheral spell casting, and that sort of thing to his copilot. But Laskar had been a prisoner not long ago, and despite his jovial demeanor, Bud still worried the man might be suffering the effects of it. Not outwardly, mind you, but internally. It was with that in mind that he thought any little perk could help.

"Sure, Laskar. Why not? You take the helm for this one," Bud said, to the man's delight.

"Excellent!"

"Just don't get too carried away and fly us into a sun or something."

"Don't worry about me. I'm the best pilot in twenty systems!"

Bud and Hozark shared a pained look. The guy really was a great pilot, but his incessant cockiness was exhausting. It was really only for his recent ordeal that they were giving him such leeway. But eventually he would be back to his normal self, and when that happened, the lunacy would need to be reined in a bit.

After a quick resupply, Corann and Hozark stepped aside from the others and conversed one last time in private before the mission got underway. Once that was done, the team regrouped and boarded the freshly stocked ship. They weren't going to be gone incredibly long, but Hozark had insisted on extra supplies, just in case.

He hoped they wouldn't need them.

"So, *navigator*," Laskar asked Bud with a ridiculously pleased grin as he settled into the pilot's seat and engaged the Drookonus powering the ship. "How far away is Obahn, anyway?"

Bud thought a moment, then consulted some star charts. "It's going to be a long trip, Laskar. A whole lot of jumps to get there."

"Then let's get going," the freshly minted pilot chirped. "Hang on, everyone, we're on the move!"

With fresh coordinates for the first of many magical jumps in place, Laskar then set the ship in motion, hurtling it through space with a burst of magic. Then he did it again. Fifteen times, in all, though they did stop to allow the Drookonus to cool more than once.

It was a robust and sturdy device, but pulling that much magic that quickly was putting an excessive strain on it. Sure, Hozark had spares, but Laskar didn't know that, and there was no sense in overloading a perfectly good Drookonus to save them only a few hours of flight time.

It turned out to be a wise choice, because once they reached Obahn and settled the ship into a low hover in the landing field, things wound up going not exactly as they'd planned.

CHAPTER THIRTY-FIVE

"This place smells funny," Laskar grumbled as he trudged off the ship.

Hozark and Bud shared *that* look. The one that is usually reserved for parents dragging obnoxious tweens on a trip they, for some reason, had nothing better to do than whine about.

Only, this child was a full-grown man and one of the best pilots either had ever seen, though they wouldn't tell him that to his face, lest they inflate his ego even further.

"Merely the nature of the environment due to the relatively low salinity of this planet's main body of water," Demelza said, taking in a deep breath of the damp air. "All of which happens to be surrounding this island, as you know."

They had landed on the island that comprised the main city of Obahn. It truly was a water world, though its surface appeared to possess much land when one made an approach from space. It was the interlinked networks of islands that did it, tricking the eye from afar. The more populated areas of the planet were often the ones where the proximity between them had made it easy to island hop either by conveyance or boat.

Fortunately for Hozark and his crew, Tikoo had made his

contract from the capital city. A city that happened to be a bit farther set off from the others, its island surrounded by deeper waters. It was ideal for an amphibian with a need for a sense of safety. It also, conveniently, limited the area the hunters would have to search.

"I will head toward the city center," Hozark said. "I possess the address of Tikoo's last known residence. However, he may not be at home, and we must keep on the lookout for him. Demelza, I think the main marketplace would be a good location for you to begin. Bud, you and Laskar will survey the less reputable establishments along the shoreline."

"Why do *we* have to go to the smelly dives?" Laskar groaned.

"Because you and Uzabud can fit in quite easily without need for a disguise."

"Hey, buddy, what're you saying?" Bud joked.

"Just that your former pirating ways will serve you well as a second-nature sort of camouflage. But, again, do not engage Tikoo if you see him. Contact myself and Demelza. We shall keep our skrees active, but on silent. Call us at once if he is spotted and await our arrival."

"You don't have to tell me twice," Laskar said. "A Council agent? No way I want to tangle with one of those."

"Your courage is quite reassuring," Demelza cracked. "I shall begin straightaway. Let us reconvene in five hours at the central square if none have located him by then."

Hozark nodded once, then vanished into the crowds.

"How does he do that?" Laskar asked.

"He is Hozark. A master of the Ghalian. There is much he can do," Demelza replied, then turned and did much the same thing.

"These two, always disappearing like that. Even without a shimmer cloak. It's disconcerting," Laskar said.

"Just be glad they're on our side," Bud replied with a grin.

"Now, come on. We've got work to do and establishments of ill repute to visit."

He may have groused about the task, but Bud was secretly looking forward to the opportunity to let his inner pirate out once more, even if only for a short while.

Hozark made quick time to the central hub of the city. Obahn was a cultured place, and a world where visitors from far and wide came to restore their energy in the numerous thermal baths that dotted many islands, as well as partake of its rather legendary seafood.

The Wampeh assassin had not come for such niceties, and he bypassed many of the local establishments offering such delights. Tikoo's last known residence was close by, and he would not take his eyes off of that prize.

The place at which he finally arrived was a gleaming building rising above the lesser ones in one of the richest sections of the neighborhood. The winds at altitude caused by the churning seas had made towers an unpopular construction design due to the slight swaying their tenants would have to endure, even with spells to counteract them. As such, more modest buildings had been erected.

Modest by the wealthy's standards, that is.

The entry hall was ornate, and every staff member wore resplendent uniforms color coded based on their post and rank within the staff. None of them wore control collars, Hozark was pleased to note. Slaves were much harder to get information from. The threat of their collars' shocks tended to make them quite gun-shy when it came to any form of disobedience. Or things that could remotely be construed as such.

The master assassin entered the building wearing the face and garb of a member of the elite. The aloof expression on his now-tanned face was that of a man so used to getting his way that the mere thought of someone objecting was utterly foreign. And distasteful at that.

It was precisely the type of man he needed to be to grill the staff while seeming like any other resident or guest. If he needed to, that is. It was his sincere hope that the man would be home and he could simply interrogate him and be done with it.

Unfortunately, life of late did not seem to be so simple a thing.

Tikoo's rooms were empty. Not of his possessions, but they had the look of a place quickly emptied of anything of real value. The layman might not notice, and in fact, it was clearly intended to give the appearance that he'd just stepped out, but Hozark had a feeling his prey had fled this particular hidey-hole.

A full twenty minutes of carefully played questioning had produced nothing. All of it had been in the guise of a wealthy guest who had prior dealings with the man and could not understand why it was so hard for the menial staff to simply fetch him so he might discuss more business with him. Even so, the staff was tight-lipped.

Hozark was impressed by their commitment to their employers, but he also saw the hint of fear in their eyes. Oh yes, they knew the sort of people Tikoo ran with, even if they wouldn't say it aloud. One servant, however, appeared to be a relatively new addition to the staff. One who might not have the same reservations as the others.

It was that one he focused on, shifting his appearance to that of a fellow worker. Normally he wouldn't have risked it, since the odds of being noticed as not belonging were great. But in this case, the person he wished to talk with was so new, it would be easy to play off their not yet having met.

He approached in the guise of a senior staff member and asked for assistance with delivering a few packages to Tikoo's rooms. Packages he himself had just ordered and had delivered to the property. Once there, the questions were casual, the conversation fluid, and the two parted ways without so much as a lick of drama. But Hozark had learned a bit of new information, and he was not amused.

His konuses were powering his shifting disguises with a degree of ease, but he had a feeling he might need a little safety net in place before they engaged their quarry. He had used up all of his internal magic escaping Garvalis, and it was time to replenish it a bit.

Of course, he would not go out and murder a random power user for their magic. For one, it was crude and tactless. For another, despite all the countless men and women the Wampeh Ghalian had eliminated, they nevertheless valued life as only those who witnessed death so often could.

But he could find a suitable mark to drink from in this circumstance. Oh yes, that was perfectly fine. Not enough to really drain them. Just enough to give himself a little backup cushion of power, just in case. The Ghalian were always ones for backup plans, and this was just one more instance.

He actually did wind up going to the thermal baths in hopes of finding a suitable meal there, but in the four different facilities he visited, not a one had a power user of anything worth taking.

It was beginning to look like he might simply have to forego his impromptu power-up when he caught wind of the faintest whiff of power. He quietly uttered the words to the spell he knew so well, his konus powering a refining tool that allowed him to pinpoint the location.

A gambling hall.

It was just the sort of place a power user might be expected to try to conceal their gifts. Typically, this was done by blatantly displaying no konuses or any other magical accoutrements while at the tables. And losing, of course. They had to lose just often enough to make their good fortune seem like luck and not magic.

The rotund, bald-headed man who sat amid the crowd at the farthest game was easy to pick out once Hozark had caught his scent. He was quite skilled at hiding his power, but the specialized Ghalian magic had locked in on him as he cast once more.

He wasn't being terribly overt in his manipulation of the game. Just enough to come out ahead. Not *too* ahead. Not enough to draw the notice of the gambling bosses patrolling the floor. But he would win enough to maintain a comfortable existence while not being blacklisted for cheating.

Hozark stepped up and placed a wager on the game. Then another. Then one more, each successive play allowing him to get a better sense of the man's gift.

Yes, this one will do just fine, he decided. *Only a low-level emmik, but he will suffice.*

The assassin pulled up from the table and went to try his luck at another game of chance. One that afforded him a clear view of his new prey. A short while later, the man cashed in his chips and stepped out into the streets.

The large man stopped at a food vendor to get a quick snack as he went. As he was wiping his lips and disposing of the wrapper in a waste receptacle just a few blocks later, a curvaceous Karuni woman sashayed out of the nearby house of ill repute and leaned in close.

What she said no one could hear over the street noise, but whatever it had been, the man seemed most intrigued with her offer. With a warm smile, she took his hand and led him into the building, all the way to the room farthest back.

"I'll be right back," she said as she opened the door and gestured for him to enter. "I just want to freshen up for you."

He stepped inside and shut the door to wait for this divine specimen of a woman to return.

He didn't even feel the fangs sink into his neck, or the

strange Wampeh magic they bore with them, knocking him unconscious before he even knew what was happening.

Hozark pulled a deep draught from his victim, a slight shiver of pleasure tingling his body as the man's power became his. But he showed restraint and broke free long before any lasting damage would be done.

The wounds healed immediately under the spell he cast by rote, having done so after every victim nearly his whole life. He then added a sleeping spell on top of that and lay the man down on the bed. After a moment's thought, he ruffled the sheets and threw the pillow on the floor. Why not let the groggy man wake to the belief he'd gotten lucky?

He would feel drained, but for all the right reasons, chalking it up to too much drink, and too much recreation. And then he would return home, or wherever it was he was heading, none the wiser.

And the woman who had been paid quite well to ensure Hozark was not disturbed would then go back to her normal business after having a rare night off, paid in full by a generous, and immediately forgotten, patron.

It felt fantastic, having some real power charging his cells once more, and Hozark walked a little taller when he stepped back out onto the streets to continue his search. This time wearing the guise of a bookmaker seeking the Fakarian who owed him money.

Even with that ploy in action, no one seemed able to help him with any new information. From what he'd heard so far, the information from the young staffer at Tikoo's home appeared the most likely to be true. But if not, he hoped the others had better luck than he did.

CHAPTER THIRTY-SIX

The marketplace was a bustling hive of vendors and patrons, both of which seemed to be spilling out from the carefully constructed buildings into the streets, which were jam-packed with stalls and makeshift stands where all manner of goods were offered for sale.

It was almost maze-like in its twists and turns, and one with a lesser sense of direction than the Wampeh woman casually looking through wares would almost certainly lose their way.

Demelza, however, was in her element. The churning mass of people moving past one another offering her myriad opportunities to eavesdrop on conversations, or slip into somewhere she might not be invited to get a better look at any potential leads.

Stalls within the vast expanse of low buildings were organized by the wares they offered, some edifices full of spices, while others contained craftware and cooked foods. Still others sold bright cloth in long bolts of fabric, their lengths hanging from high above and fluttering in the breeze.

Then there were the stalls and stables spread across the farther ends of the marketplace. A series of loud, and somewhat strong-smelling, buildings and pens housed all manner of creatures. Some were to be sold as pets. Others would become someone's meal.

And just a few of the vendors had animals for sale whose various bits and pieces possessed some purported magical use. It was near that particular group of stalls Demelza was questioning people, casually inquiring about any products that might be good for the dry skin rashes Fakarians were notorious for when away from water of the correct salt content for too long.

It was a simple fact. This world's water was distinctly lacking in that regard, and there was no way Tikoo had not acquired something to help with the itch.

It was a good idea. If a vendor had made any such sales to a local, she'd suss out the details with pleasant flattery, small talk, and a deceptive smile. But so far, she was not having any luck. And the vendors hawking their bogus wares were beginning to wear on her nerves.

"I tell you, friend. All it takes is a tiny pinch of Azmokus horn added to your daily tea and your manhood will grow bigger and harder than the very horn itself!"

She finally had enough.

"Really? You're selling Azmokus horn for people to make tea out of?"

"It is nothing that concerns a *woman*," the vendor sneered, not at all approving of one of her gender interrupting *man talk.*

"You don't think flaccid erections and bumbling incompetence around our private bits concerns *all* women?" she shot back with a disarming laugh. "You're selling junk magic to desperate men, and you know it."

It wasn't exactly the most stealthy thing to do, but it had been a tough morning. She had spoken to nearly everyone present, and it seemed a certainty that whatever Tikoo had used for his undoubted ailment, it had not been procured here. And this man was being an ass.

"You don't know what you're speaking of. This is the finest Azmokus horn in ten systems," the vendor retorted.

"I'm sure it is. And that means it is just as useless as it is in the other nine." She turned to the potential client to whom the man had been hawking his wares. "It's just a growth of dead tissue shaved off of the poor beast and made into a tea. Why, you would likely get as much of an erection, or perhaps even a stronger one, chewing a wad of callouses."

The vendor glared at her with venom in his eyes. She realized that perhaps despite the dead end this had turned out to be, she had nevertheless overdone it, bringing the man down as she had. Ignoring him, she turned and strode off into the marketplace once more.

"Wait!" a voice called out.

Demelza paused and turned. It was the poor man she had just saved from wasting his coin on junk magic.

"Is it true what you said about callouses? Do they truly enhance erections?"

"What? Are you serious?"

"Of course I am. This is nothing to joke about," the man said. "Do you know where I could get any?"

"Callouses? Start with your feet," she said, rolling her eyes in disbelief as she walked away.

The man could be heard talking with another who had overheard the exchange. And, amazingly, they seemed to be discussing whether it might be a good idea to open a callous stand.

"Enough of this," she sighed, then turned and headed in the general direction of the rendezvous point.

Ten minutes later, she paused at a depressing sight. An older Ootaki woman, her skin no longer that vibrant, pale-yellow of her kind, and her golden, magical hair shorn to a close buzz cut, was sitting on a stool. At first, she seemed to be just resting, but then the control collar around her neck became visible as she shifted her top.

The woman was a slave, and she was for sale.

But one thing about slaves. People spoke freely around them, often ignoring them as if they were just part of the furniture. Slaves, the Ghalian knew, often heard far, far more than any would expect, and they were often great sources of information.

Demelza stopped near the woman to look at some magical baubles on an adjacent table. She turned casually to the Ootaki and smiled.

"You wouldn't have happened to come across a Fakarian recently, would you?"

The woman smiled and shrugged her shoulders.

"Fakarian? Blue-green amphibian people with two sets of eyes and a tail?"

Again, the woman smiled and shrugged. Then Demelza realized what was happening.

"You can't understand me, can you?"

Another shrug.

"Always cheap with the magic," she said of the slave vendors as she cast a very small translation spell.

They were always trying to save some coin, and more often than not, by leaving their slaves essentially mute by taking away their translation spells. It was the only way all of the myriad races in the galaxy could talk with one another, but these were seen as less than people. Property. And property did not warrant the spending of additional coin for something as pointless at talking.

"There, now you should be able to communicate a bit," Demelza said soothingly. "Have you seen a Fakarian lately?"

The woman's eyes widened with palpable joy. It had apparently been some time since she was able to communicate with *anyone*.

"Listen," Demelza said when she saw the emotion in the woman's eye, "you can keep this spell, but you must be quiet about it. Otherwise your master will notice and strip you of it, do you understand?"

"Yes," the woman said, her voice rough from disuse. "Thank you. Thank you so very much."

"I'm glad to be of help," the assassin said. "But perhaps you can help me. A Fakarian? Blue-green skin?"

"I've not seen any matching that description. I'm so sorry."

"Do not be sorry. Just be safe with your secret. And thank you for your help."

Demelza then turned and walked away before the emotional woman might make a scene and subject them both to more scrutiny. She made quick time distancing herself, diving deeper into the marketplace.

She still had a great deal of time to kill, however, so she took the circuitous route through the lesser-traveled rows of stalls. At least there were some novel things to look at on her walk. And the flash of blue-green skin briefly exposed from the pushed-up sleeve of a man several tables across the stalls was suddenly something she very much wanted to look at.

A Fakarian. And he was about to slip out of her sight.

Demelza took off at a quick pace, gently slipping between shoppers, avoiding raising a scene as she pursued the oblivious man. Some eyes flashed to her as she went. Apparently, chewing out one of their fellow vendors so publicly wasn't such a good idea.

Hozark would chalk it up to a mistake of youth if he heard about her little outburst, but *she* knew what she'd done. She was a Wampeh Ghalian. She knew better.

But there was nothing for it at this point. All that mattered was catching her prey.

The cloaked man was still visible up ahead. He moved fluidly, easily weaving through the crowd. It was all Demelza could do to keep up without raising suspicion. Her prey slowed and entered a market building. Moments later, the Wampeh hot on his heels followed.

He had actually put more space between them in his short time inside. It seemed he knew his way around this place *very* well and was making quick time through the less-traveled side paths between vendor spaces.

Demelza forced herself to stop when he did, though. Perusing wares, even buying knickknacks from a few stalls while waiting for him to move to somewhere more private. Somewhere she could take him without anyone being any the wiser.

It took a full twenty minutes for him to finally exit the marketplace and head into the residential areas toward the water. The paths were smaller there, and presented the best opportunity Demelza would have to make her move. Quickly, she surged ahead until she was right on the person's tail, matching their steps with her own silent pace.

She hurried ahead, as if she were merely another shopper in a hurry, her shoulder hitting the man just right, spinning him to face her.

Shit.

"Watch where you're going!" the man said.

"My apologies," she replied, then watched the annoyed man vanish down the road.

His hands were not at all webbed, nor did he have two sets of eyes, one each for land and water. And as she got a better look up close, she could see there was no tail hiding underneath his cloak.

His skin was similar to that of a Fakarian, but this was obviously a different race, and she was no closer to finding the evasive Tikoo than when she'd started.

CHAPTER THIRTY-SEVEN

The waterfront was expansive, as the entire city was an island, but the former space pirate and his smart-mouthed sidekick were steering clear of the hoity-toity rich kid areas in favor of the rough-and-tumble dives where the real action took place.

The kind of bars and clubs where you were likely to be stabbed or hit with a blast of particularly nasty magic if you eyed the wrong person in a way they took offense to. It was violent, it was gritty, it was dangerous, and for Uzabud, it felt a lot like coming home.

After a few hours sticking close by his friend's side and learning the ropes, even Laskar was starting to enjoy the wondrous houses of ill repute, though, despite all of his tough talk and bravado, he just didn't quite fit in among the rabble. It was his natural tendency to come off like some sort of high-bred snob who was rubbing people the wrong way more often than not.

Fortunately, Bud was more than able to compensate for his friend's shortcomings.

The great thing about the dens of iniquity was the way in

which information flowed. It was a world of gossip and tall tales, for certain, but also a place where valuable tidbits could be acquired.

For a price.

Bud had greased more than a few palms by way of purchasing many rounds of drinks––courtesy of the extra coin the Ghalian had given him with which to better carry out his task––and they felt like they may have actually gleaned a bit of useful information in the process.

It was thirsty work, and Bud had found himself drinking shot-for-shot to loosen those lips, but he was a pirate, after all. Unfortunately, his tolerance was not quite what it used to be. In any case, they'd acquired intel, and that made the inevitable hangover worth it.

Hozark likely wouldn't like what they'd found out, but at least progress was being made.

"We should be getting back. It's almost time for the rendezvous," Laskar said.

"I know, I know," Bud said, tossing his skree in the air, catching it lazily in his hand as he had been for the better part of the last hour. "But we can always call them and say we're going to be a little late, right? I mean, we're making good progress down here."

"If by progress, you mean bad news and you getting drunk, then sure."

"Oh, lighten up, Laskar. Work and play don't have to be separate things, you know," his drunken friend slurred.

"Yeah, but at least my play doesn't require a full battery of decontamination spells afterward. I mean, look at these people," Laskar said, gesticulating at the crowd.

The man whose beverage he just knocked from his hand with his waving arm was anything but amused.

"You're going to pay for that, fancy boy!"

"Hey, now," Bud said, stepping in front of his copilot. "Thass no way to talk to my friend. And come to think of it, didn't I already pay for that drink?"

"You know what I meant," the man growled.

"No, I really don't," Bud said, abruptly getting right up into the man's face. "Because so far as I could tell, it was starting to sound like some little bitch was trying to start a problem with my friend. And *that* would be a mistake of fucking epic proportions."

"Epic, you say," the man shot back, not retreating an inch. "You? Epic? What are you going to do, little man?"

"Normally, I'd have already dropped you like the sack of shit you are. But since this is a respectable establishment—"

The patrons watching the exchange all chuckled.

"—I'm waiting to teach you a lesson outside."

"Why wait?" the man replied, much to the delight of the crowd.

It was going to be a fight, and by the looks of things, it would be a good one. The crowd was amped up and ready to go as well. In just a moment, an all-out bar brawl was going to be unleashed.

"Enough!" Demelza said, shouldering her way through the crowd.

The angry man glared at her, perfectly happy to strike a woman just the same as a man. "Who the hell do you think you are, bi—" he started to say.

She lay her hand on his shoulder. "Drop dead."

The man instantly crumpled to the ground in a heap. The bar patrons scattered in a panic, their bravado gone in an instant.

"Dark magic!" people shouted as they ran.

It was simply impossible. No one could cast in anything but the arcane, almost gibberish language of spellcasters. Plain-speak couldn't do a thing, no matter how powerful a person was. Or, at least, it shouldn't. But this woman had just dropped one of the toughest men in the bar without batting an eye. And she'd done it using plain-speak.

Bud stared as well, though his gaze was more of annoyance than anything else.

"I could have handled it," he slurred.

"I would have expected a foolish altercation from Laskar," she shot back. "But from you, Bud? *You* know better."

"Hey, what's that supposed to mean?" Laskar asked.

"Oh, you know precisely what it means. But it seems Uzabud here managed to out-mouth even you."

Laskar started to protest, but Demelza held up her hand, and judging by the look in her eye, he decided perhaps silence was the better option at this particular moment.

"How did you even find us, anyway? Aren't you supposed to be in the marketplace?" Bud asked.

Demelza reached out and snatched the skree from his hand. "You've been keying this on and off for over twenty minutes, Bud. If not to stop you from starting a bar brawl, I'd have tracked you down to simply shut you up."

"Hey, that hurts."

"Be glad it is only your feelings that are experiencing that sensation."

Laskar bent down and examined the man on the ground. "Hey, hang on a minute. He's not dead. I thought you cast a killing spell. A totally new one I didn't even know could be done, I might add."

Demelza looked at the slumbering ruffian with disgust. "That was no magic. Do you see the spots on his skin beneath his hair? This man is an Ohkran, and their people possess a vulnerable nerve bundle at the base of their neck. Fortuitous, as it negated the need for any *real* violence."

Bud looked at Laskar, then back at Demelza. He then started to laugh. And not a little chuckle. A full-on belly laugh, tears welling in his eyes. "Oh, the looks on their faces. They all thought you were some deadly visla come to kill them all."

"Tempting as it may be, no, Bud."

"But you're a Ghalian. Why would you blow your cover like that when we're stalking someone?"

"Because I have it on good authority that our prey has already fled this world."

"Oh? What have you heard?"

"That Tikoo did indeed make his contract with the order from here, but when Aargun was slain, and Master Prombatz managed to escape, he got spooked and skipped out of here, heading off as far away as he could."

"We heard pretty much the same thing," Bud said. "But where does that leave us? We haven't the faintest idea where he ran to."

"*Kraam*," a voice said from a dark corner of the bar.

"When did you get here?" Bud asked as Hozark stepped into the light.

"Some time ago, actually. You really must take care not to activate your skree like that, Bud. Next time, someone else might take notice."

"Wait, you were watching all this time? And you let us almost get into a fight?"

"I was curious to see how Demelza would defuse the situation. And while it was not exactly how I would have done it, her method was nonetheless effective in its swift efficiency." He turned to Demelza. "Help me get Bud back to the ship and sobered up. We have a long flight ahead of us."

"I can fly," Laskar offered. "I only had one drink."

Hozark studied him a long moment. Uzabud's copilot did indeed appear sober, to his pleasant surprise.

"Very well," he finally said. "You will start the jumps that take us to Kraam. We will then begin preparations."

"Preparations for what?"

Hozark smiled, darkly. It was a grin devoid of true happiness. "We prepare for a *far* more challenging hunt."

CHAPTER THIRTY-EIGHT

Where Obahn had perhaps been an odd-smelling and somewhat damp world, it was also a hub of travel, trade, and culture. The cities were clean, for the most part, and the air free of the reek of factories and pollution. And as for the rougher parts of the populace, they tended to stick to their own neighborhoods, tussling and brawling well away from the more well-heeled of their fellow citizens.

Kraam, however, was something completely different. Something that was going to make tracking down Tikoo quite a bit more of an ordeal. For Kraam was a smuggler's paradise, tucked away in a tumultuous solar system with an unstable blue giant at its center. And even in the main city, searching could prove quite an ordeal.

The magic from the sun was benign, but its flares could wreak havoc on a person's skin and eyes if they weren't paying attention to the magical warning tabs mounted to every building and carried by most people.

They would give enough notice to head for cover, but every so often one would find themselves stuck outside during a solar event. They weren't fatal, but a particularly strong one could lead to some time out of commission, and with substantial coin spent on a healer.

The cloudy regions were largely protected from the effects of the flares, the particular composition of the mists managing to break up and disperse the harmful rays.

The same could be said about the undersea communities. They were fewer in number, but the underwater caverns were protected by not only the waters above, but also the thick stone and minerals that formed the vast spaces.

A few hidden tunnels would typically connect them to the surface, but for the most part, access was made by water. *Under*water, that is. And underwater travel for more than a minute or two required a particular type of magic that very few possessed.

The robust communities in the open-air surface cities and farmlands were the ones that typically felt the brunt of the sun's impact. It was there that Demelza would be conducting her survey of the main towns, flaunting her zaftig, bronze-skinned tavern worker persona to coax information from the lips of those who dwelled in that area.

Given the relative safety of the elevated, cloudy region looming above the main city below, Hozark had felt Uzabud and Laskar would at least be less likely to suffer from any adverse damage should a random solar event pass through.

Undersea would be the safest, in that regard, but also by far the deadliest. That was why Hozark had taken that network of townships beneath the main city's coastline for himself.

The toughest of the tough would be found down there, and if things got hairy, it could quite possibly require all of his considerable skills to complete the task and apprehend the man. Should he even find Tikoo, that is.

"How is it that you knew where to go before we even told you?" Laskar had asked as they departed Obahn and made the first jump toward their new destination. "I know Bud didn't transmit that bit over the skree."

"No, he did not," Hozark replied. "But I acquired some intelligence from a worker in Tikoo's residence tower. With that helping direct my further digging, I was able to piece together our quarry's flight from that world, and his eventual destination. Kraam."

"And I also acquired a similar bit of information in my search," Demelza said. "Though the name of the world he had fled to had not yet been revealed to me. Only that he had departed, and in some haste, I might add."

"Yes, after Master Prombatz escaped the trap that had been set for him, it seems our friend Tikoo wisely deduced someone might come looking for the man who had arranged that contract."

It had been a fluke that an additional Wampeh Ghalian had been present on the contract with Master Prombatz. And an even more surprising twist was that it was the younger, weaker assassin who was attempting to complete the contract.

Blind luck, bad timing, whatever you'd call it, having Aargun completing his final test had been the unforeseen variable that had allowed the master Ghalian to escape. And even then, only barely. But the repercussions would undoubtedly be great.

"Seems like we were all pretty successful with that information gathering, if you ask me," Laskar said when they dropped out of the jump.

"I would agree with that assessment," Hozark noted.

The copilot looked at the star charts and confirmed their location while Uzabud slept off his buzz, then began plotting the next jump.

"I mean, sure, Hozark, you were the one who learned the actual name of the place first. But I think we were all on track to find out soon enough."

"Again, I would agree. But that is neither here nor there.

What matters is that we have a location and whereabouts of our target. I know if he is still on this world he is within the main linked cities of the capital of Kraam, but it is still a spread-out area. Fortunately for us, Fakarians are not a common sight, though on a somewhat wet world such as Kraam, it is possible we might come across others."

"Or similar races," Demelza noted.

"We'll kill 'em all!" Bud slurred, lurching into the command room.

"Oh, my friend. We need to get that out of your system," Hozark said. "And I am afraid it will not be pleasant."

He rose to help the drunken man back to his quarters, where he would use a rather uncomfortable bit of magic to rid his body of the toxic fluids.

"So, all killing talk aside, we split up and somehow track this guy down. That's the deal?" Laskar asked. "Seems a bit tough in a place that big."

"It will be, but I have faith in you all," Hozark said, pausing in the doorway, supporting Bud's semi-conscious bulk. "But whatever happens, remember, this is an interrogation mission, not an assassination. We need Tikoo alive."

"It's not *him* being hurt that I'm worried about," Laskar said as he dialed the last coordinates of the jump into the Drookonus. "All right, hang on. We're jumping," he said, then uttered the little spell that engaged the device and once again set them in motion.

CHAPTER THIRTY-NINE

"Remember, this is a capture and interrogation mission," Hozark reminded his crew as they strapped on all manner of weapons, both magical and conventional.

Going after Tikoo, and on the rough world of Kraam, no less, was *not* going to be easy. Not by a long shot.

"Give it a rest, Hozark, we've got it," Bud grumbled, still feeling the effects of the abrupt voiding of alcohol from his system.

It had sucked. Even more than he remembered from the last time Hozark had done it to him, though on that occasion he had nearly wed the most comely daughter of a Bazarian warlord of sizable holdings seeking to expand his territories.

Bud had thought it a good idea in his drunken stupor. The girl was nice enough, he supposed. And it was true, she did possess huge tracts of land––something more than one suitor had taken note of.

What Bud had neglected to realize in his drunken zeal was the price from his side of the bargain. Namely, he would become a communal brother-husband to the other members of the family, helping keep the bloodline fresh and strong.

When he had been forcefully sobered up and saw what he had very nearly signed up for, Bud nearly vomited again, and not from the effects of any alcohol or food poisoning.

"So, you feeling like yourself again?" Laskar asked. "You got a bit carried away back there."

"I was fine. It just hit me harder because I had an empty stomach, is all."

The other three looked at one another but let his lie slide.

"All right, then. Let us load into my shimmer ship and depart for the main city. Uzabud's mothership will be safe where it is. There is no likelihood of any suspicion being drawn with it parked this many islands away."

Laskar had set them down expertly, right on target in a quiet and remote landing area on a small farming island. He had stepped off the craft and paid a local youth to keep an eye on it while he and his friends supposedly descended to the underwater city nearby.

The mothership was too large to have fit in the small undersea tunnel leading to the alleged destination, so that part of their ruse was solid. And the boy was young enough to not run with the truly dangerous types who frequented that particular locale.

He might talk to locals up top, but no one with direct contact with them would be around to identify either their presence or absence in the cavern. This left them free to take off in the invisible ship when the coast was clear, then make the quick hop over the few islands to their true destination.

Hozark set down a few minutes later and tucked his ship carefully atop a small rocky crag surrounded by an animal refuse dumping site. No one was around for quite some distance.

"This is so disgusting," Laskar moaned when the stench hit his nose the instant the door opened. "Why *here*, of all places?"

"Because no one ever lurks around an open sewer," Demelza said.

"Exactly," Hozark agreed. "The ship is invisible, but that does not mean people might not bump into it on a bustling island such as this."

"Do not worry, Laskar. The air in the higher altitude region you will be investigating is fresh and clear. You'll have the smell cleared from your sinuses in no time," she added.

"Come on, man. Stop jabbering and start moving. The quicker we get out of this muck swamp, the sooner I can scrub this nasty from my nose," Bud said, quickly hopping across the rocky patches that led to dry, non-fecal land.

"I'm going as fast as I can without falling in!" he shot back.

It was a perfect place to hide the ship, and this just confirmed it for Hozark.

"We will rendezvous in two days. Keep your skrees on silent alert at all times. And, Bud, please do take care not to activate yours so carelessly this time."

"Yeah, yeah," he replied, then set off on foot toward the base of the small volcanic mountain at the center of the island that rose above them into the mists.

The rest of the trio quickly followed suit and separated, each heading off toward their respective areas of operation.

The path toward the main city center was clearly marked and would prove an easy, and quick, trek for Demelza. She wasted no time donning her disguise. One never could tell whom they might encounter on the road, and if she could begin gathering information while hitching a ride to town, all the better.

Hozark's journey would require a bit more planning, as well as an expenditure of both coin and power as he found the best way to reach the underwater cavern city most likely to contain his prey. He had a faint sense of the man's proclivities from a quick scan of his personal rooms back on Obahn, but finding the man himself would be another matter altogether.

He pulled his hood over his head and picked up the pace toward the coastline. Soon enough he would be in the company of some very rough men. Shortly thereafter, if all went according to plan, he would have the Fakarian in sight and get his interrogation underway.

Or things could go completely sideways on him yet again, as had seemed to be happening with alarming frequency of late.

Bud and Laskar were making the hike to the mountain together. It had been decided they should definitely stick with one another as a team for this mission. Hozark had said it was because they were a mean and efficient fighting force when together, but the reality was he needed each to look out for the other.

Both were somewhat impulsive men, though Bud's recent lack of restraint had been something of a surprising break in his normally rock-solid character. The strain of the job seemed to be getting to him a bit. After this task, Hozark would see to it he had some proper R&R time to recharge himself and restore his spirits.

"Stupid fog," Uzabud said as he stubbed his toe on an unseen rock on the path thanks to the difficult visibility.

"Come on, Bud, I think it should clear up a bit not much farther ahead," Laskar urged, falling in next to his friend.

And sure enough, just a minute later the damp mists seemed to push back from the men. Not by much, and surely not enough to grant them any semblance of good visibility, but enough to make the trek at least somewhat more comfortable.

"Looks like fortune is smiling on us," Bud said, his mood lightening slightly. "Finally."

"Yeah, finally," Laskar agreed, glad that Bud hadn't noticed him casting the tiny spell to keep the mists at bay.

It wasn't a great expenditure of magic, but Laskar had found that sometimes the smallest creature comforts made all the difference in the world. And right about now, his friend seemed to really need *something* to go right.

"Hey, what's that?" Laskar wondered when a faint blue light became visible in the mist.

A moment later another did, then several more. A whuffing breath could be heard as the glows began to resolve in shape from the swirling fog.

"Malooki?" Bud marveled. "There are Malooki down here?"

"Yes, friend! Magnificent beasts to carry you to the top of Mount Flagaris," a man wearing a rather ridiculous hat said, his form materializing out of the mists. "I do assume you are traveling to the summit, yes?"

"Aye, that we are," Bud replied, slipping back into his pirate ways.

"Then these can save you quite a lot of walking. For just a pittance, you can each ride one of these beautiful creatures to the top, where my associate will be waiting to take charge of them from you upon your arrival."

"One-way rentals?" Laskar asked. "No extra charges?"

"Nary a one," the man replied.

"How much?"

A price was given, which Bud haggled down to where both he and the Malooki keeper knew it would arrive. But haggling was as much a social thing as a business one, and goodwill had been established by the time the price had been paid and the Malooki saddled.

"Remember, their hair changes color depending on their mood. Blues, greens, purples, even yellows are all good. If you see them turning orange or red, though, that signifies agitation. In that case, be ready to jump clear in case they bolt."

"Sound like wonderful beasts," Laskar joked.

"Oh, but they are, friend. Marvelous creatures who wear their thoughts on their sleeves. Or, their hair, as it may so be."

Uzabud let out a low chuckle. "If only wedding bands were made of such a material. It would help spouses across the known systems avoid a great many arguments."

"Believe me, friend, you are not the first to have this idea," the Malooki master replied with a grin. "Now, they are well familiar with the path, so just let them do what they know and deliver you up top. You should be there in no time."

"Thank you," Bud said as the animal began its trot up the trail. "We'll see you on the way down."

"I look forward to it," the man replied.

If things went well, Bud hoped so. But if things went awry, their return trip might be much faster, and much more violent than desired. Only time would tell. But for now, they rode.

CHAPTER FORTY

The dampness in the air would undoubtedly be comfortable for the amphibian man they were pursuing, Uzabud thought as they climbed through the mists higher and higher atop the backs of the great, gentle beasts.

The Malooki were making good time, plodding along with the men seemingly such an insignificant weight to their powerful flanks that they moved as if entirely unburdened.

The fog had not let up for moment as the trek went on. The mists that hugged the volcanic mountain seemed drawn to it like a moth to a flame. There was actually something to that observation, for the winds gently blowing in from the shoreline pushed the moist air up against the warm hills, causing an up-flow of the rapidly cooling vapors.

While there was humidity to the air in the main city below, as well as along the coast, the condensed nature of it rising up the mountain made for a downright moist environment.

Condensation dripped from the Malooki's glowing, faintly blue hair. The animals shook abruptly, sending a spray flying.

"Yeah, this place is right up that guy's alley," Laskar said, wiping the surprise blast of water from his face with disgust. "Freakin' amphibians. It's just weird, is all I'm saying. Like, why can't he choose one or the other?"

"Because that's the way he grew up," Bud replied. "Just like you and I were raised to breathe air and use konuses for magic, this guy was brought up breathing both above and below water. Just like how power users cast like it's nothing, while the rest of us have to use konuses."

"Hey, I have magic of my own," Laskar griped.

"Sure, buddy. Sorry. And your tricks come in handy at times, making fires and lights and stuff. But I'm talking about *real* magic. The powerful stuff."

"Stuff like *that*?" Laskar asked as a glow became visible up ahead.

"What is that?"

"Looks like a bubble of power. Light. Warmth, even."

"But how?"

"We'll find out soon enough, I guess," Laskar replied as his Malooki kept walking right toward the increasing brightness.

He was right, in a way. It was akin to a bubble in some respects. But rather than popping and disappearing into nothing when pierced, this bubble remained intact when the visitors' mounts rode through it.

A rush of heat and light washed over them as the air abruptly shifted from damp and misty to clear and sunny. This was the city they had been seeking. A glowing pearl of warmth and comfort tucked away at the very top of the inactive volcano.

And above it, a clear vortex of fresh air opened up to the sky. A window of blue without a trace of fog or mist.

"Now *that's* some impressive magic," Uzabud said as he marveled at the sight.

"Not magic, friend," the man walking toward him said.

The Malooki veered his direction instinctively. The Malooki wrangler down below's counterpart, obviously.

"Not magic?" Laskar asked. "Then how is it doing that?"

"Well, there is *some* magic, truth be told," the man said as he took the animals' reins and led them to the stables. "But that just buttresses the phenomenon. What really causes it is the shape of the hills. Ya see, it acts as a wind vortex, spinning around the volcano. By the time it reaches the top, it flares out, pulling the mists apart. All we do is add a little magical push to keep the hole open."

"So you always have clear skies up here?" Bud asked.

"Mostly. Of course, if there's a solar flare up, we reverse the effect to pull the mists in tight. They block it out, you see. But it's the sun's lesser power that buffets our atmosphere up above most days that gives this place that nice glow I'm sure you noticed."

"I was wondering about that," Bud admitted.

"You'll see it better when the sun falls below the horizon. And tonight should be a pretty good show. It's a dancing aurora some nights, and it's a sight to see."

"So, it's a magical power?" Laskar asked. "Can it be harnessed?"

"No, nothing like that. It's just a reaction between the sun and our planet's far lesser innate power. Nothing anyone can use, but it does create a lovely, rippling glow many nights."

"So, it's useless, then?"

"I wouldn't call it that. Just not useful to man, is all. But it sure is pretty to look at. And who doesn't need that from time to time?" He thought a minute. "Though I do recall hearing someone say Ootaki could store a tiny bit of the power, but so little it would take them decades for it to amount to anything significant."

"Huh," Laskar said as he dismounted. "Interesting."

The two visitors thanked the man, then asked if he had by any chance seen a friend of theirs. A blue-green fellow they were supposed to be meeting in a few days.

"Perhaps he got here a few days early," Bud said. "Anyone like that up here?"

"Not that I've seen," the man replied. "But I was down below most of the week. You might want to check the Blue Wind Tavern in town. Most travelers wind up there eventually."

Bud and Laskar tipped the man, then headed off into town to survey the area and see about accommodations for the night, as well as finding this Blue Wind Tavern to get something to eat and rest their weary bones.

In fact, the more they walked, and the more dead ends they came across inquiring about the amphibious man, the more the latter sounded like a good idea. Soon enough, they gave in to the temptation.

The Malooki might have saved their muscles from the exertion of hiking, but their backs, legs, and buttocks were unaccustomed to riding, and an entirely different type of soreness had settled in.

"There it is," Bud said with relish. "At last. The Blue Wind. Looks like my kind of place. And let me tell you, I am sick of walking."

The two men sauntered into the establishment, where, to Bud's delight, it did indeed appear to be his type of tavern. They took seats at a communal table and warmed themselves with food, drink, and festive conversation with a rather gregarious group of travelers who had been atop the volcanic mountain for nearly a week.

"A Fakarian? Nah, we'd have definitely seen one o'those fellas 'round here-parts," a stocky fellow with bristling quills for hair said. "Any o'you come across one o'them fishy types? The blue-green ones?"

His comrades likewise voiced their lack of contact, further driving home the likelihood that Tikoo was nowhere to be found up atop the mountain. But they would still carry out their full survey.

These men and women had essentially done their legwork for them, meeting and greeting just about everyone in their time up top. But there was still nothing to replace looking with one's own eyes, and that was something they would most definitely do.

In the morning.

Night had fallen, and the temperature outside had dropped sharply. To go out now would be courting substantial discomfort. As such, all of the residents and visitors were indoors for the evening, and gambling and merriment were the order of the day.

After hours of festivities and good company, it had gotten quite late, and in the course of many conversations, it had become increasingly clear that the odds of Tikoo being anywhere nearby were slim to none.

"It's late, Laskar. We should go find lodging."

"Why don't we just stay here?"

"Because this place is where visitors stay. They'll charge us double."

"So? It's not our coin, anyway."

"But we can't be frivolous with it," Bud replied, glancing across the bar where a lovely, pale-green woman flashed a brief smile, then looked away.

"It's cold, and it's late, and I'm tired. Come on, Bud. Let's just stay here. Just this one night."

The woman at the bar was staring at Bud more assertively now, and when he smiled at her and gave a little nod, she smiled back.

"You know what? You're right. Why don't you go get a room? I'll be along later," Bud said.

"Really?"

"Yeah," the former pirate said with an enthused grin. "I don't think one night will be an issue."

"And we could use the sleep."

"Huh? Oh, yeah. Sleep. Right. That'll be happening. Sure," Bud said, slipping some coin to his friend. "Go get your room. I'll see you in the morning."

CHAPTER FORTY-ONE

While the two travelers had ventured up the mountain into the mists, Demelza had spent the day being productive in the town down below. Extremely productive, in fact.

With no chilling fog to deal with, she made good time across the flatlands, visiting farm stands, shops, merchants, and trading outposts in a great many of the neighborhoods making up the city. In her disguise, the beguiling charms of the buxom dancer Alanna were enough to loosen the tongue of many resident tough guys.

And several of them said the same thing. Her friend the Fakarian? They'd seen someone matching that description recently, but they'd not been around for a few days. Perhaps she would like to join them for a drink to talk about their helping her find the person––after they got to know one another better, that is.

With great skill, she extricated herself from their interest–– often with a digestive distress spell applied just at the right moment to allow her to slip away when her suitors stepped off to use the restroom.

It seemed that on this world, her gypsy dancer persona was a hit. And in the quest for information, dance she would.

Establishment after establishment, she drank and caroused and danced with abandon, drawing the attention of everyone present. For an assassin, it was pretty much the opposite of her usual tactics, but in this case, the most visible, most desired person was able to control those around her, all vying for her attention.

And what got her attention? Information about her friend.

Drinks flowed, and more than one burly fellow wound up under the table as she bested them shot for shot. Of course, her shots were vanishing as soon as they passed her lips, the alcohol re-materializing in an alleyway on the other side of the block. Hozark's trick spell was proving quite useful in a place like this.

It wasn't just a house or town of ill repute. It was an entire world.

This was becoming a rather interesting experience, she mused. And one that was testing her skills, but in a most enjoyable manner. And Hozark had taken her under his wing, as much as one of the Five ever would, of course. It seemed that working for the leaders of the order had quite a few benefits for a woman eager to learn and improve her craft.

She was a full Ghalian, but that didn't mean there was not room to better herself.

Hours and hours were spent prying information from inebriated people who took a fancy to her. By nightfall she had left a trail of lustful and unconscious men and women in her wake.

Most had succumbed naturally to the copious quantities of alcohol they were attempting to ply her with to gain advantage. But the liquid cut both ways, and she was getting quite a lot of information from the men of ill repute who took refuge on this world.

Unfortunately, while Hozark would undoubtedly be

interested in some of what she'd learned, almost none of the information pertained to Tikoo. Yes, he had definitely arrived on Kraam, as their information had led them to believe. But once there, he was visible but for a short time, then became increasingly elusive until he seemed to drop off the map entirely

The man knew his craft. He was an agent of the Council of Twenty, and as such, he was incredibly slippery, it seemed. And of the few Demelza questioned who had actually seen him, none, it seemed, knew his current, or even most recent whereabouts. Or, at least, so they claimed.

Demelza glanced up at the sky and the dancing aurora illuminating the mountaintop. It was a lovely place, she thought, and under different circumstances, possibly a good location to rest and revitalize, far from the scrutiny of any who knew her.

But tonight, she was not Demelza of the Wampeh Ghalian. Tonight, she was Alanna the dancer, and without another moment's reflection, she strode off to yet another establishment, ready to dance and drink and cajole yet again. Someone, somewhere had to have a lead. The question was, would she find them tonight?

Morning would bring with it an entirely different set of locals to pry information from, and with a very different persona. Alanna was good for this sort of evening work, where heavy drinking was involved. But for those with sharper brains, not addled by alcohol, the guise of Indirus the crippled widow tended to prove more effective.

Of course, *that* character had a backstory worthy of a world of scum and villainy, and was by no means a pushover. Indirus was a pirate's woman. A raider. One of the Warhammer fleet that had burned so brightly, but for such a short while.

They'd all died at the hands of the Council of Twenty nearly five years past, the Council's plans for expansion proving far more important than any short-term alliance with a band of rebel pirates.

After they'd done their part and helped the Council claim their prize––in this case, a resource-rich world at the far end of the Bogadeh system––they had received their reward.

Death at the hands of their employers.

Of course, the Council made it seem like they had perished in noble combat, and with none to witness their true fate, no one knew how the Council reneged on their offer of an entire world for them to call their own, opting instead to unleash a deadly poison through their ranks, hidden in their casks of celebratory alcohol.

When the men were dead or dying, it was then child's play to destroy their ships in such a way that made it seem to have been combat related.

But rumors got out. No facts, of course, but some rumors. And a widow of one of those brave men would always be given a certain respect, even by the roughest sort.

But that would be in the morning, and Demelza couldn't let herself slip into the mindset that shifted her entire physical demeanor to inhabit that character. Not now. For now, she was Alanna, wild woman of abandon and no reservations. Tonight she would dance and frolic and leave a trail of damaged men and women behind.

And in the morning, she would be gone.

CHAPTER FORTY-TWO

While the others were enjoying, to varying degrees, their labors within the great expanse of the city and its mountaintop cousin, Hozark was on a more difficult path. One that took him through the filthy shantytown along the shoreline as he sought out their amphibious target.

He might very well still be on the surface. There were plenty of hidey-holes, nooks, and crannies where he could tuck away and stay out of sight while maintaining contact with whoever happened to be within his network on Kraam. But Hozark had a sense of the man. A feeling. *This* one was a wily one. *This* one was crafty.

Having the sea at his back would provide the water-loving Fakarian with a degree of comfort he would be unable to achieve within the city proper, and certainly not atop the high volcanic mountain looming above. Hozark had thought it a near impossibility that he would be found *that* far from the water. That was why he had sent Bud and Laskar there.

Yes, the unlikely duo *might* actually find him, and yes, he and Demelza *might* have to make a hasty ascent of the mountain, but there was more to this mission than just capturing the Council agent.

There was intelligence to gather, and those a little bit farther from the man's normal haunts might be more inclined to loosen their lips. And Bud had proven himself rather talented at making new friends and prying loose information from them without their even realizing it.

The dampness of the shoreline was only slightly uncomfortable, largely due to the relatively warm temperature of the waters in this region of the planet. It was why the sealife was so plentiful, which in turn provided a steady food source for the hungry mouths come to rest and hide out on Kraam.

Unlike the main city's marketplaces and bazaars, the water's edge was populated by fishmongers and vendors of less savory wares than you might find in the city proper.

This was where the roughest men and women spent their time on the surface. But Hozark was following his instincts, and his instincts told him he needed to dig deeper still. Or, swim, as the case may be. For deep in his gut, the assassin was all but certain his prey was lurking beneath the warm waters, hiding out in one of the cavernous undersea townships.

And *that* was where the truly dangerous types congregated.

There were fourteen caverns surrounding the island. Fourteen places Tikoo could be hiding out. But Hozark immediately eliminated eight of them for being either too remote for the Council agent's purposes, or not possessing more than one entry and egress.

Escape routes were a valuable tool of the assassination trade. Vital, in fact. But assassins were by no means the only craftsmen of nefarious skills who utilized them. And it was utterly unthinkable that a Council agent would corner himself in a sequestered cavern of his own free will.

That left six possible locations where the Fakarian might be hiding out. Hozark had picked up some chatter from locals on the surface before descending into the first of them. It seemed that four of the potential hideouts possessed multiple surface tunnels leading to their depths.

That degree of ease of access led the Ghalian to the conclusion that Tikoo would be hiding out in one of the remaining two. Yes, those two also possessed surface accessways that did not require one to pass through the waters around them, but from what he had sussed out, those routes were both dangerous as well as hidden. Precisely the sort of thing that would prevent most from venturing down below.

And it was precisely there that Hozark went.

The largest of the two was going to be his best bet, he reasoned. More people and a larger underwater tunnel for ships possessing the rather uncommon magic required for subaqueous travel to more easily arrive unseen. And a larger tunnel meant larger ships. Potentially Council vessels, even.

The easy water egress would also put Tikoo at ease. Having a water escape route so handy would give him a confidence that Hozark could exploit. Very few possessed the spells for this environment, nor the requisite training and skill to wield them underwater.

The issue was that spells were tied to spoken words, the combinations of the gibberish-sounding phrases slowly stumbled upon and refined over tens of thousands of years as the people of the diverse worlds scattered throughout the galaxy learned what they did by trial and error.

Somehow, the arcane combinations failed spectacularly, setting back that chain of knowledge for generations. But others were rapidly developed and shared, such as the spells for levitating items. It was the reason the wheel had never been invented. Being able to float items rather than roll them, the round device had simply never been needed.

In fact, to suggest something so crude as pulling or pushing any item of weight along on a wheeled contraption would draw laughter from one and all. It was simply so inelegant, unlike nice, clean magic.

An early issue, however, was that not all possessed innate magic within them. Casting and imbuing items with magical power had initially been confined to a smaller set of men and women who possessed the ability.

But the means to channel power and store it, allowing others to then tap into it, was found. It was highly inefficient at first, but over time, that too was refined until the konus was developed as a catch-all tool that pretty much everyone had these days, though of widely varying power.

But even with a konus on their wrist and a few spells in their tool bag, the power to protect oneself from the crushing weight of an ocean's waters was incredibly specialized magic known only to a few, and capable of being cast and controlled while underwater by even fewer. For to cast, again, the spell had to be spoken. No easy task while submerged.

Amphibian races could create an air bubble, allowing the vocalization, but land-bound races had no such ability. It was what would give his amphibian prey a bit of overconfidence. And that, he could exploit.

Hozark had an ace up his sleeve that only a few could manage. He had trained under Master Garrusch in his early years. The man was incredibly knowledgeable in arcane spells, and had spent a long, long time practicing and experimenting with them over his decades as a Ghalian master.

And though he had died while Hozark was still young, Master Garrusch *had* taught several of those obscure spells to a pair of young aspirant Ghalian who had shared his thrill in practicing the arcane magic. A Wampeh named Hozark, and his sometime paramour, Samara, both of whom showed great aptitude for the unusual arts.

It was their drive for self-betterment that helped that pair rise to the top of their peers and graduate to full Ghalian early. And that knowledge from so long ago might very well come into play today, for Hozark knew the spell to craft a small air shell across his nose and mouth.

It was not enough to allow him to breathe underwater for any great length of time, but it *was* enough to allow spells to be enunciated, even while submerged. And with that little trick in his arsenal, he was the deadliest assassin under the seas.

But for now, he would stick to the above-water areas of the town in the cavern.

The streets were illuminated by the gleaming stalactites above, the minerals comprising them having absorbed background magic that seeped down from above and percolated up from the planet's core over millennia. The glow they cast off provided ample illumination round the clock, though additional magic had been put in place to light the more heavily traveled pathways.

And the town itself was nice and cozy, the geothermal activity of the currently inactive volcano beneath them providing a comfortable degree of heating for the entire area, including the waters, which took up a full third of the vast cavern's space.

Pens containing sea life for harvest were found at the far end of the watery area, while pirate vessels of various makes, carrying crews from myriad systems, floated lazily near the shore. The captains of those craft had studied long and spent much to possess the magic necessary to travel beneath the waters.

Hozark emerged from the water at the far edge of the docking area, silently stepping ashore and forcing himself dry with a carefully placed surge of magic. He had come by neither ship nor the tunnel system, and his arrival had gone entirely unnoted. Just as he wished.

He quickly altered his appearance. A Wampeh in a place such as this would raise suspicions quickly, even if he or she was not a Ghalian. It was simply not the sort of environment his people frequented. And one as cheerful and harmless as Alasnib the trader would not do so well in this place. Instead, he took on the guise of a swarthy pirate, similar in look to Demelza's preferred visage.

Bronze skin and sandy hair completed the look, his own firm muscles already adding to the appearance of a man of action. And that he was, only not the type they expected.

And from what he'd managed to suss out in just his first few minutes within the cavernous township, the presence of a blue-green person residing nearby seemed to point to one thing. He had come to the right place. And things were about to get interesting.

CHAPTER FORTY-THREE

Hozark had caught wind of a blue-green-skinned individual from several lines of inquiry. Yes, he was on the right path, and the confirmation he had received––while utilizing a handful of relatively similar disguises to validate his findings––meant one thing. The time for the inevitable confrontation was almost at hand.

But Tikoo appeared to have friends in this place. The Fakarian was liberal with coin, and the resulting goodwill his generosity had generated would make merely snatching him off the streets impossible. It had been a clever use of funds, and one Hozark approved of, despite it forcing him to alter his plans.

He was getting close, though. And once he found the wily Fakarian, he would either get him drunk, or simply hit him with a spell that made it seem that way, then remove him to somewhere they could chat more privately. And what an interesting discussion that would be.

A flash of blue-green skin caught his eye far off down a roadway. He couldn't be entirely certain in the unusual light of the cavern, but Hozark was willing to bet that was his man. He altered his course and made quick time in that direction.

His pursuit was a subtle one. One that used several disguises as he followed his quarry across the undersea township, always shifting to a different face as he drew nearer and nearer to his target. Finally, several minutes later, he saw the Fakarian step into a seedy pub.

Given, *all* of the pubs down there were seedy, but this one possessed an extra layer of seediness that made it feel even rougher than the others.

Hozark waited a few minutes, tucking into a dark alleyway, not to await a victim to mug, but to change back to his pirate disguise. The bronzed visage firmly in place, he then stepped back out onto the street, walked up to the pub, and waded right on into the establishment's crowded entry, pushing his way toward an empty seat at one of the long communal tables.

He grabbed a passing bar wench and ordered a hearty seafood stew, then tore off a piece of the loaf of bread in the center of the table as he greeted those around him. They exchanged the crude pleasantries people in this sort of gritty establishment so often did, then, determining the newcomer was a source of neither coin nor hostility, went back to their meals.

The Fakarian was across the establishment, seated at a table against the far wall. He seemed at ease in the room of rough adventurers. Just as a Council agent would be.

Hozark began forming a plan. He would find a way to apply a spell to the man's food, causing some gastric distress. He would then follow him to the restroom and see what information he might pry out of him while seeming to help the poor, ill fellow.

Then he saw *her*.

This is not good, he thought as the *second* Fakarian caught his eye. *What are the odds?*

The answer to that silent query was slim. The odds were really, truly, exceptionally slim. But it had happened. And now, of all times.

There was another Fakarian here.

Hozark's expression remained unchanged, even as his mind raced. The two were seated at opposite ends of the establishment, and they didn't seem to be acquainted. At least not outwardly. It was just stupid luck.

Adding another layer of confusion to the mix was that the Fakarian nearest him was a female. Normally, that would have made his job easier. Tikoo was definitely a male, and that should have taken the other amphibian out of the equation.

Unfortunately, Fakarians were one of the only known races who could switch genders. And for a Council agent, especially one on the run and not wishing to be found, changing not only one's attire, but also one's gender, could prove an incredibly effective means of throwing off the scent.

Hozark settled into his seat and slowly chewed his bread, taking his time to formulate a new plan.

This was going to be interesting.

Both Fakarians seemed to have arrived roughly when he did, and their food came out at approximately the same time. That allowed him a nice cushion to settle on a plan. Finally, as he was finishing up his meal, Hozark set into action.

Belching with gusto, he rose from his seat and swaggered over to where the female was sitting, plopping down beside her and leaning in close.

"Hey, I saw you from over there and wanted to buy you a drink."

The blue-green woman ignored him, focusing on the food in front of her.

"I'm Garamush, by the way," Hozark said, offering his hand.

The only way he could employ the little spell that would detect a recent shift in gender would be through several seconds of uninterrupted contact. Again, she ignored him. His little ploy to take her hand, or at least get a name, had come up short.

"You know, you have some really beautiful skin," he said,

pressing on, adding an increased hint of inebriation to his swagger. "The blue and green are incredibly flattering. And those eyes. Oh my."

Her eyes were indeed something to look at, their coloring being rather striking in contrast to her skin. All four of them, in fact. But his flattery didn't so much as cause a glance his direction.

"So, about that drink? What're you having?"

A long silence ensued. One so uncomfortable, those around them even flashed sympathetic looks.

"Fine. But if you change your mind," he said, flagging down the barmaid.

The woman stopped at his table and took his order. Hozark pulled out all the stops, ordering a glass of the most expensive liquor in the house, dropping ample coin on the table as if it were nothing.

Now *that* had gotten her attention. This was a den of scum and villainy, after all, and this drunk seemed like an easy mark. At least for a very, very expensive drink. He might not be good for much more, but the useful idiot would at least provide her one perk for the annoyance of his company.

"Okay," she said, turning to the barmaid. "Make that two."

A casual glance at the other Fakarian told Hozark two things. First, the man was watching. And second, he seemed pissed. Apparently, the assassin had just unintentionally cock-blocked the poor fellow.

"Garamush," he said again, once more offering his hand.

This time, she took it, his warm grip holding hers firmly as she politely replied.

"Dintza," she said, letting the awkward man hold her hand a moment longer before politely pulling it free.

It had been enough. The spell Hozark quietly muttered had told him all he needed to know. She had not changed gender recently. Dintza could not be his target. That meant the man watching them with an annoyed glare was Tikoo.

But the confirmation didn't give him the freedom to act. Not now. Not like this, surrounded by at least a few of his target's likely friends and cohorts. Hozark would have to bide his time and strike when the moment was right. But for now, he would chat, drink and play the part. Soon enough, it would be time for action.

CHAPTER FORTY-FOUR

It was a painfully slow ten minutes, but Hozark forced himself to smile, chat, and act like the casually flirtatious pirate he'd made his approach as. But inside, he was aware of every second as he bided his time before he could act.

He needed to break free of this engagement with the Fakarian woman, but once she'd seen the coin he was willing to spend, her attitude had warmed to him. He was a pirate, yes, but possibly an easy mark desperate for some female company.

"I've gotta have a slash," he finally said, excusing himself and heading to the restroom. That would give him a break from the intent stare Tikoo had been subjecting him and the Fakarian woman to ever since he'd sat down and begun his flirtatious questioning.

Just a few minutes later, Hozark returned from the toilets, only to see Tikoo had left his table. As nonchalantly as he could, Hozark made his way toward the establishment's front doors. Why had the man chosen *now* to leave, of all times?

"Hey, where are you going?" Dintza called after him as he made for the exit.

"What? Oh, I was just getting some air, is all," he replied.

It was only then that he caught a glimpse of the blue-green-skinned man watching him from the shadows at the back of the pub.

It had been a test.

Somehow, Tikoo had thought something was amiss, even though Hozark had played it entirely right, leaving no hint of his true nature. But the man had sensed *something*, and that was all that mattered. He was a skittish, and very wary target, and now it seemed that the constant paranoia from his many years as a Council agent had finally paid off.

The two locked eyes from across the tavern, separated by tables and patrons. Then the Fakarian bolted out the back door, while Hozark, maintaining his disguise, stumbled drunkenly out the front.

He rounded the corner as if he were about to vomit, then took off at a run as soon as he was out of sight. Hozark knew which way his target would flee, given what had just happened. And he had plotted out the fastest routes to the water's edge when he first arrived.

A few quick turns down small side alleys shaved time off of his pursuit, and he was hot on the amphibian man's tail in moments.

"Seal the tunnels!" Tikoo yelled to a deep-yellow-skinned man as he raced past.

The man did not hesitate, but instead took off at a run. Obviously one of his comrades in this undersea realm, he was about to cut off the only terrestrial routes to the surface.

Hozark pushed hard, but the Fakarian was a surprisingly fast runner. So fast, it seemed, that the street in front of him leading to the water's edge was already empty. He had already made his escape. Or had he?

There was something about the water, Hozark noted as he raced closer. The water was still. As if no one had recently jumped in.

This doesn't look right, he realized as a powerful tail lashed out from behind a vendor's cart, striking him square in the chest and sending him tumbling backward onto the ground.

Hozark had kept a grip on his magic the entire pursuit, protecting himself, just in case. A habit that had probably just saved his life, though it felt like one of his ribs might have broken regardless.

Tikoo was already on the move as Hozark pushed himself back to his feet. With a final jump as he reached the shore, the fleeing man dove the remaining distance, disappearing into the sea.

He was in his element, his tail free of his clothing, powering him ahead through the undersea tunnel and out into the open water. The odd man, whoever he was, had been shaken loose. And with the tunnels to the surface sealed, even if he did manage to get them open, Tikoo would be long gone.

He'd have to alert the Council, though. Someone had tracked him to Kraam. And that meant they had to clean house and ferret out the loose-lipped traitor. That, and move on to one of his other safe worlds on which he could lie low until he was called to meet with his masters.

Tikoo slowed his pace once he hit the open sea, relishing the feeling of the water flowing against his body. He'd been on land too long this time, he realized. He would have to make a point to take full advantage of the waters of the next world he stopped at.

Amused with his skillful escape, the Fakarian lazily swam to shore, rising from the sea like an oceanic deity walking out of the surf line and into the seaside shantytown.

Down the long, main pathway he walked, heading toward the parked conveyances lined up near the local eateries. One of which he would steal, finalizing his escape as he headed to board a departing craft.

Tikoo turned the corner and stopped in his tracks. An intact, dry, and very annoyed man was standing in his way, blocking the path. The man he had just left under the sea. The place he couldn't have possibly followed from.

"Impossible," was all he managed to say before a powerful stun spell blasted him to the ground, unconscious.

"What...? Where am I?" the dazed Fakarian said as the waking spell more or less slapped him across the face.

Magically, that is.

A moment later, panic set in as his eyes opened to darkness, and he felt the restraints around his arms and legs holding him quite firmly in place. There was a blindfold over his eyes, he realized, hence the darkness, and he could tell by the weight of his clothes and how they lay on his body that every last one of his hidden weapons and magical devices was gone.

A true professional, he stopped struggling and focused his hearing. He was inside. Quiet, as well. Too quiet. He was on a ship. And there was the faintest hint of a smell.

Shit.

Just a whiff, but it was there. Only a few places on the planet smelled like that, and none of them were good. Yes. Shit. He smelled it, and he was in it. Deep.

Sitting quietly, Hozark watched the subtle microexpressions on the man's face shift as he worked out his situation. Or so he thought. The Wampeh had abandoned his disguise and was now back to his normal coloring and attire. That of a Wampeh, and a Ghalian by the look of the weapons he chose to allow to be seen.

Hozark reached out and pulled the blindfold from the man's eyes, allowing him a moment to adjust to the light. His underwater eyes were squinting a bit, but his land pair shifted to handle the illumination quickly, the assassin noted.

Rather than blurt out questions and beg for his release, the Fakarian shed his initial discombobulation and merely observed, quietly sitting in his seat, though on that matter he didn't have much of a choice.

Hozark looked at him calmly for a long moment.

"You know," he finally said, "I only wished to speak with you. There was no need for all the fuss."

Tikoo said nothing, but he recognized who had captured him. *What* had him in his control. Hozark noted the subtle shift in his irises as his adrenaline flushed in spite of himself.

"I do appreciate the bit of exercise, though," Hozark continued. "It was nice getting to have a little jog and a swim."

Still nothing from his captive.

"There's no need to worry. Contrary to popular belief, Wampeh Ghalian are not all about killing and torture, you know."

"Really?" the man said, finally breaking his silence at the thin lifeline dangled in front of him.

Hozark grinned wide, his fangs sliding into place. "No. But I thought it might make you feel a little better," he said with a frightening laugh.

He had absolutely no intention of draining the man. Nor did he intend to kill him, but the effect the sight of his fangs had on prisoners was the same regardless. But this one would live. And he might even prove to be a great source of Council information beyond this one issue at hand. But there was no need to tell *him* that.

"Now. Let us discuss this contract you placed, shall we?"

CHAPTER FORTY-FIVE

"Well, that was a wild Bundabist chase," Laskar grumbled as he and Bud joined up with Demelza in a small town square. "You have any better luck?"

"No," she replied. "Though I did hear some other interesting tidbits. But Tikoo appears to be a far harder man to find than we anticipated. How did you fare atop the volcano? Any news of worth?"

"A few rumblings, a few rumors, but all in all, it was a waste of time," Laskar said.

"Not a *total* waste," Bud said with a dreamy smile.

Demelza looked at the man, perplexed. Laskar noticed her stare and let out an exasperated chuckle.

"He got lucky."

"Repeatedly," Bud added with a wicked grin.

"Oh. Well, then, good for you." She turned to Laskar. "I hope you had a nice time as well. It is not as if we are in the middle of a vital fact-finding mission or anything."

"Ha. I should be so lucky," Laskar said, looking around the square off the beaten path that they'd chosen as their rendezvous point. "So, uh, where is he, anyway?"

"Hozark? He is at the ship," Demelza replied.

"But that wasn't the plan. And he didn't skree us. Did he call you?"

"No. But he left a note for me here."

"Where?"

"You would not see it even if I pointed it out," she replied. "Suffice to say, Hozark awaits us at the ship." She adjusted the small pack of supplies she had acquired during her time among the locals. "Shall we?"

Laskar and Uzabud fell in line behind her, and the trio made their way out of the city, heading back to their hidden ship. Their ship hidden in the shit.

They took a circuitous route, doubling back several times, pausing to ensure they were not being followed. But no, they were alone, and soon enough the smell of their ship's hiding place alerted them to their proximity long before they could see it.

Or not see it, as was the case with the shimmer-cloaked craft.

They approached carefully, Demelza reaching out to ensure no wards or traps had been tripped. All was in place, as expected. She cleared the path, and they made their way to the hidden ship, then stepped inside, having first ensured they were not tracking anything foul inside on the soles of their boots.

"What the hell?" Bud blurted when they stepped into the small holding room adjacent the ship's galley.

The others hurried in and saw what the fuss was about.

Hozark was sitting comfortably in a chair, sipping a cup of herbal tea, waiting for them. He also had Tikoo, their target, trussed up and unconscious, bound to the chair beside him.

"Hang on. You got him?" Laskar blurted. "We rode all over that stupid mountain, up and down in mists on those stupid Malooki, freezing our stupid butts off, for nothing? You didn't even call us on your stupid skree!"

"You do seem quite fond of that word. Stupid," Demelza noted with a grin. "It seems you and that word have a bond."

Bud chuckled. Of course, after the time he'd had atop the volcanic mountain, not much could sour his mood. In fact, he was quite glad they'd been sent on that futile mission and would gladly head back up again with the slightest urging.

"I am sorry I did not contact you," Hozark replied. "I was under the sea. And quite busy, as well."

"I noticed," Demelza said, leaning in to observe the slumbering prisoner. "A *sominus* spell?"

"Your instincts are correct," he replied.

"He seems intact."

"Yes. The man is a Council agent, but even they have their weaknesses. It only required a pathetically small amount of torture, and the threat of far more, before he was spilling everything he knew."

Hozark paused.

"So? What does he know?" Laskar asked.

"He was a decoy," he finally said.

"A what, now? A *decoy*?" Bud interjected. "Hang on. You're saying he didn't actually make the contract?"

"Oh, he most certainly did. Our friend here was very forthcoming about that fact. However, in the course of our '*discussion*,' it also came to light that he was in fact hired by another party to make that contract. However, in that instance, the person hiring him let a little detail slip."

"What kind of detail?" Bud asked.

"The kind that was most careless on that individual's part. A casual comment was made that allowed Tikoo to become privy to a most interesting wrinkle in the job. Namely, the person who hired him was *also* hired by a third party."

Bud's eyes widened. "Holy shit. Are you saying they're part of a daisy chain? For a freakin' Ghalian contract? That's insane. I...I've never heard of such a thing."

SCOTT BARON

"Nor have we," Demelza said. "It is a firewall of deniability. Akin to a blind drop, protecting the identities of those farther up the chain. If this is true, the actual party behind the contract could be anyone."

"Potentially," Hozark agreed. "We most certainly have our work cut out for us. For the moment, however, we need to deliver our friend Tikoo to one of the order's facilities for safekeeping until the Five determine what to do with him."

"And in the meantime?" Laskar asked.

"And in the meantime, the four of us figure out what is *really* going on here."

CHAPTER FORTY-SIX

Kalama was the woman's name. The one who hired Tikoo. The one who had poor information security and had let slip that she too had been hired to pass along the contract to him. A woman with high cheekbones and curly orange hair, courtesy not of genetics, but a lot of expensive modification spells.

Tikoo had been a good Council agent. His operational skills were top-notch, and he had proven a very worthy adversary. Hozark would have caught up with him eventually, of course. He always did.

But without the help of his associates, it would have taken longer to survey Obahn, which may have led to Tikoo fleeing from Kraam before his arrival. It would have resulted in something of a wild Bundabist chase, and at the moment, time was something they did not have in abundance.

Those who were responsible for ambushing Master Prombatz and his young aspirant had things in motion, and whatever it was they were planning, there was an urgency to finding out what it was, and what could be done to stop them.

Why someone would purposely target the most deadly assassins in the galaxy was anyone's guess. But when they were found, guesswork would not be required. The Ghalian had many, many ways of making people talk.

"You sure this is the place?" Bud asked, tugging at his high-collared coat as the four of them made their way through the largest shopping district of one of the wealthier cities on the wealthiest planet in the system.

He did not like dressing up as if he were some high-class buffoon. He had been a pirate, after all, and the world of fashion had never made much sense to him. Clothing designed by people who obviously never actually wore any of their miserably uncomfortable creations themselves.

Yet to infiltrate and fit in on this world, he, and the others, had no choice but to appear as any other casual shopper might. And that meant fashion.

Hozark and Demelza looked amazing, of course. No matter if they were clothed in the finest garb in all the land, or draped with rough cloth and covered in muck, they were masters of infiltration and disguise, and this was simply one more job.

Laskar, however, was different. He seemed quite at home in the fine threads. In fact, his attitude had even improved a bit, and his posture straightened slightly. For him, playing dress up was apparently a pleasure, though he might be wary to admit it to his rough-and-ready associate.

"We stay together for this," Hozark had said to the group when they dropped into atmosphere. "Numbers and proximity will allow us to block any escape attempt and keep from necessitating a pursuit."

"Good. My ass is still sore from all of that Malooki riding," Bud said. "Running does not sound particularly appealing at the moment."

"You sure it's not from that little green––" Laskar started to joke.

"No. She wasn't that sort of woman."

"Whatever you say, Bud," he cracked back. "Whatever you say."

The approach to the city had been normal. No crazy maneuvers or subterfuge required. Just jumping into the system, dropping out of orbit, and landing in the immaculate, elevated docking facility. It was spotless, and even had multiple accessways leading directly to the stores and merchants.

Visitors to this city would not have to wait any longer than necessary to start spending coin if they did not wish to. And spend they did.

The opulence on display was staggering. And so too was the waste. So much spent on things, the generic of which cost a fraction of the price on other worlds. But there was social standing attached to these bits and baubles, and that commanded a premium.

And somewhere amid all of this consumerism, their target awaited them.

Kalama was a socialite. How and why she, of all people had been chosen to play a part in this twisted plot was unclear, but Hozark assured his friends the information he had acquired from Tikoo was most certainly accurate.

"The woman probably ran up some sort of debt from her spending habits," Laskar said. "I bet getting that contract to Tikoo was offered as a way to make good on it."

"You think?" Bud asked. "Seems kind of odd for a high-class society woman."

"Nah, it's not at all uncommon for that sort of thing. I mean, think about it. It's done with gamblers in over their heads all the time, so it makes sense that the same should apply to other kinds of overindulgence and indebtedness too."

"I have to admit, it kinda makes sense," Bud said. "Hand off a simple message and be free of that looming obligation hanging over your head? Who wouldn't step in and make a quick delivery for that sort of thing?"

Hozark and Demelza merely nodded their agreement as they walked, smiling and laughing, blending in with the crowd while their trained eyes scanned every face and storefront for the woman in question.

They had an address for her, and that was their destination, but the Ghalian knew full well their prey might walk right into their grasp. Literally, in some instances. But as they strolled, there was no sign of the woman on the streets.

Porters were all around them, pushing the floating conveyances loaded with the purchases of the elite. Shopping Sherpas, of a sort, but rather than mountaineering adventurers, they served a far different kind of master.

None appeared to be slaves, though, despite the Council of Twenty spreading the use of them until it was rather commonplace. In fact, all across the city, only a handful of the gleaming control collars were to be seen.

It was a bit unusual, as the owning of staff was almost the norm. But the shops seemed to have actually employed workers for the task, allowing patrons to leave their own at home.

It was a testament to just how much coin was flowing through their coffers, for owning an enslaved laborer was often cheaper than hiring one, in the long term.

Slavery had long been an issue for the Ghalian, and they had taken more than a few jobs at discounted rates when the outcome might weaken the hold of the Council's terrible practice. They never took sides in conflicts and wars, but they did have their own agenda at times, and they would quietly work to further it.

"Hey, is that the place?" Bud asked, staring up at the gleaming tower with a small series of floating gardens surrounding it, held aloft by a very expensive bit of magic.

"Yes. Her residence is within that building. Thirteen levels up, adjacent to that garden," Hozark noted, pointing to one of the floating outdoor spaces.

"Damn. The coin this place must have cost. Now I can see how you could get in debt *really* easily," Bud marveled. "It's like an addiction for these people."

"Of a sort," Demelza agreed. "In any case, it is something that can be leveraged against those who fall on hard times, as we suspect Kalama likely had. But you never can tell."

"True. And for that reason, we must remain vigilant," Hozark added as they stepped into the building's lobby area.

It was quite over the top. Gaudy, one might even say. But whatever one's opinion on the display of wealth, none could argue it was not impressive.

Enormous sculptures acted as supporting columns for the mezzanine level, and magically powered lift discs would silently whisk passengers to the upmost reaches of the edifice. A fountain quietly burbled, the sleek stone behind the flowing water immaculate, kept free of moss or algae by a series of expertly placed spells.

And that was just a taste of the layers upon layers of magical opulence surrounding them. One could spend hours looking at the marvels around them, time permitting.

But they were not here on a sightseeing visit, and they didn't have the time for it even if they wanted to. And they were certainly not residents, though the group's attire allowed them to blend in as though they were. Even their konuses and blades selected for this mission were fine and ornate, pulled from the little stash Hozark kept handy for just such types of infiltration.

"This way," Hozark said, heading toward the lift discs. "We need to go up."

CHAPTER FORTY-SEVEN

The ride up was as smooth as it was fast. The lifts traveled at a normal speed and were designed for average people, not power users, it seemed. Vislas, and even emmiks, could pull from their own internal magic stores to counteract the negative effects of a much faster ascent. One that might cause others to black out from the speed and forces that accompanied it.

Thirteen floors passed in a flash, and moments later they stepped out onto their target's level. Only a third of the way up the building. She had money, no doubt, but was not wealthy by the upper floor residents' standards.

There were only a few residences per floor, however, and with that type of footage, even those of just average means were still living in a degree of luxury not afforded to many. It seemed Kalama had done well for herself. At one time, anyway.

"This is it," Bud said, pointing out her door.

Hozark saw it as well—before Bud had—but he had paused a moment. Something felt off.

"You sense it too?" Demelza asked.

"I do."

"What are you guys waiting for? Let's do this," Bud said impatiently, moving toward the door.

"No, not yet, Bud," Hozark said.

The pirate froze. When Hozark got a vibe, it was almost always to your benefit to listen to it. The assassin studied the door a long moment, Demelza doing the same.

"Ah, that's it. There it is. Do you see?" he asked.

"Yes. Clever, I must admit," she replied. "Nicely done, for a layman."

"See what?" Laskar asked. "I don't see anything; it's just a door."

"Just a door, yes. But also *not* the door we want."

Bud cocked his head as he studied the door. "It's numbered. This is her door."

"*One* of her doors," Hozark replied, pointing to the dust around the doorjamb. "This is not an entrance. It is a secondary doorway to the unit. But it is not meant to be opened. Not from the outside, that is."

"Why in the world would you do that? Build a second doorway?" Bud asked.

"It would normally have been a second unit, I would wager. Two must have been combined at some point, and this door became an emergency egress for the resident," Hozark explained. "And as it is not meant to be used as an entrance, it has alarm spells and wards placed upon it."

"Huh," his friend said. "I would never have guessed."

"Most would not. And they would set off the alarms, summoning the building's security detail."

"What kind of security we talking?"

"Nothing impressive by our standards. Just run-of-the mill hired muscle. But then, we are used to dealing with a different type of adversary, are we not?"

"Yeah, I guess you could say that," Bud replied with a chuckle.

Over the years, they'd had a great many run-ins with all manner of people wanting to do them some harm. In some cases, far worse. Compared to them, a couple of rich people's security goons weren't any real concern.

But they didn't want to raise a fuss, even a minor one. No alarms, no conflict, just in and out. Stealthy. That was the order of the day.

"So, what do we do?" Laskar asked. "Do you disarm the wards or something?"

"No, Laskar. We shall follow the course of least resistance," Hozark replied. "We go in through the front door."

The four of them stepped away from the false entrance and followed Hozark down the corridor. If Kalama's home was actually the combination of two units, her actual entry could be in either direction. But which one?

It was a coin toss, but with only two doors as possibilities, at least it wouldn't take long to find their mark.

"Excuse me," Demelza said, a warm smile on her face as the door opened. "I have a package delivery for a Denna Kalama."

"Denna?" the orange-haired woman asked. "I'm no denna. I'm not part of a visla's family."

"Oh, I'm sorry. My mistake," Demelza replied. "But you are Kalama, yes?"

"Yes. But what delivery do you have? Those are usually dropped with the man at the front reception area and brought up by Marisko."

"Marisko called in sick today."

A look of surprise crossed the woman's face, then a split-second later she attempted to slam the door in Demelza's face. The Wampeh's reflexes were far too fast, and she, along with her three associates who had been waiting against the wall out of sight from the doorway, all rushed into Kalama's home.

"What the hell do you think you're doing? Do you know who I am?"

"We do, actually," Bud said with a grin as he grabbed her by the arms. "Kalama. Not *Denna* Kalama, though, right?"

She flashed a hateful glare at him but stopped struggling. She knew the odds were horribly against her and a fight might just make it worse.

"Please, have a seat," Hozark said.

Kalama obliged, sitting quietly in the offered chair. *Her* chair. Bud strolled through her home, admiring the trappings of wealth in every room.

"Nice digs you've got here," he said, meandering across her main living space in the direction of the lift they'd taken up to her floor.

The flustered woman glared at him as he looked around.

"You've already broken in. Just take what you want and leave."

"We do not want your possessions, Kalama. We want information."

A perplexed look blossomed on her face. "Wait, isn't this a robbery?"

"Nothing of the sort. If you cooperate with us and tell us what we wish to know, we shall leave you and your possessions as they are."

"What do you mean? What kind of information could I possibly have that would be of any use to your sort of people?" she asked with disdain.

"Hey, watch it. I like my sort of people," Laskar said.

"You performed a task recently. Delivered a message to a Fakarian. A man named Tikoo. Does this refresh your memory?" Hozark asked.

"The one on Obahn? Yes, I remember him. But I don't know him. Whatever he did, I can assure you, I had nothing to--"

"Who hired you to deliver your message to him?" Hozark said, cutting her off.

"That? Just a man named Bitz. He runs a local import shop. Shoes, clothes, that sort of thing."

"And where can we find this Bitz?"

"He has offices at the distribution building. It's the big white one a few hundred meters from the arena."

"Well, shit. That was easy," Bud said, walking toward the door.

"It was," Hozark agreed. "*Too* easy."

"Just truss her up and let's get out of here," Bud said, reaching for the door.

"No! Bud, don't!" Hozark called out.

But it was too late. The door burst open as soon as he touched it, and a team of burly men swarmed into the space, weapons at the ready.

Despite his natural instinct to fight, the point of a blade immediately thrust up against his back convinced Bud that perhaps this was not the time for heroics. Hozark could take them, sure. But he was not Hozark. He was good, but not that good.

Hozark, Demelza, and Laskar all had their weapons in their hands in an instant when the men burst in, ready to go. But they paused at the sight of Bud with a dagger pressed against him. Further inspection confirmed Hozark's initial concern. These were not building staff. Not by a long shot. These were professionals.

"Drop your weapons," Kalama said with a knowing smile.

"This was a trap," Bud realized. "No wonder it was so easy."

"And now you are *my* prisoners," she replied. "Gantz said someone might show up after I did his job. I thought he was being paranoid, but who argues with him? But it seems he was right. And now my debt to him is paid in full."

"And this Bitz person?" Demelza asked.

"There is no Bitz, idiot." She turned to the mercenaries. "Bring them to the cells, and go fetch your master," she said.

"Cells? Who the hell has cells in a luxury residential building?" Bud asked.

Kalama raised a brow and grinned. "Oh, you'd be surprised."

CHAPTER FORTY-EIGHT

The cells within the luxury tower were both immaculate and well stocked, as one would expect of so high-end a building. If one were to expect in-house torture facilities as part of your housing package, that is.

It quickly became apparent that the entire thirteenth level of the building was empty but for its lone resident. But so far as Hozark could tell as they were ushered down the hallway toward an imposing double door, the other residents were likely moved to other levels in the building, judging by the faint signs of moving scrapes to the door frames.

There was no appearance of forced relocation, though. Nothing broken, no telltale marks from a scuffle as people resisted. That meant they moved willingly, and likely to nicer units higher in the building. And recently. Likely only a few weeks prior, when Master Prombatz had been attacked. To move that many so quickly meant a lot of coin had been spent to achieve that goal.

Someone had gone to some length to ensure that Kalama was backed up by a team of men of action who would complete their tasks regardless of the woman's competence. The way things were set up, even if she had failed horribly in her job, the mercenaries under her would have stepped in and completed it anyway.

Whoever had paid for all of this had anticipated the eventual backtracking of Tikoo's contract. And that person had left Kalama where she was as a honey pot. And she had done as intended, pulling in her victims like flies to honey. It was all perfectly arranged, and the would-be interrogators were now captive. Captive and about to be tortured, more than likely.

Only there was one small flaw in that plan. The enemy did not realize something of the utmost importance. They had no idea who exactly they had captured. Two of their prisoners were Wampeh Ghalian. And they were only prisoners because they chose to be for the moment.

"You thinking what I'm thinking?" Bud asked as he sat in his cell waiting for the torture to begin.

"That you really must learn when to listen to my warnings?" Hozark replied with a wry grin.

"Ha-ha. Very funny. But no, I'm talking about what comes next. I mean, look at all the gear on the walls. And on that table we passed on the way in."

"Seriously. These guys are ready for some serious torture sessions," Laskar agreed.

"Nothing of the sort. It is merely for show," Hozark said.

"Really? 'Cause it looked pretty damn real to me," Laskar shot back.

Hozark smiled at him as one would a child. "Dear Laskar, if you'd more carefully inspected the items on that table when we arrived, you'd have noticed all were not only new, but also possessing not a speck of dust on them. The equipment is real, no doubt, but it is merely there to evoke a visceral fear response. A response you are presenting at this very moment, I would add."

Laskar was about to say something, but Bud caught his eye

with a little head shake, and he thought better of it. This was not the best time for snark.

"So, what do we do now?" Bud asked.

"Now? Now we wait."

Five hours had passed before the door to the holding cell area finally swung open. A short, stocky man with enormous hands for his size and leathery, brown skin, strode in, flanked by a pair of Tslavar mercenaries. By the look of them, they were the largest he could find.

"Well, well. What've we got 'ere?" he drawled. "A buncha wannabe tough guys tryin' ta be cute. And in my town, no less," he said, surveying his captive audience. "Pathetic lot, all of you. Pain in my arse, you are. But you'll be makin' me some good coin at least."

"Excuse me, but there must be some mistake. No one will pay a ransom for us, so you might as well just let us go," Hozark said.

"Let you go?" the man said. "Let you go? You've gotta be pullin' my leg. And it's not a ransom I'll be seekin'."

"But, if not a ransom, then what?"

"Hell if I know. I was just to catch whoever came and messed with Kalama. But once I hear back from my contact, I know he'll pay me a handsome bonus for snarin' you an' your friends."

"So, you are in charge here?" Hozark said.

"Damn proper, I am."

"Not many people have your kind of clout around here. You must be Gantz."

"The one and only."

A Tslavar mercenary strode through the doors in a bit of a rush. "Sir, there's been a little incident at the warehouse. A shipment is light."

Gantz went from jovial intimidation to unmasked rage. "It's

what?" He spun toward the door. "You skree Tormal and Trisk. Have them meet us there."

With that, the angry man stormed out of the holding cells, his interrogation interrupted by something apparently far more interesting.

The prisoners remained silent a long moment before finally speaking.

"So, that was him," Bud said.

"Yes. The one who hired Kalama," Hozark confirmed.

"And he just showed up like that."

"Indeed. It seems, in his case, that his overconfidence saved us a bit of searching."

"But we still need to get out of here," Bud noted.

"Obviously, Bud. And once we do that, we shall have words with Gantz. On *our* terms."

"Guys?"

"Hang on, Laskar," Bud said. "All of our stuff was taken, Hozark. Our weapons and konuses. And we're locked in here. We're kinda screwed, unless you have some secret Wampeh Ghalian trick to get us out."

"I am working on it," Hozark replied. "A solution is bound to present itself if we but open our eyes to it. There is *always* a way, if we are willing and able to see it."

"Uh, guys?"

Bud flashed an annoyed look at his copilot. "I said, in a minute."

"Whatever," Laskar grumbled, then walked to the cell door and placed his hands over the magical lock.

He stood there like that for a good, long minute, his hands held in place. Then, without warning, the door unlocked and slid open.

"How did you do that?" Bud marveled.

"Just a trick I learned a while ago when I was running with some guys who got caught more often than not."

"Impressive, Laskar," Demelza said. "Quite a skill you possess."

"It's nothing, really. Just a little manipulation is all."

"It is not nothing," she persisted. "You just saved us a great deal of time with that 'little manipulation.' Well done."

"Indeed. What Demelza has said is correct. Well done, indeed," Hozark added. "Now, we have things to do."

"Yeah. Get revenge," Laskar said.

"No, not revenge. We stalk our new target, acquire him, and have a little chat with him on our own terms."

"I hope that includes at least a little revenge," Laskar griped.

An amused smile tickled the corners of Hozark's mouth. "No revenge. That is an unproductive path. But rest assured, the implements at my disposal are *not* for show only."

CHAPTER FORTY-NINE

Hozark led his team out of the building through a service lift, avoiding prying eyes that might report them to Gantz, tipping him off to his captives' escape. The door panel opening to the small floating disc shaft was invisible to the eye, its seams perfectly blending in with the lines of the wall where Hozark ran his fingers.

There was an inaudible click, the only confirmation of his hunch slightly moving beneath his fingers. The panel slid open without a sound, and a moment later, the lift disc dropped to floor level and stopped, awaiting its passengers.

"How did you know that was there?" Laskar asked. "No one could have seen that, and you're still not wearing a konus."

"Years of training," Demelza answered for Hozark as he checked the shaft door for any hidden traps or wards. "Just one of many things we have drilled into us from an early age."

"It is safe," Hozark said, turning to the others. "And to answer your query, Laskar, if you look carefully at the floor, you will notice the slight difference in texture from wear and foot traffic. The way the light catches it. Do you see?"

Laskar squinted and scrutinized where Hozark had pointed. "I don't see anything."

"Hang on a second," Uzabud said. "I see it! Holy shit, I can actually see it."

"See what?"

"Look, right there. Unfocus your eyes and just let the blurry highlights steer your gaze. You see it?" Bud asked.

Laskar stared a long moment. Then a bit more.

"Gentlemen, I appreciate this is a novel learning moment for you, but we really must go."

"In a second," Bud replied. "Come on, man. You see it, right?"

Slowly, a grin spread across Laskar's face. "I see it! No way! There it is!"

"Nice for you both," Demelza said. "Now, get on the lift disc. Time is wasting."

The two men piled in with them and shut the panel. Hozark cast the descent command, and they dropped all the way to the service area of the building, a level below the lobby. From there they quickly exited the building, walking as if they belonged there and were above questioning as to their presence. And dressed as they still were in rich people finery, the servants averted their eyes and made a clear path for them as they walked.

Whatever it was that had brought people of their status down to the service level, no one wanted to fall under that umbrella of scrutiny. More likely than not, someone had screwed up, and there would be hell to pay. That was the usual reason for such a visit, and more than enough reason to steer well clear.

"The warehouse. It would likely be in a central location. Gantz strikes me as too much of a control-obsessed individual to allow its operation far from his watchful eyes," Hozark mused.

"Yeah, but there have to be a bunch that fit that description around here. Looking at all the shops and commerce?" Laskar said. "I bet there are dozens of them."

"How do we figure out which one it is before he finds out we're gone? We don't have time for this," Bud said. "Do we track down Kalama and pry it out of her?"

"You are making this far more difficult than it needs to be," Hozark replied. "Come."

He led them to the nearby thoroughfare and flagged down a hovering conveyance. "Excuse me, sir. We're seeking a particular item the shops don't seem to have. My wife, here, is absolutely set on its acquisition. I was told that a fellow by the name Gantz likely had possession of one in his warehouses. Might you know how to get there? We are in something of a rush."

The driver looked at their attire and was thanking the gods for such a good fare. "Gantz? Of course I know him. A lovely fellow. Most delightful," he lied.

He did know him, of course. Everyone knew him. Namely, what a tyrannical asshole he could be to any who worked for him, and the wrath he would rain down on any who crossed him.

"That's fantastic. Could you take us to him?"

"Of course. Please, step aboard."

Hozark held out his hand, chivalrously helping Demelza––his 'wife'––into the conveyance, then climbed in with her. Uzabud and Laskar boarded behind him and they were underway. It was a several-minute ride, but given the layout of the city, the warehouse wasn't really all that far from where they'd been captured in Gantz's trap.

"That's the place," the driver said, pointing to the building they'd stopped in front of.

"Thank you ever so much. What do I owe you?"

The driver relayed the price, and Hozark dropped coin in his hand, plus a healthy tip for his assistance.

"Where did you get coin?" Laskar asked as the man drove away. "They took everything from us."

Uzabud laughed. He'd known Hozark a long time, and there were certain Ghalian tricks he'd seen on several occasions, and this was one of his favorites. "Let's just say if he ever wanted to give up the assassination game, our friend here could have a very lucrative pickpocketing career."

Laskar stared at the Ghalian master with a questioning look. Hozark merely smiled and shrugged. "Come, we have work to do."

Entering the warehouse through the front would have been the fastest and most direct way, but as they were most certainly unwanted guests, a more surreptitious entry was warranted. Hozark and Demelza split up while their friends tucked into a shop, pretending to examine the wares.

They returned a few minutes later from opposite directions. The pair joined up and stepped inside, acting as though they were a couple once again.

"There is a rear entrance, but it is warded," Hozark said quietly as they walked past Bud and Laskar. "Too many layers of protections for our needs. But there is another way in. A small worker's access on the near side down the side alley. Meet us there in five minutes."

Hozark turned to Demelza. "Come, darling. I want to check out the shop we passed down the road earlier."

"Of course, my love," she replied with a radiant smile, wrapping her hand through his arm and strolling out of the establishment like a pair of lovebirds.

Bud and Laskar shared a quick look. Say what they might about the cold and stoic ways of the Ghalian, their friends had to admit, these two could really turn it on when they had to.

Five minutes later they joined up with the pair at the side entryway.

"We move fast. Stay behind Demelza and I. We take down Gantz as quickly as possible, then clean up his men. Clear?"

"Clear," the men replied.

Hozark didn't wait a moment longer and plunged right into the building, the far weaker wards disabled before their friends had joined them. It was a thing to see, a pair of Ghalian moving with speed and precision, laying out over a dozen henchmen without breaking stride, and with no weapons to boot.

All that the trailing men could do was quickly bind those who had fallen––and were still breathing––and collect their weapons. By the time they reached their friends standing over Gantz in his office, the man was bleeding from the nose, bound to his chair, and entirely devoid of his prior aggressive demeanor.

It seemed that when faced with not one but a pair of Wampeh Ghalian, and Ghalian he had so recently imprisoned and threatened, no less, he became quite the trembling coward. And the poor man now realized their capture was almost certainly because they permitted it rather than through any skill of his own,

It was a somewhat nasty discussion they had with the captive man. Perhaps a little rougher than needed, truth be told. But Gantz was more than just a source of information. He was someone they didn't like. It wasn't personal, but it still was, at least a little.

He gave up the name of the person who hired him almost immediately. Given his resources, and the likelihood of him posing a threat in the future, those were his final words, and his body would not be found.

It was a quick flight to the nearby world the man who hired him was located on, and that one was *not* expecting company. He was taken completely by surprise, and without a fight, and was downright eager to tell these mysterious assailants whatever they wanted to know.

He was then stunned and packaged up, handed off to a Ghalian agent on that world to be transferred to the same holding facility as the others. As for Kalama, she had already been bundled up and taken as well. No loose ends to talk. No one around to even hint at their plans.

"Well, that makes your head spin, doesn't it?" Bud said with a perplexed laugh.

"That it does, my friend. That it does."

"So, he was also hired."

"So it seems."

"He was hired to hire the person who was hired to hire the person who hired the person who made the contract. Damn, that's just crazy. I mean, who'd have thought? And we're still not at the head of the snake yet."

"Indeed. It is most perplexing. Perplexing, and yet impressive in its thoroughness. Someone went to great lengths to ensure they would not be found out."

"No shit. I tell ya, Hozark, if it keeps up like this, the Ghalian holding facility is going to have a whole menagerie of messengers pretty soon."

Hozark nodded with a somewhat amused grin. Little did they know how accurate that assessment would prove to be.

CHAPTER FIFTY

More than a half dozen leads.

More than half a dozen new prisoners sent to the secret Ghalian holding facilities.

It had been a mess. A busy, hectic, time-consuming mess.

They'd followed the leads presented by each successive target, chasing down the next link in the chain leading back to the original contract maker, sometimes literally, the pursuit spanning cities, planets, and even systems on one occasion. That particular target had nearly slipped by them, and it was only Bud's brilliant flying that had allowed their capture.

The whole ordeal had taken them weeks, and none of them had been simple. And though differing levels of interrogation had been needed, every single one of them had essentially the same story. They'd been hired for just one task. To hand off a package to the next person in the chain. Nothing more, nothing less.

They didn't know what the package they were carrying contained, or even the name of its recipient for that matter. Not until they opened the sealed letter within *their own* package that they'd been handed by *their* courier. And that was only opened upon arrival on the next recipient's world.

And so it went. And it turned out that each successively smaller package contained the same instructions for the next person. Deliver the package inside, then go back to your life. And that was what each of them had done.

"A double-blind method of engaging an entire network of unwitting couriers," Demelza mused as they reviewed what they knew thus far. "It is a rather clever way to ensure one's anonymity."

"Yes, most clever. Ingenious, even, though also quite a time consuming process. Someone went to a great deal of effort to achieve this goal. It was not a casually planned attempt," Hozark said.

Bud leaned back in his seat, thoroughly enjoying the seemingly rare bit of downtime, given the flurry of activity of their past weeks. They had another lead to follow, but for the moment at least, they could enjoy a tiny moment to themselves before diving back into the pursuit of the truth.

They hadn't drained the Drookonus powering Uzabud's mothership, but if this kept up, with this many jumps so close together, Hozark wondered if he might have to tap into his emergency backup cache to help the man continue to fly them on their task.

At least Bud was in good spirits. The frustration of this seemingly endless chain of couriers continually springing up was wearing on them all, but it was amazing what a simple bit of self-enforced downtime under pretense of giving their Drookonus a break could do for one's spirits.

It was why Hozark had suggested it. Under the guise of a necessary stop to prevent the device from overloading, of course. No one wanted to be the one taking a break when there was work to be done. So Hozark gave them an excuse. And all were perking up for it.

Especially Bud, who had been so focused on his flying after the one man's near escape, Hozark actually worried what effects of such constant focus might have on the man.

"Casual? Hell, this was clearly a Council attack. I mean, from what we heard about what went down, it seems pretty obvious. The number of power users who attacked them? No way it's anything else. No one has those kinds of resources."

"I'm afraid I must agree with Uzabud," Demelza said. "Someone planned this out long in advance." She paused, giving Hozark a sympathetic look. "Someone who understands the Ghalian."

"Samara?" Laskar asked. "You think it was Samara? I shot her down."

"You shot down a craft. We never saw who was inside. Or if anyone was, for that matter," she replied.

"Good point. And she is the only one I can think of who could have pulled off this sort of thing. And from what Hozark says, she's had what, ten years or so to plan it?"

"I still do not believe her capable of this degree of treachery," Hozark said.

"She tried to kill you, man," Bud reminded him.

"Yes. But only when I was on task to slay her employer, Bud. Remember, I sought *her* out, not the other way around."

"Which doesn't change the fact that she tried to kill you. Like, not playing around, *actually* tried to kill you. Mel, back me up here."

"I must admit, he is correct in that aspect," she agreed. "Having watched the two of you battle, I can say with confidence she was pulling no punches."

"Of course not. And I'd expect no less of her. But, again, it was I who forced her hands into action that day."

"Yeah, man, but there's no wrath like your ex's wrath," Bud noted.

"She is not my ex. We grew up together within the order. We

were close because of it. And, yes, there were times we were intimate. But we were not bonded."

"I didn't think you guys ever got your freak on," Laskar mused. "That must be some kinky, violent, scary shit."

"Dude, please," Bud grumbled.

"What? You know you were thinking the same thing."

"Yeah, but how about a little tact?"

"I prefer being blunt and to the point, thank you very much."

"We've noticed," Demelza said. "There is not an ounce of subtlety or tact within you, is there, Laskar?"

"Maybe. Maybe not. But I can sure fly a ship."

They all hated to admit it, but he was right about that. His piloting skills were on point, and they were fortunate the normally reclusive pilot had happened to meet the man and agreed to take him on as a copilot.

That temporary alliance had blossomed into a full-fledged partnership, and though he annoyed Bud to no end, Laskar also gave him a skilled backup. Something that let him take his eye off the ball for a few moments from time to time. Something he hadn't even realized he needed.

"So, about your *not* ex," Laskar said. "You gotta admit, it really seems like she's the only one with the knowledge and skill to pull this sort of thing off."

Hozark paused, mulling over their situation a long moment. "She left me––the *order*––ten years ago under the guise of her own demise."

"Right, and now she's getting even," Laskar said. "Right, guys? I mean, it makes total sense."

"No, it does not," Hozark said. "Had Samara wished for revenge for some unknown reason, I can assure you, we would have heard from her long before now. Someone else is in play here. So, we keep digging."

Demelza was ready for it. They'd already paused long enough, and she was anxious to continue the hunt. Bud and

Laskar, however, looked as if they had deflated, just a tiny little bit.

"All right. I'll fire up the Drookonus and get us underway," Bud said. "I just hope we get to the end of this chain sooner than later. This shit is getting old."

CHAPTER FIFTY-ONE

The prior couriers had been vastly different sorts of people. A socialite, an agent, a mobster, and so on. No real defining thread to bind them, aside from the tasks each had been retained to do.

After weeks of running down leads, sometimes literally, the group was more than a little tired of the seemingly endless stream of lower-tier lackeys.

"We need to finally hit something concrete, or I'm gonna kill someone," Bud lamented as they flew to their next destination.

"Isn't that *their* job?" Laskar joked, nodding toward their Wampeh associates.

"At this rate, I might give them a run for their money if our luck doesn't change."

Hozark looked up from a parchment he had been studying with a curious expression lingering on his face a moment, then rolled it and tucked it away once again. The Wampeh Ghalian had been contacted for a bit of assistance from their network, and that assistance had come. Their spies had located the person whose name did not exist, it seemed.

The message had been delivered in person, as was the

order's way in all but the most absolutely unimportant communications. Skree calls could be intercepted––though the general public believed that form of magic was tamper-proof––and only face-to-face meetings were truly secure.

The Council of Twenty had kept the skree vulnerability secret a long, long time, and only a tiny handful of them even knew it existed. But the ability to listen in to any conversation they wished was something they wanted very much to keep under wraps. A tool that could be incredibly useful in a moment of crisis.

That the Wampeh Ghalian also knew of this exploit was an even closer guarded secret. One that had dictated they continue to use what seemed like outdated methods to communicate.

"Uzabud, I think you will like what I am going to tell you," Hozark said. "Though its ramifications we do not yet fully know."

"What do you mean? What did your Ghalian buddies have to say?" Laskar asked.

"The name our last target revealed to us did not exist. No one had ever heard of them."

Bud rolled his eyes. "And this is supposed to make me feel better, how, exactly?"

"Because our spies are very, very good at what they do, Bud. As are our Ghalian brothers and sisters and allies who are secretly embedded in a great many of the Council's strongholds."

"You have spies in Council facilities?" Laskar asked, surprise on his face. "Well why didn't you say so earlier? We could have used them."

"Because they are in deep cover. Some for years. Those are not resources we call upon lightly, lest we burn their identities over a trivial matter."

"But this isn't trivial."

"No, it is not. And Corann reached out to them on our behalf."

"And?"

"And our people have found out the *true* identity of the man who contracted our last target. And with that bit of knowledge, we are, in fact, heading into a far more dangerous situation than any of our prior leads have taken us to."

"What am I flying us into?" Bud asked. "I just cast for the coordinates you gave me, but you didn't say anything about––"

"It is okay, Uzabud. Our arrival will not be the dangerous aspect of this mission."

"So, tracking down this scumbag is," Laskar said. "Great. Who are we going after this time?"

"A man by the name of Drazzix."

"*Emmik* Drazzix?"

"You know of him?"

"Of course I know the guy. Drazzix the Terrible? Drazzix the Stone Fist? Drazzix the Crusher of––"

"We get the point, Laskar," Bud said.

"What I'm saying is, the guy's a high-ranking lieutenant in the Council, and one hell of a target."

"Your assessment is accurate," Hozark noted. "And he is a rather potent emmik possessing some degree of power. Not visla level, of course, but significant nonetheless."

"Obviously more than a lackey, then," Demelza mused. "This is good. If any were to have actual useful information this one would."

"Uh, hello? You're forgetting the whole Council enforcer thing, aren't you?"

"Dear Laskar, we have dealt with Council issues in the past, and this will be no different," she replied. "Just wait until we reach his system and land. All will work out for the best. You shall see."

. . .

Uzabud had drawn no attention to their ship when they arrived in the Council-controlled system, flying in the calmest, unnoteworthy and relaxed manner possible. He was just another ship landing on just another world.

A world overseen by an emmik who had killed dozens of his pirate brethren and hung their preserved bodies out along the ramparts of his stronghold as a warning to any others who might come to his world looking for an easy score.

Not just his city, but also his planet was protected, and there would be no repeat warnings.

They set the ship down in a landing field in an industrial section of the city. It would take a little longer to arrive at the walls of the emmik's abode, but that would give them a bit of time to get a feel for the city and ask questions of the locals as they drew closer.

It was a surprisingly bright place, the sun's yellow rays casting a warm light that lasted nearly through the night. It was a fluke of the world's poles that had it canted at such a degree as to only let the sun set for a mere few hours every night.

It was a trait of this world that made agriculture a booming business. It also meant a stealthy approach to the moat-protected grounds of Emmik Drazzix would be nigh impossible.

Between the guards patrolling the grounds, the vast, watery gap separating his estate and the rest of the city, and the pair of Zomoki standing guard at the front gates just across the lone long bridge, entering this place would be no easy task.

"You were saying?" Laskar said to Demelza, a victorious look plastered to his face when they had completed their circuit of the city and arrived at a discreet alleyway looking out onto the moat. "Not a problem, right? It'll all work out for the best, right?"

Demelza merely shrugged. "I appear to have been mistaken. This emmik is far better protected than those of his rank should be."

"Yes, it is more than a little disconcerting," Hozark noted. "And also quite intriguing, wouldn't you agree?"

"Oh, indeed."

"And there are additional wards along the cliffs above the moat––do you see them?"

"I did note them when we first arrived, yes. As well as the irregular shifting of the guards at the bridge and gate. And the Zomoki appear to be a particularly nasty pair," she added, just as one of the great winged beasts belched out a stream of magical flame, charring the ground beside the bridge.

By the look of the blackened terrain, it was a regular habit of this particular creature. Possibly out of boredom, but more likely because the magical control collar around its neck urged it to periodically let out a fiery blast to give any would-be intruders second thoughts.

"We must complete a full loop of the compound. Demelza and I will circumscribe the moat in opposite directions," Hozark said. "We will then meet back here to go over what we have managed to learn."

"And us? What about us? Do we just sit around and do nothing?" Bud asked.

"No, Bud. You and Laskar will buy a few simple items in town, posing as travelers new to the world. Purchase foodstuffs and strike up a conversation with the shopkeepers and casually mention the stronghold and the man within. Perhaps you will get lucky and glean a bit of useful information for your troubles."

"So, you go do deadly spy stuff, and we go food shopping?"

"More or less," his Wampeh friend replied with a toothy grin.

"You're a dick, Hozark. I ever tell you that?"

"On a regular basis," the assassin chuckled. "Now, you'd best get to it. Demelza and I will take our time in our survey, but even, so it should not take terribly long, and I would very much like some sustenance waiting when we return."

Bud let out a frustrated groan. "Such. A. Dick."

"You keep saying. We will see you shortly," Hozark replied, then the group split up and went about their tasks, as stealthily as they could in this dangerous city.

CHAPTER FIFTY-TWO

"They're really big," Bud said.

"We saw, Bud," Hozark replied.

"*Really* big. And they eat people. A *lot* of people."

"Yes, we heard."

"And there's only one bridge to the compound."

Hozark sighed and took another bite of the local pastry the duo had procured from a nearby vendor. "Bud, are you going to keep reciting things Demelza and I noted on our survey, or do you have any relevant *new* information for us?"

"He's just reiterating the key point here," Laskar chimed in. "Namely, that there's pretty much no way in through those gates if they don't want you to pass. And this won't be like that time you snuck past those Zomoki in stolen Tslavar cloaks."

"We are well aware," Demelza said. "There is quite simply too much power in use here to hope a mere scent distraction with a familiar guard's cloak would gain us ingress."

"And some Zomoki are said to be able to see right through shimmer cloaks," Laskar added.

"That is just a tale," Hozark replied. "But undoubtedly one based on bits of reality. They do possess an excellent sense of smell, and that, combined with sharp hearing and even sharper eyes, means that nearly any shimmer would be inefficient if we were forced to utilize it so close to one of them."

"Two, Hozark. There are *two* of them."

"Yes, Bud, we know."

"Two Zomoki. On either side of the gate."

"We are aware."

"There's no way you can get past them."

"I wouldn't say *no* way. But given our time constraints, Demelza and I shall utilize an alternative means of entry."

"Alternative? There's only one way in. And what about me and Laskar? How are we supposed to get in without winding up Zomoki food?"

"You are not."

"Excuse me?"

"No, Bud. You are not going to be eaten. Nor are you going to go anywhere near those Zomoki. You and Laskar will standby with the ship, keeping it ready for a quick escape, if need be."

For once, Bud was not going to argue being left behind as the getaway driver. Hozark had taken him on plenty of dangerous contracts in the past, and they'd always managed to survive.

More often than not without coming *too* close to meeting a horrible demise. Given the odds they were up against this time, leaving the Wampeh to do his thing seemed like as good a job as any to the former pirate.

"What are you planning to do?" Laskar asked. "Come in from overhead? Drop into the walls from above?"

Hozark smiled his enigmatic grin. "Let Demelza and I worry about that. You just keep an eye on one another and be ready. If things go sour, they will do so with great speed."

"Then let's hope they don't."

"Agreed."

Hozark and Demelza rose and walked off down the alleyway

to prepare for whatever crazy plan they had in mind, leaving their friends to watch and wonder.

"You two be safe," Bud said to their backs.

A moment later they were gone.

The moat surrounding the fortified estate was an enormous affair. Not some little swampy pool of stagnant water like might be found on some backwater estate, but rather, a massive, deep trough, swirling with the fresh waters channeled in from the nearby river.

It was over a hundred meters across at its widest point, and not much less at its narrowest, making any sort of improvised crossing device useless. And should a boat or hovering conveyance make an attempt to reach the other side, they would be struck down with immediacy and accuracy from the team of guards, both magical and not, stationed within the external walls.

And if for some reason one was foolish enough to try to swim across, hoping their smaller shape would go unnoticed, the deadly Nazgari living in the waters would rise up from below, snatching the hapless victim like they were merely a floating snack.

The Nazgari were rarely seen from the surface, though. They were bottom-dwellers, content to feed on whatever happened to settle down in their chosen domain. More often than not, that would be the bodies that had floated out of the dungeons via the wastewater system.

But with the illumination above silhouetting anything on the surface, they would also instinctively swim upward at great speed to take down living prey, whatever that creature might be.

And it was into that water that Hozark intended to descend.

"Are you certain about this?" Demelza asked as Hozark tightened the strap holding his vespus blade firmly to his back.

The weapon was still charged with a substantial amount of magic, and should things get truly out of hand, Hozark had decided it would be preferable to have it within reach than tucked away on their ship. If he needed the weapon, then it was a life-or-death situation anyway, and notice of its use would be the least of their concerns.

"I am certain," Hozark replied as the two sat casually at the water's edge, waiting for the tiny window of darkness to make their attempt.

It was going to be a first for Demelza. An underwater infiltration, and with another Ghalian, no less. She'd heard of the arcane magic used to provide one with a safe corridor through the water, but none could cast for long enough to sustain it for any significant time.

Normally, a second or even third caster might attempt to overlap their spells, creating a linked tunnel of force holding the waters at bay. But even that was a rather specialized bit of magic. One she did not know.

At her request, Hozark had attempted to teach her the very old and very difficult spell he would utilize to provide them air and safe passage, but Demelza was simply unable to manage the arcane magic.

"Do not doubt your talents," Hozark said after her tenth failed attempt. "Only Samara and I had any aptitude for them back in our youth. We were always eager to master difficult spells. The rare ones. The arcane power few knew how to control. Master Garrusch shared our love of this sort of magic, and he taught us a great many unusual spells before his demise."

"Including this one."

"Yes. Including this one. And with it, we will possess a self-contained bubble of protective air, allowing our ingress through the stronghold's outflow system."

"Are you certain it will sustain for the two of us?"

"Without problem. If it were just me alone, I would use a different spell. One that allows for rapid movement through water—a very helpful tool, as I was recently reminded. But it only contains the caster, whereas this spell can expand to encompass a larger space. Namely, that in which we both reside."

"And the Nazgari?"

Hozark's confidence only wavered an instant. "We will be on the bottom, and will possess no scent of food. I believe we should be fine. It is only on the surface that we would present a tempting target for them."

Demelza was not entirely thrilled with that lackluster reply, but this was Hozark she was dealing with, and if she was going to die in the belly of an underwater beast, at least it would be at the side of one of the greatest Ghalian masters of her lifetime.

"Very well, then. I am ready."

"As soon as the sun sets, we will descend," he replied.

It was a long, boring wait, but eventually, the sun dipped below the horizon, providing not total darkness, but a dim enough ambient light to allow them to slip down the ten meters to the water's edge unnoticed.

"Prepare yourself," Hozark said, then began casting the spell around both of them.

A few moments later, he took her hand and stepped free of the safety of land and into the deep, dark waters. It hadn't looked like there was anything around them on the surface, but as soon as they were submerged, the protective spell became quickly apparent.

Namely, when they didn't drown.

They sank to the bottom rapidly, remaining close to the moat wall as they did. The only really dangerous moment was at the very beginning. They were against the side, and the light should not show a silhouette, but sometimes life laughs at your plans, and in this case, a Nazgari's jaws would be the ones delivering it.

"Are you good?" Hozark asked as their boots touched the muddy bottom but remained within their protective bubble.

"I am."

"Then we continue."

The two walked quickly across the bottom of the moat, passing the occasional bone or partly eaten corpse as they did. It seemed not all of the emmik's cast-offs became Nazgari food.

A blur flashed by them in the dark water. Hozark motioned for Demelza to freeze. The assassin did as she was bid instantly, not moving a muscle as the man in front of her drew his vespus blade within their little bubble of magic.

The blue blade was glowing faintly, but not crackling with power as it was wont to in battle. But it was ready. Not for a fight with the emmik, but to defend them from the creatures in the deep.

A massive mouth full of razor-sharp teeth lunged at them from the side, the spell bubble stopping it, at least for a moment. Hozark thrust the blade through the magical membrane slowly, sweat beading on his forehead from the concentration.

He had shifted his magical source for the spell from just his konus to his vespus blade as well. And as the blade was now part of what was powering the spell, it was able to pass through it without disrupting the casting.

The point sank into the Nazgari's gaping maw, drawing blood, but not causing terrible harm. The creature jerked back in shock and quickly swam away. It was an instinctive reaction, not a rational one.

It had always been the biggest, baddest thing in its own little fishbowl, but suddenly, there was something else there with it, and it had a far more painful bite.

"Come, we must hurry," Hozark said, pushing ahead but keeping the blade in hand.

It only took a few minutes to reach the other side, but locating the opening of the wastewater system's opening required a bit more searching.

"There!" Demelza pointed out, spying the dark hole in the likewise dark rock wall.

"Good eyes," Hozark complimented her.

There was a grate in place, but not so narrow as to prevent their entry. The opening was too small, however, for a Nazgari to pass, and they proved a far better deterrent than any blocking spells could ever be.

The pair quickly made their way through the winding network of tunnels, following the stronger flow of water and waste until they emerged in a small dungeon lagoon.

This was where those bodies had come from. The lowest point in the grounds. And the least frequented.

They climbed ashore carefully, scanning the area to ensure they were alone. Only when they were certain, did Hozark finally drop the spell.

The stink of the air around them hit like a damp fist. It was a familiar stench. The smell of death. Emmik Drazzix had apparently killed far more than anyone realized within these walls. But once they had the answers they sought, he would do so no more.

CHAPTER FIFTY-THREE

Moving their way up through the lower levels of the dungeons, Hozark and Demelza noted they were locked with only the most perfunctory of spells. A somewhat more robust warding system would have been expected, but it seemed the emmik was a bit overconfident in his security team.

That and the people in his dungeons would typically not be in any sort of condition to effect an escape.

There were, however, a few signs of a moderately recent scuffle, though those would be invisible to the average person's eyes. For Ghalian assassins, however, the marks were telltale. Some violence had occurred here, and recently. More likely than not, a poor soul struggling for their life as the emmik's guards hauled them off to their demise.

Climbing higher, they exited the dungeon levels into the most basic of storage and servants' areas. Again, sparsely populated and infrequently traveled, and those who were in the area were easy enough to avoid, even without their shimmer cloaks.

"Do you smell that?" Hozark asked.

"An Akarian," Demelza replied.

"I agree with the assessment. Are you up to date with your animal fighting spell practice?"

"Not as much as I would like to be. These are somewhat specialized predators, after all. But I believe myself more than adequately prepared."

"Then we move quickly and without pause. Stun them if you can. Slay them if you must. We wish to preserve the appearance of a quiet house if at all possible."

Demelza nodded and followed as Master Hozark led the way.

The beasts they caught wind of were Akarian death hounds, though they weren't actually hounds, and they tended to wound and maim more than kill. But the name had more of a ring to it than Akarian injury critters, and so it had stuck.

Whatever they were, the animals were fast and bitey, and more than capable of crippling a fleeing attacker caught in their sights. It was what made them great guard animals. A violent play instinct that just so happened to lead to intruders being partially shredded but left alive for questioning, more often than not. They were unusual, though, and neither Hozark nor Demelza had run across one in ages.

It was looking like that out-of-practice magic was going to be put to the test, and soon.

The pair raced down the narrow hall, the musk of the animals growing stronger by the second.

"Now!" Hozark hissed as they passed the threshold from the hallway into a large gathering chamber.

The Akarian were at rest, not wound up and expecting company, and thus, the stunning spells directed at them flew true. But these were an unusual type of animal, and normal magic would not do. All a regular spell would accomplish was to irritate them. And an irritated Akarian was a dangerous one.

More than usual, that is.

"Two down, two still standing," Demelza noted.

Apparently, an additional pair had been in the room. Four was just such an uncommon number of them to find in one place. Someone must have really been worried about stealthy intruders.

But the animals seemed a bit slow off the mark, and the follow-up spells hit them full force, driving them to slumber along with their friends.

"That was close."

"Yet too easy," Hozark said, wondering if someone had perhaps drugged the beasts. "Be alert."

Demelza nodded once and took off at a run, following Hozark as he raced through the next chambers. A few guards were napping, so they slowed their pace and quietly maneuvered around them. No sense in having an alarm raised if it didn't need to be.

Two rooms later, however, they came across a patrol. Four guards, Tslavars, all of them, rounded the corner and stepped into the chamber just as they entered from the other side. There was nothing to do for it but engage, and quickly at that.

Demelza cast her silencing spells, muting the sounds of fighting as best she could given such short notice, while Hozark tore into the mercenary guards, his vespus blade a streak of blue, laying waste to the poor men before they could even cry out.

"A bit much," Demelza noted, looking at the dismembered guards.

"Yet effectively silenced," Hozark replied, wiping the blade clean and resheathing it. "We must dispose of the bodies, quickly."

He cast a cautery spell, sealing their oozing wounds, keeping the remaining blood on the inside rather than the outside, then heaved them up and placed the dead men's remains in a pair of large footlockers against the far wall.

They appeared to be decorative only, as there was nothing

stored inside of them. At least, nothing until they'd been filled with bits of dead people, though Hozark doubted that was the owner's original intent.

"We are close," he said as they came upon a more ornate series of doors and gaudier decorated rooms.

Silently, the two assassins slipped into Emmik Drazzix's private chambers, both of them holding multiple powerful disabling spells on the tips of their tongues, ready to drop the man if they could before he could cast against them.

It would be a tough fight, but they hoped that, together, they could take him down. Then they could question him, and hopefully, finally, find out what was really going on. Who had actually set the contract in motion.

The man was there, as expected, but something seemed wrong. He was slumped over at his desk. And he did not appear to be moving.

Hozark moved to his side and carefully tipped his head back. What he saw shocked even him.

Emmik Drazzix had been drained.

"How––?" Demelza blurted in confusion.

"A Ghalian did this," Hozark replied. "And recently. That explains the hounds."

He leaned in and studied the wound. Had the man been allowed to live, it would have been healed, leaving no trace, his mind wiped of the event, leaving him to wake groggy and confused, and a little weak. But unaware he'd been drained.

But this man had been drained dry. Someone had taken all of his power in the process. And only one race possessed that ability.

"It is appearing more and more as though Samara in fact lives," Hozark reluctantly admitted.

"And by the look of things, she is cleaning up loose ends," Demelza added. "But at whose behest? She is obviously not working alone. She has no motive."

A parchment on the desk caught Hozark's eye. Carefully, he pulled it from beneath the others and studied it with great scrutiny.

"What is it?"

"A sloppy bit of work, for one," he said. "The emmik's personal papers were rifled through but left in a mess. As if someone, perhaps, interrupted the intruder. And this is the clue we've been looking for," he said, holding the paper's heavy seal for Demelza to see.

There was no name signing the order to hire the next person down the line for the contract, as with the other unwitting participants. But this was different. This had a seal marking the page. And not just any seal. A Council of Twenty seal. And a most specialized one at that.

"Is that a validity seal?" Demelza asked. "I've never actually seen one in person."

"It is," he replied. "And this tells us at least part of what we need to know. The chain ends here. Emmik Drazzix was the first man hired. And he was hired by an actual member of the Council of Twenty."

"But we do not know whom."

"That we do not," Hozark replied, studying the paper and its seal.

The validity seal was a clever tool of the Council members. A specialized mark only the Twenty possessed. One that lay the full force of the Council behind whatever document carried it, but while keeping the drafter of the message anonymous. A trick employed by the ever-scheming Council members.

"Could it be a forgery?"

Hozark studied it a moment longer. "No. And what's more, the power to set this seal is strong. There are only traces, and incredibly obscured, but it's clear a visla sent this."

"So, we've narrowed it down but are no closer to the truth."

"I simply do not know," Hozark replied. "But the emmik is

dead, and I fear this may be a trap. We must depart immediately."

Having said it aloud, the universe must have heard his concerns, for moments later the compound alarm sounded. The two assassins looked at one another and drew their weapons. Hozark's vespus blade glowed an intimidating blue.

"Well, that is unfortunate," he said, steeling himself for a fight. "Seal the room tight when we exit. It seems we might have to be leaving in a far greater hurry than planned."

CHAPTER FIFTY-FOUR

Guards, staff, and a few high-powered visitors all raced about the compound in varying degrees of aggressive readiness or startled panic. The Tslavar mercenaries geared up in their kit as quickly as they were able, ready and eager for a fight.

The staff, however, knew better. They'd survived more than one altercation between the emmik, his friends, and someone with a bone to pick. It was far safer and far less likely to get them killed if they just tucked themselves into the farthest and quietest corners of the estate.

As for the visitors, many were significant power users themselves, but aside from their own personal retinue of guards, they were relatively at risk. And for all they knew, this could just be a clever plot to draw them out and remove them from competition by the emmik himself.

Treachery was not the order of every day, but many of them had done similar things in the past to claw their way up the ranks, and they wouldn't put it past the man. It was a funny little bit of nature, that. Those who had back-stabbed others tended to expect the same treatment to be applied to them at some point. It led to a rather paranoid existence.

The alarm seemed to have set the animals off as well. The Zomoki at the gates were bellowing with agitation, their collars glowing bright as they were urged to spray their magical flames. This made escape for those lacking smaller ships within the stronghold's walls near impossible.

Several were well enough acquainted to acquire rides on one another's craft, though some had to leave behind a few of their staff in the rush due to limited space aboard. When whatever was happening was over, they would send their own ship to return to collect them.

The unspoken part of that message were the words, "If you survive."

A great sloshing rumble rose from the deep stairwells to the dungeons, and a clattering of claws on stone and gnashing of powerful jaws could be heard echoing off the walls.

"It would seem the emmik's defensive spells included opening the bars blocking the effluence tunnels wide, allowing the Nazgari to enter the lower levels and dine on whoever might be so unfortunate as to be present," Hozark said. "I believe our initial means of egress has been removed."

"So, we fight, then."

"Yes. We fight. But in the chaos, perhaps we will be able to avoid much of the conflict if we adopt a generic Tslavar appearance. This seems too sudden to be a specific reaction to the emmik's demise. Something else caused this alarm."

The two assassins had not had any time to stalk and replace any of the actual mercenary guards on staff, but each had a few go-to faces they could don in times of crisis, when they needed a quick bit of cover. This was most certainly one such time.

Hozark and Demelza then followed the noise of rushing footsteps and joined the panicked staff as they raced for a safe bolthole.

"You there! Stop!" a small squad of Tslavar guards said when

Hozark and Demelza hurried past with the staff. "We are regrouping at the inner courtyard. You're going the wrong way."

"We are ensuring the emmik's people get the hell out of our way before heading over there," Hozark said with a disgusted snarl. "We need the place clear before we start our sweep."

The Tslavars nodded in sympathetic agreement.

"Good point. The halls will have to be empty for the sweep. We'll help. It shouldn't take long with extra bodies," the thick-necked man said, turning to his men and gesturing for them to step in and assist. "Hurry up and move, you lot!" he yelled to the panicked workers, ushering them along. "You know the drill!"

Had Hozark attempted any other excuse, he and Demelza would almost certainly have been outed as intruders on the spot and forced to fight off all of the Tslavars while caught in the middle of the rushing laborers.

It would have been a mess.

But his excuse for not immediately joining the other guards was a logical one, and it bought them a bit of leeway with the Tslavars. And tying it to what was standard operating procedure for these types of general alarm situations––namely, a full-property sweep––had not only provided them cover, but also pulled the actual Tslavar guards onto their side.

The procedure would be to ensure all staff and visitors were accounted for, then move through the property room by room, hallway by hallway, until they had covered the entirety of the grounds. But the latter would only be once the garrison commander told them what exactly it was they were looking for.

Judging by the lack of scrutiny the Tslavars were exhibiting, it was clear no one had found the emmik's body yet, so at this point it was more of a fire drill-type scenario than an all-out manhunt. But that would change soon enough. Once they discovered their employer had been slain, and by a Wampeh Ghalian, no less, none would escape scrutiny.

Hozark was just glad that the deadly Balamar waters were

incredibly rare. At least he and Demelza would not have to face that sort of a threat, as he had so recently. So they blended in with the others. But they were disguised as generic Tslavars, and once they started examining identities closely, they would be discovered.

The whole process of ushering the staff took only a few minutes, after which the two assassins found themselves marching along with the real Tslavar guards to the inner courtyard. Over a hundred had gathered, many only partially geared up, having rushed to their positions from wherever they'd been enjoying their off time.

The disguised assassins fell in line with the others and stood silently. At the moment, they were relatively safe. But if––no, *when*––they found the emmik's cold body, that would change in an instant.

"Listen up!" the heavily armed captain of the guard shouted out, silencing the murmuring men. "The general alarm has been sounded, and you all know what that means. Possible intruders in the estate. Now, I know there was a false alarm just the other day, but we're still doing this by the book. Start at the assigned positions and move through the grounds. Don't lose contact with your group. And don't get sloppy. Emmik Drazzix will personally punish any who are found slacking off. Is that clear?"

A chorus of 'yes, sir' rang out.

"Then get to it."

The guards quickly split off into groups, spreading out to begin the search.

"They do not know," Demelza quietly said.

"It appears not. But we do not have much time until they do."

"Over a hundred, by my count. And keeping in contact. We cannot simply wander off and make our escape without being seen."

"No, we cannot," he agreed. "An admittedly surprisingly

sound system for the likes of Tslavars to employ, I must admit. Whoever put it in place must have dealt with the order in the past."

"It seems that way. So long as they maintain visual contact among the group, it will be near impossible to remove and replace any of them."

"So, we join them for now. Even in our less-than-perfect disguises."

"Risky," Demelza said.

"Unfortunately, yes. But this may work to our advantage," Hozark said, a plan rapidly forming in his mind. "If we embed ourselves with the group moving in that direction"––he nodded to the far walls––"we will be working our way toward the bridge, eventually. Their check will include ensuring it is secured."

"So, we will cross it surrounded by a large group of actual guards performing their search. It will be enough to get us past the Zomoki. Clever," Demelza said.

"It should work, if all goes well."

"And if they discover the emmik before that?"

Hozark paused in thought. "*Then* things will get *much* more interesting."

CHAPTER FIFTY-FIVE

The disguised Wampeh were making good time moving through the inner sections of Emmik Drazzix's grounds. The group of Tslavar guards they had joined were a fairly professional bunch, which was saying a lot for the normally thick-skulled and quick-to-fight mercenaries.

But these had been well trained, and as a result, their survey of the chambers, storage facilities, and winding corridors located in their assigned area had been moving smoothly. That there were two new faces among them only raised eyebrows for a moment when they began the sweep.

"We were tasked with cleaning out the dungeons," Hozark had told them. "Mizzah an' me, we'd just finished dumping the last of the bodies into the runoff and were making our way upstairs when the alarm sounded. They grabbed us and said to go with you lot, so 'ere we are."

"Yeah, it were a real mess down there," Demelza added. "But we got it sorted. Bloody tough work, that is. Hey, can I get a swig o' that?"

The man they'd been speaking with pulled his flask from his hip and passed it over. Demelza took a draught, then handed it to Hozark, who did the same, then passed it back with a happy grin.

"Thanks, Brother. It's a thirsty bit o' work, that's for sure."

"You've got that right," the Tslavar replied. "I was helping watch the kitchen staff bring in an order of supplies when this all went down. Was going to get me a nice snack out of it, too. But what can we do, right?"

Hozark and Demelza laughed in agreement with the man.

"Is that new one still there?" Hozark asked. "You know, the young one who's plump in all the right places? What was her name again?"

The Tslavar's grin turned into a full-fledged smile. "Oh, you mean Elzah."

"Yeah, that's the one. Is she still working the kitchens, then?"

"Oh, she is. But I've got dibs on that one if anyone does."

Hozark laughed. "Okay, okay. But there's no harm in a man looking, now, is there?"

"Ha. None at all. And there's a lot to look at."

"Ain't that the truth. What did you say your name was? I'm Faloon."

"Torvak," the man replied, shaking his hand with a strong grip. "Good to know ya, Faloon."

It was a wild guess he had made. They'd only been in the emmik's grounds a few hours and had not had a moment to do any recon of the staff, but it was a common scenario that played out across all of the many estates and compounds they'd infiltrated over the years.

There was *always* some sort of romance going on between the staff and guards, and more often than not, it involved the kitchen and housekeeping workers. It was just one of those things that had proven out regardless of world or system. And that common bond of lustful male lechery had just further endeared Hozark to their new friend.

"Well, come on, then," the Tslavar said. "We've got a lot of boring work to do before we can get back to our real jobs."

"And hopefully Elzah, right?" Hozark added with a conspiratorial elbow and wink.

They both laughed and shared a knowing look.

"Come on, you two," Demelza said. "We've already cleared most of this part of the building. We'd better hurry up and finish up in here so we can check the bridge and then get back to it."

The two men grunted their agreement and continued on their way.

And that was all it took for Hozark and Demelza to pass that initial bit of scrutiny. The flimsiest of cover stories, and a pathetically transparent bit of superficial bonding. But as the grounds were simply being swept for intruders, there was no real sense of urgency or pending threat to the affair, so it worked.

The guards were at ease, doing this by rote. Another false alarm, no doubt. If something serious had been going down, surely they'd all know about it by now.

So they walked, and they searched, and then they searched some more, always edging closer to the front gates. And from there, it would be a survey of the lone bridge as their last step before declaring this portion of the estate secure.

Hozark and Demelza would stay close to the others, the stench of the large group of them masking the two Wampeh as they made their escape. And by the time the others noticed the two new additions to their numbers had disappeared, the intruders would be long gone.

Or so they had hoped. Oh, if only it could be so easy.

A shrill blast filled the air, and everyone's skrees alerted at once. The guards pulled the devices from their hips and listened to the group broadcast, and Hozark mimicked the action, bringing his skree close to his face as well.

He and Demelza were not tied into the staff's

communications, but they could hear the announcement easily all the same. The emmik had been slain, and from the look of it, a Wampeh Ghalian was to blame.

Suddenly, this had become much more serious.

The guards all looked around, on edge and ready for a fight from a potentially invisible enemy. Eyes turned to Hozark and Demelza.

"Who are you two, again?" the nearest guard asked, a blade ready in his hand.

"She's Mizzah. An' I'm Faloon. Torvak knows us," he said, nodding to the man with whom they'd just shared a drink.

"Well, we did only just meet," he replied, unsure.

"Oh, are you fucking serious? You think me an' her are Wampeh? Think about it, there are two of us, an' everyone knows they only work alone."

The others hesitated, unsure what to do next. It was true, everyone knew Wampeh Ghalians' reputations for always striking alone. And these two had been with them from the start of the search as well.

Slowly, the on-edge Tslavars lowered their guard. Not entirely, but just enough to remove the threat of imminent violence against what were very likely their own people.

"You've got a good point," the leader said. "But you're new to our group, so we'll need to confirm your identities all the same. I'm sure you understand."

"Of course. I'd be surprised if you didn't," Demelza replied. "But be quick about it. There's an assassin loose in the grounds, and we've got to stop their escape."

"Shit, she's right," Torvak said. "If the Wampeh makes it past the Zomoki, then it's a clear shot across the bridge."

Demelza's suggestive little seed about the bridge had just sprouted. All it needed now was a little water to make it grow. Water that would be provided not by she or her accomplice, however.

"How can anyone get past the Zomoki?" one of the guards asked. "Those things are terrifying."

"Who knows? You know how tricky they are," another replied. "Come on, let's—"

He had only taken one more step when a brutal spell lashed out and removed his head from his body. Apparently, it had been set within the walls, a booby trap for those heading toward the gates.

"Itzall!" the leader shouted. "Dammit, come on! They had to go this way!"

"This leads right to the bridge!"

"Alert the others!" he said, then took off down the hall, casting his strongest defensive spells as he moved.

The others followed in his tracks, unsure whether he was brave or foolish or both. But with all of their defenses overlapping as they moved, only the strongest of trap spells would be able to harm them, and the one that had taken down their comrade was a rather simple one with not much power behind it. He'd just been caught with his figurative pants down.

"Do you feel that?" Demelza asked as they ran with the others, more trap spells bouncing off their shields.

"Yes," Hozark replied. "This is Ghalian magic, but it is incredibly weak."

"Barely enough to harm anyone but those who are caught totally unaware," Demelza agreed. "But it was certainly enough to get their attention, it seems."

Another series of spells were triggered when they reached the mighty doors leading out to the front entryway. There, the Zomoki would be scorching the ground between the gates and the bridge as their control collars shocked them into action.

"Stop with the damn Zomoki!" the leader shouted into his skree. "We're in pursuit of the assassin, they've set booby traps and are making for the bridge. Tone down the spells making them spit fire and have them focus on sniffing out Wampeh. And send the others to meet us out front."

He then charged ahead, his team of Tslavar guards close behind.

"This changes things," Hozark said as they stepped out onto the spacious entryway.

The Zomoki were dead ahead, one on either side, but they were facing the bridge in front of them, sniffing the air, their collars glowing bright. Whoever had shifted the spells, the deadly animals were now intent on smelling anything non-Tslavar. Even in the middle of a pack of them, the two Wampeh would be detected.

Hozark glanced at Demelza as they ran with the others, growing ever closer to the looming mass of the great beasts. They slowed their pace a little, allowing others to overtake them until they were at the back of the group. But more would be following shortly.

Hozark abruptly turned, and the two ran to the left, hugging the wall of the stronghold as he and Demelza raced toward the narrow path between it and the cliffs leading to the moat below.

The nearest Zomoki spun its head, but it did not spew flames. Its collar spell had been changed to prevent it from roasting their own men, and a shock ran through its neck the moment it even tried. The others took note, however.

"Hey, where are you going?" Torvak called after them, a confused look on his face. "We're going this way!"

A moment later, the group's leader was racing toward him, the others close behind in his pursuit.

"They're *both* assassins, you idiot!" their leader growled as he sped past. "Hurry! There's no way off that trail. Have the others go the opposite direction. We'll box them in."

It was a foot race, and though the assassins had a head start, they had been seen. More importantly, they had nowhere to run to. And with the full force of Emmik Drazzix's guards now closing in from both directions, there was simply no way they would escape. Not even two of them could handle that many men.

Then, as he watched with confusion, the two fleeing intruders abruptly turned at a sharp angle, racing not along the path or toward the stronghold's wall, but to the cliff's edge.

"They're not stopping. What are they thinking?" the man wondered as he watched them, dumbfounded.

None who landed on the water's surface had ever survived more than a few moments. The Nazgari were keen hunters, and the splash and commotion of that first impact always drew them in like hunters to their prey within seconds. To jump was suicide.

And yet, side by side, the fleeing duo did just that, launching themselves from the safety of land into the open air. They fell out of sight, plummeting toward the water below.

But there was no splash.

The guards raced to the edge, magic ready for anything. Anything but the large ship that quickly rose in front of them and flew off in a flash, two escaping killers already dropping through a hatch to the safety of the vessel's interior.

"Send our ships after them!" the guard yelled, but it was already too late.

Bud banked hard, then climbed steeply toward the relative safety of space. And as soon as they were kissing the atmosphere's edge, they jumped, the ship vanishing in a magical flash.

"Where are we off to?" Hozark asked as he and Demelza shed their disguises while entering the command chamber.

"We're headed for a backup location. Laskar jumped on it and plotted it out as soon as you skreed for that emergency pickup when the alarm sounded."

Hozark nodded his thanks to the copilot. "Well done, Laskar. You have my thanks."

The ship dropped out of the jump in a distant system. One where no one was looking for them or trying to kill them. At least, not at the moment. The way things had been going, that could change at any time, it seemed.

Hozark relayed what had happened to the others, who listened with rapt attention.

"A Wampeh Ghalian did it? You're sure?" Bud asked.

"It would seem that way," Hozark replied.

"And Drazzix was hired by the Council?"

"A member of it, yes."

They all sat silently a long moment before the pilot spoke again.

"So, what in the worlds do we do now?"

"Now?" Hozark said. "Now we inform Corann."

CHAPTER FIFTY-SIX

The flight back to regroup with the leader of the Five was diverted unexpectedly. Hozark had directed Uzabud to stop at a seemingly innocuous little world along the way. A world that just happened to also be a hub for Ghalian communications.

But so far as Bud and Laskar knew, they had merely stopped for a short respite and to pick up some fresh provisions. It wasn't that he didn't trust his crewmates, it was that this was simply one of those things Ghalian *never* spoke of. It was part of what kept them alive this long. A secret network in plain sight in systems all across the galaxy.

And only full-fledged Ghalian knew where they were.

With the concern that a Ghalian was potentially working off-contract, cleaning the trail for the Council of Twenty, now a very real threat, word had to be passed along, and an entirely new set of passcodes enacted while the Five decided how best to deal with this situation.

Their communications were secure, as they were locked within the minds of those carrying them, though occasionally on parchment as well, the words typically self-destructing with a magical flash upon reading. Whatever was going on, those working for the order had to be kept safe.

But as he handed off the message to be forwarded to the network at large, something unexpected happened.

"A message waiting for me?"

"Yes, Master Hozark."

"But none knew I would be coming to this world."

"That is correct, Master Hozark. For this reason, the same message has been transmitted across the systems awaiting you at whichever world you should arrive at next. And now that it has been relayed, I shall inform the others, and the message will be purged from the collective."

It was most unexpected. And it was also disconcerting. For Corann to have gone to these lengths, something quite serious must be afoot. And in light of what they had just learned, he could only wonder what that might be.

"Wait, we're going where, now?" their pilot asked.

"You heard correct. We are changing our destination to Etratz."

"But that's nowhere near where we were planning on—"

"I am aware, Bud. But this is where we are going now. Laskar, will you please plot the new jump for us?"

"You got it, Boss," the copilot said, confused but not about to step into the middle of that conversation.

"It's not normal, man. Up and changing things so abruptly when we've got such pressing information," Bud said.

"I am aware. And I appreciate your concern. Truly, I do. But this is a directive from Corann herself."

Laskar paused from his task. "How did you even hear from her, anyway? I mean, it's not like you skreed her. At least, not that I've seen."

"It was a fluke," Hozark lied. "I happened to spot a fellow Ghalian when we were resupplying, and they relayed that she had departed her residence and was now on Etratz. Had we flown to her on Inskip, we would have received the same message, only several days later. So, you see, this good fortune saves us many extraneous days of travel."

"You spotted another Ghalian here? The most secretive, elusive order of assassins in the galaxy, and you just happened upon one of your buddies?" Laskar asked.

"It is not quite so wildly unlikely as that. You see, we have certain systems in which we often resupply. Nothing terribly exciting, but the odds of encountering one of the order drastically increase given that fact. Still, you are correct, it is a rather rare occurrence. Fortune, it seems, was smiling upon us today."

Whether or not Laskar bought the story was unclear, but Hozark didn't much care at this moment. What he did care about was that they needed to get to Corann as quickly as was reasonable.

Three days' transit was how long the re-routing had taken them. And in that period, Hozark and his friends had spent a great deal of time going over what they'd learned thus far.

Someone had started a ball in motion. One that would ultimately lead to the capture of Aargun and the near-fatal wounding of a master Ghalian in the process. It was something a great deal of care and planning had gone into. But it was more than just that. Someone had fairly intimate knowledge of several aspects of Ghalian contracts. Not necessarily how they were handled from start to finish, but enough to take advantage of their unlikely intelligence.

The final group truly had no idea what they were doing besides handing off a package to someone as they'd been instructed to, or setting a trap for any who would perhaps retrace those steps.

What their prey had apparently not anticipated was the

degree of perseverance Hozark possessed. It must have put them quite on edge when they realized just how close the assassin was getting to unmasking them and discovering their true identity.

And when Emmik Drazzix was found dead, slain by Samara, most likely, the clue as to his hiring to begin the whole process had turned things quite on its head. It hadn't just been a Council-affiliated person seeking to make a name for themselves by taking out a Ghalian. It was one of the Council of Twenty themselves who had targeted the order. And *that* had greater implications.

Implications that could draw the entire order into a conflict.

But with the anonymous seal, it could be any one of them who set that plan in motion. And with all of the backstabbing and plotting within the Council, there was simply no taking action until they had something more concrete in hand.

And that was about to materialize.

"Master Corann," Demelza said as she strode into the cozy bungalow the leader of the Five was currently calling home. "It is good to see you."

"Demelza. I am pleased at your return," she replied, but her signature warmth seemed particularly forced today. Something had unsettled her, and for that to happen, it must have been significant.

"Hozark," she said as her associate joined them.

"Corann."

"The others?"

"I have instructed them to offload some supplies and then load some others," he said with a grin. "It should keep them occupied for a little while. Now, what is this all about? We have information you will find most interesting, but something tells me your news may be more pressing."

Corann cut right to the chase.

"Aargun has been located," she said, a flash of rage flickering behind her motherly gaze.

"And he is alive?" Demelza asked.

"So far as we know, though not for much longer, I fear, given where he is being held."

"Where is he, Corann?" Hozark asked.

"Actaris," she replied.

"That is not good."

"No, my friend, it is not."

Demelza was a little surprised by the two master Ghalians' demeanor. For them to react this way was unusual, to say the least. "What is Actaris?" she asked. "The name is familiar, but I don't recall why, exactly."

"A Council black site and stronghold," Hozark replied, sharing Corann's grim look. "One of the worst. It has always been something of an off-book facility. An interrogation and torture location available to Council members should they need it."

"So, it's not a normal Council operation?" Demelza mused. "Then perhaps it is only minimally staffed. We could––"

"We *will*," Corann interrupted. "It is fully staffed, and those within its walls are armed and trained. But we are going to Actaris. We are going to retrieve our brother and deal with those responsible."

The look in the woman's eye told Demelza all she needed to know about her commitment to the plan. She was an angry mama bear, and heaven help whoever it was who had harmed her cub.

"Actaris? You've got to be shitting me!" Laskar said when he learned of their destination. "It's a freakin' Council stronghold. You said so yourself––it's a fortress."

"And the Council's overconfidence in their safety will be their undoing," Corann said. And her word was final.

In this one, rare instance, even Laskar knew when to keep his mouth shut.

The beginnings of the plan were already in motion before they had arrived. Corann had called in many of their vast network of spies to facilitate their entry into the fortress. Any information, any revisions to the security protocols, would need to be gathered before they struck.

"The information will be awaiting us on Vandorag," Corann informed them as they boarded the ship to stow the last of their supplies. But they wouldn't be leaving. Not yet.

Her own shimmer ship would soon be docked alongside Hozark's on the hull, another craft ready and waiting to be deployed in this assault. But for the moment, it sat by, awaiting her.

"Okay, plotting a course to Actaris," Laskar said.

"Not just yet," the Master Ghalian replied, composing herself and turning to Master Hozark. "First I have something I must do. And Master Hozark, I need something from the Three."

"The what?" Laskar asked.

"It is a Ghalian thing," Hozark replied, not elucidating any further.

The Three were the members of the order tasked with keeping the location and access secrets of the Ghalian cache of weapons and wealth. It was a deliberately small number, and access to those items was likewise complex and required some effort.

The Three had set the wards and defenses on the hidden vault, and they had likewise hidden several sets of magical passkeys in systems across the galaxy. No one could access the vault without the right combination of them. Defenses had been layered upon it for millennia. Deadly magic only the Three could disarm.

With all of the magic piled upon the facility, even if someone were to learn its location, any serious attempt to break in would result in their demise. And if someone of a visla's power were to try to overcome the defenses, not only would their actions incinerate the contents, but they would quite possibly destroy a chunk of the planet in the process.

"I will handle it, Corann," Hozark said. "Come, let us discuss this further before we depart."

They stepped away from the others and walked to a quiet room. One with ample muting wards in place to prevent any from overhearing what was said inside.

"The Three, Corann? What do you have in mind?" Hozark asked.

"I need something special from the vaults," she replied. "I need you to fetch me a claithe."

Hozark nearly blanched at the suggestion, and for him, that was saying something. "A claithe? Are you sure?"

"I am."

"But you will need to feed, then. And a lot, at that."

"I am aware, Hozark."

"And the risk––"

"Despite the risk, it must be done. You are one of the Three. Reach the others and make this so."

"I will," he replied, more than a little reticent at the thought of unleashing such a weapon.

"And while you are there, do stock yourself up for the incursion," she added with her trademark smile. "We will not be leaving any living, I think. And now, I believe I will see to that feeding you mentioned. You will be back before I am, so when I return, be prepared to depart immediately."

With that, Corann left to drain several power users she'd kept track of for just such an emergency. Bad men and women she would drain dry without a contract taken out on them, despite Ghalian norms. Sometimes, one had to work outside the standard ways of doing things. This was one such occasion.

As for Hozark, he steeled himself for the task before him. It would be easy to contact the other members of the Three. None were in deep cover at the moment. But a *claithe*? It was a weapon so powerful and dangerous, even most vislas did not dare use one, lest they kill themselves along with everyone around them.

Corann possessed the will to control it, yes. But could she hold onto that when things got crazy and the spells and projectiles were flying? He sincerely hoped so, for if not, they would all meet a rather grisly end.

CHAPTER FIFTY-SEVEN

The Three were a known part of the Ghalian order, yet only the Five were ever privy to who actually made up the Three. Sometimes, one, or even more, of the Five were members of the Three, but, more often than not, it was other high-ranking Ghalian who made up their ranks.

Of course, in a profession such as theirs, one of their number would fall from time to time. In such instances, the Five would select a replacement, and the remaining two would individually meet with and reveal the secrets of the Three to the new member.

It was a way to ensure no one would ever be able to pillage the order's vast stores of wealth, weapons, and power. And should the location somehow become compromised, there were backup portal egresses to remove and salvage the most valuable of their items.

Portals, however, were incredibly rare, insanely hard to cast and open, and they required such massive amounts of power that none even attempted them except in times of absolute need, and even then, most failed.

The Wampeh Ghalian, however, had been acquiring power

for millennia, and though they never took Ootaki hair from the poor slaves they occasionally freed from their ill-intending owners, they did possess quite a quantity of previously shorn Ootaki hair, likewise taken in the course of their contracts.

To leave it behind would have been foolish, and to destroy it a waste of a perfectly good resource. One that they now used to power the last line emergency defenses of their secret vault, as well as a few of their training houses.

Hozark had been one of the Three since before he was made one of the Five, though the two events had happened in fairly rapid succession when a large number of Ghalian fell while completing their contracts during an enormous flare-up of violence against the Council of Twenty.

The order was not part of the conflict, but sometimes even peripheral players could fall victim to the machinations of war's brutality. It was part of the reason the Ghalian did not engage in war and never took sides.

They did, however, give preferential treatment to contracts that might negatively affect the Council of Twenty. And now they were doing so once more, it seemed. And not a lackey or peripheral player, but an actual Council member, no less.

Hozark had sent the fastest couriers on hand to get word to the other two members of his exclusive group. Their keys were needed at the stronghold vault, and he would meet them there. Fortunately, both were relatively nearby, no more than a day's travel at most.

"I will be gone for two days," Hozark informed his shipmates.

"Hang on. You guys made it seem like this was some crazy urgent thing we were doing here. Now you and Corann are both going off and leaving us here for a few days? What's up? This doesn't make any sense," Laskar said.

"Resources are needed for our task, and we are both fetching them," was the reply.

That didn't mean much to the non-Ghalian, but for Demelza, it was confirmation of something interesting. From what had been said, Hozark was one of the Three. And he was getting some of the truly big weapons for this mission.

"Do not worry, my friends. They will be back soon enough. This is but a brief delay, and one that will allow you to entertain yourselves in town a little before we engage in this task," Demelza said.

Hozark nodded to her once, well aware she knew what he was and what he was about to do. "I will return shortly," he said, then turned to Bud and Laskar, flashing an amused grin, though he was anything but amused. "Do try not to get *too* drunk while I am gone."

With that, he strode off and boarded his own craft, disengaged from Bud's mothership, and vanished into the sky.

"Well, he said not to get *too* drunk," Laskar mused. "So, I guess we'd better pace ourselves. Starting now. You coming?"

"In a minute," Bud said. "I'll meet you at the tavern. The one down the road on the left."

"See ya there," his copilot said, then trotted off to drown his unexpected boredom.

"Is everything okay?" he asked Demelza when Laskar had gone. "I know Hozark, and he wouldn't delay something this big for no good reason."

"Just be comfortable knowing his absence for this short period will eventually increase the likelihood of our success," she replied. "Now, go join your friend and relax. There will be plenty of stress soon enough."

Several systems away, Hozark was walking the back streets of a tiny town on a tiny moon that most had forgotten about long ago. It was a place of last resort. A world no one visited by choice. Where those with nowhere left to go came to drown their sorrows and draw breath from day to day while waiting for the end to claim them.

There were many places across the galaxy where the members of the Three had hidden the enchanted keys to the Ghalian vaults. No member knew all of them, and multiple keys were needed to safely access them. That meant each would be retrieving the one nearest their location and heading to the world on which their secret vault was hidden.

The system was working as planned. All of them were in separate ships to avoid a catastrophic loss, and the keys had remained undiscovered and magically hidden. And even if they were found, none would know what they were, nor what to do with them.

Most of the keys were relocated from time to time as a simple precaution, but one set had not moved for centuries. Those were the keys of last resort. But Hozark was not collecting one of those today.

He walked the slick stones of the damp streets to a run-down bath house toward the center of the grimy town. It wasn't anything like the relaxing spa-like facilities on most worlds. This was a *true* bath house, as in, many who used it were simply in need of a bath.

Some of them greatly.

The gray water runoff that flowed into the sewers attested to the level of filth many of the patrons had shed on their visit. Coin was hard to come by, and when it was acquired, the choice between cleanliness or alcohol was often an easy one. The bath typically lost.

But every month, the small group overseeing the town funded one free bath for all who needed one. It was a way to, at least slightly, quell the stench that permeated the city and reduce the likelihood of the eruption of a plague.

This was not one such day, though, and the baths were mostly empty. Hozark paid the entry fee and trudged past the little stalls toward the slightly larger one he had spent a piddling amount to use. He stepped inside and closed the flimsy door behind him.

The massive stone tub was already full of steaming water––the magic providing the hot water to the facility was perfectly functional, at least––though the dark ring around the edge said something for the place's attention to cleaning. But that was of no matter.

Hozark quietly murmured the secret spell only he and two others knew, the power pulling from the konus on his wrist. Silently, the huge carved tub lifted into the air as easily as if it were a child's balloon, rising nearly a meter before coming to a stop, resting there, the tub not spilling a drop.

Hozark grasped a thick, damp tile beneath it and pulled it free, then reached into the hole beneath, removing a small, magically sealed box. He replaced the tile, then uttered another spell, lowering the tub back to its original position.

He washed his grimy hands in the clear waters, turning them a bit muddy. Perfect to complete the impression of his having washed himself of the daily grit and muck. Then he rose, pocketed the small box, and headed out of the facility, never to come back.

Once a key had been retrieved from its hiding place, that location was finished. After he visited the vault, he would give the key to one of the other Three to be hidden anew. He'd do it himself, normally, but his task with Corann was a priority, and despite this delay, time was still of the essence.

Hozark trudged back to the outskirts of town and boarded his ship, his next stop, the secret vaults of the Wampeh Ghalian.

CHAPTER FIFTY-EIGHT

Hozark arrived at the bustling world of Omatza in good time. He had been pulling a bit harder from his Drookonus than he'd have liked to make longer jumps, but time was of the essence, and the other members of the Three would be arriving shortly, and it would not do to keep them waiting.

Omatza was clean, where the world he had just come from was dirty. Bright where it was dark. Its buildings tall and inspiring where the other's were squat and depressing.

And the wealth. Oh, this was a world of the elite and powerful. It hadn't been quite so opulent when the Ghalian overseers of the order's treasures had selected it a few hundred years prior, but it was a classy environment even then.

Every several hundred centuries the Three would relocate their vast wealth and powerful treasures to a new location, often on a resplendent world but sometimes not. Wealth led to tighter security and reduced the likelihood of war or strife bringing about an unexpected fall of the city. Its own nature provided the first line of defense, as it were.

But there could be too much of a good thing, and this particular location was gaining a bit too much traffic for their purposes these days, all three noted when they met at the appointed location. Once this current affair was completed, they would relocate again. Perhaps to a more backwater location this time.

But that would be dealt with later. For now, they had work to do.

"Marsoon," Hozark said, greeting the skinny man of roughly his same age as he joined him at the little outdoor cafe.

"Hozark," Marsoon replied with a wide grin and a warm hug.

This was *not* the Ghalian way, and it was precisely why he had done it. They were just a pair of Wampeh meeting for lunch. Nothing to see at all, for Wampeh were merely another race among the many on this world.

Nothing gave away their Ghalian nature, and nothing would, unless they were to let their fangs slide into place. And any who saw that, would not be around to spread the tale.

"Is Pintohk joining us today? I see you have a third place setting," Marsoon asked, taking a seat.

"Indeed, though I do not know how long she will be delayed."

"Hopefully not long. I am famished!" the rail-thin man said, leaning into his naturally occurring disguise that was not a disguise.

"By all means, order something. I know she would not wish for us to wait," Hozark said.

The two procured a few small plates of local delicacies as well as a pot of rare, hand-picked tea from the misty peaks of the nearby mountains. It was not a cheap meal by any stretch, but they were men of great wealth, and dropping coin like this was nothing to them.

Precisely the impression they wished to convey. And among the other elite out for a meal, they blended right in.

"Cousins!" a musical voice chirped out with joy.

Hozark and Marsoon rose to greet their "cousin" as she rushed to them and gave each a big hug, dropping her shopping bags clumsily at the table.

Wampeh Ghalian were anything but clumsy.

Her act was a very convincing one, and no one paid her the slightest mind as she blended in with the others perfectly. They snacked, drank tea, and chatted about this and that, all the while communicating by careful phrasing and word choice.

The conversation may have sounded like one thing, but the content of it was most certainly something far different than what any observer would overhear.

"Shall we go for a stroll? It's a lovely day!" Pintohk asked when they finished their tea.

"Sounds like a fine idea. Hozark, are you game?" Marsoon asked.

"Why not?"

The Three dropped ample coin on their table and wandered off into the city's busy streets, eventually arriving at an artisan's shop specializing in sculptures actually carved by hand, not magic. They entered and passed through the workspace.

The proprietor had been called away on a job, leaving the place empty. Precisely as intended.

Each of the Three took a small box from their pockets and opened them. The keys were not keys, exactly, but rather, magical implements whose combined power would unlock the entry to the vault. Improper use of them, however, would trigger the fail-safes.

The city outside had no idea just how close they were to annihilation at that moment should anything have gone wrong.

But the Three knew the order and manner in which to utilize the keys, and within a few moments the massive stone column that seemed to be supporting the building itself pivoted away from the wall, exposing a wide staircase to the secret vault below.

"I shall return shortly," Hozark said, taking to the stairs.

The others turned and faced outward, standing guard and ready to slay any who should stumble upon this scene, regardless of their intent. While the Ghalian avoided needless bloodshed, there were a select few occasions where outright slaughter would be required. Protecting this vault was one of them.

Fortunately, no one came into the shop. Their magically locking the doors had seen to that, but you never could tell when the unforeseen might happen. A friend with a special key, or a delivery person venturing in, for example. But not today.

Hozark emerged from the depths of the magically reinforced vault with two crates on a pair of floating conveyances.

"That is all," he said, and the Three sealed the vault, adding more power to the already massive layers of magic protecting it, as their predecessors had always done, then tucked away their keys, each to be re-hidden once more.

Hozark slid one of the crates to his comrades. "Weapons," he said. "The good ones. Make sure the other Masters receive them, and be sure to arm yourselves as well. Things may become tense with what is about to occur, and the order may need this additional power at hand."

"And the other?" Marsoon asked.

"That is for Corann," Hozark replied, eyeing the crate, so normal in appearance but containing, aside from a number of interesting toys, a weapon of the most horrible power.

"Understood," Pintohk said. "If you and she are embarking on a task together, we will take extra care to watch over the order's affairs while you are gone."

"The other masters will likely be fine, but with Master Prombatz's recent encounter, every bit of assistance is appreciated," Hozark replied. "Now, let us do what needs to be done."

"Good luck, Master Hozark," Marsoon said. "May your task be successful."

"Thank you, Brother. I sincerely hope we are."

The trio exited the shop pushing the floating crates along on their conveyances. Having exited a sculptor's workspace, the size of the crates was nothing of note, and most shoppers used the magically powered mode of transit to move items from place to place. Why carry with your arms what a piddling amount of magic could do for you, after all?

The Three said loud and warm goodbyes in the nearby square, then parted ways, as happily as if it had just been another lovely day shopping. But once Hozark was safely back aboard his ship, his false smile faded.

There was deadly work ahead, and the crate he had just retrieved would play a large role in it.

CHAPTER FIFTY-NINE

Master Corann had returned early and was already waiting for Hozark when he returned to Etratz with his deadly booty in tow. While Uzabud would not sense the power she contained from her feast, Hozark and Demelza could feel the utterly huge amount of magic she had acquired in such a short time.

Laskar, though a pretty weak power user, was a magical being nonetheless, and he had also made note of the woman's overflowing power.

"What the hell did she do?" he asked Demelza when the woman had rejoined them.

"To prepare for our pending action, Master Corann has utilized some resources at her disposal," she replied.

"Resources? You mean she just went and fed on people?"

Demelza stared at him calmly. "Yes, that is precisely what I mean."

"So, what? The Wampeh Ghalian just have a bunch of vislas and emmiks sitting around waiting to be eaten if you guys need a top-up? That's insane."

"Nothing of the sort. Master Corann is one of the Five, and as such, she has knowledge of the whereabouts of many who would otherwise not attract attention. Men and women, *powerful* men and women operating outside of the normal system. Bad people the galaxy would not miss."

"So she killed them? Took their power for herself and just left their drained bodies behind?"

"More or less."

"That's messed up. I don't care how much she needs her fix, stealing power like that, it just feels wrong."

"I can assure you, this is not the Ghalian way. For her to do such a thing only reinforces how dire the situation is," Demelza noted. "We are killers, yes, but not murderers with no conscience."

"Murderers with no conscience? Is Hozark back?" Bud joked as he joined the others.

"He landed a short while ago," Demelza replied.

"I didn't see him."

"Because he set down by Corann's ship, near her lodging."

"Why didn't he just come straight here? We're going to be docking him to my ship anyway, so why not save a step?"

"I could not say. Perhaps he had something he wished to say to Corann before we depart. In any case, he should be joining us shortly."

"I'll get him," Laskar said. "No sense in us yapping around here for another day when we could be talking en route, right?"

The copilot took off at a trot down the alleyway shortcut to the little landing spot where Corann had previously parked her ship. Where Hozark had apparently just joined her.

He and Bud had spent their waiting time dropping a fair amount of coin in the tavern, drinking and gambling and having a pretty good time of it. They might be flying off to their death, after all, so why not do as their friend suggested and live a little before possibly dying a lot?

But they'd sobered up and were ready to go, and with that

sobriety, a buzzing anticipation arose. The sooner they were in motion doing *something*, the better.

Hozark had met with Corann at her ship not only because he wished to discuss a few elements of this mission with her in private, but also because he had to transfer his deadly cargo to her, to store in her craft straightaway. A claithe was not the sort of thing one wanted to hand off on a busy street by any means.

"You retrieved it, then?" Corann asked as he brought the floating crate to a halt before her.

"I did," he replied, opening the outer lid.

She reached inside and recited the release spells for the bonds holding the claithe. The crate was far oversized for the magical weapon, but given the contents, additional protections around it were warranted, layered and nesting within one another. Only after opening all of them was the device finally revealed.

It was larger than a konus or slaap, though some elements were similar. The band around the wrist, for one. But a claithe also possessed a brass knuckle-like portion, linked with a powered gauntlet across the back of the hand tying it all together.

Corann focused her mind as she carefully removed it from its cradle, concentrating hard to ensure there would be no chance of accidentally allowing any of her newly acquired power to bind with the weapon.

"Beautiful," she said, admiring the craftsmanship as she slid it over her hand and wrist.

A thrum of deadly potential vibrated up her arm as it rested against her skin. This was a weapon of incredibly powerful, but also unstable magic. It was why no one ever used them. Why they were hardly even spoken of.

Laskar was jogging down the alleyway toward them,

approaching their secluded meeting point, when he saw the shine of *something* on the woman's wrist.

"Hey, guys! We're all ready and waiting for you!" he called out as he drew nearer.

He was so focused on his friends, he failed to notice the footsteps falling in time with his own. Footsteps right behind him. Hozark, however, caught a glimpse of the mugger's blade flashing in the light as they exited the dim alley.

"Laskar, look out!" he called to the oblivious man.

Laskar spun and jumped aside, startled by Hozark's abrupt warning but knowing better than to doubt the man. The attacker had likely only planned on taking his coin, but now with the man on guard, his attitude turned more deadly.

Corann did not even think about what she was doing when she cast her spell. She intended to kill the man, yes, but only a quick little flash of her deadly magic to not only protect their ally, but also ensure none spoke of what she possessed.

Things, however, did not go exactly as she had planned.

The claithe felt her power and clamped onto it, the device almost reveling in its use of magic, despite being inanimate. The spell that burst forth was magnitudes more powerful than Corann had intended. In fact, it was arguably the most powerful she'd ever cast, and the would-be mugger vanished in a cloud of red mist, obliterated with brutal efficiency.

The woman strained and fought against the claithe, forcing it to disconnect from her power. She quickly pulled it from her hand and placed it back in its protective crate, closing it and sealing it shut. She appeared all right, but Hozark could sense the drain it had been upon her. She would not need to feed again—she was overflowing with power to begin with—but it had taken a sizable amount of power.

"That was foolish," Hozark said, quietly.

"And completely unintentional," she replied. "Though it does serve as an impromptu test, I suppose. At least I now understand it better and have more of a sense of my boundaries."

"A test I do not approve of, obviously," he said. "But your point is a sound one."

Laskar, unlike the two assassins, was flabbergasted by what he'd just witnessed. A man had literally exploded into nothing before his eyes. It was unlike any use of power he'd ever seen.

"What in the hell was that?" he blurted, eyes wide with shock.

"Just a Ghalian spell, is all," Corann replied with her usual sweet smile.

"Yes, and a good thing she cast it," Hozark added. "That man would likely have killed you, Laskar. Why would someone be after you? What exactly did you get up to while we were gone?"

The stunned man blinked a few times, clearing his head before his power of speech settled back into full function. "I don't know."

"Laskar?"

"No, really. I mean, you left, and I went to the tavern," he began. "I mean, I did drink a fair bit, but nothing too excessive. And I gambled a bit, of course."

A look of understanding settled onto Hozark's face. "Did you win?"

"Oh, yeah. I actually cleaned up. It was amazing."

The two assassins shared a look, then Corann turned and pushed the crate into her ship.

"You were marked for your winnings," Hozark said, walking over to better see the remains, or lack thereof, of the attacker.

There was nothing left but scraps of cloth and a bit of red powder on the ground.

"He followed me from the tavern?" Laskar asked.

"Undoubtedly. And had you not spun on him, he might have slain you. Or he may have merely robbed you. In any case, the point is now moot. However, you would do well to learn from this and pay better attention to your surroundings in the future."

"I will."

"Good. Now, come. Let us join the others. We have a long flight ahead of us."

CHAPTER SIXTY

Actaris.

It was an unusual world with an unusual history. One that made it particularly well suited to play host to an off-book Council of Twenty black site where mere torture was likely the least of the unsavory things going on.

In the past, the rocky world had been a stronghold used by various space pirate conglomerates. It had served that purpose for hundreds of years, in fact, hosting a great many adventurers and doers of nefarious deeds.

It was a dry world, with limited water but a breathable atmosphere, though its slightly stronger-than-normal gravity did have the tendency to make one's lungs burn all the same. But, in time, one would grow accustomed to the additional pull.

It had been a safe place to take refuge. The naturally rough terrain, with massive spires of stone jutting out at all angles across the globe, made any sort of large-scale attack from space nearly impossible.

That is, until the Council of Twenty took note of it one unfortunate day. Normally, they'd have written it off as being too magic and troop costly a target to claim as their own, but Visla

Trixzal, the leader of the Council at that time, was a prideful man with an overdeveloped sense of self-worth.

And the pirate leader holed up on that world had not only stolen one of his prize ships, but had also taken one of his brides prisoner. And she had been his *favorite* of the lot.

Rather than let an offense so great as that go, he rallied the Council's forces and stormed the battlements of Actaris, the fight laying waste to tens of thousands of both his own as well as his enemy's men before the remaining pirates surrendered and threw themselves on his mercy.

It was at this point, the appropriateness of using that particular world for evil deeds became set in stone. Trixzal accepted their surrender, the many thousand remaining relinquishing their weapons in defeat. But once they had been taken into the visla's custody, he reneged on their deal.

The men and women were returned to the surface, and they were tortured and slain, the thousands of bodies put on display along the rocky outcroppings as warning to any who would ever dare attack Visla Trixzal or the Council again.

For obvious reasons, no one went anywhere near that world after that day. And while the elements and time had claimed almost all signs of that conflict, a few skeletons still dotted the rocky slopes as a gleaming-white reminder of what had happened there in the not too terribly distant past.

And that was where they were now going.

The old junker Uzabud had sourced was a scavenger craft. It flew, but only barely, and its loss wouldn't be too great a concern. His mothership was tucked away at the far edge of the system on a cold and barren moon none ever visited. As for the Ghalian shimmer ships, the sheer amount of magical power employed around the stronghold on Actaris meant even they would not escape detection.

One might be needed, however, and Hozark parked his ship, fully cloaked, hundreds of miles away, just in case. If they had to steal a vessel from the Council, it would be a relatively short hop to surreptitiously drop them at the hidden craft while making it appear the stolen ship had either escaped or crashed.

In any case, it was a backup. And Ghalian always had a backup plan.

Corann shadowed Hozark when he deposited his ship, then the two flew back to the distant moon to park her craft and join the others aboard the junker. Then it was just a short flight to Actaris, where either success or death awaited them.

"You guys ready for this?" Bud asked as they neared the prickly world.

Even from space, the giant rock spires made it look like an uninviting ball of danger.

"We are prepared," Corann said as they approached the Council stronghold.

"Speak for yourself," Laskar gulped. "Look at that place."

There were several powerful craft in a low hover nearby, always stationed there to protect whichever Council member should choose to visit, if the need arose. And the facility itself was protected by layer upon layer of spells. That, plus everyone's general aversion to the world made this a place where members of the Council felt safe.

But it was also not often used, and for that reason, security, intimidating as it seemed, was somewhat lax in its own way. The infiltration would be difficult, no doubt, but not impossible.

"Never fear, dear Laskar. We will succeed in this effort," Demelza said, patting him on the shoulder in an attempt to comfort him.

It didn't work.

Laskar and Uzabud were clothed as salvage traders, as were the others. But the three Wampeh knew full well that any of their race's complexion would receive additional scrutiny in this place. And with all of the magical protections in place, their usual disguise spells would be ineffective, leaving them but one option.

The old way.

The makeup was good, and though they were all a bit out of practice in its application, by the time they were approaching the landing area they'd been directed to by the control facility, all three bore no resemblance to their normal selves.

All were armed with the usual accoutrements one would expect of salvagers. A konus, a sturdy blade to pry and cut with, a sword, though little good that would do them against trained Council guards, and a pouch for whatever treasures they might come across in the course of their work.

In essence, they were not seen as a threat. They'd be allowed to pass with these, but nothing more.

But Hozark's vespus blade would most certainly be needed, as would Corann's claithe. It was with extreme care they applied the golden strands of Ootaki hair Hozark had recovered from the Ghalian vaults, wrapping them carefully around their weapons, casting obscuring spells of the greatest power.

It was a huge amount of power being spent for a mere shielding spell, something that no one would ever waste Ootaki hair on. But that was what would make it so effective. None expected it.

But the Ghalian were a wealthy order, and this was a small cost in the big picture of their efforts. Once the hair had been properly affixed and the blocking and glamour spells cast, the pommel of the magical sword seemed boring. Plain, dull, and unworthy of note.

And Corann's claithe was covered by gloves and her sleeves, the Ootaki hair masking its magical presence, but only just. Concealing a weapon like that took far more power than the vespus blade.

"What've you got there?" the guard at the landing site growled as they approached carrying a pair of floating crates.

"And why aren't they using a conveyance? I don't see any slave collars."

"It's good stuff, in there. Quality trade, that is," Bud replied, opening the crates to show off the miscellany on the top of the pile. "And they're carrying them because that idiot gambled away the last functional conveyance we had," he said, flashing an angry glance at Laskar.

Having been in the pirate game a long time, he knew the ins and outs of scavengers and their ways, and now that knowledge was coming into play.

"Trade? At Actaris?" the guard asked, incredulously.

"Believe me, I don't want to be here," Bud said with a friendly laugh. "Probably no more than you do, am I right?"

The guard didn't smile, but his agreement with the sentiment was almost palpable nonetheless. No one wanted to be stationed here, and guard duty, outside no less, was the worst.

"But we're short on options. If it wasn't for our ship being in such dire need of repair, we'd have just as soon passed right by this whole system," he continued. "But as it is, we find ourselves in need of parts. And we all know the saying about beggars."

"They're not worth killing because they have no coin," the guard replied.

"What? No, no," Bud said. "They can't be choosers. Beggars can't be choosers. Surely you know that one."

"Mine's better," the guard said, stepping aside and gesturing them toward the nearby entrance. "Go on, and hurry up about it."

"Thanks, Brother," Bud said with a smile. "Come on, you lot. You heard the man. Get a move on!"

"Okay, Boss," Hozark said, lifting his side of the crates with a grunt.

The former pirate led the way, walking to the waiting entry. They were about to enter the belly of the beast, and if they hoped to survive once inside, success was the only option.

CHAPTER SIXTY-ONE

Inside the corridor there were no further guards to be seen. In fact, there was *no one* anywhere.

"This is some pretty lax security," Bud noted as they walked deeper through the long tunnel into the main heart of the stronghold complex.

"They feel safe here," Hozark replied. "A stronghold build into the very rock of the planet, the entry guarded by Council ships, and a reputation surrounding this world that keeps all but the most foolish, or the most desperate, away. It is no wonder."

"I guess so. It's just weird, is all. I'm used to people trying to kill us when we do stuff like this."

"Give it time, dear Uzabud. I'm sure they will start soon enough."

"Come, divide the crates, and let us begin," Corann said, quickly separating the containers, lifting a third from where it had been hidden within the original two.

This smaller crate held more than just salvage junker material. It contained several items of great value from the Ghalian vault. And one rarity that would be certain to grab the attention of whoever was really behind all of this deceit.

"Uzabud. You and Demelza will take the larger crate of trade and see what you can learn of Aargun's location on your way to the quartermaster. If you should happen upon him, skree me at once."

"We shall, Master Corann," Demelza said as she and Bud lifted their load.

"Laskar, you will take this other crate, as we discussed. Your idea was a good one, so activate the hidden conveyance and act as though it is just a routine foodstuff delivery. Once in the kitchens, talk with the staff and see what you can learn."

"Getting people to talk is my strong suit," he replied.

"*Talking* is your strong suit," Bud chimed in. "Just stick to the plan."

"When do I not?"

"Do you really want me to answer that?"

That left Corann and Hozark with the smaller crate. One they would carry by hand. And that crate would be taken to the heart of the stronghold. To the visla's chambers. There, she would unleash the power of the claithe if necessary and do whatever it might take to reclaim their captive brother from this place.

"Be safe, and be smart," Hozark said. "The workers here have no reason to expect an attack, but they are also very familiar with the Council members and their aides, so be cautious what you say and to whom. Remember your role, and stick to your part of the plan."

The group nodded as one and headed off in different directions. The basic layout of the place wasn't much of a secret, since it was simply occupied when the Council took over this world. Yes, modifications had been made over the years, but the foundational design was the same.

The interior of the stronghold possessed a multitude of outdoor courtyard spaces, some quite large, a holdover from the old days when pirates would host great feasts and festivities, the smaller ships actually landing in some of the larger ones to offload alcohol, food, and entertainment.

That aspect was largely unchanged, and the route toward the inner chambers the visla would most likely be using was as they'd expected it to be. What they hadn't expected was the cries of a beast ringing out through the walls. And this was not a guard animal; it was obviously captive and in pain.

"Is that a Zomoki?" Hozark mused as he and Corann moved along as if nothing was wrong.

"I believe so. But what could they be doing to such a beast to cause that reaction?" she replied.

Neither had a clue, but that question was soon answered when they passed out into one of the courtyards on their way to their destination. It was the fastest route, avoiding twists and turns of the corridors inside. It also lay bare the mystery of the crying beast.

Zomoki were there. Medium-sized specimens, but quite large regardless. Hozark and Corann shared a look as they passed the still creatures. Both of the Zomoki lay there with eyes open but not seeing. They would never see again, it was quite clear.

Someone had killed them. But not an outright slaughter. No, these magnificent, magical animals had clearly been experimented on. And while they were still breathing, from the looks of it. Just like the dead Wampeh Hozark had seen at the smelting facility. Now the cries of their cousin made sense, but the machinations at work did not. Someone was engaged in dark things, but to what end, they could only guess.

The two Ghalian carefully avoided the deadly Zomoki blood that had dripped onto the stones and made their way to the far doorway leading back into the halls.

Inside the hallways once more, Hozark and Corann made good time toward their goal, walking with purpose, but also the casual demeanor of one not at all concerned about anything.

343

Anything like breaking into a Council stronghold to fight off guards, mercenaries, and a visla, for example.

"Hold there," the nearest guard said when they arrived at the doors to what had to be the visla's chambers. "What are you doing here? This area is off limits to all but the visla's staff."

"Oh, we're here to see the visla," Corann said in her sweetest tone. "We have a valuable delivery for him."

"No one makes deliveries here. Only at the depot." He turned to the other guard. "Scan them."

The guard summoned up a scanning spell, reciting the words with the bored tone of years of repetition. But the intent behind the words was there, and that was what made a spell work, ultimately. A faint green glow encompassed the two interlopers and their cargo, then abruptly flashed bright red.

The guards drew their blades at once.

"Show me your hands!"

"What seems to be the problem?" Corann asked in her motherly way.

"You're wielding magic, that's what."

"Oh, young man. We are not *wielding* magic. We're *delivering* it," she said, slowly opening the top of the crate to expose the contents within.

"Is that––" the guard said, his eyes going wide with disbelief as he lowered his blade, a hand reaching out in disbelief.

Inside the crate, a thick braid of golden hair lay coiled with several other items of great value. Items sacrificed from the Ghalian vaults that were now playing their part as intended.

"Don't touch!" Corann chided, smacking his hand like a mother would a child reaching into a cookie jar.

Little did the man know, the contents were set to burn in a magical fire if anyone but she or Hozark were to touch them. A safeguard in this deadly place.

"Yes, it is Ootaki hair," Corann continued. "Not first cut,

mind you, but a respectable length just the same. We were told to deliver this."

This particular Ootaki hair had fallen into the order's possession during an assassination not too long ago. Once the target had been eliminated, it would have been foolish to leave so potent a source of magic for his replacement to find. And so, it had been stored in the Ghalian vault.

Until now.

The Ootaki magic had set off the scanning spell alarm, as intended. And as their real weapons were masked by strands of that same hair, the impression was maintained that it was simply the braid making the alarm trigger.

Corann kept her distance, though, being sure not to touch the golden braid. If she were to handle it while wearing the claithe, there was no telling what might happen.

It was a very weak bit of magic-storing hair they had brought from the Ghalian vaults, but even an old and largely drained length of it could still have unknown effects on the unstable weapon, and *that* was the option of last resort.

"I'll take it to them," the guard said, coming to his senses.

"We were given explicit orders to deliver it personally. Where is the visla?"

"Which one?"

Corann flowed with the startling revelation that not one but two Council vislas were present. "The visla, of course."

"Like I said, which one? Visla Torund or Visla Ravik?"

"Visla Torund, of course. Is he available, or is he with that captured assassin we've heard word of?"

"How did you hear about that?" the guard asked.

"The guards at the landing site were talking about it. Is it true? So exciting––it's a rare thing to capture one alive, you know."

"They should've been keeping their mouths shut," the guard said. "But no, that one's held in the upper cells."

Corann and Hozark shared the briefest of glances. That was what they needed. Aargun's location. All they had to do was slay these meddlesome guards and they could——

"In any case, the visla is in a meeting in the topmost courtyard with the other Council representatives at the moment," the guard added.

"A meeting?"

"Yeah. Weird, we don't usually have so many here at the same time," the other guard said.

"Shut it," his counterpart hissed. "We're not to talk about that."

"Oh, right. Sorry. I just figured since they're delivering Ootaki hair it would be okay. I mean, he'll be thrilled to get that, right?"

"He will, I'm sure," Corann said, again catching Hozark's eye. "We'll bring this to him in the courtyard, then. It's one of the upper ones, you say? On the terraced rock areas?"

"He's not to be disturbed. But you can wait here."

She looked at Hozark a long moment. Aargun was close. Within reach. But there was not one but two vislas from the Council present, as well as who knew how many other representatives of the other members. It was an opportunity they simply could not miss.

"We were told to keep direct contact with this crate at all times," Hozark said in a bookish way. "So we can't just leave it here until he's done. But is there a kitchen nearby where we might get some food while we wait?"

The guards looked at one another and decided this pair was harmless enough. And if they were bringing such an item to the visla, they'd best be treated well, if not as honored guests.

"Down this hall, take a left at the intersection, then the third doorway on your right. There should be someone there to help you find whatever you crave."

"Thank you so very much. You've been an absolutely lovely

pair to speak with," Corann said, even going so far as to pinch the man's cheek.

She and Hozark lifted their crate and headed off in the direction the man had bade them. Once out of sight and earshot, they drew close and quickly adjusted their plan.

New things were afoot, and they were going to improvise.

CHAPTER SIXTY-TWO

The two disguised Wampeh carried their crate of riches down the hallway toward the kitchens, following the guard's instructions, but abruptly changed course when they were out of his line of sight, heading toward the smaller, upper courtyard where he had said the unexpected meeting was taking place.

Hozark pulled out his skree from the crate and called out to all three of their counterparts, notifying them that Aargun had been located and to pull back from their current locations and convene at the uppermost courtyards in the rocky estate.

It was a dilemma, of a sort. The goal of their incursion was near. Aargun was alive and being held in the upper cells, likely rather near the location of the meeting, if previous layouts of the stronghold were still accurate.

But this was an opportunity to do more than save an aspirant and slay his captor. This was the chance to actually find out what was going on in Council affairs. Affairs that appeared to encompass this kidnapping, as well as the torture of, and experimentation on, Zomoki.

It was too important an opportunity to risk missing that

information. And with the visla engaged with other Council members, Aargun would be safe in his cell. For now, at least.

"We determine the number of adversaries, their power, their weapons, and any ingress or escape points. Then we strike," Corann said. "We have the advantage of surprise. And there are *three* of us present," she added with an anticipatory grin.

"They will never expect that," Hozark agreed. "This is most unusual."

"And unusual times call for unusual actions, Brother Hozark. Now, let us draw closer and see what we might discern of this meeting."

The duo knew it might take the others a little time to reach their location, but they could not wait a moment. Too much valuable information might be revealed, and there was no telling when the meeting might end.

"I see four participants in the discussion. Two appear to be vislas; the others are emmiks," Hozark said, reaching out with his power as he peered out the small window that gazed out onto the courtyard from their location.

"Others?"

"A dozen Tslavar guards, most near the lesser of the magic users. Only one of the guards is near the vislas. Hooded, but the shape of weapons is clear through their cloak."

"Typical visla overconfidence," Corann said, feeling the power of the claithe resting on her wrist beneath its covering.

She reached out, carefully, sensing the magic in the air. Yes, there was a substantial amount of it out there, and any head-on fight before their backup arrived would likely result in all of their demise. There were simply too many powered people to deal with at the same time as their guards, even with the element of surprise.

But if they could get closer, somehow, close enough to overhear the conversation, then they might at least glean precious intel while waiting for the others. And from that distance, if they had to, they could likely strike one or more of the key players down, rendering them unconscious and leaving them free to deal with the lesser combatants.

A plan was hatched, and while it was somewhat audacious, that was the nature of their life. A pair of clean cloaks of the basic type Council staff used were pulled from the crate and slipped over their salvager garb. The two then stashed their crate in a nook in the wall.

Some might notice it, but none were expecting trouble in this place, so they would almost certainly just walk by, assuming it had been placed there for a reason.

Hozark took the Ootaki braid and wrapped it around himself. He was still very low on internal power, but the small amount still remaining in the hair would help him power more spells if they were needed.

He made a note to himself that he and the other members of the Three really must put some resources into fully recharging the remaining cache of Ootaki hair in their possession. Its use was not called upon often, but this occasion reinforced the usefulness of it.

With the hair safely secured on his person and safe from Council discovery, Corann led the way back to the kitchens below.

"Drinks and refreshments for the emmik," she said in a commanding voice. "Chop-chop."

The staff knew they had visitors, so the appearance of what had to be one of their aides, judging by her cloak, along with her tone of voice––that of one used to ordering staff around––set them to work at once without question. In just a few minutes a large tray was brought forth.

"Hand it to me. I will bring it to them. Now, back to your work," she said, then spun and stormed out without paying them another thought.

It was almost as if she had actually served in this capacity before. And on several of her deep cover contracts, she had.

Hozark was wearing his sword, but beneath the cloak, secured as it was, its shape was barely noticeable. He took the tray from Corann and acted as her porter. They would quietly and humbly offer refreshments to the attendees, then strike when the moment was right, dealing a blow to the Council, then freeing their Ghalian brother.

"The others must be close," Hozark said.

"No time to waste," Corann replied, then opened the door to the courtyard and stepped out into the light as if it were a totally natural thing to do, walking into the lion's den, so to speak.

It was not a huge space, perhaps twenty meters across, but it was large enough. Not so large as the adjacent courtyard nearby. That would have been overkill for a gathering of this intimate size.

The guards turned, as did one of the emmiks, taking note of the new arrivals.

One of the Tslavar entourage stepped away from the others and met them halfway to the group. "What are you doing here? This is a private meeting."

He had stopped them just out of clear earshot, and neither assassin dared utter their enhanced hearing spells with the man staring right at them.

"I was told to bring refreshments," Corann replied with her warmest, kindest smile.

"You're not part of Uratza's staff," he said, eyeing the interlopers more keenly.

"No, we are not. We were pulled from our other tasks to assist," she said, not daring to go so far as to claim to be part of one of the participants' entourage.

There was no telling which of them this guard was attached to, or whom he knew among his peers.

The guard looked over the tray in Hozark's hands, then cast

a scanning spell. The food and drink was clear of poisons or enchantments. It was just food and beverages, it seemed.

Corann took one of the smaller, less ornate cups intended for the staff and offered it to the man. "Here, you must be thirsty."

He reached to accept the offering, then abruptly stopped.

"What's that on your wrist?" he asked, grabbing Corann roughly by the arm, her sleeve pulled up by the act, revealing not only her claithe, but also her pale, Wampeh skin.

The look of shock on his face was immediately replaced with alert action as he shouted out, "Ghalian!"

Or, *attempted* to shout out, for Corann slit his throat with a concealed blade before he could complete the word. But it had been enough. The other guards raced to his aid.

It was twelve-on-two, which was ridiculously unfair to the twelve under any other circumstances, but power users were present, and they were the real threat.

"Stop the assass––" a guard shouted, then fell as a thrown dagger pierced his skull.

Hozark recognized the handiwork, and a moment later Demelza was in the fray, Bud racing in right behind her, the two's arrival allowing the Ghalian masters to focus entirely on the magic user threats.

An emmik was the first to act, casting a violent death spell, hoping to shatter Corann and Hozark's bodies. Even if they'd recently fed, it should be enough to cripple them, at least.

But he hadn't counted on one thing. Corann's claithe.

The Ghalian master countered his spell, drawing the power within her and obliterating the casting while crushing the man who had sent it her way, leaving him in a writhing, broken heap on the stone.

It was far more powerful magic than she had intended to use, and costly, especially with others to still contend with. But the effect was immediate, and it made quite an impression. Even the strongest power users feared the dangerous device.

"A claithe?" the shorter, dark-haired visla said, the realization of just the sort of weapon his would-be killers possessed flashing across his face.

Rather than fight, he turned and ran, as did the remaining emmik, both fleeing into the stronghold.

"Ravik, you coward," the remaining visla shouted after him. Torund, it would be.

"Laskar! There are an escaping visla and an emmik heading toward the inner sanctum," Hozark quickly transmitted over his skree. "Stay safe but track them and find where they go. We cannot let them escape. We will come as soon as we can."

He would have said more, but Corann was weakened from the sudden, massive draw of power. And they still had another threat to deal with. A visla, no less. And he still had his one guard, the lone lackey who had not rushed into the fight with Demelza and Bud.

Slowly, the guard lowered their hood, revealing a pale woman with long black hair and silver eyes. Eyes Hozark knew all too well.

Samara stared at the disguised man with a knowing look, a faint smile cracking the corners of her lips. She knew Hozark. She'd know him anywhere, disguised or not.

The visla hissed something to her, and the smile faded as she drew her own glowing vespus blade from within her cloak.

Hozark glanced at Corann as she tried to recover her strength, the two sharing a knowing look.

Samara was most definitely alive. And she was with the Council.

The former lovers circled one another as Hozark drew his own vespus blade from beneath his cloak.

"Hello, Hozark," she said.

"Samara," he replied.

"Here we are again."

"So it would seem," he replied.

She stopped in place, the little smile creeping back onto her face. "Well, then. Shall we?"

He nodded once.

Then all hell broke loose.

CHAPTER SIXTY-THREE

The men who had engaged Bud and Demelza were the cream of the crop of Council guards. Not mere Tslavar mercenaries tasked with standing around and looking tough—and dying magnificently from time to time. These were very well -trained men, and very well-armed.

On his own, Uzabud would have fallen straightaway, but with the curvy dervish fighting beside him, he stood a chance. Demelza was a blur of action, handling multiple highly skilled opponents at once, and doing it with great efficiency.

Normal guards would have stood no chance against her, but these were fighting her in a constant stream of attackers, overlapping their efforts rather than waiting for individual opportunities.

Due to the proximity of their fellow guards, no magic was being used. The likelihood of hitting one or more of their own was simply too great. But the swords and knives were out in force, and despite her skill, Demelza had received more than a few cuts in the process.

Of course, three of the guards now lay dead, and another

was quickly bleeding out, but the remaining eight were hard at work against her and her compatriot.

Not far away, Hozark and Samara were engaged in a furious exchange of their own, the sparking magic of their vespus blades flashing out across the courtyard as the glowing blue metal struck its counterpart.

Ghalian swordfights typically ended in seconds, not minutes, but these two had trained together. Grown up together. Slept together. They knew each other's movements as well as their own.

And while Samara had always been the better swordswoman, in the decade since her alleged demise, Hozark had committed himself to bettering his swordplay, partly as a way to honor and remember his friend. Little did he know all that training would come into play against the dead woman herself.

The visla she was guarding would have ended the fight immediately with his powerful magic, if not for one utterly unexpected thing. Corann and the claithe she was wearing. She had recovered quickly enough from the weapon's initial use and was now carefully casting powerful counter-spells with it, stopping the visla in his tracks.

But she was draining the stolen power within her faster than anticipated. At this rate, it would not be long before she ran dry completely. But the alternative was casting with more force.

However, she was not a visla. She was only using the visla's power she had absorbed. And she was not a skilled claithe user. No one was, not these days. To attempt a spell of the magnitude needed would very possibly result in the death of them all.

So she defended herself and her comrades while they fought as best they could, hoping that somehow, they would manage to seize the day. But the outcome was looking increasingly grim.

Samara's blue vespus blade struck the slightly brighter metal of Hozark's. His weapon possessed more power than hers, but both had drained the magical blades significantly not long ago and had not fully replenished them.

"You've gotten better," Samara said as she slid her blade free while delivering a front kick to her opponent.

"And you've remained impressive," Hozark replied, his dense muscles absorbing the blow. "But why, Sam? Why work for the Council?"

"I have my reasons," she said, launching into a furious attack that drove Hozark closer to the visla's dangerous magic.

A tendril of power lashed out past Corann's defenses, knocking Hozark to the ground. It wasn't enough to kill him by any stretch, but it had put a hurt on him to be sure. Samara saw her window of opportunity and lunged at the fallen man, but her blade stopped short, blocked by a far lesser weapon, but a moderately enchanted one.

Demelza had taken the sword from one of the guards she had slaughtered, the lot of them now unmoving on the ground, save the one their former pirate friend was still dealing with. The enchanted sword was more powerful than her own, so the upgrade was quite welcome. Especially as her opponent had a vespus blade.

Samara's eyebrow cocked slightly with both surprise and curiosity. She then launched into a full-fledged attack on the much stockier woman. But Demelza moved with the speed and grace of a woman half her size, the years of hard training honing her into an elite killing machine.

She wasn't as good as Samara was, but few were. She could, however, hold her own long enough to allow Hozark to regain his footing and do what needed to be done.

The master assassin looked at his comrades, each fighting for their lives, and knew his only option. He reached out to the weak braid of hair wrapped around him within his cloak and pulled its power in close. Then Hozark did the unexpected. He turned from Samara and Demelza's fight and charged the visla.

Corann, seeing what he was doing, shifted from defense to offense, casting a powerful blast of harmful magic, forcing the visla to shift his own defenses to counter the magical attack. He saw Hozark rushing toward him, but remained unafraid. The man possessed a vespus blade, yes. But it was not fully charged, and he quickly cast his own spells to stop it. And when they did, he would take the assassin's life with great pleasure.

But he hadn't counted on one thing. The Ootaki hair.

It was an entirely different type of magic than the vespus or claithe. A type requiring a different defense. And Hozark had channeled it through himself and into his blade.

The visla's eyes went wide as the unusually charged sword pierced his protective spells one by one, then drove into his body up to the hilt. His casting ceased at once, the physical shock breaking his grip on his magic.

Hozark did not hesitate, leaning in close, his jaws clamping down on the man's neck. A great deal of the visla's power had been expended fighting off Corann's claithe, but a significant amount still remained. And that power was now flowing into Hozark. And as it did, his vespus blade grew brighter, replenishing itself just as its owner did.

Samara was the better fighter, and Demelza would soon fall, she could see. Her opponent knew that to be the case as well, but when her eyes flicked away for an instant, a little smile forming on her face despite her impending demise, Samara realized the tide had turned.

With a blast of power from her konus, she created space between herself and her surprisingly talented foe and turned to see what had happened.

The visla was dead. Well, dying, anyway. Drained by her former lover while this other Ghalian distracted her. The visla was a lost cause, and so, this fight served no purpose any longer.

Samara pushed out another stun spell, this time far greater, forcing Demelza back on her heels. She then turned and ran into the stronghold corridor leading to the adjacent courtyard at full speed, leaving the woman she'd been about to kill both dazed and confused.

Hozark broke free the moment the visla's heart stopped beating. Once the life had ended, no power remained, and no Ghalian actually enjoyed drinking blood. It was merely a means to an end. That end being taking another's power.

He glanced around at the carnage. The others had done well, he noted with pleasure. Bud was bloody, as was Demelza, but both still drew breath. And from what he'd seen, Demelza had stood firm against Samara in bladed combat and survived. It was no small thing.

Corann had drained herself dangerously low on power, the claithe nearly killing her in the process, yet somehow, she was still standing. Unsteady, but standing.

Hozark swept her up in his arms––something neither would ever speak of––and hurried her to the broken body of the emmik she'd crushed so violently.

"Drink, Corann," he urged, lowering her beside the emmik.

The man did not have long to live, and his body had already begun shutting down, but his heart still beat, and he was an emmik. The power was still there for her to take.

She bit into the man's neck and drank greedily, her overtaxed body replenishing and healing as she did. The force of her feeding hastened the man's demise, but she didn't care, and when he went cold, she broke her thirsty embrace and rose to her feet, renewed.

Corann looked at Hozark and flashed a bloody smile. "Thank you, Brother Hozark."

"No, thank *you*," he replied.

"The other Council members?"

"Unknown. I skreed to Laskar to tail them, but––"

The air around them stirred as a shadow fell across the courtyard as a small Council transport ship rose overhead.

"It must have been in the adjacent courtyard," Hozark said as he watched the ship pivot above them.

A familiar pale woman was standing in front of the observation window beside the escaped visla. Ravik. This one was Visla Ravik. And Samara was with him.

Was it possible *he* was the real mastermind behind all of this? It would take a lot of work, but they had names now. And eventually, they'd know for sure.

"They're getting away! We've got to get them!" Bud shouted.

"Our ships are too far away, Bud. And we still have to make our way outside these walls."

"Damn!"

"Let it go. We will find them eventually, my friend," Hozark said, standing over the fallen body of yet another Council member Samara had been guarding. Guarding, but abandoned to protect another now, it seemed. It made no sense.

To call it vexing would be an understatement.

The ship above began to turn, and Samara and Hozark shared a final look as the ship lifted high into the sky.

She had tried to kill him. *Again*. But Hozark found himself smiling nonetheless. Samara was alive. What it meant, he was unsure, but they would definitely find out.

But for now, they had a Ghalian to rescue.

CHAPTER SIXTY-FOUR

"Where's Laskar?" Bud asked as he limped after his friends into the surprisingly empty stronghold. "I didn't see him out there when we were fighting, and I can't reach him on skree."

"It is entirely possible he was discovered while chasing our quarry," Hozark replied. "If he received my message, that is. I only hope he was not captured and taken aboard Visla Ravik's ship. That would be a most unfortunate turn of events."

"We will look for him after we rescue Aargun," Corann said, hurrying along the corridor.

The stronghold was startlingly quiet, given what had just happened. But when word of a Ghalian assassin in the grounds got out, a great unease had spread throughout the grounds. When they heard that not only one of the visiting emmiks had fallen, but Visla Torund as well, that unease rapidly turned into all-out panic.

Making it worse, Visla Ravik had fled, taking his ship with him. For a visla of the Council of Twenty to depart so suddenly, this Ghalian must be a terrible foe, indeed.

None knew there were multiple Wampeh within their walls, fortunately, nor were they aware of the fact that a vespus blade was in use. But there had been buzz about a claithe being brought to bear on the Council's men. A *claithe*. It was unheard of. A weapon of that power could kill them all in the right hands. Even faster in the wrong ones.

And with the visla abruptly gone, the hired help suddenly had very little impetus to stand and fight an enemy who could grind them to a pulp with the snap of their fingers. That a claithe didn't really work that way was of no concern to them, just what the end result might be. Namely, their death.

The four bloodied combatants moved quickly into the depths of the facility, heading toward the likely location of the cells, when they heard a man's voice cry out from just up ahead.

"Maktan!"

"What was that?" Bud asked.

"I do not know, but we will find out momentarily," Demelza said as they rounded the corner, her weapons ready.

Laskar was there, crouched over the emmik who had fled at the sight of the claithe. His hands were covered with blood as he held the dying man, a look of confusion in his eyes.

"What do I do?" Laskar asked.

Hozark moved close immediately. "Step aside," he said, then set to work attempting to stop the man's bleeding.

They had slain the others, but that had been in the midst of combat. But they still needed answers, and this man could provide them. If he lived. Hozark called upon the magic now flowing within him to try to staunch the emmik's bleeding, but even as he worked, he knew it was too late.

Before any of the Ghalian could even salvage the man's magic, the light went out in his eyes, his power gone forever.

"What the hell happened, Laskar?" Bud asked, staring at the dead power user with confusion. "The guy was an emmik. An *emmik*. Who the hell could have done this to him?"

"I don't know. I was searching, like Hozark asked, when I found him."

Hozark surveyed the scene. The signs were clear, this was a very recent kill.

"It could not have been Visla Ravik, nor Samara," he said.

"Wait, Samara is alive?" Laskar asked.

"Yeah, and Hozark's ex just took off with Visla Ravik," Bud replied.

"She is not my ex."

"Yeah, whatever. I saw how she looked at you."

"You mean while she was trying to kill me, I assume?"

"Hey, you Ghalian have your own kinks, I'm sure. I'm not one to judge," Bud chuckled.

"She is not my ex. Regardless, that is inconsequential at the moment. What matters is, who possesses the power to do this to an emmik?"

"You just said Samara and Visla Ravik were here," Laskar pointed out.

"But we saw them depart, and this man was struck down *after* their departure."

"How do you know?"

"The nature of the injury, as well as the quantity of blood lost, paint a clear picture. He was slain after they had already fled."

The group looked at one another with confusion. There had been two vislas and two emmiks in the meeting, but could another be on the grounds? And if so, one who would kill one of the Council's representatives to protect, what, exactly?

"He called out a name," Bud said. "Just before we found you."

"Maktan," Demelza added. "He cried out, 'Maktan.'"

"What does that even mean?" Bud asked.

Hozark studied the dead man a long moment. He had died in their friend's arms, and with his last breath, he had called out that name.

"It means that as he died, he gave up the name of the one

who slayed him, most likely to keep his own involvement in whatever is going on here secret," Hozark said.

"But Maktan?" Corann said. "It is just so unlikely."

"Who's Maktan?"

"*Visla* Zinna Maktan is a member of the Council of Twenty, Bud," Hozark replied. "But it makes no sense. He is one of the most benign members of the Twenty. To be involved in the experimentation and vivisection of Zomoki? And the kidnapping of a Wampeh Ghalian? It just does not seem likely."

"Little does, in games of subterfuge and deceit," Laskar noted. "And things are quite often not at all what they seem."

"Well said, Laskar," Corann said. "Now, come. We still have unanswered questions, and rescuing Aargun might clarify a few of them. Everyone, weapons at the ready. If there is another visla lurking around these grounds, we must be prepared."

The group as a whole was on edge as they moved up the stairwell to the upper cells. Something very strange was afoot, and they were walking into it even more blind than before.

The corridor at the top of the stairs was empty, the missing guards having apparently caught wind of what had happened below, as well as the fate of their comrades and employers. They entered the holding area with great caution, Hozark and Corann taking the lead, both ready for whatever might be lurking in wait.

But no one was there. At least, no one who could do them any harm.

A row of cells lined one side of the large chamber, and several shorn Ootaki lay cowering against the walls, pulling their thin coverings over themselves in a futile attempt to protect themselves from whatever torment might be coming next.

There was blood at the opposite end of the room. Multiple types by the look of it. Blood, and a solid examination table, modified to allow for all manner of restraint, both physical and magical. It too was spotted with the blood of more than one race.

A pair of pale-yellow Ootaki bodies lay underneath a thin cloth against the wall. Recent kills, by the look of it. Still warm, in fact. Perhaps *that* was what the meeting had been about. A discussion of whatever it was they had been trying to accomplish here.

By the look of it, the Council was trying to find another means of tapping into Ootaki power besides their hair. Trying, and failing, apparently. But why kidnap a Ghalian?

"Over here," Laskar said. "I found him!"

Corann rushed to the locked cell, and with the ease of one who had done so countless times, disabled the locking spells and opened the door faster than he ever could. Laskar had heard of the order's efficiency at such things, but to see it in practice made him realize the tales had been understatements.

"Oh, Aargun. What did they do to you?" Corann sighed as she examined the unconscious man.

His blindfolded face was a mess of bruises, as was his body, the different shades of color each telling its own tale as to how long ago, and how severely he had been beaten.

There were strange markings on his torso as well. Some sort of device had been used on him, the puncture marks not healing despite the Ghalian's naturally speedy recovery time.

Carefully, Corann unwrapped the blindfold, the material pulling free with a wet smacking sound.

"His eyes," Bud said, nearly gagging. "They took his eyes."

Corann gently pried his mouth open. Broken teeth where fangs would have descended met her gaze. As did the crusty stump of the man's tongue.

The three assassins looked at one another, a shared rage filling each of them. They knew torture was a risk of their profession, but this had been something more. Whoever did this had been experimenting on their brother. Him and the poor Ootaki as well.

What had been done to him was not to gain information. It was to prevent him from ever revealing who had done it to him should he survive.

Like the Zomoki they'd found down below, these people had been subjected to all manner of experimentation. And someone would pay.

But for now, the survivors needed to be tended to. Aargun would live, and most of his physical wounds would heal, in time. The mental damage, however, might never.

As for the surviving Ootaki, they would be taken and delivered to one of the secret enclaves of their people, *free* people, where, hopefully they would regain some semblance of a normal life, if ever they could let go of what happened to them.

The remaining Zomoki had been too badly injured to save, and so it had been put out of its misery, swiftly and humanely. Corann then turned the power of the claithe on the stronghold itself, setting every last inch of non-stone surface ablaze with magical fire. It cost the remainder of her stolen magic, but it was worth it.

Whatever was being done there, it was no more, and all traces were destroyed. She took the claithe from her wrist and placed it in its warded case for return to the vaults. Once they had gathered the shimmer ships and were all safely back aboard the mothership, she then went to one of the private rooms to sleep, allowing her body to recover from the drain of the weapon.

It had done its job, but it had nearly been the end of her for it. The claithe would now return to its hiding place, hopefully never to be used again.

The Council plans had been disrupted, and they had won. At least this battle.

"Whenever you are ready," Hozark said to the pilot and his sidekick.

Bud and Laskar glanced at one another and shared a nod of solidarity. They'd survived, and their unlikely team was stronger for it.

"You got it," Bud replied. "You ready?"

"Jump spells are locked in," Laskar replied.

"Okay, then. Let's go home."

CHAPTER SIXTY-FIVE

Master Prombatz was the first to meet the ship when Uzabud landed on the quiet world where Denna Finnleigh the healer resided, and it was he who personally carried the unconscious form of his young student into her home.

The Ootaki were also ushered into the woman's chambers, though their healing would likely require somewhat less effort than that of the poor Wampeh. Once they had recovered their strength, Finnleigh would ensure they reached their new secret Ootaki home safely.

She had worked with the Ghalian in that regard for many years, and it was their shared distaste of slavery that partly led to such a long-lasting relationship between a healer and an order of killers. For not all killers were the same, it seemed. And these had saved not just Ootaki, but members of her own family as well, over the years.

"What now?" Bud asked as he aimlessly strolled around outside the ship.

They'd been on tasks for so long that it felt utterly foreign to have no concrete direction or goal. Yes, things were in the air, but for the moment at least, their jobs were complete. The

Ghalian spies would be at work, but he and Laskar could most likely return to their normal lives, at least for a bit.

"We are done here," Corann said after the last of the Ootaki were taken inside. "Master Prombatz has his own means of transport and will meet us when he is ready. And Hozark, Demelza, and I have already retrieved our craft from the mother ship."

"And what about us?" Laskar asked.

"The immediate threat has been neutralized, and their plans disrupted. A day will come when we revisit these goings-on, but for now at least, your work is done," she replied.

"But what about this Maktan person? I mean, you know he's really the one pulling the strings, right? So it would make sense to take him out before he can cause any more harm."

"Dear Laskar, we are killers, yes, but not indiscriminate murderers. All we have at the moment is a name. A name spoken by a dying man, but no more. This Zinna Maktan is an odd fellow, no doubt, but he has never been one of the troublemakers within the Council of Twenty. Some strange things are afoot, no doubt, and he may be involved, but first we must investigate and verify before taking any further action."

"But he killed that emmik. You need to kill him," he persisted.

"Yes. But Visla Ravik was also present."

"You said he couldn't have done it, though."

"No, he could not. But he is part of whatever was going on in the Actaris stronghold. We have much to learn, Laskar, and the best way to do that is to observe. For now, anyway."

Hozark walked over to the copilot and rested his hand on his shoulder. "You did well, Laskar. Admirably, in fact. But the threat has been handled. Why don't you and Bud go and relax a bit? I know after all of this fighting, he could surely use it. And I would wager, so could you."

Laskar thought it over a bit, then nodded in agreement. "I

guess I got caught up in the 'go-go-go' speed we've been living these past weeks."

"It happens to all of us. But have no doubts, when we learn more about this affair and have a plan, you will be the first ones we contact." He took a pouch of coin from his pocket and tossed it to Bud. "Go and have some fun, my friend. And make sure this one enjoys himself as well."

Bud felt the weight of the coin in his hand and smiled. It seemed they would be living large for some time, and all it had cost them was a few weeks of fighting and nearly losing their lives. Not a bad trade-off, all things considered.

"Be seein' ya, Hozark."

"Not if I see you first," the Wampeh replied.

It was a common saying, but when deadly assassins were involved, it could, at times, have a more menacing connotation. But not today.

"Come on, Laskar. Let's go and get ourselves *properly* wasted."

"I like the sound of that," he replied, following his pilot into their ship.

A moment later, they rose high into the air and were gone.

All five of the Ghalian masters were gathered at the hidden training house on a bustling but unexceptional commerce world. Master Prombatz had taken the longest to join them, having spent a significant amount of time at the side of the young Wampeh who had been forcibly taken. A horrible error by assailants who had intended to capture the Ghalian master instead.

Aargun would pull through, but some of his injuries were so severe that it was clear he would never again return to Ghalian life. The order would provide for him, though. He had been taken from them in the course of honoring a contract, and for the rest of his days, he would want for nothing.

"Your contracts are valid once more," Corann informed the others. "After a thorough review of all contact that was made between the various players employed in the Council's little scheme, it is now clear that they had only planned the one attack. The other contracts are legitimate."

"Of course, we double-checked their makers as well," Master Varsuvala added. "It only made sense to do so while we were already investigating the other."

"This threat is neutralized, but for how long?" Master Prombatz asked. "We have seen what they have done, but we still do not know to what end."

"No, we do not. And your concerns are shared. But our people are hard at work to track down the threads of that mystery."

"And we are keeping very close tabs on Vislas Ravik and Maktan," Hozark added. "Though the latter seems quite harmless."

"The most dangerous often do, as we well know," Varsuvala said.

"Indeed," he agreed. "And I am sure we will have more surprises to come. For now, however, we have recovered our lost brother and stopped our enemy in their tracks. The rest will unfold in due time." He rose and gave a little nod to the others. "Now, if you will excuse me, I have one other matter to attend to."

Demelza was drenched in sweat, running through all of her sword techniques back to back, over and over. She had been at it for hours. But after coming so close to defeat at the hands of Samara, she would be at it for hours more. Every day until she felt she might, possibly, stand a chance against her.

Hozark watched her from the training room doorway a bit while she flowed through the forms.

"Are you just going to stare, or do you plan on joining me?" she finally asked, spinning to face him.

"I was just admiring your technique. You know, not many have ever been able to hold their own against Samara. She's one of the greatest swordmasters the order has ever seen."

"And yet, you did."

"I have the benefit of training with her since our youth," he replied. "You, however, threw yourself into a situation you had no hope of winning and performed exceptionally."

"Thank you."

"No, thank *you*. You saved my life, Demelza, and it is something I will never forget."

A slight blush threatened to rise to the stoic woman's cheeks. With great effort, she forced it back down. Hozark turned to leave her to her practice once more, but paused before exiting the chamber.

"Oh, and I thought you would like to know, I sent word to Master Orkut of your impressive service to the cause, as well as the substantial harm you dealt to the Council's plans."

"It is appreciated, Master Hozark."

"And the least I can do. While I do not know when you will have pleased him enough to earn a blade forged by his hands, as I know you so greatly desire, at least know this. I received a reply message just before coming to see you. And Master Orkut wished you to know that he expressed great pleasure with your efforts, and he looks forward to seeing you again soon."

At that, despite all of her training, Demelza's cheeks began to redden with a surge of joy, though only slightly. She was a Ghalian assassin, after all.

Hozark smiled. "You know what?" he said, shedding his coat and drawing his sword. "A little sparring never hurts."

"*Much*," Demelza said with a broad grin, then launched into her attack.

EPILOGUE

In the quiet of her modest home tucked away on the outskirts of a city forgotten by most, and ignored by the rest, Samara sat quietly at her small desk, staring at her recent delivery. It had arrived while she had been out hunting. Not hunting animals, though. At least, not the normal kind.

She poured herself a tall glass of arambis juice and drank deep, cleansing her palate and removing the last traces of dried red from her lips. She took a deep breath, then opened the mysterious package and looked at the instructions within.

Her jaw flexed involuntarily as she read, her pulse rising ever so slightly. This was no easy task. But, then, she expected nothing less.

Samara rose and walked to the little, innocuous trunk resting against her bedroom's far wall. She opened it, removing the false contents and revealing the wards and locks hidden beneath. Carefully, she cast her spells, unbinding and releasing every trap and ward, one by one, until, at last, it was safe to open.

The secret panel slid back, and she reached her hand inside. A necklace of fine metal hung from a little peg, but she pushed that aside. With care, though. It may have seemed like nothing, but it had been a gift from Hozark, many, many years ago. And in addition to being pleasing to the eye, it also contained a substantial amount of deadly magic.

A faint smile touched her lips at the memory of long ago, then faded. Her eyes hardened, and she dug deeper, drawing forth her vespus blade. Its blue metal was brighter than during her recent run-in with Hozark. She had been feeding it as much power as she could acquire. And she'd just gotten more.

Samara focused and pushed the stolen magic from within herself into the powerful weapon. She'd fed well, and like a baby bird taking its meal from its mama, the sword greedily absorbed what she offered it.

The metal was radiant, gleaming a bright blue. She had dumped a massive amount of power into it, and it showed. She gently tucked the blade back into its cradle and replaced the lid, her fingers brushing against the necklace as she did.

The vespus blade was as ready as it would ever be. And so was she.

PREVIEW: THE GHALIAN CODE

SPACE ASSASSINS 3

Ornate boots crunched loudly, their steps echoing in the silent halls as they ground deep into the debris littering the formerly opulent estate's tower. Delicate sculptures lay in ruin, smashed to shards, and artwork and decorative wall hangings depicting brighter times rested on the ground where they'd fallen in the chaos.

Blood was everywhere. Red blood, green blood, even some blue blood. All manner of men and women had fought and died here, some by magic, but most by far more primitive means.

Blades and cudgels had cut a brutal swath through the poor house staff who happened to be caught outside of the defensive lines on the ground floor. They had been slain with no discrimination, and with no mercy. The attack had obviously been swift and had taken them unaware, despite their state of general readiness.

Smears of green blood on the floor where the attackers' bodies had fallen were sticky testament to the efforts of the estate's security teams. They had fought well, the man thought of the slain staff at his feet. Only his guards lay there, however.

The enemy had taken their dead and wounded with them,

leaving neither overt signs of who had led the attack, nor whom they worked for. But he knew. Who else would dare to do such a thing? And in his own home, no less. A show of force in a visla's estate while he was away on business.

It was a ballsy thing to do, and against Visla Dinarius Jinnik, it was particularly so. The man had *power*. More than any visla for at least thirty systems. Someone had made a calculated choice in this attack.

Visla Jinnik kept moving, stepping over the cold bodies of his men. The magical lift discs to the upper floors seemed to still be functional, but he cast a protective spell around himself as he boarded, just in case the intruders had left behind any little surprises for him in the way of wards or traps.

He went straight to the top of the tower. The level containing his personal quarters. A place staffed by his most trusted men and women and protected by his most skilled guards. Just as was the case down below, the scene was one of carnage.

Here, however, the fighting had apparently been far more intense. The walls, he noted, were greatly damaged by some dangerous magic gone astray. It was one of the reasons magic was almost never used in close-quarter fighting.

While spells could be greatly effective against an approaching enemy, once you were in the thick of combat, those same spells could just as easily take out your own men by accident as well as your intended target.

And while that was bad on land, it could be even worse in space, blasting a hole in the side of a ship and venting attackers and defenders alike into the frigid void.

So, no one used spells in this kind of fighting except as a last resort. Which, judging by the stray damage, it had been.

That little quirk of magic was what led to the development of enchanted blades. While they were somewhat limited by their wielder's reach, the magical weapons could slice through armor and flesh alike.

All of Visla Jinnik's personal guard carried them and were well trained. And their proficiency with the weapons was apparent by the corpses and limbs strewn about the place.

The fighting had obviously been fierce, as a few of the Tslavar mercenaries sent to invade his home still lay dead on the floor, their comrades unable to retrieve their bodies in the heat of battle.

Despite the horrible loss of life, Jinnik smiled, though it was pained, not one of joy. Merely one of appreciation. His men had served him well, and their surviving families would be well taken care of for it.

He looked at the uniform on one of the few mercenary bodies left behind. No markings. Nothing to tie the man to any one cause or organization, as he had expected. They were an anonymous fighting force, and if seen or even captured, their true loyalty would be easy enough to deny.

On he continued, crossing the wide foyer by the lift discs and heading into his personal chambers. Furniture was scattered and smashed, and the signs of fighting were even more intense in the narrower confines of the corridor.

Something caught his eye. Something horrible. A servant's head had been severed and placed carefully on the leg of an upturned table. The visla paused and stared at this new horror, his boots now slick with gore.

"Poor Sidisa. You did not deserve such an end," he said to no one in particular. Not for lack of ears around him, but because all of them were dead.

He felt his already bubbling rage grow even stronger. Even in the heaviest of combat, this was just not done. There was no tactical purpose for such a thing. Except one.

Someone was making a point.

He carefully scanned the area, taking in every detail he could. Then, with a heavy heart, he walked to the doorway of the room adjacent to his own suites. Four of his most trusted guards lay dead at the threshold, fallen where they had made their last stand.

He took a deep breath, then stepped over their bodies into the room.

The damage inside was minimal. Barely noticeable, in fact. All of the violence had taken place leading up to this place. The crux of it all. The true reason for the assault on so fortified an estate.

There were bloody bootprints marking the floor, but only one body in the room. Her name was Willa, and she had been with the family a long, long time. A gentle soul, and a wise teacher. And now she was as dead as the others, long cold where she lay on the floor.

Visla Jinnik bent down and picked up a doll. It was the likeness of a man called Suvius the Mighty. A great gladiator warrior, and his son's favorite. His grip tightened around the doll as his emotions threatened to take control.

The static buzz of agitated magic around him began to thicken into a dangerous crackle of power and rage as his anger grew stronger. It was a family condition. His father had it, his father's father had it. And more likely than not, his son would too, one day. If he lived.

Jinnik breathed deep, calming his mind and heart as he'd been trained since his powers began to truly manifest and grow in strength when he was only twelve, just a few years older than his son. Slowly, the dangerous magic receded back into the visla, but only just.

He forced himself to look at the room with a clear mind, pushing emotion aside, at least for a moment. Then he saw it. A single, sealed note on the small table placed in the middle of the room where it could not be missed.

He picked it up. Not a speck on the envelope, not a drop of blood or smear of soot. This had been left for him *after* his son was taken. He turned it over and stared at the seal. One he knew all too well.

Jinnik strode from the room, jaw tight as he headed to his personal study. He would open it there, and then he would plan what to do next.

A bit of motion caught his eye and he stopped and turned, his gaze falling on what he had missed when he entered. A column had tumbled in the fray, and beneath it a Tslavar mercenary lay pinned. His injuries were severe, but not fatal.

"Please, help me," the man asked, exhausted from days of struggle to pull free of the enormous weight.

"Help you?" Visla Jinnik said, the angry magic crackling around him once more. "Oh, I'll help you."

He raised his hand, focusing his power, and released it with one barking spell. "*Hokta!*"

The green man didn't even have the opportunity to scream as he was crushed into an unidentifiable bloody pulp.

Jinnik lowered his arm. An arm that was not wearing a konus or slaap. This was his own power, not that stored in any magical device like the unpowered needed. It had been a fair expenditure, but not enough to completely deplete the crackling, angry excess magic buzzing around him.

But the violence had helped. At least a little. And slowly, the magic began to pull back into his body. He had killed the one witness he could have interrogated, but with the letter in his hand, there would be no need.

For now, he needed to sit and to think. And once he had a plan, then, and only then, would he would act.

ALSO BY SCOTT BARON

Standalone Novels

Living the Good Death

The Clockwork Chimera Series

Daisy's Run

Pushing Daisy

Daisy's Gambit

Chasing Daisy

Daisy's War

The Dragon Mage Series

Bad Luck Charlie

Space Pirate Charlie

Dragon King Charlie

Magic Man Charlie

Star Fighter Charlie

Portal Thief Charlie

Rebel Mage Charlie

Warp Speed Charlie

Checkmate Charlie

The Space Assassins Series

The Interstellar Slayer

The Vespus Blade

The Ghalian Code

Death From the Shadows

Hozark's Revenge

The Warp Riders Series

Deep Space Boogie

Belly of the Beast

Odd and Unusual Short Stories:

The Best Laid Plans of Mice: An Anthology

Snow White's Walk of Shame

The Tin Foil Hat Club

Lawyers vs. Demons

The Queen of the Nutters

Lost & Found

ABOUT THE AUTHOR

A native Californian, Scott Baron was born in Hollywood, which he claims may be the reason for his rather off-kilter sense of humor.

Before taking up residence in Venice Beach, Scott first spent a few years abroad in Florence, Italy before returning home to Los Angeles and settling into the film and television industry, where he has worked as an on-set medic for many years.

Aside from mending boo-boos and owies, and penning books and screenplays, Scott is also involved in indie film and theater scene both in the U.S. and abroad.

Made in United States
North Haven, CT
14 February 2025

65839554R00233